LEAPING BEAUTY

BY REBECCA FOX

Cover design by Cherie Chapman
Cover images © Shutterstock.com

Illustrations by Sally Parker

Produced by Softwood Self-Publishing

Printed and bound by CPI

DEDICATION

For my friends and family (and anyone
recently told off for daydreaming)

PROLOGUE

RAIN

Celador Castle, the South Realm

Red Felian looked up at her father and said clearly, 'I have no intention of being left behind.'

The king of Landfelian was stunned by his young daughter's declaration. And the king of Landfelian was not a man who was stunned easily. There was a considered silence as he rubbed the slightly battered crown on his head. He took off his spectacles, which were small and round, and peered down at the princess.

'Your horse will miss you terribly.'

The candles in Red's chamber burnt low. 'He will come on the quest too.'

'I see.' The king tucked her in and tried to change the subject as Red shivered beneath her blanket. It was a bitter night; a terrible fog stalked the castle grounds. 'Are you warm enough? This infernal fog will get into your bones.' He paused and listened. 'Although I think the rain has finally stopped.'

There had never been rain like it. No one in Landfelian could remember a rain as full or sad as this one. It had rained before, but it had never cried. The skies over Landfelian had wept for seventeen days and had indeed now stopped, leaving the entire South Realm silent. Only the fog remained, shrouding the castle of Celador like an illness.

The rain had started when Red's mother disappeared. On that day, there was shouting below the Princess's chamber, urgent and raw. The Queen was gone. She was simply gone. No one saw her leave. Her horse was missing. The deluge continued, and the roads turned into rivers, making it impossible to send out a search party. The king returned, half-drowned and feverish, after three days and nights of hunting the surrounding estate for his wife. The servants thought the rain was a bad omen and would not venture outside alone. The weather even upset Rose, the chambermaid most prone to singing 'Goodnight Irene' and other progressive folk songs around the castle. Now, Rose only whistled forlornly which annoyed everyone. The animals were subdued; they slept in circles, like wolves, and cried if they lost sight of one another. It would be fair to say, from the morning the Queen had disappeared, that nothing sat right in the Four Great Realms of Landfelian.

After her mother vanished, Red had spent the days

in Celador's library – returning each morning to the walls of books and searching for answers. She sprawled out before the fire and read while the rain drove on, keeping the household custody. The light was muted and dim; it was impossible to tell the time because of the fog.

Red had searched the library for a record of any incidents concerning fog and unexpected disappearances, but she found no passage to explain them. There was nothing to help her turn what had happened over in her hands and understand it clearly. She had crept downstairs and overheard her father make a private declaration to his herald in the antechamber of the throne room.

'Has there been any news, Richard?'

'No, Your Highness. I'm afraid we are still unable to send out messengers. This rain, it's … quite unnatural.'

There was an audible sigh. 'I must do something. Call on the seven heroes and a hundred able men and women. We will leave as soon as possible. There can be no further delay.'

'What do you plan to do?' the herald stammered.

'Launch a quest until I find her.' The door had slammed, and Red heard the herald hurry away. She had returned to the library and looked up the word 'quest' in the most dust-ridden and ornately bound books.

Quest

An expedition led by a hero to seek out a truth or to accomplish a prescribed task for an interminable length of time.

She'd lifted herself up onto her elbows, frowned, and turned more pages.

An act or instance of seeking.
Endless or apparently endless.

She'd lain back and stared at the ceiling. *Endless,* she thought. *That wasn't good.*

Red had discarded that book and returned to a leaf-green tome of fairy tales she had read often. In the musty pages she usually found comfort and sense – not on this occasion. She'd read about a knight who went on a quest to find the most beautiful maiden in the land. That same knight had died aged ninety-seven after giving up and returning home, only to discover the most beautiful maiden in the land had in fact lived next door, above the dairy.

'So, quests are long and not always successful,' she'd said to herself, sucking on the end of a lock of hair and sighing. That was not very comforting. She'd climbed a ladder and wheeled herself around the great room to the cartography section, where maps of all sizes were rolled up with faded silk ribbons. Here she'd found the journal written by her godfather, Peter Weatherby: *The Nether Regions: What Lies Beyond Landfelian – A Cloudbuster's Guide Thus Far.* Reading until her neck ached and her eyes grew tired, Red determined that if there was to be a quest, she would be a part of it.

And yet, although the king knew he could not take his daughter with him, he couldn't quite bring himself to say goodbye. He considered her determined eyes and noted how her hand held on to his sleeve.

'I've decided something,' he said to her. 'We will go on our very own quest as soon as I return with your mother.'

A short while later, there was a tentative knock on the princess' door, followed by a polite cough.

'Come in,' the king called.

The herald stepped quietly into the room, which was illuminated only by candlelight. He could not see the king, who had gone there to bid his daughter farewell. In fact, he could see very little, for he was a very short herald.

'Your Highness?'

'Yes, Richard.' The king's voice came from somewhere within the half-light. 'Is it time?'

'Yes, Your Highness. The rain has ceased. The heroes are assembled. Everything is ready.' The herald walked further in and came face to face with a large tent. Its structure was quite something: a statue of a lower-ranking goddess, a miniature-sized throne, a hat stand, and a wolfhound held up several acres of sheet, and a lantern flickered within, casting shadows from inside of the king with his daughter.

'What do you think of my den, Richard?' the young heir asked, her tangles of red hair stuffed beneath a cavalier's hat. 'It's a rhombus.'

He rocked on his heels and whistled. 'It's quite remarkable, milady.' The herald's job was to find everything delightful, even ruff collars and falconry. 'A visionary design.'

'Atlas helped.'

The wolfhound thumped his tail once and walked solemnly towards the door, lowering the canopy by several feet.

'I believe it is your best yet. Forgive my intrusion, Highness.'

The herald bowed to all in the tent and hurried down three dark floors of the castle and out of the side door of the Family Wing. He continued across the courtyard to the stables, and here he stopped to mop both his eyes with a handkerchief. Heralds do not weep, it was their job to smile through adversity, and Richard Losley was one of the best. He never blubbed on the job – with everything being so delightful, there was simply no need. Times however had changed.

'Are you quite well, sir?' came a voice from behind him.

'Yes, yes. Thank you, Rose, terrible sinuses.' He sniffed his way past the loveliest of the chambermaids and told himself to get a grip. 'Would you be so kind and tell Angus to bring round the king's horse?'

Inside the den, the king was still trying to leave for his quest and making a real hash of it.

'It will all end well. You'll see.' He sounded sure. Kings always sound sure – it's part of the training – although this one's eyes gave him away somewhat.

'How do you know?' Red studied her father's face and waited. He looked tired. He smelt of smoke, suede, coffee, and horse.

'Do you know what makes a hero truly, truly great?'

Red sat up in her makeshift bed. 'Their horse.'

He smiled and gently shook his head. 'Not all heroes have a horse.'

He received a curious look from a pair of clear green eyes. 'What then?'

'A true hero never, ever despairs.' He squashed another pillow under her head awkwardly. 'Try to sleep now.'

'Let me come with you, as far as the Lake of Stars.'

The king's smile became lopsided, and he kissed her head. 'If the weather improves, I will send for you. Now, curl up well. I may return by morning.'

The wolfhound followed him out, and Red blinked furiously as half the canopy descended and the door closed. She crawled out and went to the window. Here, she waited until her father rode out. She watched as his tall figure quickly became lost to fog and imagined him riding through the night and for several days to meet his seven heroes and the one-hundred able men who had volunteered to join the quest. She closed her eyes and told the moon to keep him and her mother, wherever she was, safe from harm.

Miriam found Red asleep against the window the next morning, the girl's feet blue with cold.

'It's time to pack, dear child. Your father left instructions. You are to leave here today.'

The sky was pale and Red couldn't hear the birds. She watched Miriam bustle about, retrieving clothes and disappearing under the bed for a dusty trunk.

'Where am I to go?'

'North, cherub, to Paloma.'

'Why?'

'The weather. It's this fog. It has covered much of the south realm, but not the rest of Landfelian.' She sniffed. 'Folk don't like it – think it's witchcraft, unnatural. And with the king away on his quest, he thinks it will be safer for you to stay at Paloma with your step-uncle and aunt.'

'But I don't know my step-uncle and aunt.' At first, Red refused the undergarments being proffered, but when met with Miriam's stern look, she reluctantly began to dress. 'How long must I stay in the North Realm?'

'As long as the quest lasts.' Miriam gave her a bright smile.

As Red put on her boots, the word 'endless' rang through her mind.

'THE KINGDOM OF LANDFELIAN'

To look down over Landfelian from the comfort of a Cloudbuster – which I doubt you would ever do, since only one existed and the inventor responsible never let it out of his sight – was to look over a green, gently undulating land. The Sea of Trees stroked the western shore, its deep green waters pouring into the wide arms of the White Ocean. Across the realms to the east lay the Wondering Waters, upon which seven islands floated, like flying clouds skipping away into the high, boundless water.

Landfelian was a kingdom bigger than Fronke and smaller than Engerlande. It was lined by the roaming tracks of man and horse. The Four Great Realms were separated by crinkle-crankle walls, meandering rivers, ancient forest, and rangy mountains, each as different from the other as the Highlands are to Hampshire. And at the heart of Landfelian lay water, the Lake of Stars gleaming cool and clear.

At this time, the farthest depths of the South Realm, an area known as the Misty Mountains, were shrouded by an unpleasant fog. No one outside of the south had given it much thought though. The people of Landfelian were generally far too busy with the business of finding food and eating it before someone else did. Not to mention rumours of an event gathering pace in the North Realm, where it appeared that the royal palace of Paloma was holding a ball – another one, which would explain where all the food had gone.

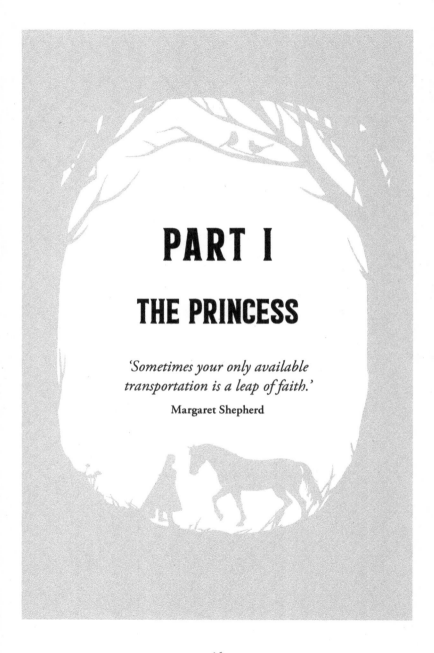

PART I

THE PRINCESS

*'Sometimes your only available
transportation is a leap of faith.'*

Margaret Shepherd

1

THE BIGEASY RIVER

Seven years later

A murmur of thunder rumbled through the Great Mirrored Hall at Paloma Palace. A white flash lit up a mass of red hair that belonged to a young woman standing by a window.

Red looked down at the manicured grass and bit her lip.

'Oh, God,' she muttered.

The ground seemed further away than it had that morning. She slipped off a pair of court shoes and looked behind her. No one in the Great Mirrored Hall paid the young woman with bare feet any lasting attention. She must be one of the poorer cousins, a relation to the half-queen, perhaps. Her wig had no height, and her dress, which was as green as a duck's cheek, had no bustle. A tiny wing carved from copper hung from her right ear. 'How heathen,' the other women remarked and moved on.

Over the sea of wigs, she could just see Richard the Herald, next to a large potted silver birch decorated with tiny gold cherubs. He stood by the entrance of the ballroom and cleared his throat. A footman banged a gong loudly. As he did so, Red swung one leg over the windowsill and glanced at the clock on the bell tower.

'Ladies and gentlemen,' the Herald trilled to the guests, 'your attention if you please. The half-queen and half-king desire your company in the grand ballroom. The evening's entertainment is about to begin.'

There was an audible 'ohhh' from the gathered courtiers and a sudden swell towards the ballroom doors. The herald was almost flattened by a wave of powdered and eager faces.

Red took her moment as the courtiers turned and began to drift away from her, towards the ballroom. She disappeared off the window ledge. It was the first in a number of leaps she had planned for that night. And not the biggest.

She fell through the night like silk, landing silently on the ground below. Clenching the grass between her toes, she looked out at the dark gardens and tried to breathe normally. There was no one to be seen. The night was still.

Run.

Red hooked up her dress and began to move. She was

covered in goose bumps. Her heart beat like a steady drum. *Breathe,* she told herself. Her legs made long, light strides away from the window. She had to be quick.

RUN.

She had dreamt of this moment – except, in her dreams, something always went wrong. The hem of her dress caught, leaving her hanging from the palace wall and flashing her undergarments at the approaching guards. Or she forgot how to run and stood frozen on the grass below until the man with the silver-topped cane found her and escorted her back inside.

But Red had not forgotten. She had seven minutes – at best, ten – to find her horse, race down the back drive, and get as far away from Paloma as possible. If the night's entertainment was as good a distraction as the herald had promised, she should be able to pass every unguarded checkpoint and escape without being seen, arrested, dragged to the watchtower – and married.

'I am ready. I am ready.' She whispered to herself as she ran.

For seven years, she had built up her strength to such an extent that she could have balanced a small pony on her stomach and sung 'Doh Ray Me'. Since moving here, she had only ever had this single purpose in mind. If she wasn't ready now, she never would be.

The poplars rustled beside her in the wind. There were two guards loitering by the fountain ahead guarding the first avenue, moaning about how uncomfortable their boots were. Red held her breath and ran around the east wing of the palace, staying in the shadows until she reached the bottom of her turret. She hovered there, looking up at the highest window, and meowed twice. After a few seconds, a bulging hemp sack landed with a thud at her feet. She slung it over her shoulder, turned towards the back drive, and continued to run, barely making a sound.

The bag bumped against Red's back, slowing her steps, but she'd packed as lightly as she'd dared: a pair of thick stockings, her boots, a tennis racket, a bag of roasted nuts, a leather pouch of something strong and courage-inducing that she'd stolen from her step-uncle's drinks cupboard, a small candle, her godmother's rubies, Father Peter's journal and map, a spyglass, her father's old riding coat, and some fake letters stating she was someone called Mary Drew. Surely everything one would need for a treacherous journey?

Red swallowed. In all her seventeen years she had never made a journey like this before. There was also the problem she couldn't leave behind: the teeth around her ankle. A voodoo charm that had been fastened there and was impossible to remove. It prickled against her skin in the heat of the summer night, but she ignored it, pushing herself on, further away from the palace.

She stayed out of sight, taking cover under a row of horse chestnut trees. But as she ran between each one, thorns pricked the soles of her feet. Red could not slow down, look behind her, or put her boots on; there was no time. Her throat began to burn as she ran, but her legs and purpose did not waver.

After a few minutes, Red saw the giant cedar that marked the halfway point of the back drive, its trunk as wide as a bothy. There, a large horse waited for its owner to arrive, nibbling at the grass impatiently. The horse's name was Face, and Face was a valien.

Valien were rare animals – their ancestry involved mountain stallions from the South Realm, flat racers from the Eastern Plains, and a third breed, which many hoped was a unicorn. Red had been introduced to Face when he was a foal, at which point the two had become inseparable. There were as few valien left in Landfelian as there were riders of valien; it took a certain amount of skill. These horses were highly sensitive, intelligent creatures – they would throw off any brute with a pair of spurs who fancied himself a rider. The king had taken his valien on the quest. There was another that belonged to one of the old heroes, but neither man nor horse had been seen in the kingdom for many years. And there were rumours of a wild herd, their whereabouts unknown, but the people of Landfelian were very excited knowing they were out there.

A groundsman by the name of Jim True stood by his wife and son, with the princess' valien. He was having enormous trouble keeping the animal still. The horse's black tail flicked up and down, and the hackles that ran across the ridge of his back bristled in the wind as Jim held the reins tight to keep the horse concealed.

'Not long now, my boy.' The valien snorted, and Jim's eyes flicked to the guardhouse not far from the end of the drive. 'We'll be discovered if he doesn't quieten down.'

'Don't worry, my lover. Got a stash of toffee pennies in my pocket. They should keep him busy,' said June, as she was flicked affectionately in the face by a thick black mane. Aside from Red Felian and leaping over bushes, the young valien loved nothing more than toffee pennies.

'She must be close,' Billy murmured, as he watched Face's velvet ears twitch excitedly.

June was now out of toffee pennies, so Face started to nibble on her apron string. 'I can't hear anything apart from that thunder.' She glanced at the night sky. 'Looks like she'll be riding out in a storm.'

The moon lit up Red like a piece of green tinsel as she darted in and out of the shadows. After slapping a stone hog, she disappeared behind the cedar tree, which snorted with elation at the sight of her.

She found her breath and gasped, 'Hello,' reaching up to stroke her horse in relief.

SNORT.

'Ready?' she looked at him and smiled.

He nuzzled her neck, a keen flash in his eyes.

GRUNT.

The valien stamped the ground, impatient to go, but Red turned to the True family and could not think of anything to say. The silence was too much for June, who could not abide quiet or very thin women for long. 'I don't like the look of that cumulonimbus,' she said finally as she attached the hemp bag to the princess's saddle. 'You'd better get a welly on.'

Red looked anxiously at the sky. 'I wasn't expecting a storm.'

'Don't worry, princess.' Jim smiled reassuringly as the sky behind them crackled. 'Your horse is about to take off like a rocket.' He looked up at Red. 'Been hell keeping the brute still. He bit the wife and nearby broke my toe.'

'He's nervous. He's not used to the disguise or being out of the stables at this hour.' She could not stop stroking Face's neck, which was now brown with mud like the rest of him. He was still obviously bigger than the average stallion, but at least now he didn't stand out with the black and white markings of a valien. He did, however, in his opinion, look like a large, hairy turd and was thoroughly put out.

'He is unrecognisable,' Red continued. 'Thank you. You've risked so much for me …' Smuggling Face out of the royal stables, lying to the guards, mixing strong North Realm tea with marshland clay, and rubbing it over his distinctive piebald coat and star-shaped blaze … She didn't want to think of the punishment they would meet if they were caught. 'I don't how to thank you', she stammered on, 'but your efforts will not be for nothing. I will find the king. I promise I will.'

June put her hand on the princess' foot to stop it shaking – the teeth around her ankle squirmed menacingly. 'Don't linger here, princess. Get away as soon as possible. Your horse may be a different colour but he's still twice the size of any other.' She then handed Red a food parcel that weighed the same as a bag of rocks. 'It's not much, just some bread, a round of cheese, some honey roasted ham, and a bag of apricots.'

'Thank you.' Red's mouth wobbled as she tried to look strong.

'Come here, you silly goose.' June gave her a squeeze. Red inhaled the woman's scent of washed linen and jam. 'We're all rooting for you, duck.'

Jim whispered into the valien's twitching ears. 'Keep her safe or, if you ever return, I'll dye you the same colour as the half-queen's wig.'

A boom of thunder rumbled over the small party. Through the branches, Jim looked up at the moon and the five virgins winking brightly around it. The air became charged and urgent. Face shifted impatiently, his ears flat.

'It's time to go.' Red looked at them and grinned as she hoisted herself up onto her horse's back.

'I should think so.' Jim slapped the valien so hard, he reared up and volleyed over the bush, which was impressive, although unnecessary.

The guards sent to patrol the end of the back drive were genuinely surprised when a large horse landed on the path and headed towards them. It shook its mane and stamped once before breaking into a stone-flinging gallop.

'What the ...?'

Their orders were to arrest anyone who looked suspicious, but most of the guards did not know how to spell suspicious, let alone recognise it, although they enjoyed arresting women.

'Does that look suspicious to you, Axe?' asked Hammar.

Axe took in the scene before him. 'That rider ain't wearing any shoes ... I'd say so.'

'STOP IN THE NAME OF THE NEW LAW!' called Hammar

The rider pounded onwards in the direction of the river.

Axe, the first guard, shook his head. 'You don't sound offishall enuff.'

Hammar tried again. 'SLOW YOU DOWN, KNAVE! We, the Blackwood Guards, command it! What business dost thou have on the back drive?' Hammar liked using words like knave and dost. He was old-school like that.

But Red did not answer, and she did not slow down. She was not stupid, and she was not a knave. She urged her horse to go faster, her heart hammering against her ribs. The sky erupted above them. She bent down low, ignoring the tearing pain as the voodoo charm bit into her ankle, and whispered encouraging thoughts to her valien. 'They can't catch us. Keep going.'

They both knew what was coming. With luck they could race past the guards, but there was no avoiding the fact that at the end of the back drive was the river – the Bigeasy – and no one jumped that. It was the wildest river in Landfelian. A game of pooh sticks here was over too fast to be any fun. The water pummelled down from the snow-crusted summit of Mount Felian, dividing the North and East Realms and ending at the great coastal city of Alba. The servants' raft was tethered to the banks and staked thrice over to stop it drifting away. The only other way to cross the river was to swim, and no one did that without a rope and someone at the other side holding it.

Either Red jumped the Bigeasy or she stayed within the palace's power. Because it had not been attempted before, it was the least watched, least guarded, and most unlikely exit from Paloma. Had she suggested her plan to any sane North Realmian, they would have dribbled in shock and assumed she had been at the meadery all day. The one thing all the people of Landfelian said about the Bigeasy River was, 'Oh aye. It's the wide one.'

But the king had always told Red there was a first time for everything. He said this most often when faced with a complicated necktie or difficult realm dispute. He had a point, she thought, as Face's hooves thundered along the stony path, shuddering her bones. She just wished on this occasion it was not her blazing the trail. As she urged her horse on, she smelt the water – cold and clean in the soupy air.

When her valien saw the river, he grew nervous and farted. Only one thought filled his mind: *YOU ARE KIDDING.*

'You can fly, Face,' Red croaked, trying to convince herself as well as her horse. 'There's nothing to it. Oh God.'

The guards had stopped shouting. They were starting to wonder what the rider had in mind.

'Bugger me,' said Axe. 'He's not going to stop. He's going to try to jump it!'

'Nah,' said Hammar, his eyes wide. 'He'll stop.'

'STOP YOUR 'ORSE, YOU TURNIP!' Axe yelled.

Face made a low, whining noise. The guards knew a determined valien when they saw it and stepped quickly out of the way, watching the horse's tail streaming behind it like a black flag.

'Did that horse look familiar to you?' Hammar watched Face thunder on.

'It can't be.' Axe stared at the retreating animal. 'Wrong colour.'

'We'll just collect the corpses from river maintenance tomorrow,' Hammar said, taking a swig from a bottle labelled *GROG* stashed in his leather jerkin.

'You've got to hand it to the lad, though – balls of steel,' said Axe.

'I'll say. Rides like a hero, if there were any left. Takes real chump to steal the princess' horse.'

'Funny thing is, could have sworn he was wearing a dress.'

It was the most impressive piece of runaway riding the guards had ever seen.

Jim and Billy True watched too, from behind the trunk of the great cedar. June had brought her needles and was knitting manically.

'I can't look. Is she over?' she asked.

Jim closed his eyes and said a quick prayer. 'Not yet, love. She's getting close now. That headstrong animal looks like he might just do it!'

On and on, June worked the needles. Oh, how that woman knitted. She made good progress with a scarf and was still going strong by the time the princess reached the riverbank.

Jim whispered fervently, 'Jump, jump, jump.'

The valien decided to close his eyes as he reached the water. There was little more he could do but listen to his mistress and push off.

Red counted down the last thundering strides.

Five.

Four.

Three.

Two.

And then she swore.

It was the longest unofficially recorded pronunciation of a swearword beginning with 'S' that the North Realm had ever heard. She felt her stomach lurch into the night in front of her and her heart rocket into her mouth as her horse pushed up into the sky. They were airborne, with the river below them. Leaping in a perfect arc, the valien and the princess reached for the stars, soaring over and over and over the water ...

'Is she . . . ?' asked June, who was creating a piece of knitwear fit for a giant and making little panting noises.

'Not quite!' Jim yelled.

'WHY THE HELL NOT?' June cried.

'It's a very wide river.'

Red held on tight to her horse's mane and hoped to God she wouldn't hear a splash. Two ducks flying by quacked at her, and then she felt Face begin to fall. She closed her eyes.

Thud.

Thud.

Scramble.

There was a long pause. Silence is not always golden,

but this one was. When Red opened her eyes, and she saw there was land beneath her and not wildly rushing water.

Face snorted and shook his back leg, which had slipped down the bank on landing. Red began to laugh as she hugged him tight. 'We did it. We actually did it!'

The sound of the princess' laughter carried over the water and back to the cedar tree.

Jim risked stepping out to get a better look, and what he saw made him fall to his knees and kiss the ground. A grin lit up Billy's face and June stopped knitting and burst into tears.

The princess was alive – alive and dry and swearing on the SOUTH side of the river.

Paloma Palace was twinkling in the dark behind Red's friends as the fireworks for the ball began. Sweat trailed down the small of her back, and her damp red hair blew about in the wind. Somewhere along the line she had lost her wig. Face's dark eyes shone, his mouth foamed, and his nostrils flared. He gave out a great, excited whinny.

'Christmas, that was close,' she said, her hands shaking as she stroked him. 'I'll never ask you to do that again.'

✳ ✳ ✳

From a howling cliff on a small unmapped island, the king looked down to see the hairs on his arms standing tall. Austin Blue Felian smiled at his wolfhound, who thumped its tail and howled into the wind.

'Yes, Atlas, there has been a leap. We must hurry … It's time to return home.'

A shrill whistle sounded from the sea below, where a great ship waited for him in the shallows.

THE WILD PLACES

The guards continued to stare at the river.

'Did you hear a splash?' asked Axe.

'No, not yet,' replied Hammar.

They listened hard, sure their eyes were deceiving them.

'I don't think it's coming, Axe.'

'Well, blow me. The rider cleared it.'

'And in a dress.'

The guards heard the sudden stab of a cane into gravel. A man liquefied into view and choked the area where they stood with his cheroot smoke.

'Gentlemen.' The man pointed at the river with his silver-topped cane. 'Can you tell me where the rider of that valien may have gone? Before I cut out both your tongues and ask them?' His voice was dead calm and a little nasally.

It was the head of royal security – the man in charge of the guards and purveyor of all things pain related, specialising in experimental torture. His name was Daniel Blackwood, and he was the son of Jeremiah Blackwood, the most ruthless lawyer in the city of Alba.

Daniel removed his gloves slowly, like stockings, as he waited for the guards to answer. He had witnessed the princess' leap. He knew she had escaped her imprisonment and pending marriage, and he was a long way from happy.

'While you formulate your answer, kindly arrest the groundsman and his family trying to crawl away from behind that bush. Take them to the tower for questioning.'

'Right you are, Captain.'

* * *

The princess was not on a track she knew. 'Which path through Boundary Hedge do we take?' *Where is the signpost?* she thought.

She stared at the dark horizon, then at Face. He was not sure either. The valien had never been out into the North Realm before, and in his excitement, he walked around in circles.

A scream of fireworks echoed across the plains. At the sound, Face reared. They heard a male voice yell, and Red fell, landing hard on the ground.

'Wha– *ooff,*' she cried, lying stunned on her back on the ground. Looking up, she saw a man on a grey mare towering over her.

Every sound grew quieter, and the world became muffled. She was aware of a pair of heavy boots thumping either side of her waist. For some reason she couldn't breathe.

'Look where you're bloody going. Are you trying to kill yourself?' The owner of the boots crouched down and looked into her eyes. 'Or just lame my horse?' He had bright eyes and smelt of hay. Two tanned hands pulled her up.

'I can't …' she gasped. The air had been knocked out of her, and she fought to breathe.

'Keep your corset on, milady, you've only winded yourself.' Though his face was worn by the weather, the man didn't look as old as she had first thought. 'Going to have a big bruise on your backside as well.' He smiled at her. He can't have been much older than her.

Red tried to remain calm, but there was a man in clothes that looked seasoned by a life living outside, probably sleeping in hedges, gripping her waist and grinning. *A bandit,* she thought, *disguising himself as a Man of the Road,* and she narrowed her eyes. He had a lot of messy brown hair, and when she looked up at his mouth, it was still grinning at her.

'Worth it though – that was some leap. I watched it from across the plain there.' He pointed further along the river.

Red took a swing at his arm and missed. 'Get away

from me!' Her voice sounded like a dying carp.

He laughed again and backed away. 'I've never seen a horse take off like that.'

Face stood protectively beside Red, his ears flat, staring at the man with all the hair.

'Yes, you, Pegasus. How did you manage it, a heavy horse like you?' He took a step closer and raised an eyebrow. 'Bit bigger than the average stallion, isn't he?'

Red didn't meet his eye. 'Is he? I really couldn't say.'

'He's almost closer in size to a valien ...' He gazed at the great horse.

Red laughed nervously. 'He's nothing of the kind.'

'Right. Well. What's this all about then?' The bandit made no move to leave. 'Didn't you like the feast at Paloma Palace? I've heard all about the menu at the half-queen's parties. Bit rich for my tastes.' He frowned. 'Not much of a wig man myself, although I wouldn't decline an invitation to the palace pantry.' He looked hungrily in the direction of the palace.

Red scrambled up and tried to mount her horse. She was struck by the sharp stab of teeth into her ankle from the voodoo charm. She stumbled right into the man's chest. It was warm and broad, but up close she could see that his shirt was covered in dark stains. Blood. It looked a lot like blood. She quickly let go and stood back, alarmed. What was she doing hugging a murdering bandit? This was never part of her plan.

The man continued to talk. 'In fairness, I'd want to get

away from there too. Those halfwits trying to claim the throne have spent precisely eighty-seven percent of the kingdom's wealth, if you believe the papers that come out of Alba.' He spat on the ground. Red looked at her boot, inches from where his spit landed, and narrowed her eyes. 'They're working overtime at the House of Gold to smelt something from nothing, from any bits that are left from the royal treasury. That half-queen's close to nailing the final thirteen percent with tonight's carry-on, I should think.'

Red glanced back at the dying fireworks over Paloma Palace. She was not aware of the kingdom's financial situation, although it was true that her step-aunt Caroline had had twenty hedgehogs stuffed and dipped in gold to use as door stops for that night's festivities. The blood-stained bandit continued to rant on about the economy.

'I've heard it said many times of late that if the king's quest goes on any longer, the half-king and half-queen will claim squatter's rights to the kingdom.'

He had her attention now. 'Impossible. They can't.'

'Milady, if King Felian keeps all his best fighting men and women away on a quest, those two pretenders can do anything they want.'

'But the law ...' started Red, but was cut off as the man laughed at her. Again.

'You should have a lie down. The law is as corrupt as everything in that palace.' He noticed the copper wing earring hanging from her right ear and the ribbon of blood beneath it, seeping down her neck. 'A big leap like that will give you quite a shock. I suggest you make camp soon, light a fire, and sleep it off.'

They heard the rumble of drums, coming from the direction of the palace.

'Actually,' said Red, 'I have to go.' She felt fine, if a little giddy, perhaps. Anyway, what did he know? She quickly gathered up her bag and tennis racket.

The man pointed carefully at her ear and took a step closer. 'You're bleeding. Right here.'

Red pressed her hand defensively against it and winced. 'It's nothing. Thank you for your help.'

She touched the valien's shoulder, and the giant horse sank down to allow her on. She whispered something indecipherable in his ear, and in seconds they were away.

The Man of the Road watched her go. Lightning illuminated her white neck as she turned to look beyond him at the river. He followed her gaze. The banks of the Bigeasy were alight with torches, held by six, maybe eight, fierce-looking men gathering on the other side. Guards, Blackwood Guards. *What has she done?* he wondered. *Was she a horse thief?* The Man of the Road smiled. That must be it, the girl was a horse thief ...

'Wait!' he called after her. 'Where are you heading?' He struggled to mount his horse. 'I know a place you can rest!' But his horse refused to stand still. The mare stamped around in circles, throwing her head about indignantly as the wind picked up across the plain. 'Will you keep still, Legs? For pity's sake.'

Another flash of lightning lit up the thief's copper wing, half trodden into the ground. 'Well, look at that. She left something behind.' The man picked it up, looked at the delicate intricacy of the engraving, and put it in his pocket.

'I would have liked to buy that trailblazer a drink. And then steal her horse …' His horse bucked. 'Oh, keep your mane on. I'd have sold it on. You're the only woman for me.' The Man of the Road, whose name was Robbie Wylde, shook his head and laughed a full-bodied, deep, full colour sort of laugh. 'Never a dull moment on the road,' he mused.

Then he adjusted his cloak, put his hat on, and rode towards Boundary Hedge to find some breakfast. The Honest Sausage was not far and did an excellent … well, sausage.

✳ ✳ ✳

Red streaked past a weather-beaten sign that offered all travellers a choice. Its carved wooden hands pointed in three directions.

THE FAR NORTH:
Paloma, Mount Felian, Giant Country
WESTWARD:
Little Snoring
SOUTH THROUGH BOUNDARY HEDGE:
Everything Else

Historically, the people of Landfelian loved nothing more than the possibility of an adventure. And before Queen Phoebe had disappeared (in the most tragic and unsolved mystery of the time), they left the house a lot more. But after she had vanished, the kingdom grew wary. Instead, people found their adventures closer to home, opening a letter, gazing into a teacup, or just digging a hole. How many full-scale adventures had there actually been involving certain death, dragons, and sorcery before the Quest? One hundred and one – but they had all been a long time ago and the majority undertaken by Patrick Dickie, the Pirate King.

In any case, every realm was still generously equipped with rest houses and inns serving good ale and sausage pie to any would-be hero, and the Men of the Road knew where to find every one of these crumbly crusts of salty goodness and each roaring fire.

After escaping the young bandit, Red did not stop until she and Face were safely beyond Boundary Hedge. They passed through the archway of the thicket that grew over twelve-feet tall with a width twice as much and out the other side, where the rest of Landfelian greeted her, dark and vast. This was her family's kingdom.

'Seven years, Face, and we have not been further than the banks of the river.'

Red took a deep breath. The night smelt of dry grass and smoke. *Smoke? Bit late for a bonfire,* she thought. Red imagined the faintly burning hearths of the many homesteads scattered over the North Realm and carried on. For the first time, she could pick a path and roam like any other independent horse-owning woman. Nothing on her journey from here to the city of Alba would be accounted for as long as she avoided the main thoroughfares, the inevitable guards – and stayed clear of men with pirate eyes and blood-stained shirts – she might even find the king. She would be fine, she thought. Just fine. The teeth around her ankle stabbed a little harder into her skin as she tried to focus on the way ahead.

The princess was wrong about the smoke, though. It was not the faintly burning hearths of warm crofts. She had just missed the great surge of beggars who arrived to wail and shake their withered limbs at the half-queen's guests as they travelled towards the ball. The smoke from their fires lingered in the air, along with the smell of tired skin. She did not notice how thirsty the crops were around her, nor how grey the corn and hungry the cattle. She could not hear the half-starved rodents that limped across her path. Instead, Red Felian got out her map and smiled. For the first time in years, she could go anywhere without being watched by guards. She quietly wished herself a happy birthday and trotted on.

3

TEETHING PROBLEMS

Red, you may sniff, is not a very princessy name. It is only three measly letters and a common primary colour. Shouldn't it be something longer, you might ask, like Alethia Hermione Esmerelda Von Troose? In truth, her full name was in fact Aubrey Tulip Matilda Friday Edward Felian.

You can understand why she shortened it. Few called her Aubrey, and those who called her Princess Edward were politely ignored. Most of the servants in the palace referred to her simply as 'milady' or 'that red one'.

But why red, why not brown? Well, here lies the tale of the princess' making.

(It should be noted here that for readers who prefer stories without the words 'love' and 'making' in them, the words 'basket' and 'weaving' have been inserted into this book instead as a substitute. It is also important to note there are no handsome princes in this tale. Not one stud on a black stallion with a feathered hat, a signet ring, and exceptional teeth. No one with a name like Sebastien Heskwithe-Goodheart of the Montague Clan or Rufus Victor-Lookinwellen to the rescue. Those idiots stopped visiting Landfelian a long time ago, after the Great Vanishing when the weather turned and very few people were blessed with good teeth (a tidy set was all one could hope for). If such a prince is what you're after, I suggest you give the person who sold you this book a slap, for this is a different lobster altogether.

There were no redheads in the Felian line, apart from a touch of strawberry in the blonde hair of Red's grandmother, Matilda. The queen's barnet was honey-coloured, and the king was blue-eyed, dark, and rangy, and neither of them had a cousin with a head of hair like a bell pepper.

So, it was not the genes that did it. It was something else. Something magical, and probably a touch pagan.

Long before the night Red jumped over the river and celebrated her seventeenth and a half birthday, the kingdom swam on a sea of romance, spawned by the true love of its king for a young woman whose name was Phoebe. This being so, on a warm Friday afternoon in September, King Austin and his future bride wove baskets on a bed of recently fallen maple leaves. After a picnic of malt loaf and a bottle of exceptional peach brandy, they fell into the sort of nuzzling sleep two people very much in love tend to do. The young couple wove baskets until dawn, and in the morning, they swam in the Lake of Stars, with scarlet leaves stuck to their skin and lodged in their hair. On Monday, after unconsciously changing the colour of the royal line forever, they returned to work like everyone else. Nine months later, Phoebe had a baby – a baby born with hair the colour of new wine held up to the light, like autumn leaves in the sun. On some days, the baby's hair was so vivid the servants found it hard to look at anything else. The princess' locks eventually inspired the bestselling rouge at the time – 'Carmine on Friday' – and unless stuffed thoroughly into a hat, she was impossible to miss.

After Red was born, Landfelians embellished the tale of her making and it was passed down as a warning to their young. 'All manner of magic and mischief can occur around that lake.'

During the reign of King Austin and Queen Phoebe, these sorts of inexplicable episodes went on the whole time. White witches roamed free, practising their healing arts. Robins left little blue eggs in hedgerows with no fear of them being stolen or scrambled for breakfast. There were no unseemly fogs. The king and queen were so happy that the entire country caught the feeling, and an age of romance was born. The queen began to build her Still Places – peaceful havens dotted around the kingdom – and she became a great patron of the arts. The king wrote a book under the nom du plume Michael Dashing: *An Adventurer's Guide to Basket Weaving*.

The Four Great Realms sat easily alongside one another. Even the small locality of Thorne in the West Realm – which could be troublesome and inclined to putting heads on spikes – enjoyed a time of peace.

As Red Felian grew up, neither her hair nor her spirit became less interesting. She could not walk into a field of frisky bulls without warming up for a sprint first, but generally, tranquillity reigned – until the year of the Great Vanishing, when everything changed in Landfelian.

After the queen disappeared, people grew too sad to weave baskets. 'What's the point?' They shrugged. Riots started outside the School for Romantic Thought. They were not very good ones, but riots nonetheless. Young women and men decided to study rocks and moss instead. Bandits stalked the highways, digging large holes and hiding in trees, hoping to catch noblemen and women to steal their food and footwear. There was very little kissing in Landfelian. Kissing was rarely seen and usually done by mistake, resulting in some embarrassment. Many forgot how to say the word and came out with 'kicking', which was entirely different.

There was only one who did not lose hope in the years after the Great Vanishing: Red Felian. Her hope burned bright. She was confident the king and her mother would return. Afterall, her father had made a promise.

What had caused the Great Vanishing remained a mystery. At first, Queen Felian simply began to have trouble sleeping. For three months, she paced her rooms at Celador while her husband snored contentedly from the royal bed. At the same time as her insomnia arrived, the weather in the South Realm turned, and a strange fog rolled in from beyond the mountains. By dawn on the first clear morning, with her nerves shattered, the queen went for a walk. She liked to walk as far as the castle gates, where a fine view of the South Realm could be seen before returning for breakfast with her family. On this day, the household woke to find she had disappeared without a word or a note, and her valien's stable was empty.

Some would say Red had no choice but to vanish; the way of her mother, the way of her father. But no one outside the palace knew the true reason for the Princess' sudden leap.

She had tried to run away from Paloma before – several years earlier, after the voodoo teeth were fitted around her ankle. It had been the night of her step-aunts Matchmaking Party (that woman did not need much of an excuse to make good use of a champagne bowl). It was also the eve of Red's sixteenth birthday and the first day of autumn. The Great Matchmaking Party did not involve lighting matches and saying, 'Ah look, there burns a good one.' It involved young men at the furry, moist stage with whiskery moustaches and voices like trumpets. Although it was preposterous, something told Red that her step-aunt was preparing to marry her off. She decided not to hang around and see what happened after the suitors finished the duck liver pâté and had a good go at the punch. Instead, the princess hatched a plan to get out of the castle and fast.

'I'll need this portable spyglass – ha, yes!' She threw it high in the air, where it hit the ceiling and broke. She put it in the hemp sack anyway and stared at the pile of clothes on her bed. A slim cat by the name of Julia purred through the maps, stockings, and wigs. She did not speak, but a cat of Julia's experience could say an awful lot with the flick of her tail and a slow blink of her blue eyes. She was wiser and cleaner than most humans, with fur the colour of a black pearl. She belonged to Red's godmother (who was possibly a witch – although her family had never been certain).

Red removed an extendable top hat and a silk snake filled with dry broad beans from the 'To Pack' pile and rifled further into her trousseau. 'Aha! Father's old riding coat.' It was arrow proof, rain proof, and it looked like it knew where she was going even if she did not. Red put it on and breathed in its familiar smell.

'And he will know it's me when he sees it.' She chewed her nail, unsure. 'Well, he'd bloody better.'

Red had not been out of the palace grounds since her journey from Celador in the South Realm. Her guardians, the half-king and half-queen, insisted it was not safe, that the Kingdom was changed – but enough was enough. She had to escape.

The voodoo anklet of discoloured teeth grazed against her skin. She could not remember the last time her right foot had felt warm. And downstairs, a selection of suitors – sons of gentlemen, apparently – were gathered to win her hand and heart, burping their way through the canapés.

Slamming a book entitled *Wild Flowers of Landfelian* into her bag, she grabbed a frock shirt, flat cap, and a pair of long johns from the dressing up trunk.

'So long, Julia.' Red headed to the door. 'I will find the king and bring him back before my step-aunt and uncle drink what's left in the cellars and turn this palace in to a Fronche court. I will live by my wits and …' She tried the knob. It was locked from the outside. 'Oh no.' Red then surpassed all expectations and climbed out the window, along the roof, down, and in through the window of another wing.

She made it all the way past the guards, down the main avenue, and on to the nearest tavern, The Parsnip's Nose. Her ankle began to bleed heavily halfway through her first pint of bitter, shortly after which she fainted. The new man in charge of royal security and a fistful of his guards lifted her from the floor and carried her back to Paloma.

It was then that Red knew what the teeth around her ankle were really for. Her step-aunt had waved away the matter after the clasp had been secured. 'A mere trinket, dear, to keep you safe.' The spell remained inert as long as she stayed on the palace-side of the Bigeasy River, but if Red wandered too far, the enchanted teeth would slowly gnaw through to the bone and darkness would consume her.

Princesses in other lands did not have to deal with this kind of rubbish They were dancing under shimmering lights and kissing the lips of fair, blue-eyed, sword-wielding princes. They were highlighting their hair with lemon juice and wearing corsets tighter than napkin rings. Not Red. She planted carrots with the groundsmen, studied her maps, and tried to find a way around the voodoo.

In the years that followed her imprisonment, Red planned her breakout in a far corner of the palace gardens. Behind the potting shed, next to the compost heap, where Jim True inspected baby pineapples and planted spaghetti squash, she drew possible escape routes in the soil. Red grew taller, stronger, and she gained breasts. They were small but convincing. Jim True's wife started feeding her wholesome stews and apple pies from the orchard, after seeing her working alongside her husband each day until the light faded. Despite not having a great deal of experience outside of Paloma, she had a lot going for her. Or a lot to lose, depending on your view of such things. The voodoo charm attached to the princess' ankle made the groundskeeper uneasy. It cast a dark shadow over her skin and could not be removed by force alone. There was something terribly unnatural about it.

Once through Boundary Hedge, Red rode for five more hours until the night began to fade and light infused the sky. *It must be close to sunrise.* She began to feel a little anxious. You see, the princess had the distinct feeling she was being watched.

'That black squirrel has followed us all the way from the Bigeasy,' she said to her valien. 'I don't trust it. Is the Head of Security training squirrels now? I wouldn't put it past him, the swine. What do you think?'

Face snorted in response.

'You think I'm being overly suspicious. Well, one has to be.'

As they passed another abandoned cottage, she prattled on to keep herself calm. The princess could talk to anything for hours – a willing tree, a cluster of basking dragonflies, some bumblebees surfing the lavender. She was less easy with people. She did not know that many and she trusted even less.

On she talked. 'What part of the North Realm is this?' She swept up a handful of white flowers and inhaled. 'Mmm, sheep parsley. Or is it nun's drift?' The half-queen had removed all wildflowers from Paloma's gardens, preferring more disciplined beds and borders. 'We must be in the Haa valley!'

It was a common-held belief that princesses across the board were on heat one-hundred-and-fifty per cent of the time. There were countless tales about it, young women hunting innocent princes by night, gate-crashing balls, eating trippy apples, messing around with spinning needles, sleeping with peas, and letting strange men kiss them. Red Felian came from a slightly different mould. She spent her days outside, running, riding, and digging. She enjoyed weeding and reading any books concerning clouds – particularly the work of her godfather Peter, who was an explorer and inventor, of sorts.

Besides a keen interest in horticulture, Red was into weather, with special credit to storms. She loved a big sky and a shakedown in the heavens. At a gust of wind through the wisteria or a tease of lightning on the horizon, she would climb onto the roof of her turret and wait for the clouds to march over Paloma, whipping her hair about so it roamed tall above her head. While other young ladies experimented with ribbons and bonnets, this princess studied the sky. She watched storms roll in, mighty and bulbous, across the White Ocean and the Sea of Trees. She had inherited this passion from the queen, who was fond of riding in turbulent weather and reading filthy novels in the rain, underneath a large parasol.

By some miracle, Red and Face were on course for Little Snoring. They were heading south-east – away from the storm, through Haa Valley, and avoiding the Swift Highway – on a lesser-known track that smelt very faintly of pigs. The Swift Highway was not what it used to be when it was a busy thoroughfare leading to the city of Alba. It had been a road full of merchants and traders, but now on either side lay blistered, stubbled fields and bundles of sleeping rags – hawkers and peasants crouched in the ditches to avoid Blackwood's Guards.

The hedgerows swayed, full of ticks the size of thimbles, filled with the blood of thieves.

As dawn grew close, Red began to feel more peculiar. She tried not to think about the voodoo charm on her ankle, but there was no denying its power. At first there was a twitching behind her eyes, and then her mouth became very dry, which developed into the feeling of having an exceptionally large tongue. Her sight was definitely on the way out. 'Why is that handkerchief flying above us?' she asked, squinting at an owl. 'Are you going blind too, Face?'

Grunt.

'Oh God, what is happening? How am I supposed to find anyone if I can't see them?'

Red tried blinking lots, but the edges of her vision remained blurry. She tried not to panic and focused on the fact that the air smelt of rain. 'We need to find shelter. The storm is coming this way.'

A cold wind found her neck and hands. It found her toes too, and her ankle rubbed painfully against her boot. She told her ankle to hold on; in a few days she'd arrive in Alba, and help was on its way to meet her there. Her stomach yowled hungrily over the wind. The valien would have given away his collection of big sticks for a trough of warm oats and sweetened milk.

She tried to block out the pain and concentrate on the countryside around her. It was then that she saw another sign. The kingdom was full of land markers, all open to interpretation. Some were utter nonsense, others more geographically sound. The results were quite startling, if you enjoyed getting lost. Most were difficult to spot and did not look like signs at all – they came in all shapes and sizes, from haunting sculptures of minotaurs to lady hares made from petrified wood and engraved with riddles.

Red approached a dead elm which was carved in such a way it resembled a towering hat stand. Old hats hung from each branch, now covered in moss and ivy, and the names of places were painted around the rim of each one in silver calligraphy. Branches then pointed the way. Red stopped beneath the tree, got off her horse, and had to climb a little to decipher the words painted upon the hats.

HEAVENHAM
THE SLEEPING HILLS
RHUM – SMALLEST CITY IN THE NORTH REALM
THIS WAY FOR THE SOUTH REALM
WATERWOOD

And on the smallest– an archer's hood covered in lichen – were the words:

THE HONEST SAUSAGE
Recommended in the Good Horse Stop Guide.
Two days amble on an ass, one on a horse, three on foot, five on crutches.
Not long at all on a valien, but if you've got one of those, I'm the king's jester.

'That's it, Face. We'll head there before we make our way to Alba.'

Sausages ... Just thinking about them made Red's mouth ache. And The Honest Sausage sounded promising – it was out of the way, and it would have a hot, pork-based menu. Sausage pie, sausage roll, sausage on toast – all things she rarely got at the palace. Her growling stomach was now riding her horse.

They rode blindly past a bony man reaching out from a tree with a knife between his teeth; further on they trotted over a human-sized lizard lying across the road holding a net. The lizard said, 'Ow' and 'Truck;' as Face stamped over him. The princess was so deep in thought and pain that she missed every one of the six bandit attempts to drag her from her horse.

Where would she go after Alba? she wondered. Straight to Celador, or her godmothers', if they were still living in the south realm ... She remembered little of them, except that they were informed in 'the whiter kinds of magic'. Yes, Maggie and Jan would know something about the hexed teeth on her ankle, and Red wanted to know where it had come from. You can't just walk into a molar shop and ask for a box of human bone containing cursed teeth and some mouthwash. She had read all she could in Paloma's library, and one thing she knew was that voodoo required sorcery. It required a hefty amount of bad energy, some chanting, a black candle, and almost always a witch. This meant someone inside Paloma knew a witch. And if there was a dark one practising in Landfelian. it must be brought to the attention of the king.

'Daniel Blackwood is not the only one behind these wretched teeth, Face, I am sure of it.' The thought of him and his silver-topped cane made her skin crawl. 'Protection, my foot,' she muttered. At Paloma, the man in charge of security would look on her as if she was something he wanted to bottle up and sniff every day. There was no escaping him. His sharp face would appear from shadows or in nearby windows. By the lake, his reflection would find hers, motionless apart from a trail of smoke from his stinking cheroot. He would curl his fingers around his cane and mouth the word, 'soon'.

Red tried not to think about what Blackwood wanted from her. There were days when he would disappear, take the barouche, and not inform the half-queen or half-king where he was going. He always returned with renewed vigour and the same hungry glimmer in his eye. One day, she had decided to tell her step-aunt and uncle how the new Head of Security made her feel uneasy. They guffawed and told her she was being wilful. 'Wilful!' She gritted her teeth and urged the valien on.

Ah, the half-king and half-queen. Red's step-uncle, Gerald Godfrey Pooter-Smythe, and his wife, Caroline, currently the gatekeepers of Paloma Palace and guardians to the only remaining heir of the kingdom. The king had made a huge error of judgement giving these two characters such a position of power. No one had expected them to get the job, and certainly not for long. Before the king had left on his quest to find the queen, he was not in his right mind. His stepbrother was family after all, and what was it that people said about family? Blood being thicker than milk and all that. What could go wrong, with them in charge while he was away?

A king should never ask what could go wrong, unless they want something unpleasant to land on the throne. And in this case, something had. Red didn't care if they were relations, a family is about trust and love. If you don't have those things, you don't have family.

The half-queen had been christened Morag. She'd changed her name to Caroline as soon as she was old enough to look her mother in the eye and say, 'No.' She was a pin of a woman with no waist to speak of and very little brain. If a stick insect swallowed a cork, its silhouette would be very similar. She had the legs of an undernourished sapling and a small, shrunken head that creeped out of her corsets like a shrew. Her lips were permanently stained rouge, behind which her teeth were yellowing. Her eyes, once a pretty blue-grey, had fallen from grace and clarity years ago. White pouches sat beneath them, and in moments of high stress, these turned purple. Too many heavy wigs had weakened her hair so much that in a high wind, without a hat, large parts of her scalp could be seen.

Red knew it was the sudden riches that had pickled Caroline and Gerald like gherkins. As soon as the herald had given them the keys to the kingdom, Caroline's first words to him were, 'And precisely where are the vaults with the gold? Could you provide me with a map?' Caroline – a former governess – gorged on her new position as steward to the throne, binging on all the beauty and wealth. And she held ball after ball. She began her day with a julep, heavy on the gin, and ended it with a shot of reduced sloe. After a month she insisted everyone refer to her and her husband as the half-queen and half-king. Once she had sat her bony bum down on the throne and looked up at the painted fresco of 'An Imagined Garden in Paradise', there was no turning back.

Unfortunately for the realms, she was the closest thing they had to a full queen. She was loathed but not hated by the locals. They could not hate her, for she did not have a complete brain; there were some important parts missing, namely a sense of responsibility beyond her own and her husband's gratification. Through Caroline's eyes, the kingdom stretched no further than Paloma's gates.

Red had watched her step-aunt and step-uncle like two balloons slowly filling up with water. As the years passed, they grew more and more intolerant, puffy, and irritable. She wondered what she had done to make her only official family tire of her so soon. At the same time, as the gout began to settle in and mouth ulcers popped up like salt piles, Caroline decided to get rid of the only other permanent resident in the palace. Red was the final snag in Caroline's fishnets. Every time the half-queen glimpsed the princess' flaming hair through a window or from the seat of her portable throne, she suffered a sharp pain in her chest and was reminded of two things:

1. What she had once been: young. (Now, under the midday sun, Caroline looked sixty-one. Anyone who enquired further into her birth date was banished to another realm.)
2. What she never would be: royal, in the true-blooded sense.

Something had to be done. Caroline thought hard, which took effort and exquisite new stationery. The servants sensed Red's doom like an approaching storm. And the more the princess tried to be liked by her guardians, attending lectures on wig maintenance and advanced topiary, the worse she made it.

Time passed, and Caroline thought of nothing else. Her charge grew tall and willowy; she slowed down, filled out until there was no getting away from the fact that Red Felian was a sure-fire fox. The young footmen forgot to polish things when the princess wandered in looking for a book. Guests stopped to gaze at the line of beauty she cast riding by on her horse. It was not an obvious beauty, and there were days she looked as rough as a bad day at sea, but she had natural grace.

The half-queen played Gin Rummy constantly, a game she was unbeatable at, to calm her nerves. One day, during a game with a young courtier called Sir Toby Mole, Caroline was on her eleventh sherry and winning. She shuffled and stared fixedly at the cards as they blurred through her jewelled fingers.

'I say, Caro,' came Toby's sweaty voice, 'you're really whipping me up this morning. I seem to have run out of gold … What can I possibly bet with now?' He grinned affably. 'My clothes, ha ha!'

Outside, the princess was riding her vast spotty beast up and down the back drive. Caroline turned away from the window and looked at her sherry with the concentration of a surgeon about to remove the appendix from an ant. 'Gerald and I struggle terribly for room here in the palace. I am at my wits end.'

Paloma Palace had seventy-eight rooms. Toby pondered this. It seemed a lot of room for three people. 'I don't see how –'

'That girl takes up all the air. I can't go outside without seeing her with that muddy man, digging,' she snapped.

Toby had never seen Caroline outside. 'But you don't like going outdoors.'

'That is not the point,' she squawked. 'I would like it a lot more if the girl were elsewhere.'

Sir Toby rolled the dice. 'You could always wager the princess away in a bet.' He smiled in a chummy way and took a slurp of his julep. He was joking, of course. Sir Toby was at his most winsome and stupid with a pack of cards and a cocktail.

Caroline looked at him and her eyes grew bright. 'What

a winning idea.' She wasted no time. 'If you win the next game, my dear man, you shall win the princess.'

'Well, I don't really think ...'

Caroline proceeded to play the worst game of her life until the job was done. She polished off her drink and clapped. 'Sir Toby, please proceed to the far easterly turret to claim your prize!' After years of seething, she couldn't believe how easy the whole thing was to resolve. 'Do you know, I think I shall have a ball to celebrate.'

Caroline was beside herself with excitement. She would make Sir Toby Mole the husband of Red Felian. He was a gentleman's son, born to Lord Christopher Mole, first of the king's heroes and heir to Mole Hall. There were a few hitches to iron out, of course – age, consent, living arrangements – but the general gist was a good match to be well and quickly made. She hurried down to the cellars to inform Gerald.

Her husband looked completely confused at the news. 'But, darling, I don't understand. How could this have happened?' He placed a tasting glass carefully down on a barrel of port and looked glassily at his wife. 'I was not aware the princess had feelings for Sir Toby ...'

'Don't be ridiculous, Gerald,' she snapped.

The half-king stared at the ceiling and tried to remember the last time he had seen his niece. 'They are rarely in the same room. But if you say she really loves him, then ...''

'This is marriage. Feelings have nothing to do with

it. He won her, fair and square, in a game of Gin Rummy.' Caroline fluffed up her wig and sniffed. 'Perfectly legitimate. The girl will be weak with excitement when she finds out. She's desperate to get away.'

'Get away? I was not aware she was unhappy.' Gerald chuckled nervously and looked upon his wife. 'You are a rare jewel. So astute.'

Caroline smiled at her husband. 'We must have a ball to celebrate.'

'Very well. You know best.' Gerald then disappeared off to run a bath, leaving his wife to design the invitations.

FORMALITIES

After the celebration of her highness' engagement at the Greatest Wigged Ball of All Time, the princess will depart from Paloma with Sir Toby Mole. They will be married in a private ceremony on the Mole Estate by Thomas Finkermeyer, the royal holy man, and Master Blackwood, the head of security.

The princess' belongings and horse will follow.

THE VERY SMALL PRINT
With the departure of the princess, the half-queen and half-king
will remain guardians of Paloma until the return of the king.
If the king has not returned by the day the quest reaches its tenth year,
they will preside over Landfelian until a rightful heir takes the helm.

Caroline got a few peasants who could not read to sign a declaration summarising the order of events. Gerald added his signature and tried to ignore a dull throb of apprehension by inspecting the contents of the cellars again.

Soon thereafter, Red found her step-aunt with a footman, measuring the dimensions of her chamber. 'What are you doing up here, step-aunt?'

'I simply wish to know if this turret could house a second wiggery.'

'But then where would I sleep?' Red laughed, nervously.

'Elsewhere, my dear.' The reply was sharp as a lemon.

Red tried not to panic. She had a plan, after all. And it had just been fast-tracked.

* * *

'I'll be sleeping elsewhere, alright,' murmured Red as Face galloped on, further and further away from the palace, away from the well-tended gardens and the final hours of the ball. 'Hateful, the pair of them.' She wiped her eyes.

Face had been galloping for half the night. He was as thirsty and hungry as a sheep in the Goby (the Goby was an area of Landfelian between the North and West Realm where nothing grew but the prison and around that a never-ending bog). As for Red's ankle ... It had moved past throbbing and was teetering dangerously close to tearing through the third of her six bandages. What Red said next would not have been understood by any creature nearby.

'Weareinrealtroublemyfriend.'

She could no longer speak properly. This had happened once before, when she had drunk a bottle of pear schnapps at a formal picnic and tried to cartwheel over the badminton net. The sky was now turning pink. 'Itsmorning.'

They were only a day's ride from Paloma and the storm. It would not be long before the roads teemed with guards. Dragging herself upright, she clicked encouragingly at her horse. 'IcansmellsausageFacewearaclose.'

Red could see the faint glimmer of lanterns ahead: a dwelling of some kind. She whimpered blindly towards it as dawn broke in the sky. Finally, they reached the back door of a dusky pink farmhouse, where, apart from the gentle pecking of some hens with feathered legs, all was quiet. She could make out some worn letters on the side of the house in front of her. **The Honest Sausage**, she read, just as the world turned black.

THE HONEST SAUSAGE

A woman called Nin Potts was in bed. She was not fully awake, but she was close. She yawned and turned over. When the birdsong outside her window reached full chorus, she yelled, 'Oh shut your pie holes,' stretched until her back cracked, and rolled slowly out of bed. She padded downstairs, opened the back door, and took a good look at the sky. 'Pink and troubling,' she deemed it and slammed the door shut. After a strong cup of tea, Nin was a different woman. She pulled on a pair of sturdy boots and said hello to her cow. Still in her nightie as the animals chirruped and snorted insistently around her, she filled a bucket with muddy spuds from the garden. She was so immersed in the tasks of the morning that she did not immediately notice the giant horse leaning against the wall of her house or a young lady slung around its neck, fast asleep and pale as the moon. Leaving her cup in the vegetable patch, she returned inside to throw cold water over her face and have a wash. Trotting back, she retrieved her tea, took a slurp, and tripped over the hoof of a valien.

'MARY, MOTHER OF MICHAEL AND MILLICENT!' Nin dropped the cup. 'What the devil are *you* doing half-dead against my house?' The horse opened one beautiful hazel eye to look at her. 'You won't find any young fillies in here my lad – only sausages.' She stared at his solemn face. She wasn't particularly interested in horses, but this one was unlike any she had ever seen. He had a long, curved neck and was twice the size of her old mare. Face flicked his left ear at her, which was all he could manage.

Nin scratched her head. Why had the condiments man delivered a horse? She had asked for sweet relish and mustard from Engerlande this month. Nin patted his nose and gathered up a few more potatoes.

'You'll get right under my skirts if you stay there. I've got an inn to run.' She sighed, looking at her jumbled garden. 'If you could call it that.'

And then a voice spoke, which sounded like a barking toad with bronchitis, and she tripped over her spade in surprise.

'Excusemegoodladyisittoo earlytoenquireaboutafullLand- felianbreakfast?'

'A talking horse, by Joseph!' Nin peered closer

and finally located a windswept girl with red hair, sitting cross-legged on the ground beneath the giant brown horse. 'Good Lord, lass! What happened to you? Come in, quick, you'll get piles sitting down there.' She looked at the sky. 'There's a storm coming from the north.' Nin put a firm arm around the princess' waist and pulled her inside the warm fug of the farmhouse. The girl had a slight limp on one side and was a dead weight in her arms. After leaning her against a beam in the kitchen, Nin set about making more tea. 'It's turning out to be a devil of a day. There's a cold wind this year from the south. And I've another leak in the roof.' She stood back and looked at Red, who was sliding down the beam. 'And now you show up. That horse must stay outside; he won't fit in my stable. I'll fetch him a blanket.'

Red mumbled, 'thank you' from the floor.

'Dear me.' Nin steered her towards the Man of the Road's bench by the fire and put a cup of tea in front of her. 'You can sleep here.' *What a strange, bedraggled thing,* Nin thought. *She must have come from the abbey in Heavenham – with a voice like that, she was bound to be holy and northern.* She looked again. The very far north – her silk dress and strong chin did not echo any of the nuns Nin had in recently. She watched as Red struggled to remain awake on the bench. The girl had peculiar, green eyes and there was something familiar about her hair, but Nin could not place it. 'I'll get you some ginger syrup for that throat.' She thought some more. Convent girls were mousey and not encouraged to ride. Whoever she was, the girl had clearly fallen on hard times. Nin sighed. Hadn't everyone?

Red struggled out of her boots. She clutched the table and winced as she pulled her left foot free.

What an ugly-looking anklet, Nin thought. She prodded the fire and threw a couple of logs into the grate. No, she reconsidered, the girls skin was too smooth for a traveller,' but the girl was too small breasted for a gypsy and her skin too smooth, which would surely make her a runaway from one of the ruined estates closer to Paloma. Yes, that was it. She was the lovechild or daughter of a disgraced landowner. A mistress to some gentleman with a thing for horrible foot adornments – a foreigner, perhaps. Nin Potts smiled encouragingly at her guest. She loved a good story as much as she loved a good sausage, which was why she was the perfect innkeeper. No one this intriguing had been left outside her back door for years.

'So, what are you running from then, my lovely?' she asked, making a start on breakfast. At Red's silence, she pressed on. 'No matter, let's feed you up and set you on your way again after a good sleep. Have you been having trouble at home?' She melted half a pound of butter in a pan, pounded and dusted a round of dough, and placed it over the fire to bake, with an assortment of other loaves. Nin set a pail of water sweetened with honey in front of the valien, and the animal dunked his head in thankfully.

Red pretended not to hear. She stopped fiddling with

her bandages and found the table laden with food.

'Eat up quick,' advised Nin, 'before any Men of the Road get here and finish the fried tats. I apologise for my spuds, they're not growing as well as they should. I only collected a dozen this morning and they were smaller than the goats balls. It's the weather. Something fishy going on in the waters of this realm at the moment.' With a flick of apron strings, Nin placed a further platter steaming with everything good from the garden in front of Red and gave her a wink. 'Wherever you are running to, no one leaves The Honest Sausage hungry.'

Red could have cried at the table before her. 'This is too much, thank you.'

'My pleasure, duck.'

There was a bowl of dark cherries, a basket of warm bread, wild berry jam, and salty butter. And there were sausages – herby and crisp – with a mountain of golden-edged potatoes. The eggs were peppered and scrambled, next to mushrooms and tomatoes laced with garlic leaves. Sleep could wait, and so could the king. *In fact, sod the king*, Red thought as she chewed bread like no other bread she had ever chewed. It was dense and rich; if butter needed a reason to be, surely it was for this bread alone. Under the half-queen's instruction, the food at Paloma had been terribly complicated. Perfumed jellies, pickled herrings, and roasted peacocks were often the order of the day.

Red sighed as she placed her cutlery together on the empty plate, sat back, and looked around her. The Honest

Sausage was nothing more than a large room filled with worn tables, high-backed benches, and two cracked leather chairs by a fireplace, which took up one whole wall. Merry flowers in glass jars stood upon gingham tablecloths, and pewter tankards hung from hooks above a worn worktop, beyond which there was a stone-flagged kitchen. A large window there looked out on to a cow and some old stables. The farmhouse smelt of homemade bread and woodsmoke.

A chocolate-coloured dog followed the innkeeper around the room, wagging its tail in a circle. Red moved closer to it as she drank her tea, and the dog came to rest its silky head on her knee.

'Sophie! Leave the girl alone.' Nin emerged from the kitchen and beamed. 'Have another sausage.'

'I don't think I can.' She laughed, looking at her plate. 'I've never had a breakfast like it.'

'Well, you should have.' Nin took a bucket of oats covered with sticky treacle outside. Face sniffed her bosom appreciatively and devoured the bucket, making happy grunting noises. 'You'll both have your twinkle back in no time,' said Nin, coming back inside. She sat down and looked at the princess. 'Now then, where are you from?'

Red covered her ankle with her dress and smiled carefully. 'A ditch, not far from here.'

Nin studied her face. It looked hunted. 'Fair enough. As long as you don't bring in any undesirables – no bandit boyfriends – you can stay for as long as you like.'

'Do you get many visitors?' It was early, and the inn appeared empty, but Red feared it wouldn't stay that way. 'Any guards?'

'You're safe on that score. Them Blackwood guards haven't been this way for months. Only my regulars come here. Mind you, I don't get much young female company.' She sighed. 'Only the odd hag.'

Red was relieved. She would stay a little longer. Nin was not at all what she had expected from an innkeeper. She was not as fat or old. Her pretty, freckled face frowned as she wrote the menu on the wall in round, well-fed letters, and Red noticed sad lines around her mouth.

Menu of the Day

LEEKY SAUSAGE
HERBY SAUSAGE
MUSHROOM SAUSAGE
ALL SERVED IN A PIE WITH HOLE, ONION
GRAVEE, FRIED TATS, TOMS, SHROOMS, WILD
GARLICK AND NORTH REALM MUSTARD FROM
OUR LOCAL CONDIMENTS MAN, CLIVE.

The Honest Sausage was hard to find if you did not know where to look. It was hidden the other side of a crinkle-crankle wall that stretched for many miles up the western flank of the North Realm. The wall concealed a hero's estate – long since abandoned, because of the quest. Over the years, Nin's blushing farmhouse had sunk a bit; the roof dipped in the middle and the windows leaked. A compost heap sweetened the air and a brood of wide-hipped hens clucked about. The farmhouse was the last inhabited place before Waterwood – an impassable basin of ancient, closely woven trees separating the North Realm from the East Realm where the Bigeasy River did not. Riders rarely travelled through this wood. Many had forgotten it was even there and just considered it a dark tangle on the map that was generally best to go around.

The Honest Sausage was especially popular with Men of the Road, when Men of the Road had been a more frequent sight across Landfelian. Nin lived alone, apart from one such man who claimed the bench by the fire and slept there between hustling for work. Most of the regulars were servants from deserted estates and farmhands – numerous chambermaids called Kitty and poor, jobless men waiting for the return of the king and better days.

Red wondered what it would be like to live in a place like this. She would have liked to stay and be like Nin, occupied by simple, physical tasks. It reminded her of spending hours with Jim in the kitchen garden listening to him talk about his family. Red took a deep, shaky breath. It would be peaceful. From her seat by the fire (she was still too full to walk), she watched the lady of the rest house prepare food for the ruddy men and women who wandered in. Only one thought occupied her mind; how long did she have before the voodoo consumed her? Now with the fire warming her bones, she suddenly felt very tired and alone. Her whole body ached from the journey. She tried to summon the will to get up and continue on but kept drifting in and out of sleep.

In the afternoon, Nin appeared in front of the fire holding her first batch of scones, their tops turned a deep nutty brown. 'These fellows had a bit too much sun, but they'll be soft as cream inside, with a good coat of butter.' She put three on Red's plate, got a whiff of unwashed sweat and skin, and bellowed BATH at her. Red dropped her scone in shock. 'How about a nice hot bath?' Nin said more quietly. 'No offence, duck, but you smell like a fox hole.'

'I do?'

'Yes. I've met tramps who smell better. And you've got half the road stuck to your face.'

'I think I may have trodden on something in that last ditch.' Red studied the hem of her dress, which was brown.

'Get upstairs. I'll bring hot water to fill the trough.'

'The trough?' Red replied weakly.

'Yes, you get in it. Folks call it a bath.'

'Oh.' Red had never washed in a trough before. The half-king bathed twice a day at Paloma, but Red avoided taking her clothes off anywhere Blackwood might find her. She made do with splashing her bits in the lake when she was sure no one was watching her swim.

'Do you have a name? Mind I've got a terrible head for names. Called my husband Bill for years, and he called me Sybil. We were both floating up the wrong estuary.' She blinked at the fire and took a big bite of a scone. 'A great bear of a man he was.'

'My name's Mary – Mary Drew.' Red tried to sound normal. She passed Nin the jam. She wasn't good at talking about feelings. She was better at staying busy before they overwhelmed or took something from her. When others cried, she normally put out an unsure hand or did something alarming like hold the person's foot and cough. 'What *was* his name?'

'Thomas.'

'That's a good name.' Red bit her lip and sat on her hands.

Nin smiled. 'Well, if he ever comes back, I'll kill him. How long does a quest take, I ask you?'

Red began to choke on her scone, showering Nin with crumbs. 'Quest?'

'Yes, love. No need to spit.'

'The king's quest?'

'Yes, is there any other? My other half was a romantic fool … He went to be a cook on board one of the hero ships that left seven years ago. Wanted to do his bit. Keep the men and women from going hungry while they searched for the queen. He left with the owner of this estate – a good man, one of the Seven Heroes – they called him the Duke.' Nin gave a sad little laugh. 'I haven't seen the silly arse since, but I've been saving the grill pan for him to wash when he gets back.' She paused. 'You've gone quite white again, duck. Not enough iron,' Nin decided. 'Have another sausage and I'll go out and pick you some spinach.'

'Have you had any news about the quest?' asked Red.

'News? Dear girl, have you been locked in a turret? No one has heard a whisper.' Nin began to dust the scones with a tea towel. 'Only rumours.' A shadow passed over her flushed face. 'The Palace Times say the hero ships are turning back and the king continues alone. The condiments man says they are lost in a cold and hopeless fog. Though my Robbie says if you can't touch it, see it, smell it, or put it in your mouth, it's a load of tripe.'

Sophie thumped her tail and looked expectantly at the door.

Red sighed. 'And how does he know?'

'He's a Man of the Road, so he knows all sorts. Probably the last of his kind in Landfelian; the roads ain't what they used to be. He doesn't have a home but helps the families left behind on all those big estates – mends things, walls, leaks.' She smiled. 'I don't know what I would do without him. My poor cow would still be in labour for one, and the roof would have caved in.' She rifled around in her apron and pulled out a handwritten card. 'He runs a tidy little business – calls it At Your Service, Milady. The tart.' She laughed.

Red thought this Man of the Road sounded like an enterprising, cocksure know-it-all.

'Travels from realm to realm, keeps the ladies' spirits up, repaints the front door, oils their hinges, that sort of thing. And he drops in to see an old scrubber like me when he can.' Nin poured Red another cup of tea. 'Take a card. May come in handy if you're ever in a bind. He's the right sort. Not a gentleman, though. I'd stay clear of those if you know what's good for you.'

Red took the card, with every intention of losing it, but glanced at it all the same. The handwriting was surprisingly fine.

AT YOUR SERVICE, MILADY
ROBBIE WYLDE – MAN OF THE ROAD
FOR HANDS-ON HELP
ASK AT THE CAT'S BACK INN, CITY OF ALBA.
PAY IN KIND, KINDLY.

She did not need anyone's help, and certainly not the sort some Man of the Road delivered with suggestive calling cards. She sincerely hoped she would not bump into him when she got to Alba. She gave Nin a clear, if slightly green, look. 'I know the quest will return.'

Nin nodded and wondered why she felt more hopeful hearing this from a runaway, half her age, who wore teeth for jewellery than she had from anyone else in years. 'Bill wouldn't die without telling me. I just wish he would get a move on.'

The princess yawned a yawn that could have housed another person and tilted towards the scones.

'Dear me, Mary, been through more than a ditch, haven't you? Have a bath before you put me out of business and have a sleep.'

'I really must be getting on,' said Red. She looked out the window at the afternoon light and tried to stand.

Nin crossed her arms. 'Whatever it is you're getting on with can wait until you're clean.'

Red lay in The Honest Sausage's trough and allowed steaming lavender water to envelop her shattered body. Her ankle stung like a hornet attack. She had to bite down on a flannel to stop from screaming, 'Ow, frock' when she washed around it. 'A few more days and this will all be over.'

Dark clots of blood had gathered below the surface of her yellow, bruised skin. She was accustomed to a general ache, but this was different; it felt darker and deeper. She rewrapped the bandages as best she could and pushed it to the back of her mind. The pain was temporary and would pass. She had to keep going. It would be dangerous to stay anywhere too long.

Sleep was the best cure, in any Landfelian's book,

to combat sickness – either that or a long bout of laughing. Unfortunately, there were still doctors who went in for leeches and cupping, and in the poorer parts of the cities, there were some worrying practices involving slugs. As afternoon faded, Red yawned, slipping further into the bath. The princess had reached what doctors called the 'toast' stage of exhaustion. In this state, a woman is a dangerous thing to be around. They can do one of three things: cry, give the person nearest to them a really hard time, or fall asleep.

Red brushed her teeth, combed the bugs from her hair, and redressed. Her green dress had been washed and dried, though Nin had given up trying to do anything with the riding coat. It was etched with what looked like a thousand years' worth of challenging terrain. She returned downstairs and sat back down by the fire to put her boots on.

The Honest Sausage had filled up with an evening crowd, but Red slipped back to her seat by the fire without catching anyone's eye. Before she could cry or give any of the quietly supping customers a hard time, she fell quickly into a soundless sleep. A plate of unfinished scones provided a pillow. It came as a relief to many in The Honest Sausage, who sensed the young woman was close to the edge and hoped to avoid a scene. Sprawled across the Man of the Road's bench, Red did not say another word.

5

THE MAN OF THE ROAD

Robbie rode up to The Honest Sausage and slid wearily off his horse. He leant against her warm, rising side and fell asleep there for a few minutes, until an owl hooted.

'Rest, lady,' he said. 'We'll sup here for a few days.' He stroked her muzzle and left her next to a hay basket. Nin's ripe garden was a welcome sight, as was the smell of sausages cooking and the figures of the old pipe smokers lit up in the window. Robbie stretched until his back made a satisfying crack, then walked towards the door without noticing the valien watching him closely from behind a plough cart. His only thought was for his bench by the fire and a tankard of honeydew ale.

There were very few genuine wanderers left in Landfelian. Men without homes tended at least to have a cart or a piece of wood they bedded down on, and even the most peasanty peasants had a gutter to call their own. A true Man of the Road did not go in for such permanence, and Robbie Wylde was one such man – and perfectly content he was with his lot. He carried no key about his person because he owned no door. He was not a roadman, a highwayman, or a travelling man trying to sell something. He was more of a young drifter. He did not know where he would lay his hat at the end of each day and until recently it had never bothered him. No ties meant no mess. As it happened, his hat and boots had often hung in the most mouth-achingly spectacular bedrooms with only the finest views of the Four Great Realms. Because of the king's quest, Robbie found himself in the company of the most powerful women in the kingdom. The quest widows were glad of his company and his strong, capable hands.

He was not a man of the street. Political men were rarely content, and Robbie never had held much truck with politics. He preferred foraging in meadows over wine-fuelled debates, questioning what was good for the kingdom. Nor was he a man of letters, like the herald. He was a man of the world, but a world thus far confined to Landfelian. Should he have the chance to travel far further afield and say, 'Speak freely, for I am a Man of the World,' he would take it with both hands and never look back. In fact, he yearned for nothing more.

Robbie thought about leaving Landfelian every day. He wondered about the colours of a foreign sky. He dreamt of places where he could clear his head from the ghosts of his past and wake up to a warm breeze full of spices. Until he acquired enough gold to afford sea passage out of Landfelian, he concerned himself with eating well, keeping his teeth clean, and caring for the most important woman in his life: his horse. A life on the road in this kingless land no longer held the freedom it once had. Robbie was one of the few Men of the Road that remained. Since the quest, most had turned to begging or been beaten and imprisoned by the guards.

'Nin! You are looking as edible as ever.' It was well after dusk when he strolled through the doors and gave the lady of the house a squeeze as she bent over to prod the fire.

'Get off me, you pirate.' She pushed him away playfully.

'Sausages, all the trimmings, a bottle of ale, and a side of you, please, tulip.'

'How are you going to pay for it this time, Mr Wylde?' Nin looked at him and tried to appear stern.

'In foot massages.' He took off his hat, washed his hands in a bucket by the door, and smiled. 'And I will sing odes about your sausages throughout the land … but for now, if you could put it on my beam, sweet lady.'

'Your beam is full.' Nin made a notch on one of the upright beams and laughed as Robbie gathered her comely body into his arms and waltzed between the tables, singing – in a husky voice – a song about a lonely pie and a hopeful sausage. It was out of tune, but it lifted everyone's spirits. Sid whistled along, and Jerry the local tramp got out his spoons. The place was full of the usual beards. Robbie had missed it. With the end of the song, he took a bow and turned to the fire. 'And what do we have here?'

There was a sleeping pile of clean, young woman on his bench.

'Shush.' Nin tried to steer him away. 'You'll wake her.'

She looked familiar. 'The redhead,' he murmured, letting go of Nin. 'Well I never.'

'Do you know who she is?'

'Not as such.' He had lost sight of the girl's tracks soon after Boundary Hedge.

'Well, leave her alone, then.' Nin retied her apron and did something high and sprouting with her hair. 'She arrived on my porch this morning and has come here for some peace.'

'But she's on my bench.'

'Well, find a new bench and sit on that.' She tutted. 'And take your muddy boots off while you're at it.'

Robbie sat at the end of the bench, unable to take his eyes off the horse thief. Her ear had stopped bleeding, he noticed. She looked softer in the light of the fire. 'I bumped into her on the road – or rather, she ran straight into me – near Paloma. I think she might have stolen a horse.'

'Stolen, from the half-queen and half-king?' Nin looked closer at Red and smiled. 'Good on her.' She turned to Robbie. 'I've gone quite grey at the edges waiting for you to come by.

There's a problem with the window upstairs again, terrible draught.'

He squeezed her hand. 'I'll stay a few days and put it right.'

Nin looked pleased. 'Sit down, you must be famished.'

Robbie stoked the fire and stared at the embers for a moment, moving Red's feet gently out of the way so he could sit down. He ran a hand through his thick hair until it stood up, then removed his boots and a pair of holey socks. Stretching out his legs, he sighed. This was the seventh year of the quest, and it was his last in Landfelian. He couldn't keep up with the ladies' needs, and they no longer had the means to pay him. He nearly had enough gold to bribe a place on board one of the anchored merchant ships, which would set sail as soon as the fog lifted. The thought cheered him. The fog had to clear soon, and then he would leave.

Red smacked her lips together and moved, like a cat in the sun. Robbie turned from gazing at the fire to look at her. Her left foot came to rest comfortably on his knee. He studied her heavily bandaged ankle and slender, bare foot. He could not see much of her face as it was hidden under a mane of red hair, which looked like beech leaves in the flickering light. The old riding coat she lay on had the royal insignia embroidered on the sleeve – a valien jumping out of a crown and the letters *AF*. She appeared young for a horse thief. She had an almost solemn face, except for its curling mouth. One long arm was draped over a pot of wild berry jam.

'What are you running from, then?' he asked her sleeping face.

Red snored faintly and turned over. Robbie looked further down, past her neck. He coughed and regretted it. She moved, and her feet furrowed under his thighs for warmth. There was jam streaked across her cheek. Robbie idly thought about licking it off. He fiddled with the copper wing in his coat pocket.

Robbie soon forgot about his bench and his tired body. He was discovering what the half-queen had spotted and gambled away. Even with food stuck to her face, the princess had something. It didn't knock him down and try and straddle him like some women; it quietly held his attention. It was in her long lashes and long legs, the freckles like cinnamon on cream that dusted her nose and the bridge of her cheeks, a mouth that wanted to smile far more than it wanted to find fault with the world.

The young Man of the Road was enjoying himself immensely by the fire, and so were Red's toes, which were warming up nicely. He gazed lazily at her and drank his ale until something sharp dug into his thigh. He saw it on her left ankle, where some bandages had come loose. Teeth – dark and sharp.

'CHRIST, WHAT THE …?'

Nin's dog howled in surprise at the sudden noise.

Robbie looked closer. 'There is a bony, scorpion thing with teeth … eating this girl's ankle!'

A few folks looked up. Robbie was always getting hot-headed about something, and the patrons of The Honest Sausage were accustomed to his rants.

'I must get it off!' he continued to yell, looking wildly around the room.

Sid asked Nin what the specials were, and she told him.

Robbie stared down in horror at Red's ankle and then at her. She did not seem to notice a part of her was being slowly chewed. He knew what it was: voodoo, it had to be. 'I think she's fainted from the pain. Milady?' Robbie shook her. 'Wake up.'

Red frowned in her sleep and said, 'No.'

He picked up the nearest jar of flowers and tipped the water over her face. 'Someone's put a hex on your ankle!'

Red leapt up, snatched her feet away, and hid them under her dress. Her ankle throbbed painfully. She scooted to the far end of the bench. There was a man staring at her and shouting. He looked familiar.

The bandit.

'YOU!' She thought about kicking him in the codpiece but noticed he wasn't wearing one.

Nin arrived with some sausages. 'Oh good, I see you two are getting on. Robbie is very territorial about his bench,

Mary. Don't take any notice.' She smiled, but it quickly dropped from her face when she heard her dog.

Sophie had stopped wagging her tail and was standing by the front door. A low growl came from the back of her throat. Her eyes did not move from the door, and the hackles along her back stood up. The regulars in The Honest Sausage slowly put down their knives and forks when they heard the noise, and all conversation dwindled to silence.

A distant drumming could be heard.

Robbie stood up and looked out the window. He could see the light of torches moving through the trees towards the inn.

Nin whispered, 'Oh no, they've found us.'

Red stood up, oblivious, and glared at Robbie. 'You followed me!' Robbie stopped her from saying anything more as his warm, rough hand clamped itself firmly against her mouth. She tried to bite it, but he shushed at her. 'Shhh. Listen.'

Red became still and heard the drums, more clearly now. Closer. It was the unmistakable sound of guards. Blackwood's Guards. Each drumbeat made her jump. Robbie took his hand away.

'I don't suppose there is a society of drummers in these parts I do not know about?' Red whispered.

'No, pet,' replied Nin, 'no drummers here, unless you count Jerry's spoons.' She sped into action, hiding the tip box, gently removing the knife from Sid's hand, and hurrying to the door to look down the lane. 'Crapper, it's them guards from the north. Sid, put your knives away! Look sharp, everyone, company's coming. And, Jerry, don't start singing, "Oh When the Guards Come Skipping In" – remember what happened last time.'

Robbie turned away and attacked his sausages. He took an angry gulp of ale and frowned as the drumming got closer. The swines were not going to interrupt his dinner. What had he done this time? He had not been caught poaching rabbits or galloping without a permit, and it was months since his last arrest.

When a Man of the Road is tired, hungry, and falsely accused of wrongdoing, they react in one of two ways:

1. Start a fight with the person nearest to them.
2. Get drunk – drunk until there is no room left to be anything else.

Robbie wondered which way the evening was going to go.

He shot a wary look at the horse thief, fumbling around for her boots and bag. The colour drained from her jammy cheeks.

Perhaps it wasn't him they were after.

He watched the girl try to tie up her laces in a hurry. 'You're making a real hash of that,' he said helpfully.

She ignored him.

'We haven't properly met. Robbie Wylde,' he said, holding out his hand. It was ignored too. 'So, what's your crime, princess?'

'I'm not a princess.' Red picked up his tankard and drained it. He noticed she smelt of bath, jam, and something else … something nice, like lavender. Her eyes were trained on the front entrance. She stood up and crept towards the back door.

'Stolen the king's coat, is that all? Or was it his horse? Don't worry – they let you off lightly for breaking and entering. They'll frisk you, strip you down to your slip, and put you in the stocks for a week.' He popped another bit of sausage in his mouth. 'Nothing to worry about.'

Sophie scratched to be let out, her teeth bared. Everyone in The Honest Sausage heard the sound of leather boots creaking towards the front door.

'You're not a princess, then?' he said, holding up the royal coat.

'No, I'm a …' Red snatched it from him and tried to sound casual. 'I … I'm a … princessgram.'

Even Jerry had trouble swallowing this one and stopped playing his spoons. A princessgram was a personalised greeting with or without a song. Often sent to wish someone a happy birthday. In the spirit of a singing telegram, they were very popular in Landfelian before the queen disappeared and took joviality with her.

'A princessgram?' Robbie raised an eyebrow, his eyes

bright. 'Not a great climate for the royalist-loving crowd. A fairly niche market, I should think.'

Red attempted to melt into the wall, but no one could mistake that there was a person with astonishing hair there, trying not to be seen. It had dried in big, shining red waves by the fire.

Nin quickly threw a shawl at her. 'Put this over your head, quick.'

'You would be surprised,' Red whispered to Robbie, covering her silk dress and hair with the shawl. 'I'm very popular at stag and faith-leaping parties. I also do weddings, birthdays, coming-of-age hog roasts, and full-moon feasts.' She searched around frantically for her hat. 'The hair dye is fairly costly – it takes a lot of beetroot and carrot pulp to get the right red – and my horse wasn't cheap, although I think it's important to commit to the role.'

The man by the fire looked doubtfully at her and then he quickly passed her his hat. Red hastily put it on as a shadow spread across the room from under the front door. The guards had gathered. She stared at the shadow in horror, stepping backwards and reaching for the door behind her. But it was too late.

The front door swung open, letting in an indulgent drumroll and a barrage of boot stamping. A guard with a thick bristle of moustache bellowed, 'That's my foot, bunion head!'

Sophie barked, and a riot of a voice roared at her.

'Shut your mouth you old …!'

Everyone heard the dog yelp. Robbie put down his knife and fork and sighed. The inevitability of pain was written on the walls.

'That brute just kicked my dog!' Nin picked up the nearest thing to hand, a hen-shaped milk jug, and stormed towards the guards.

Robbie reached out and held her back by an apron string. 'Don't waste your good china on them,' he said under his breath as the door was kicked wide open by a thigh-high boot and one fat purple jodhpur. The hinge broke (the hinge knew it would happen; it happened every time).

'Greetings to the foul and the poor. We hail from the palace!' This short announcement was followed by another lobe-numbing drumroll.

When it finished, Sid put his hand up and asked, 'Which palace?'

It was a fair question, there was more than one, but he should have known better. The nearest guard slapped him.

'We, the Blackwood Guards of Paloma and the North Realm, come with grave news in faith!'

A Quick Word about Blackwood's Guards

1. They rode about the North Realm shouting.
2. They were not nice to trees, the poor, or their horses.

3. Each possessed a drum that they could not play but persisted on hitting.
4. Many suffered from impaired hearing.
5. Their uniforms were made from black leather, purple jodhpur, and studded cuffs shaped like spear heads (the half-queen was responsible for the greater part of the design).
6. They were hired by Blackwood to protect the royal legacy and secure the kingdom in the absence of the monarch. Before this, they were self-employed criminals serving time at Hard Place Prison and on Landfelian's Most Unpleasant List, although no one was supposed to know this.
7. Perhaps most surprisingly, the majority of the guards were married, although there was nothing loyal about them at all.
8. As former prisoners, they were never trained in the art of fencing. Instead, they threw things.

There were no further questions. Everyone in The Honest Sausage fiddled with something. A few tables shunted back a couple of feet.

'Princess Felian is missing!' the moustached guard shouted.

There was a genuine gasp amongst the assembled. Nin sat down in the nearest chair. 'Oh, the poor mite.'

The guard spat on the floor and rocked back on his heels, pleased at their reaction.

Robbie turned to look at the redhead trying to disappear further into the wall and raised an eyebrow. She pulled the shawl tighter around her.

'Last night, during the ball, Princess Felian was kidnapped! We come here with a warment.' He frowned at the writing on the scroll. 'No, that's not right. A warm ant to search every premithis... Every prometheus... Oh arse it – every inn in the realm!'

'And try every sausage!' the fattest guard added. 'Until we find her!'

'YEAH, THAT'S RIGHT,' the guards all jeered.

The girl was still frozen by the door. Robbie looked at the selection of drums and gristly men in front of him and stood up. 'Gentlemen, I'm afraid I can't let you do that.'

Ten pairs of eyes swivelled round to look at him, and ten pairs of leather boots squeaked in his direction. Sid swallowed audibly and crossed himself.

Robbie clenched his fists. His arms hung loose by his side. He looked about ready to burst into flame.

'What's it to you?' a guard barked at him.

'Oh dear, not again,' Nin muttered and said farewell to her crockery.

Red tried to remember how to breathe. There was going to be a fight. The bandit was going to start a fight, and maybe then she could open the door.

A foul, pockmarked figure ignored Robbie and leered over to Nin. 'Madam.' He dribbled with sour breath. 'Are you the propeye … The pulpiter …The woman in charge of this rest house?'

'I am.'

'Have you had any princesses in of late?' The guard had taken a shine to Nin's breasts, which were heaving nervously. He leant closer. 'You haven't noticed nothing a bit … curly? You know … off?'

Nin took a polite step back. 'I'm not really on the royal route. You only have to look at my regulars to see that.' She gestured to Sid and Jerry, who did their best to look deranged. 'Not one of them comes from Paloma, and to this day I've never served a princess.'

'Aye, she's got a point there.' The room tutted in agreement.

The guards were not so easily deterred and started eyeing the crowd more closely.

Red tried to turn the doorknob silently. If she left quickly, no one would be hurt.

Nin drew the guards to the corner. 'I'll introduce you to everyone. This is Rod and Regina – they make curd from a small herd of bearded goats in the Misty Mountains. Quite delicious, if you like your yoghurt on the goaty side.' One of the guards made a note. 'Leslie here collects interesting stones, from which he makes pendants. He has a stall at the Lake of Stars festival this year, if you are interested in a token for someone special.' Nin moved the guards on to the next table. 'Eddie and Eileen are travelling minstrels. They play a total of thirteen instruments between them, all from the fiddle family.'

One of the guards came forward and beat his drum at Eddie, who looked terrified. 'How about, "Good morning, sunshine"!'

'What about him?' The moustached guard pointed at Robbie with his club.

'Oh him … He's just a young Man of the Road.' Nin floundered. Robbie mouthed something at her, and she frowned. 'He … he's a fine storyteller. Today, he … claimed he can fly.'

Everyone in the room began to flap their arms and make bird noises, as familiar glances were passed between them.

'It is true, my friends,' said Robbie. 'I'll show you.'

Sid took his teeth out. The tables edged further back.

'There is no need to show them, Robbie.' Nin stood in front of him. 'You will find no princess in here, Captain, only loonies.'

The captain looked at Nin warily and noticed a flash of green in the gloom at the back of the room.

'You!' The guard pushed Nin roughly out of the way and headed towards the silent figure at the back. 'What's your story?'

Robbie quickly climbed onto the nearest table and stretched out his arms. 'Look, I'll show you how I can fly!'

The Man of the Road dived off the table. He flew in the way only a falling man can – that is, not at all. He landed, spread-eagled, on the majority of the guards. Drums got pushed into codpieces, boots squashed against faces, and things that shouldn't be pressed on, were. The scramble of guards grunted in pain as Robbie punched his way free.

Before anyone could work out what had happened, Regina's goat slipped its collar and charged the guard with a prominent Adam's apple. The remaining upright guards fell over like dominos. They suffered from a considerable lack of traction in their leather boots, and Sophie lunged on the one who had kicked her. Biting his shoulder pad, she shook it like an animal possessed – such was the widespread unpopularity of these uniforms. The Adam's apple guard cracked his whip at Regina's goat, wrapping it around his own leg by mistake. Eileen strummed a nervous jig on her ukulele. Leslie took the opportunity to have a good cry, and Robbie did a great deal of damage to anyone underneath him.

Nin looked out the window. The young runaway was hovering outside, looking unsure. She quickly closed the curtains and stood down hard on a guard's hand, but it was too late.

'Captain!'

'What!' He was busy kicking Robbie hard in the ribs.

'The lady by the door. In the green dress. She's escaped!'

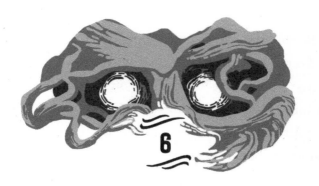

TIMOROUS BEASTS

Red took a deep breath, crossed her heart, and hoped not to die as The Honest Sausage groaned and smashed behind her.

She ran further into Nin's paddock and whistled, but her horse did not come to her. Stood alone in a dark field, she tried to recall where she had parked him. The wind hurled around her, and there was rain in the air. The storm from Paloma had caught up with them.

'Where are you?' The princess felt afraid. She was missing her only ally. A cow sniffed her arm with its wet nose, making her jump. 'FACE!' she hissed. 'We're leaving – right now!' And then she whistled.

Red had many kinds of whistle for many different occasions. This whistle said, *HURRY THE CUP UP.*

The king had taught her about the power of whistles when she was small. '*It is a common misconception, rosebud, that kicking, spurring, and whipping an animal will get it to move faster. This is unnecessary and employed only by oafs.*' She remembered how he could imitate nearly all the native birds and instruct his valien to sit. Where the hell was her father now when she needed him?

Red's whistling had alerted a large male hedgehog to her, and it was this – and not her horse as she had hoped – that ran out to meet her in the dark.

'YOU'VE TASTED YOUR LAST SUGARLUMP!' she screamed.

Sometimes a good threat does just as well as a whistle. The valien appeared behind her and snorted. He'd smelt the guards and waited right next to the back door for Red. The muddy colour of his coat had concealed him so completely that she'd run straight past him.

'Oh, thank God.'

He flicked his tail at her as she climbed onto his back.

There was a sound from the kitchen window. The back door swung open, and the Man of the Road landed on his front, halfway down the steps. He looked up and gave Red a painful smile.

'Hello.' Blood dripped from his nose.

'Hello.' She looked down at him.

'What are you doing?' A meaty fist grabbed hold of

his shoulder, and Robbie called out as he was dragged back inside. 'Run!'

She didn't move. It was only her first day on the road and she had caused a fight. Innocent people were being beaten with maces because of her. She couldn't just leave ...

Robbie yelled harder. 'GO!'

'Yes.' Red pulled herself together and whispered into the valien's twitching ears. They left at a gallop (only a valien can do this with any success), jumping clean over the trough and the garden wall. Red's horse kicked over Nin's potato bucket and woke up the hens. Fleeing from The Honest Sausage, they skidded out onto a lane and turned left in the direction of the East Realm.

Minutes passed before Red realised something was missing. 'My bag!' she yelled. 'The map! My book on wildflowers. We have to go back!' Face kept his course; he was an intelligent horse. Red howled.

There is nothing more upsetting for a woman than leaving her bag behind, apart from perhaps the crushing feeling of having no option but to go back and retrieve it. It is a grievous situation to be in. She checked behind her in case the inconspicuous hemp sack had climbed on somehow in the rush, but it hadn't.

Red would have to continue without it. The princess could hear the guards yelling orders at one another. They were outside now, mounting their horses and rearranging their drums in anticipation of an uncomfortable chase. She narrowed her eyes against the wind and pulled the rim of Robbie's hat low over her face. The guards' horses formed a pack in the distance behind her.

'They think they can catch us,' she whispered to Face. The valien flattened his ears. 'Good luck to them.' Red smiled and leant into his gallop. They flew over the ground. Her knuckles grew white with cold. Sharp twigs nicked her skin, and dust swirled across their path.

The guards' horses were not like hers; not even half like hers. If they caught up with the valien, it would be something to tell their foals one day. They pounded on, grunting with the effort to keep the mighty horse in sight. Red rode light and fast, but the distance between her and the guards remained steady. They refused to give up the chase, following her around every bend and hill and gully.

Realisation dawned on Red. 'We'll never lose them. We need to get off this path – it's too exposed.'

Face couldn't say much by way of a reply, although he did agree.

'What an earth is …?' Red started, before screaming, 'DUCK!'

A signpost soared over their heads in the wind and smashed against the trunk of a strange-looking tree. Red made out the words:

Take the next left for Waterwood
~~(although no one has for years)~~

(A very honest bunch, Landfelian's sign-writers.)

Red looked behind her to see the wind had formed a small twister between her and the guards. Their numbers appeared to have doubled – another clutch from Paloma had joined in the pursuit. She realised the route ahead to Alba would be swarming with Blackwood's men. The thought of him turned her cold. 'He'll cut us off at the city gates.'

Red became aware of the odd-looking trees looming over the road to her left. The ancient wood smelt sweet and mossy, like a den. It would be a good place to hide until the guards passed by. Red saw Waterwood as a helpful, if slightly wizened, hand extended in help. What harm could come to her in this wood? There would be nothing but trees – lots of trees, and she loved trees. Although she recalled reading something about the wood in Father Peter's journal … She wished she had her bag with her to check what it had said.

A second sign came into view, poking out of the ditch at a jaunty angle.

THIS WAY FOR WATERWOOD
TREAD SOFTLY

And in very small, anxious writing that ran off the edge of the sign:

NORTH REALM SIGN MAINTENANCE TAKES NO RESPONSIBILITY FOR THOSE WHO DECIDE TO ENTER WATERWOOD AND WILL NOT BE HELD ACCOUNTABLE FOR THE CREATURES THAT LIVE WITHIN IT.

The princess had seconds to decide. Seconds. She knew there was nowhere else for her to hide. Her horse was not sure; the place didn't smell right to him. Red shifted to the left and, hanging from Face's neck, she reached out and yanked the sign from view, throwing it as far as she could into the darkness. 'It's a harmless old wood,' she whispered to him. 'Let's go.' She urged him inside, and they disappeared down the now unsigned, overgrown, and very easy to miss turning.

Waterwood swallowed them whole.

'It's pissing windy.' Some way behind Red, the guards roared at one another over the storm.

'Can't see nuffink, either. Where'd that woman go?' they yelled, peering at the windblown road ahead.

Visibility was poor with the driving rain and debris thrown about by the wind. Their drums bounced uncomfortably against their jodhpurs. The guards wished they'd taken some sausages to go. They rode on, straight past the turning to Waterwood and on to the borders of the East Realm.

As soon she heard them pass, Red's heart slowed down, and her horse stopped to have a pee. The pair continued into the woods, along a trail – which grew narrow, then extremely narrow, the further they went. It continued to grow narrower, forcing Face into a cautious trot as the curling trunks of trees brushed against his side. Very soon the trail gave up being a trail altogether. With Robbie's hat slipping jauntily over her eyes, the princess wove slowly through the ancient trees, feeling a lot better about the night ahead. It felt nice and safe under his hat. It smelt of hair, hay, and garlic. Red wondered if she would see him again to return it. He'd started a fight to help her escape, and with that thought in her mind, she no longer felt so alone.

There are two types of dark. The first is dark with light bits. This dark contains stars, moons, fireflies, and the friendly cooing of little owls. It's the sort of dark where you will find a shining lantern hanging from a branch in a snowy forest, marking out an inviting clearing and, if you are lucky, a talking faun. Then there is the other type of dark. This is the dark that people are afraid of, and Red was in the thick of it. She pushed Robbie's hat up, but it made no difference. This dark had very few light bits. She could barely see Face. This worried her as she was riding him, and she believed that everyone should know what they were riding, no matter how dark it is.

'Crikey, it's dark. Where are the stars?'

When people are afraid, it is probable they will say something obvious like, 'Oh dear, I'm bleeding,' or 'Is that sheet flying all on its own? Surely not.' And so forth. As they crept further into Waterwood, Red realised neither the moon nor the stars were visible in this wood. Not even the shooting ones. The sky must have left this part of Landfelian hundreds of years ago as soon as the trees grew tall and their leaves concealed all that lay above. She had never been in a wood quite like this one. Red reached inside her father's grubby coat pockets and found what she was looking for, a dented tin. Travel matches. There were three left.

The king of Landfelian had travelled a great deal in that coat, on long journeys to the edges of his land, and often further – to the crumbs that had dropped off the edges of his land and floated away into the White Ocean. He had travelled to barren, bleak places, where trying to start a fire would pose a problem and not being able to see the darn fire to blow on it would be an even bigger problem. After one bout of bronchitis too many, the king had summoned Father Peter, the wisest man he knew, to Celador. The two men met in the Chamber of Serious Discussion, with a pot of coffee, to do something about it. The queen was not a cook, but she was good at cakes. She made a sponge filled with blackberry jam and left them to it. In four days, the men invented the first travel match. The match was longer and thicker than the ones that came later from a gentleman named Ship. It was made from the swamp trees of the marshlands in the West Realm, which had a very oily, sweet sap and were highly combustible. Its flame was the colour of a blood orange, growing up to ten inches tall and burning for precisely three hours. The shaft of the match was as thick as a pencil.

The princess thought about her godfather as she continued carefully through the wood, holding her lit match and feeling a lot happier. 'Look,' she said to Face. Written on the barks of the watertrees were fat, silvery letters, as if a giant snail had painted the words with its belly.

WELCOME

TO WATERWOOD.

IN HERE IT IS BEST TO

KEEP YOUR

MOUTH CLOSED

AT ALL TIMES.

What's that supposed to mean? Red wondered. She had no intention of eating anything she found here.

They were no longer being chased, and they were out of the storm. While her ankle was still pulsing with pain, she had all her limbs and two travel matches left. Under the circumstances, there was a lot of bright side to look on. Whoever had written those words was scaremongering. It was probably just local children playing.

Still, Red thought as she looked around, she would not be returning to this wood in a hurry. Sliding off Face and leading him, she limped on. It was becoming impossible to ride through the intimately woven trees. There was an ominous sort of garbling coming from above, and the ground underfoot was oddly springy ... She decided not to dwell on the one question glaring at her through the leaves as the garbling noise got louder: what else lived in this wood?

The trees that surrounded them did not look like they belonged to Landfelian, at least, not to any part of the kingdom Red had seen. Their great, pale trunks curled out of the ground like giants arms and legs weaving up into a swaying roof of fan-shaped leaves. The roots of the trees frequently tripped Red up, bubbling up in places like drowning limbs. Face's ears remained flat against his head. She stroked his nose and made reassuring noises. Branches cast snake-like shadows around her. 'Woods are not evil,' she reassured Face. 'Woods are friendly places filled with birds …' She tried to relax. 'Imagine what lovely woodland creatures are making this noise. Possibly a frog of some kind. I do hope so. I love frogs.' The noise was quite loud for frogs, but Red didn't want to think about any of the bigger creatures it could be. She patted her horse, who looked wide-eyed with fear. 'Goodness what unusual roots.'

Face thought the tree roots looked like they wanted to reach out of the ground, pull them under, and strangle the life from them. But he said nothing.

As they bounced on, across the springy land, Red began to hum. Her ankle knocked against a branch and her eyes watered in pain. Leaves fell from the sky and stroked her neck, making her jump.

Face was nervous too. The whole place felt wrong to him. It did not sit right. It smelt too sweet, like a place the wind had forgot. After two hours of being utterly terrified, Red stopped humming and agreed with him.

'This wood is the pits. We won't stay long – if we head straight, we'll find the other side soon enough.'

Her horse stopped. He sniffed the air, stamped his foot, and farted. This was valien for, 'I'm not having a good time.' He could not see the way out in this soupy air, he could not read the way of the stars, and, far more worryingly, they were being watched. None of his valien instincts could help them here.

The treetoads were indeed watching. They watched the young woman with her bright tangle of red hair and the furry beast that was walking behind her. They watched the pair go deeper into their wood, and they could not have been more delighted. The creatures watched, and they crowed a welcome song to the hairy beast and the princess. All through the night they crowed their song. When the new guests did not appear to notice, they sang a bit louder and began to crawl slowly down the tree trunks to get a better range.

Guests! It had been so long – years – since the last. Those guests had left the woods in a hurry, not looking nearly as attractive or interesting as these two. How wonderful!

The last Landfelians to come out of Waterwood had been an intrepid pair of well-seasoned explorers – Red's godfather, Father Peter, and his apprentice, Paddy Burridge. The men wrote a detailed account of the experience in a journal, which would later appear in a chapter entitled 'All Creatures Large and Amorous', in a book on the lesser-known corners of Landfelian, called *The Nether Regions*. Father Peter sent a couple of first editions to the king and queen shortly before their disappearance. Red had found one in Celador's library and squirrelled it away in her bag for her journey. She'd only read the first half before leaving the book and her bag in The Honest Sausage. She could have done with it now – and her bag of nuts. Life is a beauty and a beast.

AN EXTRACT FROM 'THE NETHER REGIONS'

A note on treetoads, fellow explorers young and old. The ominous sound that reaches a rumbling crescendo in the very heart of Waterwood is in a fact a Song of Welcome. Do not be alarmed, dear friends, it is the call of the species native to Waterwood. It is a species that has lived there since water and tree began; these creatures are as ancient as the fluff in my cardigan pocket. TREETOADS are neither as unpleasant or as large as their singing voice suggests. They are in fact very shy and the size and weight of a grapefruit. They hide themselves from view in the highest branches, where they nest amongst the wide leaves that fall in abundance and gather in thick layers between the roots of the trees. Thousands of years of fermentation creates the sweet odour of the wood. Little light can fight its way through the jabberwocky trunks, but you will be quite safe, do not worry. There is almost *nothing to fear. In the presence of humans, the treetoads become emboldened. Shyness withstanding, they are an extremely amorous and social species. They basket weave all night, reserving their days for sleeping and feeding. Brave treetoads may drop down from their nests with a great plop, landing as near to you as they dare. They do this with one thing in mind: kissing, as poor Paddy discovered. It is important to remember that if a falling treetoad lands near you, do not under any circumstances let it approach. Move on quickly, and politely explain that you have a pressing engagement. The reason for this is simple. Treetoads are toxic. They feed on a sap that oozes from the watertrees. One kiss from a treetoad turned my apprentice into a walking, talking, romancing fool for several hours. The kiss consumes a person's common sense, and any worries or fears they might have had before entering the wood are soon forgotten. If too much slumbersap is passed on by the treetoad to the nervous system, an overwhelming desire to sleep will take hold of its victim. In Waterwood, one risks falling into a permanent slumber and losing all desire to leave the woods, where nothing grows for humans to eat. The effects of the kiss wear off after several hours, though this can be shortened with very sweet, strong coffee and a firm slap about the face.*

TO AVOID BEING KISSED
An umbrella or parasol works as a friendly, effective barrier from the diving treetoads.

AN IMPORTANT NOTE
The real danger of this wood is not the treetoad or its kiss. It is the leaves that make this bewitching place fatal. What

Paddy and I discovered, my dear Landfelians, what has gone
unrealised since time began is this: Waterwood is floating.
The leaves and roots conceal a great reservoir that has been here
for centuries. Therefore, what you must avoid at all costs is

But it didn't really matter what Father Peter had to say, because Red was unable to read his journal at that time. It was Robbie Wylde who had it, amongst her other things, her bag, her book, her scrunchie, and he had just finished off her nuts. The hound.

Red and her horse continued on their way, almost certainly lost and definitely terrified.

Fear can be prompted by all sorts of things. King Felian turned white and had to sit down at the sight of offal. He didn't think anything's internal organs should be pan-fried with butter and sage and then eaten.

The queen was terrified the sun would leave. Shortly before she disappeared, this irrational fear had disturbed her so much the king kept a fire glowing in their chamber all night and asked Sir Toby to paint a vast mural of a sun on the ceiling.

Nin Potts of the Honest Sausage would not be in the same room as a crab. They walked sideways – enough said.

Robbie Wylde had always struggled with parsnips. Fibrous, white fingers that tasted strongly of rubbish. He couldn't stomach them. His biggest fear was staying in one place.

Fear can be prompted by all sorts of things. For a princess, Red was not as highly strung as royal tradition tended.

She did not enjoy spending any length of time in confined spaces. Rooms without windows made her nervous. She tried her best to get on with the rest, like these woods.

Face was a fearless valien, but like many fearless creatures, he also had his hang-ups. He did not like amphibians or anything warty with a stretchy mouth and goggly eyes: frogs, toads, newts, and the lizards that appeared out of nowhere and left important bits of themselves behind he could not handle. As a foal, he was very shaken by a frog that had made a nest in his stable and crawled out of the straw one day to say hello. He now had a tendency to bolt at the sight of one green-padded foot. Waterwood was doing nothing for his confidence.

Red was running low on travel matches. She had dropped the last one when she fell on a twisted root. A symphony of gruboling rained down from the treetops. It sounded as if one excitable person had been left alone with an organ, underwater.

'A piece of toast and a cup of tea would be nice.' Thinking of tea and toast helped her relax. They were comforting thoughts. Toast-sellers were as common in Landfelian as squirrelgrams and condiments men, and by far the most popular. Scalding bread at breakfast had only been discovered in the last decade and was still considered a hoot.

'Whatever is making that noise will be more scared of us than we are of it,' Red told Face. People say this. But in the case of dragons and ravenous, wild beasts, it is not strictly true.

'And those silly signs … When has any sign in Landfelian been reliable? Take every one with a pinch of snuff and follow your nose.' One of her godmothers had told her that.

The valien kept quiet and followed the princess, hating every minute. He could sense the creatures crouched above him, and he did not like the way the ground seemed to move underfoot.

No one, not even Father Peter, knew when the trees had begun to take root over the reservoir to form Waterwood. But the trees had been there before people. That deserved a certain amount of respect and folklore. The most popular tale about the wood was that it was the home of a Nimff – a beautiful Nimff who had lost her true love in the tightly woven trees. The Nimff had called and called for him, searching the woods for years. He never came to her. So she waited, singing her song until all that was left was the sound of her voice (now rather rough and bitter) and her fingernails. Landfelians loved a grim tale about a Nimff as much as they loved toast.

* * *

Robbie was going straight after his hat, with blood drying in his nostrils and a swollen lip from fighting the guards and catching Regina's goat. He had not been beaten to a pulpy mess and left for dead this time; it seemed the drummers had bigger fish to fry, and the red-headed princessgram was that very big fish. They had left him standing and able to go in pursuit of her himself. Robbie had known she was not a princessgram from the moment he saw her stretched out by the fire on his bench. It hadn't been the royal crest on her coat or the piece of ghoulish jewellery on her ankle but the look she gave him right before she'd called him a thief and a bandit.

That's a princess, alright, he'd thought. And she'd left without paying for her sausages. Typical princess behaviour. Then she went and unwittingly saved his neck by taking every one of Blackwood's Guards away with her and saving him from a broken nose and probable arrest.

Robbie soon found himself thundering down the path that ran along the edge of Waterwood. He tracked the guards at a distance, watching as they sailed straight past the shattered sign in the ditch. Slowing down to get a better look, he spent a few minutes fiddling about in the undergrowth, where four enormous hoof marks and a piece of bloody bandage lay not far from the buried sign.

'Waterwood, eh? Well, she's got balls, I'll give her that.'

Waterwood did not feature on the guards' radar; woods did not serve women or ale. Robbie had not forgotten about Waterwood. He was a Man of the Road, and he knew every nook of the kingdom. He had camped amongst the pale trunks with the treetoads many times when he wanted time to think. The flame from his torch discerned two tracks in the mulch, leading into the trees, one from female-sized boots, limping a little on the left side, and the other, four reluctant hooves.

'Clever girl.' Robbie smiled. Waterwood was impenetrable against spying eyes. As long as she remained inside, she would not be seen. Although how safe she was would be a matter of debate. The woods were no place for an inexperienced traveller, especially one being tracked by a Man of the Road.

✱ ✱ ✱

The princess felt her way through the leaves, telling herself she would return to the rest house once she found the king and pay for her sausages.

'How could I have forgotten? You have to pay for things outside Paloma.' She would leave the bandit's hat with a thank-you note, too. She was so deep in thought, composing a polite but playful note, she forgot where she was, until a treetoad dropped down and landed on her.

'ARHHGRL!'

The treetoad screamed back. *'Crow, grubol, click-click-click-click!'*

Face whinnied. The treetoad pressed its mouth against the princess for a long, wet moment, shook itself excitedly, and leapt away. It landed on the valien's face, not the branch it expected, whereupon all manner of hell broke loose in the quietly seeping wood. Face reared up and tried to shake off the treetoad, which clung to his snout, omitting very urgent clicking noises (the sign of a treetoad in great distress). The creature clung to the velvet nose of the valien, with its splayed sucker-padded feet. Face bounded off, shaking his head, trying to remove the heavy blob, deep into a part of the wood no one had mapped. Red was left behind holding her travel match. She waited until his hooves dwindled away before screaming for him to return.

'Come back! It was a leaf!' she lied. 'A toad-shaped leaf!' She ran after him, following the signs of panic and horse. Her light faltered. The ground swayed under her. She wiped away the residue that the treetoad had left on her lips. 'Urgh, what was that? Oh God, Face, wait for me!'

Red had never lost an animal before, and her valien had never lost her. Suddenly, she was in an unknown shadow of the land, alone. Calling until she was hoarse, she tried not to whimper, although one or two escaped. The voodoo charm tightened against her skin the further she ran. What if he fell and broke his leg? What if he was hurt? She stumbled desperately on. A strange, heavy feeling began to take hold of her. It was as if with every step a warm, thick blanket wrapped tighter around her. Waterwood clicked and thrummed. The odd *CAW CAW* joined in.

A little further on, Red giggled. What was funny? Absolutely nothing about her predicament was funny. She snorted again and slowed down to a saunter. How calming this wood was, she thought, yawning. It was a magical place with friendly creatures. The next yawn was so long, it caused her to stop and lean against a trunk, where she took the moment to ask it a question.

'Are you a daughter of Eve or a son of Adam?' She put her arms around it and gave it a hug. 'What's happening to me?' She shook her head and tried to gather herself, which was difficult because she was suddenly very sleepy. The leaves clung to her. She peeled one off her chest, and a few others unpeeled themselves and slapped to the ground.

'I give up.' She stood unsteadily. 'We can all stick together.' She slapped another branch and winked at a treetoad watching her. 'You too, you sly old toad.'

The princess took a deep breath of the swampy air and strolled dreamily on until she reached a clearing. In the middle of this break in the trees, a circle of yellowing leaves greeted her. She took a step further and the ground sprung back beneath her feet.

'A leaf mattress.' She laughed in wonder. Red tried a star jump and bounced easily. She shrugged off her father's old coat and threw it towards a tree. The treetoads could not believe their luck. They leant out of the trees to watch, and some dropped down in delight to join in.

Bounce.

Bounce.

BOUNCE.

'I really like your wood.' Red continued to bounce upon the fallen leaves until she heard a whinny. 'Face!' She lifted the last travel match in the direction of a familiar pissed-off horse noise. There was another whinny, louder and more impatient this time. It was proving difficult to stop bouncing. She laughed giddily, 'I must not get carried away.' And then, with a polite plop, the princess disappeared down a leafwell.

A leafwell was not good. A leafwell in this wood was a death trap. A leafwell was the wood's way of protecting itself from cutters, poachers, and sappers. It started to come back to Red now like a terrible dream. Sappers used to stalk Waterwood for its slumbersap, the molasses-coloured goo that oozed from the watertrees and made the whole place so soporific. The treetoads drank it. It sent them quite mad, falling from their nests and kissing every Stan, Trip, and Paddy. Sappers sold the goo at the black market in the docks of Alba, disguising themselves as coffee traders.

'One teaspoon will send you into a cloud of ecstasy,' they leered at passing gentlemen. 'Stir this into tea and sail away on a boat called Bliss.'

It was the opium of its time, until the sappers began disappearing and all goo-dealing stopped. Waterwood was left alone. If that Nimff and her lover had existed, you can bet your last sticky bun they'd ended up at the bottom of a leafwell, along with all the sappers.

'Oh dear,' Red whispered. The leafwell was not as fun

as she first thought. She found herself sinking faster than an innocent woman at a witch trial. 'This is turning into quite a memorable evening.'

Thankfully, she was stopped from dropping to the bottom of the waterlogged tomb by something soft but buoyant at her feet. She bobbed up and down, her head just above the leafy water, coughed up several mouthfuls, and gave her horse a reassuring wave. The valien watched in disbelief from the edge. 'Don't worry,' she told him. 'I've landed on something. I think it's a log.'

She stifled another yawn. It wasn't cold in the leafwell – it was like being in a warm bath. The leaves glued her in a tight, leafy hug. Her boots balanced on the log, stopping her from falling any further down. Red held the travel match high above her head like a hippie at a peace rally and smiled gamely. 'It's going to be alright.' And she believed it, too – until she remembered another part of Father Peter's book.

SLUMBERISM:
An overriding desire to sleep; the after-effect of consuming too much slumbersap or 'goo'.

Her face fell. On second thoughts, it was probably not the best time to sleep, and yet she could not keep her eyes from drooping. All the bouncing, running, sausage eating, and river leaping had taken the stuffing out of the princess.

'No, I mustn't.' She forced her eyes to open. 'I have to get to Alba. I have to remove the voodoo, and I have to find the king!'

Her horse prodded the leafy well cautiously, and his hoof sank. He looked helplessly at his owner.

'Don't come any closer, Face, you'll sink.' She sank a few inches. 'Oh, crap it. Do something distracting! My eyelids keep shutting.'

The valien did his best. He flicked his tail around and around in a circle, which made Red dizzy. He tapped his hoof against a tree in a game of Guess that Tune. Then he got angry and snorted.

'I know, I'm thinking. Do we have any rope?' She yawned hard and sank down another inch. Her horse yawned back. 'Not you too.' She threw a leaf at him, which landed not far in front of her. 'We have to stay awake!'

Her log lurched, and water flew up to her chin. Thoughts of leeches and drowning caused the effects of the slumbersap to wear off a little.

'Go and find a long branch or an ivy tail.'

The valien closed his eyes.

'Don't give me that look.' She swallowed a mouthful of water and tried not to think about what was in it. Closing her mouth, she glared at her horse – a glare loaded with desperate instruction.

Robbie found the mighty horse before Face found an ivy tail or a long branch. The valien backed straight into him as it tried to drag away a root that was still attached to a tree.

'You're not going to get very far without an axe.'

The valien flattened his ears and tried to kick Robbie.

He dodged the enormous hoof. 'You're definitely a royal horse. Where is she? I have her things, look.'

Face sniffed the hemp sack and gave Robbie a rough lick before he turned towards the clearing, where a faint humming could be heard. It was female and slightly hysterical. Robbie followed the valien. The noise did not conjure up thoughts of Ring a Ring a o' Roses. He had never been this far into Waterwood before – they must be only a day or so from the other side. How had she got this far without falling into a leafwell? The whole place was floating. Then he saw the flickering flame, his hat, and just enough of the princess' shoulders to realise she had not avoided the leafwells after all.

'Oh, Christmas,' he muttered. Trouble seemed to follow this girl around more than him.

It would be fair to say Red was looking pretty feral by the time the Man of the Road reached the edge of the leafwell. Her hair hung in bedraggled clumps beneath his hat, which was almost all you could see of her head.

'Fancied a swim, did you, princess?' It was the largest gathering of leaves he had seen. It was a lake.

She tried to turn around to see who had come to rescue her. 'YOU!'

Her hopes of a hero had not been answered. The enterprising Man of the Road bandit-thief had followed her instead. 'Why are you here?' she whispered, and her match went out.

A flaming torch was shone in her face, making her squint. 'Glad to see you have been taking care of my hat.'

She tilted her head up to the light and gave him the driest look she could manage, which was hard considering the circumstances.

'Did you find anything else to steal from my bag?'

'Only some nuts and this map.'

'From all the following, stealing, meddling ... Well, you can kiss your hat goodbye, bandit, because I'm drowning and it's coming with me!' Red fumed.

'I can see that, princess.' He took a step closer, and his boot sank. 'I'm here to rescue you. Hold on.' As soon as he had said it, Robbie realised he had no idea how to save her. The valien dropped the root at his feet and stared at it.

'I don't need your help!' Red shouted this a little too loud. She was so relieved to see him. 'I'm fine, really. It's not as bad as it looks.'

Robbie knew never to believe a woman who says she's 'fine'. 'Fine' is usually the stage just before something gets thrown and someone cries. He had much to learn, but this had been made clear by his mother. Still, he'd expected a slightly warmer reception. Weren't princesses supposed to swoon? Right before they said, 'How can I ever repay you?' and a breathless, 'I owe you my life.' This princess was not the run-of-the-mill distressed maiden he was accustomed to and enjoyed meeting. The ones that invited him in for stew and dumplings, followed by a good rub-down. 'It looks pretty bad.'

'My horse has gone to find an ivy tail.' Red could barely see beneath the bandit's hat now. It covered her eyes in a very devil may care way.

'Your horse is right here.'

'Good. We're leaving then. Be on your way and I will be on mine.' She gasped as her ankle grazed against something sharp in the water. 'I don't have any gold to give you.'

'And I thought you were a princess.' Robbie began to unravel his whip.

'No, I told you, I'm a very poor princessgram.'

'And I'm the King of Fronze.' Robbie laughed. 'But if you don't need rescuing, I'll be on my way.' He paused. 'Before I do go, though, I would like my hat back.'

'You TOAD ...' Red roared.

How was she supposed to throw his precious hat back with only one hand? The arm not holding the match was pinned to her side by the heavy, leafy water. Couldn't he just get another hat and move on? It was hard to keep a sense of control in her position. The great surge of hope at the sight of the Man of the Road had thrown her. It made her nervous, although he did have a trustworthy nose and seemed to be alone. It was his mouth she was wary of. She would let him haul her out and then she would hit him over the head and make a run for it. She took a reluctant breath. 'Wait.'

Robbie untied his boots and removed them and his socks. 'Speak up, princess. I can't hear you.'

'Please.' Water began to run up her nose. 'Help.'

'There are conditions.' He gave her a frank look. Gathering up his whip, he began to spin it in lazy circles above his head.

'Conditions!' she gargled.

'Would I be right in saying that you're the missing princess, only known heir to King Felian and the Vanished Queen.'

'I am no such thing!'

Robbie turned away. 'I'm not interested in rescuing a pretender.'

'I told you, I'm a princessgram,' Red tried weakly. 'And my name is Mary Drew.'

'The going rate to help a stranded female of royal blood is five hundred gold pieces.' He smiled. 'I'll give you a moment to think about it.'

'A rescue fee! What about common kindness? What about chivalry!'

Red grew very still. At least, the top of her head did, and that was all Robbie could now see. She was quiet, the kind of quiet that is busy filling up with expletives. Snorts of disbelief were fired into the water and lost on Robbie, whose whip was gathering momentum.

'Must have been a while since you got out, tulip. Landfelian doesn't go in for common kindness anymore, only paid.' He gave her a friendly smile. 'You have about ten seconds before you're swallowed and five before you find out that log you're standing on is in fact the rotting corpse of a sapper.'

Everything was silent apart from the odd plop of a treetoad. Red tried to take a deep breath and reply, but she lost her footing and disappeared.

7

IN DEEP WATER

The princess was sucked downwards. The leaves pressed heavily against her and pulled her further down. In a small way, it was a relief. She was so tired; no one wanted or expected anything from her under the leafwell. She struggled briefly then grew calm, slowly losing the energy to fight.

If this was it, she considered, she hadn't lived much. She hadn't danced a jig on a table with a bottle of mead. She hadn't galloped across the great plains of the East Realm. She hadn't skinny-dipped in the Lake of Stars or tried a mooncake. She hadn't even kissed a man with a feather in his hat and sun-weathered skin (Red had got these ideas from eavesdropping on the laundry room back at the palace). She hadn't told her horse to leave Waterwood and not wait for her, and she had not paid for her sausages.

NO, Red thought. *This cannot be it.* She had to find the king. She had to stop her step-aunt and uncle claiming the throne. Drowning was not the answer. It would not get anything done – she had to live and save her horse from being stolen by the Man of the Road. Red began to reach out for her life.

It wasn't enough.

The leafwell made a terrible sucking noise and then fell quiet as the leaves settled over the princess' head.

Face kicked Robbie in the shins, and he stumbled on to the leafwell, throwing his whip in her direction.

'Bull spit!' he crowed, landing with a loud slap, face down upon the leaves. Robbie scowled at the valien and stretched further out, towards the exact spot she had sunk. He inched over the wobbly surface, afraid of sinking and unsure if the thick layer of leaves would support him. The treetoads watched from above. Robbie felt her panicked tremors below as she fought with the water. 'I can reach you – don't panic!' he called, panicking freely.

Red was sinking too fast to hear him. Water trickled into her lungs. Her mouth and nose filled with mulch. She made one mighty attempt to pull her arms up, but they were stuck to her sides by the weight of leaves and water. She wanted desperately to find the world above, even if the Man of the Road and her valien were the only ones to share it with her. She didn't want to remain here alone. Every part of her screamed against the drowning.

Robbie was yelling now, scouring the leafwell for any sign of the woman below. 'Where is she?' He grappled about in the leaves.

The valien made a noise behind him that was horse for, *FIND OUT.*

He searched for an arm, an ear – anything to grab on to and haul out. A moment later, a hand covered in brown slime pushed to the surface, and he was glad to see it was attached to a slim wrist. 'I've got you,' he called.

He didn't. Not yet.

Sweat dripped into his eyes. Robbie flicked his whip out and wrapped it around her wrist. Gently, he pulled her towards him.

Face whinnied.

'Hold on.' Robbie filled his lungs and thrust his torso under the surface until he felt her shoulder. Tucking his arm around it, he pulled Red slowly to the surface. She slid up like a reluctant cork, sodden and covered in brown sludge.

A hole closed behind her with a noise that rested somewhere between a *SHLOOP* and a *LURRP*. She did not move, not even to scowl. She lay flat, very still, and quiet, on the edge of the leafwell.

'No time to play dead, Highness,' he called to her.

No part of her stirred.

'Open your eyes and break my nose – I know you want to.' Robbie leant over her. She looked fragile. 'They must need you back at the palace for cello lessons ... or ball practice ... or something ... Come on. Open your eyes and hit me.'

He propped her up against the trunk of a water tree. If she had swallowed too much water, she may not wake up. If he had inadvertently killed the heir, *he* would not wake up once the king found him. This would not be good for his law-abiding record. Robbie couldn't quite believe this young woman was the *princess*, looking at her. He gently removed the slime from her hair and waited. He had caught many wild animals before – his horse, wounded birds, lame hedgehogs, a fair few ladies – but never a royal. He had no idea what to do.

Red's green dress was heavy and sodden. Her ankle was bleeding through the bandages. The voodoo was still there, casting a shadow that appeared to be spreading over the skin around it. He propped her head up. The valien nudged her shoulder and breathed heavily in Robbie's face. 'She's alright, fellow,' he assured the horse. 'Just swallowed too much of the local brew.' He knew what he had to do. She wasn't going to like it. He checked her pulse. It had fallen to a faint flutter. Her lips were going blue. 'Forgive me for this,' he whispered. Robbie laid her flat, opened her mouth, and began to breathe for her. 'Come on, milady, wake up.'

The horses watched the Man of the Road take another breath and fill her lungs. They waited, and they waited. Time slowed down. The treetoads made no sound. Robbie's heart thumped hard against his chest. The water on her lashes brushed his cheeks as he bent over to breathe for her again. Then, after what seemed like hours, two surprised, relieved, and infuriated green eyes stared up at him.

Red blinked. 'What are you doing?'

He jumped up and backed off. She coughed up three lungs worth of peaty water and struggled to sit up. Red looked unsteadily at the whip curled around her wrist and then at the man holding it.

'Where is my horse?'

The valien whinnied and her eyes lit up. 'Face.' She reached out for the animal's warm, soft muzzle and buried her face into his neck.

'I'm sorry I frightened you.' She kissed him and stroked his worried nose until he was still. Finally, the princess turned and gave Robbie a cautious smile. 'Thank you.'

'Thought you were a goner.'

'So did I.' She looked at him suspiciously. 'Who are you?'

He held out his hand. 'Robbie Wylde, and this beautiful lady is my horse, Legs.'

She reached up to stroke the chestnut mare. 'I'm Red.'

Bit of a short name for a princess, he thought. No HRH, flowers, hyphens, trumpets, or foreign bits. 'That you are.' He gestured at her bedraggled hair.

She picked up his now shapeless hat from the ground and

handed it to him with a sombre expression. 'I believe this is yours.'

Robbie took the wet felty lump and smiled.

'I'm sorry it's a little out of shape.' She tried to stand and noticed his hands. 'You're shaking. Are you hurt?'

Robbie slapped on his hat and put his hands behind his back. 'No, no. Fit as a fiddle.' He didn't look at her. 'Just prefer dry land. I'm not a great swimmer.' Retrieving his boots from Legs' mouth, he began to gather up his things. Red put too much weight on the wrong ankle and winced. He reached out to steady her. 'What did you do to deserve the voodoo?'

Red looked up in surprise and brushed down her dress. 'The water here tastes very strange,' she said changing the subject.

'It's full of slumbersap,' explained Robbie. 'You should rest before moving on. You've swallowed enough to kill a troll.'

'Something kissed me.' She touched her mouth and looked at him.

He smiled. 'Treetoads. Amorous little suckers – they live off the sap.' He pointed to one crawling along a nearby branch and then looked at her mouth. Making a gruff sound, he began gathering up as many dry twigs as he could and stuffed them into his bag. The horses watched, puzzled.

'How did you know who I am?' asked Red.

'You don't get many princessgrams in these parts. And not one that would incite an army of Blackwood's Guards away from The Honest Sausage.' Robbie had never been much of a royalist. From what he remembered of the king, this redhead bore no resemblance. Except there was something familiar about her eyes. 'They never come by the hundred for me. And as for that horse …'

Face bared his teeth.

'Well, he's no donkey. No matter how much tea and clay you dunk him in. That's a valien. No other person in their right mind would ride such a fine animal into Waterwood without light, a compass, and some strong, sweet coffee – unless they were fairly high up in the blue-blood line and related to that gold-digger who calls herself the half-queen.'

Red wished she hadn't asked.

'Besides,' went on Robbie, 'only royal types run off without paying for their breakfast and voodoo jewellery.' His hands still shook. He felt angry. He'd nearly lost her to the leafwell, and, more importantly, he'd nearly lost himself and two fine horses, too.

Red stared at him, then at the ground and fought the hot urge to cry. She began to pick up twigs, too. 'I see. Well, I'm sorry to have inconvenienced you.'

She had nearly died, her ankle was in agony, and a man with unruly hair was questioning her ability to care for her horse. If he mentioned her mother, it was floodgates, people.

'And from what I remember, you have your mother's eyes,' he added.

She looked at a tree, clenched her jaw, and blinked a lot. Robbie was thinking he should probably apologise for being so insensitive and was about to when she started to walk away.

'Well,' said Red, 'thank you for the loan of your hat and your honesty.' She put on the old riding coat. 'I wish you a good day, Robbie Wylde.' She dropped the twigs she had gathered and walked unsteadily away. Her horse followed meekly behind. Trying to focus on leaving is hard for anyone who has recently died a bit. She swallowed a lump constricting her throat and wiped her eyes. Red didn't need his help, but it would have been good to have some company.

'Don't forget your bag, princess.' Robbie was filling it with something. 'Take this food for your journey. You need to soak up the rest of the slumbersap. And drink some coffee as soon as you can. It will help.' He handed her the hemp sack and smiled.

'Thank you. I meant to pay for my sausages, you know.' Red sniffed.

'I haven't paid for years. I know I owe Nin more than my weight. Take it.'

She looked desperately at their pile of twigs and fiddled with the part of her dress where a sleeve used to be.

Her uncertainty softened him. 'Let me help you. I can get you wherever you need to go. I know this land like I know my horse.'

'I have a map,' said Red.

'How is that working out so far?' He began to lay a fire and unpack items for what looked like tea.

Tea.

'There have been a few blips, but on the whole ...' She felt tired and dizzy.

'Why don't you stay awhile and warm up? I'm not a guard, you know, and I am an exceptional cook.' He watched her hesitate. 'Just for a minute. You'll feel stronger after a cup of sweet tea. If I wanted to drown you, I would have done it already.'

Red sank down against a tree to think and put her head in her hands. It *would* be less conspicuous travelling with someone. The guards were not likely to notice her with a Man of the Road and his regular-looking horse. She was too exhausted to leave straightaway, and he could keep watch while she rested. There was no need to stay with him further than the outskirts of Alba, so she wouldn't have to trust him for long ... and if he stepped one eyebrow out of line, she would hit him over the head with her tennis racket.

'What are your terms?' Red had never used this expression before. She hoped it sounded worldly and mature, like she knew what she was doing, which she did not.

'My terms?' Robbie tried not to laugh.

'You mentioned a rescue fee.' Red watched his face change.

'Ah ...' He stood up and began to pace. 'Yes, five hundred gold pieces to escort you to Father Peter's Folly.'

Red turned white. 'How do you know about that place? No one knows.' So he *was* following her. This Man of the

Road was one of the palace spies. She was sure of it. One of Blackwood's spies. She looked around for her racket.

'Father Peter's Folly is circled in red on your map, and I found a copy of his *Landfelian Journal* in your bag, so I guessed you might be aiming for there. He's the old Cloudbuster inventor, isn't he?' Robbie's eyes were bright. 'A friend of yours?'

She knew she should have used invisible ink. 'He's my godfather.'

'Godfather? I never got one of them. Bet he's an interesting man – and the only one to have travelled beyond Landfelian, over the Sea of Trees and the White Ocean to foreign lands.'

'Thousands have,' Red pointed out. 'There are merchant ships leaving all the time.'

'Not in the fog. Not for years, and not with a Cloudbuster.' Robbie stared up through the trees. 'Your Father Peter is the man to ask if you don't want to swim out of this kingdom. He can fly away anytime he wants in that balloon.'

'Fog? Where?' Red remembered the morning after her father had left. The rain had stopped but fog had quickly settled over the South Realm.

Robbie sighed. 'It lingers around the coast of this kingdom like a curse. But it wouldn't pose a problem for a Cloudbuster.'

Red could see where this was going. 'He won't let you take it.'

Robbie looked at her. 'No. But if I arrive with the king's daughter, it might push me to the front of the queue.'

The quiet sound of treetoads crawling up to their nests indicated that night was drawing to an end. Red sat down, suddenly exhausted. She had not been aware a fog had settled around the whole kingdom, as well as her home realm in the south.

'It's going to take more than a travel match to get that fire to light.'

'True.' The Man of the Road tipped the contents of her hemp sack on the ground. 'But someone packed liquor.'

She watched as Robbie threw her step-uncle's hipflask in the air and poured a little brandy over the twig pile. He struck a flint over a spear-shaped steel that hung around his neck. Soon the wood quickly licked into flame and any lurking shadows melted away. The fire warmed her pale, face and her hair shone like rubies in a cave. Robbie knelt in front of her and offered the remaining brandy with a smile on his lips.

'Do we have a deal, princess?'

She took the flask with shaking hands and drank, making a face as it found her throat.

'To Alba ... Beyond that, I don't know.' Her ankle throbbed beneath the bandages, and she wondered if she would be able to walk by then. 'I've got to find a way to remove this voodoo charm from my ankle.'

'Excellent.' He clapped his hands. 'We rest here for now.' He paused. 'I hope that horse of yours doesn't snore.'

Red was too tired to argue. She had no clear idea of how she had ended up camping with a Man of the Road, but she felt safer in his company than she did alone in the woods. She checked the ground for treetoads, kept hold of a small fork, and threw Robbie a wary look, telling him to stay on his side of the fire.

After a pot of fried potatoes and sweet tea, she moved close against the rising belly of her horse and, safe in his familiar smell, fell into a restless sleep.

Robbie stayed awake. He stared at the flames of the fire. Gazing up at the ancient trees, he waited and watched over her. The anklet of teeth made him uneasy. She stirred occasionally but did not wake.

Dreams kept Red busy in sleep. The trauma of the last twenty-four hours opened the door to a memory buried deep, and she dreamt of the day she had met the witch.

✳ ✳ ✳

Red dealt with her mother's sudden disappearance and her father's quest the only way a child in a draughty castle could think of: she crawled back inside her den and remained there, wrapped up tight like a recently cooked prawn. No one in Celador did anything to mark the young heir's birthday. They were far too busy packing. The servants forgot about all balloons, butter icing, and musical thrones after the king gathered his heroes – one hundred able men and the best horses – to sail away.

Red decided to stay inside her den until Miriam came to take her to the carriage, hoping, with luck, she would forget.

Later that morning, Red took a shuddering breath, wished herself a happy birthday, and let herself be bundled into the first carriage making the long journey north to Paloma. She waved goodbye to the den. Something pulled at her chest as the soft grey walls of the castle disappeared from view. Then she turned away and told herself, 'It will all be a great adventure.'

One month later, the royal party arrived at Paloma. Red waited in the entrance hall until night fell, while footmen smiled politely and hurried in and out with condiments that had been ordered by the half-queen. No one came to greet her. Inside, several rooms away, her step-uncle was busy sampling cheeses and too busy to notice his niece was outside. His wife, Caroline, was upstairs opening every door, drawer, and cabinet in the palace. She was planning her first ball; when housesitting a royal palace, one simply had to entertain.

Red found them the next morning, having breakfast and looking greedily at the silver.

'Oh, it's you.' Caroline sniffed. 'I completely forgot you were coming. Did you remember, Gerald?'

'No.' Gerald looked up briefly from his plate. 'You've grown.' A hug was out of the question.

The turret room they assigned her was cold and unfamiliar. Apparently, Caroline wanted the family wing for herself and her wigs. Red decided to make a new den outside in her horse's stable. The young valien slept with his hooves crossed and his haunches sticking out of the tent-like structure. He rested his long nose at her feet. The unexpected arrival of her godmother's grey cat, Julia, cheered Red's spirits. She appeared in the palace grounds after a week and wandered straight in to the stable as if sent especially. The cat purred and licked the girl's hand. A small family of house martins nested in the eaves. The animals' noises gave Red comfort. She clung to them like a rock in a storm, although they could not hold her in the cave of their chests as her father had. She ate the last bits of the food given to her by Miriam from the Celador pantry – a few sugared almonds, some cold tea, a handful of dwarf apples, a piece of hard cheese, and some dry bread – and Red made a wish.

'I wish that this bread doesn't give me or anyone else in this stable indigestion.' The animals had been thinking the same thing. They chewed on quietly. 'For my next birthday, we shall have a cake,' Red promised them. She slept with her hands clenched, wrapped like a mummy in a mix of her mother's and father's old clothes. After a few nights, fleas began to make homes in her hair.

It is a common misconception amongst many that when something bad happens – something really terrible –those suffering need to be left alone.

'He'll be fine in a few days. He just needs to be alone.'

'Don't worry, she's had a shock. What she needs is some time alone.'

What most humans need is to be held. They need someone to shout at, to cry and wipe their nose on.

The princess stayed in the stable for thirteen days before Gerald and Caroline noticed something was missing. Caroline was convinced it was a lamp in the Yellow Room before she realised.

'Have you seen the girl? I am certain she arrived some time ago.'

Gerald looked up from his newspaper and frowned in confusion. 'Girl? What girl, dearest?

They were both feeling a little loose, since it was after six o'clock and a Monday. Caroline was on her third sharpener before dinner. (A sharpener was a small glass of barely diluted liquor consumed before a public event, and the half-queen liked to be very sharp by dessert. It oiled her marriage along nicely.) Gerald had spent the day deep in the cellars, sampling the royal wines and making detailed notes for another order.

The princess was deemed missing. There was a flurry of concern in the palace. It had been weeks and not one of the servants had seen her. Had she eaten anything? The head of the household, a woman called Elvira, asked the cook to make a butter cake, in the hope the smell of it baking would draw her out from hiding. The herald told everyone to stop what they were doing and look for her. The half-queen and king did nothing, though Caroline began to bubble a little at the sides of the mouth when no one answered her bell.

'How can I run a palace of this size without a single

servant to hand?' she lamented. 'It's really very selfish of the girl.' Her eyes narrowed so much, she looked like a bit of the Morse Code.

It was Jim True who found the princess, with the help of his wife. They peered into a tent in the stables.

The only thing Red had grown was thin and as quiet as a cup. She could not move, open her eyes, or say hello, even to Jim, whom she had always liked. Her head was hidden inside a tea cosy the shape of a hedgehog; the rest of her was covered in a colourful assortment of her parents' clothes. The princess was what they call in the industry 'locked'. Jim was worried by what he saw, and before informing the half-king, he went straight to the kitchens to tell the herald.

'You'd get more life from a statue,' he concluded. 'She needs a doctor.'

It took mere minutes for a tray of hot milk with honey, butter cake, and lavender bags to arrive at the stables. Jim's wife, June, crawled inside to see the quiet lump and tried to make it eat and drink. The princess did not stir.

'Oh, bless me,' she said again and began to cry. The half-queen and king were informed.

Red could hear people come and go. A few peered in and muttered, others scribbled down long words in notebooks and left quickly. Several other doctors arrived, sniffed inside the den, sprayed things over her, and whispered furiously. They spoke around her and then compared notes. Her eyes remained firmly closed, though the light inside her eyelids denoted red-brown for day or dark red for night. Either that or a fox had sat on her. Red sent messages to her feet to kick free her mother's shawl and her father's riding coat, but she felt too heavy to move.

After thirty days of being locked, she thought it best for all concerned if she just floated away. This was not what they in the industry call 'progress'.

Her step-aunt and step-uncle began to panic when she grew cold and clammy. It would not look good if the king's daughter died on their watch. Using gold from the palace vaults, they invited the most expensive physicians and frighteningly advanced medicine men to look at her vital signs. While this was going on, in a sheltered corner of the kitchen gardens, the herald and the groundsman met. The herald re-potted a tomato plant to keep his hands from shaking, which made the other tomatoes quite anxious.

'How is she today?' He looked grave. 'Not one of the physicians can tell us anything.'

'The animals keep her warm, but I think she's lost,' said Jim.

'Lost where?'

'In grief,' said Jim.

'Oh dear,' the herald whispered and wiped his brow. 'I thought as much. Though the king is not dead, it must feel like it to the young child. And with her mother gone as well ...' The herald sat down on an upside-down pot. 'It's terribly sad.'

This was very serious. There are some places no one wants to get lost – not even the most optimistic of creatures, like the rainbow-tailed chichaw. No one would want to find themselves lost without a map in Grief. Grief was the pits.

'Any news from the king?' Jim passed the herald a large dock leaf.

'Not a word.' He blew his nose hard into the leaf.

'He'll come back to check on his cub soon enough.' Jim was a very rural man. He saw every human as an animal, particularly his wife, whose behaviour was almost entirely peahen.

'He won't return. Not without the queen,' the herald assured him. 'He's quite determined.'

'The godparents, then? What about that Father Paul something? The old man who visits with his owl.'

'Father *Peter*. I have written, but there has been no answer from any of them. Though that strange cat belonging to the godmother arrived here not long ago. I do not understand why not one of them will come.' The herald threw the snotty dock leaf in the compost.

Red's godmothers and Father Peter never received the herald's letters. 'There is no need to send out a splay of squirrelgrams,' Caroline had answered when the herald suggested she write to the family's trusted circle of friends immediately to tell them the princess was unwell. Ignoring this order, the herald sent letters anyway – but their couriers met with untimely ends, encountering hawks, traps, and the heavy boots of Blackwood's guards.

'There are rumours the king is lost, run mad,' said Jim quietly. 'I hope they're wrong. For her sake. For all our sakes. I hope he hurries up with this quest.'

'The king can be a stubborn wretch when he wants to be.'

The herald and the groundsman looked back towards the stable.

Jim grunted. 'The wife thinks the poor newt needs a witch.'

The herald raised an eyebrow. 'Mmm. That's not a bad idea. She could certainly do with a better menu.'

'Have you seen what they're trying to force down her? Wouldn't give it to the dog. Perfumed pâtés, peacock puffs, poached goldfish, and some terrible green syrup. She needs a baked potato and the work of a white witch.'

The herald agreed – the nutritional value of the palace pantry left a lot to be desired since the half-queen had taken over. 'I will make some enquiries. We cannot give up.'

Red slipped into what they call in the industry 'a coma' while her step-uncle was in the bath. The doctor by her side at the time said, 'She has fallen into the sleep before the end. There is little we can do for her now.' Whatever they called it, it wasn't good.

The next morning, a woman with eyes the colour of

140

cornflowers in a storm came by the very anxious village of Little Snoring. The woman had the sort of wayward dark hair that moved independently from her as she walked. She did not look like a peasant, although she had the hands of one. The people of Little Snoring did not remember her coming there before. It was full moon day, and the village was preparing for the monthly Moonlight Realm Feast. The woman set up a stall with the help of a wild-haired boy, unloading a cart heavy with muslin-wrapped pastries and baskets of applejacks, crumb cakes, and syrup pie – warm slices of deliciousness. Jars of scented honey and wild figs dipped in chocolate and stuffed with spiced cream were laid out on pretty plates and cloths. The smells that came from the market square greeted the villagers like sweet peas on a grey day.

The herald hurried from the palace over the Bridge of Minstrels to the village, straight through the festivities. He had to get help. The princess was barely breathing.

In the village, Landfelian flags and coloured lanterns hung across crooked rooftops. People milled about drinking steaming cups of mead and licking buttery crumbs from their lips. Jim turned pale and took a pensive swig of hot cider when he saw the herald's pinched face through the crowd.

'They do not think she will last the night,' the herald called out to him. 'Come now if you wish to see her once more.' He tried to catch his breath and bowed his head.

'Oh, bless my soul,' muttered Jim, gripping his wife's hand.

The woman watched them, a curious look in her eyes. 'It sounds like the lady needs some maple and pear crumble.'

Before the herald could politely refuse, he was drawn closer to her stall by the scent of nutmeg on her skin. A boy with dirty feet was fast asleep next to a large dog that may have been a wolf. June, Jim, and the herald were passed delicate bowls filled high with crumble. A heavy jug of eggy custard followed. No one said a word as they ate. They appeared bewitched, so entranced by the taste were they. When the herald had finished, he stood up slowly and considered the woman of the stall. She had the most extraordinary eyes.

'Goddess of all things sweet and crumbling, angel from the cloud of golden baked things, can I persuade you to move into my chambers and make a small herald very happy?'

The witch laughed, and so did her lovely hair. 'Did you not send out enquires for a witch?'

The herald's eyes widened. 'By word of mouth only, madame. No one knew of one still practising.'

'The birds hear many things. You asked, and here I am.'

'Well, better late than dead.' June heaved herself up with a sigh. 'Come. Down that hill, across the river, and up a bumpy drive is a young heir in desperate need of some of your custard.'

Jim licked the last smears from his spoon and gave the witch a hopeful smile. 'A humble crumble might just do the trick.'

The herald began to usher her in the direction of

Paloma. 'The half-king will reward you richly, dear lady, and frankly, if they don't, I will. But we must hurry.'

'Very well.' Before she left, the woman kissed her son's sleeping face. 'Behave yourself, Robbie.'

She refilled the custard jug and wrapped up another crumble, a dented silver flask of hot chocolate, and a rich beef stew. The group returned to the palace stables laden with goods and in the company of a white witch.

It was fortuitous that, at that moment, Paloma Palace was quiet. A few servants stood about in worried clumps. The valien did not flatten his ears when a woman with curious eyes came in. She scratched his nose and said, 'Hello, Face.' Then she lit a candle that smelt of lemons, crawled inside the den, knelt next to the princess, and removed the tea cosy from her head. She gave Red a look that some would say verged on stern.

Beneath her shadowed skin was a girl whose heart was still beating, although faintly. Her hair was dull and colourless. The woman unravelled her thin, cold body from the womb of clothes and held her in her arms until she grew warm. She began to sing and sway gently. It was a song that no one had heard before because she had made it up. It was a happy song; her voice was lived-in and safe. She began to talk to Red, as well as sing, as if there nothing wrong with her at all. She talked to her as a mother might.

Jim squeezed June's hand as they watched the witch, and the herald prayed, something he never did.

The witch gently stroked Red's head. 'My favourite colour is the sky at six o' clock, and the best smell, in my book, is coffee, although one cup turns me quite mad. Dear me, you have grown cold.' She rubbed Red's arms and bundled her up closer. 'That's no good. We'll have to start in the middle. I love that time of day when the birds are roosting and my son is soft and quiet. He's not much older than you. In fact, you're just as dirty as each other!' She looked at Red's troubled face and smiled. 'I imagine your mother and father think of you more than anything else.'

The conversation rolled on like a pleasant story, and the princess began to take notice of the good words being spoken to her. The witch blew on Red's hands. She talked about flower remedies and crumble. June poured some tea, and right before the moon came up, Red opened her eyes and found a woman with dark hair and bright eyes describing the smell of her son's feet.

'Like buried blue cheese – and he's only fourteen.' She looked into the princess' eyes and winked. 'That's better. You're warming up, and just in time for pudding.'

The witch's crumble worked a small miracle. Everyone in the den took a moment to toast its magnificence. This one was made with butter, brown sugar, oats, almonds, and pears. I would be lying through my back teeth if I didn't add that there was also a generous slug of brandy. It had crunch and it was lovely. Bottles of anchovy liver oil and other such slime from the Gentlemen of Medicine were thrown into the compost, along with a bowl of leeches. Red tried to stop the tears from coming, but tears never listen. 'I'm sorry,' she whispered. 'I think I have fleas.'

The lady smiled, leant in, and whispered, 'I think we'll all have them after a night in this den.' She held on to Red and continued to sway.

Red clung as tight as she could, which wasn't very tight at all. Once she started to cry, she found she couldn't stop. Tears streamed, hot, down her cheeks. She made an aching sort of noise, and all the while the witch held on.

'They left me behind.' Red tried to stop the feelings that overwhelmed her, but she couldn't; there was a lot to come out.

'No, no, they took you with them,' the woman insisted.

The princess wondered how.

'In their hearts, in everything they see.'

Red considered that she would rather be with them somewhere a little more tangible, but she was not inundated with options.

'Have some more,' said the witch. 'A good cry works up the appetite.'

June ladled out the stew.

There was a lot of snot and hiccupping. The lady remained with Red until she had eaten and was still and sleeping peacefully.

The sun rose. Jim stretched and looked at the morning. The sky was blue, brushed with pink.

They helped the witch pack up her candle and pots. 'You are a very, very white witch,' June told her. 'Never thought I'd meet one. I imagined the ones left were all hussies from the West Realm.'

'Oh, most of us are.' The lady's eyes shone.

Before leaving, she touched Red lightly on the head and whispered, 'Dear me. Someday you'll break hearts with all that red in you. Never forget you are loved.' She smiled. 'I hope my son never meets you. I'll return at the next full moon to see how you are growing. Don't bottle up your feelings – throw them as high and far as you can for the birds to see.'

The witch did not return. No one knew why or how to reach her. The herald was most upset. June reminded him a woman like that would have a very large client base and was likely to be on the road. Red never forgot her. She promised to find her one day and thank her. She left the stable, had a bath, and went to meet her step-aunt and step-uncle for the second time. The reception was not a great improvement on the first, but she felt strong and healthy again. Eating like an eighteen-year-old farm boy, with the True's help, each day she grew taller in spirit.

In Waterwood, Red shifted in her sleep before the campfire, remembering the plan she had made then. She was going to find her father. He needed her help; he was lost too. She lived in his old riding coat, wearing it day and night until the pockets became soft and baggy. If she wore it, she thought he would know she was thinking of him and feel comforted. It trailed along the ground, the sleeves swinging in the wind, sometimes catching small birds and leaves. She could hide herself entirely within its suede, tawny smell.

'It's not practical to walk about looking like a tree stump, Your Highness,' commented Jim as she helped him in the gardens one day. 'I might mistake you and chop you down.'

'If you call me Your Highness again, Jim, I will pee on the rose beds.'

He laughed. 'It's what you are, though. No getting away from it.'

Every evening they walked down the back drive together to look at the river. She liked to watch the servants take the raft across on their way home. She sat next to Jim on the banks as he smoked his pipe, blowing the smoke into interesting shapes.

'What is it like after Little Snoring?' she asked him.

'After?'

'Yes. Beyond the gates.' She would gesture at the horizon dramatically. 'In the other great realms.'

'I don't know much of beyond. June and I visited the Lake of Stars once – what a glistening place that was.' Red's eyes grew wide. 'Never had much need to leave the North Realm, though. This is my home.' He took a satisfying suck on his pipe.

She frowned. 'I want to explore every mountain and valley.' Her valien trotted around them, bucking with excitement and making them laugh.

'You'd better start soon then,' said Jim, smiling.

But that would never happen. On her next birthday, when she had grown as tall as Jim and almost as long as her father's coat, an old hag arrived at the gates of Paloma Palace. She asked to speak to the princess' guardians, and not long after the visit, Red's ankle was placed in a ring of teeth. New guards arrived with the son of a famous lawyer, a gentleman called Daniel Blackwood. It soon became clear that she would need more than her horse to get out of Paloma and into the wild. She needed someone from outside. A maverick. She could not take on the palace guards and the head of royal security on her own.

'I have an idea,' the herald announced precisely three months before the half-queen's ball. 'I know a man.' Aside from Jim True, Red trusted only her father's herald with her most guarded secret: her plans for escape.

Red looked up from re-bandaging her ankle with a clean muslin. The last attempt to cross the river on the servants' raft had ended with a slight infection. Once on the road, she would have to remember to keep it clean and dry. She would not have long, days only, before it crippled her.

'Oh yes? And what does this man do?' She frowned. 'Some sort of fighter, I presume … I'm not interested.'

'Certainly not. A fighting man would only get you covered in blood.'

'What then?'

The herald twinkled at her. 'The finest of actors. William English.'

'I don't think theatre can help me now, Richard.'

'If you will permit me to explain, Princess. I believe what you need is not muscle. You have those in abundance.' It was true. She had been pushing herself hard. There was not one valet who succeeded in winning against her in an arm wrestle or a thumb war. 'The only way to disable the voodoo around your ankle is to leave Paloma and have the spell removed.'

'I know.' She winced as the teeth pressed against her bruised skin. 'But it's impossible. I need to find the hag to break the hex, but the matching set of teeth are kept in the Clock Room here, and to break the curse they must be united. The Clock Room is guarded night and day by guards. I cannot find a way in to take them without getting found out.'

'Precisely.' Richard nodded. 'For these teeth to be taken, we need to create a distraction. We need to open a window of opportunity to allow you to make a run for it while a professional thief enters Paloma Palace.' He looked excited.

Red smiled kindly. 'And how will an actor, no matter how fine, succeed in this?' She wiggled her left foot in his face. 'Taking anything from this palace unseen is impossible.' She shuddered at the thought of the grey, watchful eyes of Daniel Blackwood. 'He sees everything.'

Richard was a patient man. 'Your Highness, William English could do it standing on his head and with no clothes on – if Amber Morningstar was available to provide the distraction.'

'What does she do?'

'She sings.'

Red stopped what she was doing and looked up. 'I'm listening.'

It was simple. The herald wrote to William English and sent the groundsman's son, Billy, to deliver the letter by hand at his most frequented place of employment, an old coaching inn called The Cat's Back. It took months to track the player down and receive a reply. (Landfelian's postal system of squirrelgrams could no longer be trusted since the head of royal security intercepted any letters in and out of Paloma, using a large bag of poisoned walnuts and a silver-topped cane.)

When the reply came, all it said was, *Miss Morningstar and I are at your service, milady.*

AN UNLIKELY ESCORT

Red's sleep was interrupted by a fit of coughing. It was her, she realised. There was smoke everywhere. It filled her nose and throat. Something was on fire.

'I'm on fire!' she screamed and wrestled free from a thick, holey blanket. She choked and looked wildly around her. It was damp and hazy. She was still in the wood. The Man of the Road was making tea over the fire, which was not setting anything it shouldn't alight. She was not on fire; the smoke had confused her sleep-fuddled mind.

'Drink this, then we go.' She saw his saddlebags were already packed.

'What time is it?' It was dark. Red tried to remember why she was in this wood with this man.

'It's sundown, Princess.' He decided not to tell her she had been delirious and talking in her sleep about crumble and a witch. 'You slept through the day.'

She looked down and frowned. 'This is not mine.' She was wrapped in a thick, woollen jerkin.

Robbie carried on brushing down his horse. 'You were shivering.'

'Oh.' Her ankle throbbed, and she gathered up her skirts, despite him, and studied it. It didn't look good. Her ankle was bleeding a bit and her foot had gone an odd shade of mauve. She re-dressed it with a slightly cleaner bandage. It only had to last until Alba.

The Man of the Road stretched and made a groaning noise. Red collected her boots. 'Thank you.' The jerkin smelled slightly goaty but was soft and warm. She slipped it off.

'Keep it – genuine yook wool. You could sleep on the mountains of the South Realm in that and not feel a thing.'

She rolled up the sleeves and splashed her face. 'From a real yook? You've seen one? What are they like?' She had only looked at illustrations in books of the vast, hairy, tusked beasts. The travelling carnival had kept one. But there was only one place to find them in the wild. 'Have you been to Giant Country?'

Robbie handed her a bowl of milky tea. 'Only by accident. Big, lazy brutes the yooks are. But very warm.'

The tea was good, hot, and sweet. As she drank,

she marvelled at the amount of kitchenware this Man of the Road packed on to his horse. Was it all necessary? The whisk? The pans? They sipped in silence, gathered their things, and then began the journey out of the woods, making slightly awkward small talk. The night passed slowly.

Hours later, Red woke with a start from a sleep she did not remember taking. She opened one eye then another, and all she saw was horse. Face was standing over her with his back legs stretched out as if he was about to pee. He did not. He sneezed. She wriggled up from under him and looked around. Her head was a nest of leaves and twigs. The Man of the Road sat, bug-eyed, by a smoking fire.

Apparently, they had made camp after five or so hours of slow walking. Robbie had not slept. He was extremely tired. He watched the princess pull on her boots, the left more gingerly than the right. She, it seemed, unlike him, was pleased by mornings. There was an alarmingly awake sheen in her eyes, and she was talking to herself as if he wasn't there at all. Thankfully, she wasn't the singing sort. Robbie had read about those women and hoped he would never meet one.

The truth was that Red enjoyed early starts. When Paloma Palace slept, she could roam free. While the servants tinkered with the fires and whisked the pillows, she was outside, galloping across the estate before any sly eyes opened and sly mouths spat out the window. Before any spurred boots began to stalk the avenues with a silver-topped cane in search of her.

The smell of their camp and coffee reminded her of Jim's potting shed. She smiled at the memory and hoped to see her old friend again soon. Red stretched, did a few lunges, and felt ready for breakfast. Sleeping in the wild was quite exciting, especially now that she had an escort of sorts. Even one who looked as tired as Robbie did.

'I don't remember falling asleep. Did I wake you?'

Robbie scowled at the fire and ran a hand through his hair, where it got stuck. 'I'm surprised you didn't wake yourself up from shouting about teeth and a cane. And when you *were* quiet, your horse whistled.' His voice scared some nearby treetoads, who stopped garboling and hid.

Red looked at her feet. 'He does that. I'm sorry.' She looked at his hands, suddenly realising she had never slept next to anyone with less than four legs before. She did not remember shouting, but her mind had been full of so many things. Had she dreamt about the witch again? She looked at the Man of the Road. 'Have you ever met a white witch in your travels?'

'White witch? There's no such thing.' He didn't meet her eye. 'I'll make breakfast.'

Robbie watched her. He couldn't believe she had no recollection of the night terrors. A shower of treetoads had landed on his back in shock when she cried out. He had wanted to wake her, but the valien stood protectively between them until she fell into a deeper, quieter sleep. Now she fluttered around like a starling, marvelling at the woods like they were on a nature trail.

'I wonder if Father Peter came this far. He loves trees, especially ancient ones. He believes trees have souls far older than ours and that many have eyes – did you know that? Always be kind to the trees; they see everything. The silver birch, especially.' She patted one gently and gave Robbie a serious look.

'Drink this coffee. It will blast the rest of the slumbersap out of you.'

She looked at the cup doubtfully. It looked more like squirrel droppings and water. She took a delicate sip. 'Oh my – PUHT!' It tasted like squirrel droppings and water too.

'Too hot?'

'STRONG!' she roared and tried another sip. It made her teeth tingle. 'And sweet.'

'I poured molasses into it.'

It was drinkable once her tongue got used to fizzing. 'I don't think I'll ever sleep again.'

He smiled at her. 'That's the idea.'

It took several difficult hours to get out of the floating wood. Robbie lost his leg down an innocent-looking puddle. Red's hair was nibbled at by several gallant treetoads. She flicked them firmly away with her tennis racket and squelched along in wet boots. She wanted to get out, to stand on dry land and see the sky. Every now and then she turned to check the Man of the Road was not holding an axe above her head, only to see him following quietly, a slight furrow on his brow, directing her on which path to take.

He made her a little nervous, so she watched him carefully. There was something she did not trust. He seemed to be wrestling inwardly, and she questioned his true motivation for helping her. He knew the wood and could do startling things with a potato and a handful of wild garlic when they stopped to rest and eat. The servant girls at Paloma would say, 'It's the quiet ones you have to watch', but Red did not know what they meant. She knew nothing about quiet Men of the Road, let alone any other kind. She had read a few books with brooding heroes, and this Robbie Wylde was nothing like them. He only appeared content when food was being prepared and then eaten. The rest of the time he said little, and when occasionally he smiled, it threw her off guard.

He caught the princess staring at him and raised an eyebrow. She picked at a bit of her hem and whistled nervously.

'I will lose him once we are out of the woods,' she mouthed to her horse.

If necessary, she had her tennis racket. She would knock him unconscious and make a run for it.

While they were packing, Red quietly filled up the remaining pouch of coffee with slumbersap and stored it in her hemp sack, thinking it might be a useful weapon later. Robbie smiled to himself and did not say a word.

By the time they felt the cold, salty wind of the coast on their skin, it was approaching dawn. It blew through the trees on the edges of Waterwood and made them both sigh with relief. Red clambered out of the last swamp, refusing his help, and was greeted by a lightening sky filled with bright stars.

'Oh, look!' Stepping onto grassland, she took a deep breath. 'I can smell the sea.' Red riffled in her bag for her map. 'Where are we exactly?'

Robbie lifted his ear to a sound travelling over the grasslands on the sea breeze and swore. 'That would be just my luck.'

Red heard it too. 'What is that faint whistling sound?'

She gazed around them. They had to be in the East Realm. There was a dry-stone wall to her left, fields of sheep, and no proper woods to speak of. Her dress was tie-dyed many shades of brown, her face was streaked with dirt, and her ankle bandage was a long way from clean. Yet she was alive and closer to Alba than she had hoped to be after only a few days on the road. What a fortunate shortcut she'd found through Waterwood. She was good at this travel lark. She willed the pain in her left foot to the back of her mind and frowned. Robbie was covering his horse's ears with his scarf.

'Whatever are you doing to your horse?'

He worked quickly. 'Preparing her for bad weather. There is a Long Wind coming. I would do the same if I were you. It's heading straight for us.'

'A Long Wind? That's impossible. There hasn't been one for years, and if it were approaching, we would hear it.'

'It will be here in minutes. We need to find shelter!' He approached the valien with a rag.

'Stop! He won't let you touch him.' Red took the rag and held on to Robbie's arm. 'Please, I need to get to Alba now.'

'Not in a Long Wind, you don't.'

'Fine.' She would go alone. She gathered up her things. 'I have no choice. I must go. I wish you well, Robert Wylde. Thank you for seeing me safely out of the woods.' She held out her hand.

He didn't take it. 'Decided to go solo, have you?'

'I have to meet someone in Alba. It's all been arranged. They are not likely to wait if I am late.'

Robbie shrugged. 'Don't trust me, do you? Well, it's your funeral, but mark my words: the Long Wind approaches. Look at the horses.' Both animals were restless and stamped at the ground. 'Keep the hat – you've got to cover up your hair somehow.' Robbie had meant that to sound a lot gruffer than it did, because he didn't care what she did. He would find another way out of Landfelian; Father Peter and his Cloudbuster were not the only way, and a princess would only bring him trouble.

'The king will see you are rewarded for your courage and your kindness.' Red looked at him. 'Won't you shake my hand?'

'If he ever returns, tell him not to bother.' Robbie took

her hand and found himself holding a smooth, red jewel the size of a robin's egg. 'What is this?'

'A ruby. It's all I have.' She climbed onto the valien. 'You saved my life.'

Robbie watched her carefully. 'You still believe he will return, don't you?'

'I know he will. He must.' Red clicked her horse to move on, but he trotted sideways. Face looked up uncertainly at the sky and did not move.

Robbie reached out and grabbed hold of her boot. 'I can't let you make the journey to Alba alone. Wait out the Long Wind with me. It's not all wildflowers and welcome signs out there, milady, not anymore.'

'I don't need your help.' She tried to remove her foot from his grasp. The pain made her feel faint.

'Very well. If you know the way, off you go.'

'Very well.' She geed her horse on.

'That's the wrong way,' called Robbie.

The valien drew to a halt, looked doubtfully in both directions and nibbled at some grass.

'I'd check your map if I were you, Princess.'

'If this is the East Realm,' she pointed vaguely ahead of her, 'then Alba is this way.'

Robbie crossed his arms. 'That will lead you straight on to the Swift Highway, right to those friendly guards you seem to collect.'

A flock of jays flew overhead, causing both horses to spook. Robbie grabbed the valien's mane.

'Take your hands off my horse!' Red yelled. She noticed his hands were covered in scars. He pulled the rag from his bag and wrapped it over her horse's head. 'Right, you offer me no other choice.' She delved into her bag for the tennis racket.

'Listen. The Long Wind is almost upon us. Look at the sheep.' They had formed a tight pack and were lying down in a dip in the field. 'If you survive it, you'll have a few hours before those nice guards with drums arrive and flood these fields, scouring every way into the city for you. It's nearly light, and this horse and your hair reflect the sun like a forest fire.'

Robbie was not the poetic sort, but when it came to her hair, it just dribbled out of him. He coughed and continued: 'Voodoo is hobbling your ankle. You're carrying rubies as currency and you're wearing the king's riding coat.' He took a step closer. 'You're also riding a valien with a bad paint job.'

Face tried to look small. Red swallowed nervously.

Robbie shook his head. 'By all means, go it alone. I'm sure you will make it.' he added sarcastically. His hair was being blown about by the wind and his hand gripped her leg. 'But promise me this: when you're done hanging from a gibbet, don't come and haunt me, because I will not appreciate losing any more sleep over your wilful attempt at playing the adventuress.'

Face tried to bite him. Red opened her mouth and closed it. She felt dizzy, tired, and, loathe to admit it, close to crying again.

'But I have to go. I have to get to The Cat's Back in Alba by Sunday to meet the man with the key to remove this voodoo charm.'

'Who is he, some sort of dentist?' asked Robbie.

'No, an actor.'

'Naturally,' Robbie sighed. 'What's his name?'

'William English.'

'Doesn't ring a bell.'

'He's very good, apparently.'

'And this actor knows how to break the cursed thing?'

'I hope so, yes, if he managed to escape Paloma with the key.'

'Who put it on you?'

'The gentleman in charge of royal security, a man called Blackwood. A man my father would never have allowed through the gates.' She swallowed.

Robbie was shocked. He knew of the man. Blackwood was responsible for the new guard and much of the terror across the North Realm. 'This Blackwood must know a witch.'

'Possibly. I was given something to make me sleep when it was fitted. I don't know how they did it exactly.' She wanted him to stop asking questions and stop looking at her. She felt cold at the memory of that night. 'Let me go.'

'That was nice of them.' Robbie held on to her.

'Have you seen this type of charm before?'

'You see a good deal on the road, Princess. My mother knew about the dark arts, and she told me, from an early age, to stay away from those sorts of meddlers. The dead must be left to rest. I've learnt never to accept a hag's trinket made from anything that was once living.'

An ominous whine filled the sky behind them. The sound of the Long Wind grew closer.

'Please, let me go.'

Robbie held on tight. 'Where is this actor now?'

'On his way to meet me.'

'At The Cat's Back in Alba.'

'Do you know it?'

Every Man of the Road did. He nodded. 'It's not easy to find, but you'll be safe there.'

'I have a map.'

He smiled. 'I know, but it won't help you get into a place that doesn't welcome palace guards, the head of royal security, or any relation to the half-queen.'

'I'll disguise myself, buy a wig.'

She had to shout above the howling wind. The horses shifted and stamped.

'Not with a ruby, you won't. They will smell you out and turn you over to the guards before you could ask for a receipt. Rubies are not common currency here, Princess. There is no currency anymore. The House of Gold's got a lot of spare room in its vaults – last I heard, it was overrun with squatters.

Bartering is how we get by these days.' He paused, looked across the fields at a hazy area on the horizon, and began to button up his coat. 'The bounty on your head is the latest game of Find a Fortune in Landfelian.'

'There's a bounty?' Red couldn't believe it. 'Why?'

He didn't answer but watched a spray of geese fly overhead, honking. Robbie covered his head with a blanket. The whole sky to the north seemed to be moving as if caught in a current.

'What is happening?'

'The birds are trying to escape the wind, Princess. If you insist on going now and going alone, aim for the old citadel at Alba – a street called Dead End. You'll find what you are looking for there.'

Red tucked her hair inside her coat and nodded nervously. 'Thank you.'

'Don't ask for directions. You can read bandit tracks, can't you? And talk your way past the city guards? And whatever you do, avoid the scraper camps.' He looked at her.

She'd never heard of those things. It was becoming hard to hear him over the roar of the sky. 'Well, I ...'

'Naturally, you know what it means if a gentleman offers you a blue drink?'

Red faltered. None of these things were on her map. He was making them up to frighten her, but unease trickled through her all the same. 'I have heard there may be a little discontent. People may have lost hope over the years, but Landfelian is good and true of heart. I will come to no harm.'

It sounded naive, even to her. Robbie raised an eyebrow.

'Fine,' said Red. 'How long before the Long Wind strikes?'

'I'm surprised you haven't read about the Long Winds in your books,' said Robbie. 'You know, in the chapter after voodoo jewellery and before –'

The valien reared up when the trees behind them began to creak in the wind. 'Please help.' She looked at him, white and stricken.

'Follow me.' Robbie mounted his horse. 'Cover your eyes and nose if you want to use them later. Stay close behind. I know a place where we can shelter, not far from here. And then we'll get you to Alba in time.' He looked up at the swirling grey sky. 'Somehow.'

PART II

THE GREAT DISTRACTION

*'There's no such thing as bad
weather – only the wrong clothes.'*

Billy Connelly

9

A ROYAL TELEGRAM

(Five months before Red Felian jumped out a window …)

Will frowned at the Palace Times. If he stared with any more intensity, it would have begun to smoke. An advertisement had been circled in black ink and the paper pushed under his door.

WANTED – A PLAYER FOR CUPID.

ENHANCE THE SPIRIT OF YOUNG LOVE AT PALOMA PALACE, AT THE GREATEST WIGGED BALL OF ALL TIME, IN CELEBRATION OF PRINCESS FELIAN'S SEVENTEENTH AND A HALF BIRTHDAY

COSTUME – CLOUD AND HARP WILL BE PROVIDED. PLEASE BRING OWN TIGHTS

'You have got to be kidding!' Will stormed out of his hovel. It was a hovel fit for a player; a hovel he was immensely proud of. His hovel was a cellar below a butcher's. There was a small corner of damp in the ceiling sporing black bumps. A wooden crate serving as a desk sported a candle he had bought from a gypsy in Kande, promising virility. A thick layer of peat served as his floor. There was one window, which was narrow and draughty, affording a view of boots and horse manure passing over the lane above. The hovel not only housed Will but a family of rats, who he liked to practise his lines with. Over time, his home had worked hard to fulfil the part of hovel, and it had exceeded his expectations.

Will did not storm far – only to the end of Short Street and then into Dead End, until he stood outside The Cat's Back Inn. The door was locked. It *was* extremely early – the toast-sellers were only just surfacing on the streets. Above him, one gabled window was ajar. He knew the window well; it had watched him attempt to climb through it on countless occasions and never once obliged.

'Amber! What in Aunt Mary's name are you thinking?' Will bellowed, throwing the *Palace Times* on the street in disgust. 'I trained with Sir Rodney Beard! The man who lived blindfolded for a year – one whole year! – to prepare for his role in "Hello, Jacqueline, It's Me, Mole".'

The people of Dead End knew Will's illustrious career and his ranting only too well. They moaned, turned over, and went back to sleep.

'The same man who after my last performance said - and I quote this to you VER-BAT-TIM - "Darling, you have it!"' He paused as a toast seller hurried by, hoping not to become involved. Will bought two slices of medium-rare toast to fuel his shouting.

'"Imagination, William," he said to me, "you have it and it will make you a star!"'

A stray dog peed on his boot, and the toast seller tried to leave. Then, quite suddenly, a beautiful woman popped her head out of the window and a soft wave of buttery hair said, 'Good morning,' to the toast seller and the dog, before directing its attention upon the player. The smile it framed was something else though; if smiles could bite, this one would take off an arm.

'Imagination doesn't pay the rent, William. You have not made a conker since you acted your way into this dead end and tried to climb into my bed!' The woman pulled her hair back to get a better range – it was doing cartwheels in the wind, which was unusually cold and strong for the time of year. 'You need to get a job. That dog knows it, I know it, and you, sir …' She smiled so sweetly at the toast seller, who dropped the butter knife and blushed. 'Everyone else in this kingdom has to make an honest living, William. Why can't you wake up and smell the toast?'

Will crossed his arms. 'I am this kingdom's greatest

actor. I WILL NOT put on a pair of tights and play CUPID for one of the half-queen's ridiculous balls.'

The beauty slammed the window and cracked the glass. The sound of frustrated woman wailed inside. Everyone on Dead End was awake now. Someone clapped, enjoying the daily drama. Will gazed up at the gabled window with longing.

'If it's income that concerns you, let me share your bed, buttercup. I will not have to pay rent and you will have no need of a fire, thereby saving outgoing costs on both sides.'

The window opened, and he smiled hopefully. Amber hurled her copy of the *Palace Times* at Will and slammed her window shut again. She pulled the primrose curtains together with such force that one side came off. This upset her so much, she burst into tears, which was very unlike Amber, who was not usually a crier. It was approaching the eighth year of the king's quest, which made it nearly eight years since Blackwood had imprisoned her family and stolen her hopes for a bright future. If there was a good morning to cry it was this one.

Will began to pace up and down Dead End, eating his piece of toast and wondering what to do next. There was no denying he needed the work; another year of glass washing at The Cats Back wasn't going to persuade Amber to marry him and move to Kande in the West Realm. He did not notice the toast seller sign for a telegram that arrived by the hand of a muddy-faced peasant boy. The toast seller tapped Will gently on the shoulder and was ignored.

'Forgive me, sunflower,' called Will with a sigh. 'I'll go to the palace. I'll put on tights and play Cupid. I'll enhance the spirit of young love … I'll do it for you.' He stared forlornly at the broken window and then frowned. 'But if that half-queen asks me to juggle hedgehogs again, forget it.' He kicked a low wall for emphasis and got a warning look from the woman standing behind it. When the toast seller prodded him sharply in the back, he spun round and yelled.

'What?'

'Telegram for you, son.' The man smelt reassuringly of an early form of Marmite, called Beefy. He pushed the young boy holding a letter in Will's direction. 'Might be good news,' he added hopefully. There were still some Landfelians who believed in good news, and most were toast sellers.

Billy True looked at Will through his mop of dirty hair. 'I have a special delivery for a William English, actor.'

Will began to walk quickly backwards. 'Is it a summons from the House of Gold?' He mentally assessed how far he could run on two pieces of toast. The gold-lenders had finally caught up with him - over the matter of a small career-development loan he had borrowed when his troop of players disbanded, which he had not paid a coin of back. A series of wigs and false noses had concealed his identity very well so far.

'No,' said the boy. 'I come from the palace.' Billy whispered and looked nervously around him.

'The palace?' Will raised a cautious eyebrow. It was a

trap. 'There is no palace in this city.'

'The royal palace of Paloma.'

'Well, boy, hand it over. I am William English, the actor,' he said, bowing with a flourish. 'This is my toast-maker and my stray dog, and if this is a trick, I will slap you.'

Billy looked at the man before him. He certainly looked like a player. His mother had told him they were all a bit curly – with ponytails and rouge and so on. This one had very expressive eyebrows and what looked like black crayon drawn around his eyes and a body stocking protecting his hair, which was the colour of conkers. He handed over the scroll.

'Who's it from then, the king?' Will laughed, unrolling the parchment. 'Has he finally returned?' He read the letter. His mouth dropped open and his eyebrows disappeared when he got to the signature at the bottom. 'Now listen, boy. This is clearly some sort of joke. Who sent you? Was it Barry at The Hog's Breath?' Will glanced up and down the street. 'It wasn't Claude, the mime artist, was it? That fool's been trying to get me back for years.'

'No. It was Princess Red Felian,' he urged.

'This seal … is it … real?' It certainly looked the part – kingfisher-blue wax on thick cream parchment pressed with the king's crest – a valien jumping out of a crown.

The boy nodded gravely. 'She's in trouble.'

'You'd better come inside.' Will scrambled over the wall into the garden of The Cat's Back. After a brief minute the back door opened and let Billy inside. 'Follow me.'

Hours later, Will English and Amber Morningstar sat around a small fire in the attic room of The Cat's Back with one curtain, a broken window, and the peasant boy from Paloma. They slurped tea and murmured to one another as night fell. It was a cosy lodging. The few pieces of furniture Amber owned were elegant. A walnut bureau stood next to a silk-cushioned armchair; her bed was covered by a soft blanket and a heap of recently discarded well-made dresses. A standing mirror served as a changing screen, from which hung long strings of pearls and feather boas. Above the fire was an old poster for the greatest travelling circus in the kingdom, the Cornucopia Carnival. Billy stared at it. A blonde siren in a sequined bodice stood alone in a dark arena, a spotlight illuminating her soulful face as, above her, the great shadows of beasts, giants, bearded ladies, and flying wonders tip-toed across a tightrope. There were two words written below: *Be Enchanted*.

Billy looked at Amber and her buttery hair and gulped. *She* was the voice of the Cornucopia Carnival, the silver-voiced wonder known simply as Morningstar. Somewhere in the city a clock chimed. He should have left hours ago. He had to make his way back to the North Realm. He forced himself to stop staring and looked expectantly at the pair. 'I must return to the palace. What is your answer?'

Will stood up and cracked his back, his eyes alight.

'Young peasant boy from Paloma, I'm at your service. You have my word.'

Billy wasn't sure he could trust the player. 'What word?' he asked carefully.

Will shrugged. 'You choose.'

'Pineapple,' said Billy, thinking of one of his favourite words.

'If you're not going to take it seriously, I will swear on my father's sword,' Will said grandly.

Amber rolled her eyes. 'Your father hasn't got a sword.'

Billy looked at them both. 'Swear on your life.'

'Alright. I swear on my life.'

Will English did not look the type of man capable of remembering his own birthday, let alone smuggling a voodoo charm out of a heavily guarded palace, but Amber winked at the boy. 'You can trust us, boy. We'll be there. The princess has our allegiance.' Her voice turned cold as she gazed at the fire. 'I have no loyalty to the new guard or the man they put in charge there. We'll see you at the ball.'

THE PLAYER

It was a sultry May evening – perfect for a spritzer. The sun had begun to fall behind Mount Felian, and the sky glowed magenta. Long lines of traffic snailed up the six great avenues that led towards the pillared palace entrance. From a grassy knoll overlooking the Curling Gates of Paloma Palace and the curve of the Bigeasy River, two peasants contemplated the lay of things.

'Looks like the Big C's having another bash.'

'Aye, they say it's her biggest yet.' In fact, it was the greatest wigged ball the North Realm had ever seen, though to anyone who asked, the hostess referred to it as the greatest of all time.

'Is it her birthday again?' the first peasant spat. 'Comes round quick. She's had four this year. Doubt there's any butter left in the buttery for icing.'

'This one's for the princess.' The other sniffed into a grotty rag. 'Seventeen and a half.'

'Well, I hope they give her fireworks. The queen loved fireworks.'

Fireworks were new to the North Realm and viewed as nothing short of miraculous. No one had discovered who was behind them; they just appeared, uninvited, at the right time, causing an 'Ahhhh' amongst the people watching. The second peasant hoicked until whatever was in his throat dislodged. 'Aye, any chance she got she'd set off a rocket.' He wiped his eyes and smiled.

'I wonder if the princess grew into her chin,' mused the first peasant. 'The king had a strong chin.'

'Poor grub. Rumours say she looks nothing like either of them. Strange hair, as red as Christmas.' The princess' hair was indeed red, although Christmas was redder.

'As long as she's got all her teeth.' It was before the days of advanced dentistry, and Landfelians relied on twig ends, a rough cloth, and chalk for dislodging a day's eating.

They were interrupted by the sight of a small man in a great hurry, who was skipping towards the grassy knoll from the village of Little Snoring. It was the king's herald. You could tell because true heralds never ran – running was vulgar – and skipping was the fastest they could travel while maintaining poise. He had begun to perspire and dabbed himself with a blue silk handkerchief. In his gloved hand, he carried a mid-length blonde wig. The small man muttered to himself in anxious, harried tones. 'Midnight, frying pan … Oh dear … There will be very little time.'

The peasants waved. 'What ho, little Richard.'

He jumped. 'Gentlemen, good day to you.'

'On your way to the ball?' They grinned and wiggled their toes. It was a comfort to see the herald. He reminded them of how it had been once, in happier times before the new guards moved in. 'Got yourself a nice wig there.'

The herald looked about the path before giving the peasants the start of a smile and bowing. 'Unfortunately, yes, I am being forced to attend.'

'Bad luck, mate. Come by and have a dram later. Tell us what the old trout puts on her head this time round.'

'I'm afraid tonight that will be impossible.' He frowned. 'All of Blackwood's guards will be out.'

The herald threw them a small pouch of silver pieces and hurried on. The peasants limped down the knoll and headed straight for The Parsnip's Nose.

'Pissing guards. Must be a pretty important bash for them all to be out on parade.'

'Maybe the king's coming home?'

'Ha! You're having a laugh.'

Richard Losley, the king's herald, would have given away his blue velvet loafers to regale the locals at The Parsnip's Nose of the taxidermy horrors that were the half-queen's headpieces. But this evening there was not a chance in hell. He had not had a night off for seven years, and never on a ball night – especially this one.

When he was over the bridge, he tucked the wig up his shirt sleeve and skipped on to the Curling Gates, where there waited two slack-mouthed men with less expression than hung meat. Richard adjusted his pink necktie, cleared his throat, and smiled graciously. The guards banged their drums at him and stamped. They wore thigh-high leather boots and extremely suspect purple jodhpurs.

'WHAT DO YOU WANT, DWARF?'

'To enter.' The herald fought the urge to add several expletives. He had to go through the same rigmarole with these guards at the gates every day, and after seven years had grown tired of it.

'WHAT'S THE PASSWORD?' They bore down on him.

'Quince.'

The guards could not remember if this was the password, and they conferred between themselves for several minutes before turning back to Richard.

'We fort it was plum.'

Richard drew in a deep breath. 'That was last month's password. Just let me in. You know perfectly well who I am.'

'Hang on there, Tom Thumb.'

The herald closed his eyes, counted to eleven, and finally there was a welcome clink. The gates moved slowly forward to reveal acres of exquisitely planted parkland. Down an avenue of gently rustling poplars, Paloma Palace shimmered, and Richard's shoulders dropped at the sight of the vast romance of a house. It was built from North Realm stone and was the colour of ripe peach. Hundreds of pale glass windows glowed from the candelabras inside. The place still had a serenity like no other in the land.

From the Curling Gates, everything looked as it should: lit up and ready to receive guests. No one would suspect anything was amiss. Apart from the guards, of course, and the watchtower, Paloma exactly looked as it had in when the king had been present, except he loathed balls and rarely hosted one. The herald took a sorry breath and skipped on. When he was halfway up the approach and out of sight of the guards, he pulled the blonde wig from his sleeve and, holding it high above his head, waved it slowly from side to side three times.

From the roof above the highest window of the east turret, a figure in possession of a spyglass and a great deal of dark red hair stood up and hopped once at the herald's signal. She watched him disappear into the palace, sat back down, and nibbled anxiously through a pocketful of cobnuts.

'The distraction must have arrived. Oh elephants. No going back now.'

Red Felian skidded down the roof several feet, in excitement. She stopped herself dropping off the edge and smiled proudly at her castle combers – two badminton rackets tied to her bare feet with a yard of ribbon, the rims of which were studded through with bristles pulled from one of the half-queen's hairbrushes. The invention had afforded her the freedom to walk along the rooftops of Paloma Palace and spy on its goings and comings without being seen or falling to her death. Around her left ankle rested a choker of teeth, which she unconsciously scratched every so often. She walked carefully around to the other side of the roof, facing the back drive and wild meadow that stretched down to the river. The wonky rooftops of Little Snoring could not be seen here, only the dark, mysterious line of Boundary Hedge in the distance. The evening wind blew her hair from her face. She thought of the night ahead, and her heart leapt.

Red watched as the guests arrived, their carriages circling the lawn.

'He's down there somewhere. My intended.' She flinched at the thought.

Hours before, Red had lain on her daybed, which was also her night bed, and declared, 'I must claim back my life! I will not spend any more time locked in this turret.'

She was not usually locked in, but for the purpose of the half-queen's so-called surprise tonight, she was. Despite the voodoo charm and the guards, Caroline was not convinced the princess would want to remain for long at the palace once she found out about the betrothal. She had not banked on her step-niece's ingenious piece of footwear. Red rolled over and howled into a pillow. She'd found out the reason for the ball months before, from the herald.

'Why are you measuring my finger, Richard?' she'd asked one afternoon, as he'd taken a tape to her hand.

'It's for your birthday present.' He'd looked guilty. 'Oh dear ...'

'Another surprise from Aunt Caroline? Oh God, what is it this time? A hairbrush?' Red made a face. 'Gloves made from ostrich feathers?'

'It is not a hairbrush, a pony, or a pair of impractical slippers.' The herald still did not meet her eye. 'There is something I must tell you, dear girl. Won't you sit down?'

'What is it? Step-aunt's been unusually civil of late. She must be planning something horrible.'

'It's a man!' Richard blurted out.

'A what?'

'She is giving you a man ... a husband.'

'NO!'

'Yes, my dear.' He squeezed her hand. 'I am so terribly sorry.'

'Who? I don't understand.'

'Sir Toby.'

'What?' Red gripped his hand so tight he squeaked. Sir Toby was harmless enough when you stood him against the rest of her step-aunt's close circle at court, but still. 'No, I'm sorry. I refuse to marry a man who wears press-on moles and sleeps in heated fir cones to curl his fringe.'

'He is your birthday surprise.' The herald patted her hand. 'It could be worse. Remember the gentleman with the big pink and white wig who proposed to you last year?'

Red wasn't listening. 'But how? Is this even legal?'

'Blackwood drew up a contract. It is the half-queen's wish that you are married immediately after the ball, before sunrise.'

'Have all the arrangements been made?' Red went cold.

'Yes. The holy man, Thomas Finkermeyer, has already been called. Unfortunately, as your guardians, they have found some ancient right to ...'

'Bloody hell.' Red was not pleased. 'We may need to fast track the escape plan, Richard.'

In fact, never had a young lady been less impressed by a surprise or a proposal. Red had no intention of marrying him. She had no intention of marrying anyone. Marriage was too risky and easily lost, and above all, it was boring. It was not for her. She would be swapping one form of imprisonment for another. Someone else to control her life and keep her confined within the walls of another rambling estate. Well, forget it.

Looking up, Red found the stars had come out in their thousands, skimming the treetops and turning their leaves silver. She glanced at the clock on the bell tower and turned to the back drive. Her step-aunt called it the Seventh Approach and alluded to it with vague hand gestures. She did not like to hear mention of the 'back passage' amongst the servants, which was odd because the woman had a gutter for a mouth. Red scanned the old road with her spyglass. It was quiet and dark. Where was the player? The road wound from the kitchens, past the stables, and on through meadows, fruit orchards, and the potting sheds before ending in a final strait at the river. She strained forward. The slow progress of a modest wagonette and the murmuring of the men on board could be heard. It had to be him. Something woke up and began to flap nervously in her stomach. Red stood up, took a deep breath, and disappeared through the window.

The princess' plan had been honed for six years, three hundred and fifty-eight days, and eight and a half hours. A slim, grey cat watched with calm eyes as Red tried to stuff her boots, a fold-up wooden tennis racket, and the king's old riding coat into an inconspicuous hemp sack – a sack that said, 'I carry potatoes. I do not break the law.'

At first, Red had held on to the hope of someone trying to scale the Curling Gates, thunder up the first avenue, and joust with the guards for her release before she galloped away with them in the direction of the setting sun.

In seven years, no one had tried.

Jousting had been banned in Landfelian, for being pointless. The heroes were all somewhere with the king, and no one else knew how to do it without being killed – the armour alone could suffocate a man. Storming castles had also been banned by the new Head of Royal Security. No one was allowed to thunder anywhere; it was a violation against the new speed law. So galloping was out completely.

Red realised that no one knew where she was and soon wondered if anyone cared to find out. She felt forgotten. And that was when the plan had begun. To escape and to find her father. She didn't need a hero; she would do it alone. However, there had been very little opportunity. But the imminent prospect of being Lady Tobias Mole was enough to make Red take the final leap. Tonight, she would cross that river or she would die trying.

Red waved at the snow-capped summit of Mount Felian, blue-white under a fat moon. The sound of lutes started up from below. She swallowed nervously, stared at her cat for a few seconds, and said, 'I hope I make it.'

The hex around her ankle twitched involuntarily. The cat hissed at it and flicked her tail. Red pinned back her hair – a job for twenty-seven pins – wiggled into the blonde wig, which Julia had dropped in through her window, then returned to her roof to sip a fine brandy – which numbed both her throat and her nerves. Now all she had to do was wait until midnight.

Below, it looked like what she was getting for her seventeenth and a half birthday was an invasion. Hundreds of elaborately painted hansoms, barouches, and cabriolets crunched slowly towards the open doors of the Great Mirrored Hall below. Red observed every four- to eight-wheeled horse-drawn transport imaginable. Horses in feathers and footmen in fascinators competed with one another in grandeur, posturing as they stopped outside the sweeping entrance. Paloma's peacocks danced between gold-spoked wheels, shaking their tails and squawking suggestively at the arriving guests.

Sir Toby Mole himself arrived in the grandest contraption of all. The Belair was a limited-edition barouche, equipped with its own minstrel and a selection of hand puppets to play with behind a small, beautiful curtain. Red thought the Belair looked like a giant aubergine on wheels. Lady Annabel, Sir Toby's mother, sat beside him, nibbling her way through a small ramekin of pickled onions. Neither were saying much of consequence.

Two elks pulled the Belair; it was simply too heavy for horses. A small, unfortunate herd had been coaxed away from gambolling amongst the sweet heather between the South and West Realm to transport the rich and assiduous to the royal ball. Their branch-like legs and graceful necks strained against the bridles and bits. Red hoped they farted all the way and turned the weak-chinned passengers inside green.

The Moles had been the last to arrive. It was so unseasonably humid that night that the elks had needed to stop for an hour to rest by the river. Nothing would move them. Sir Toby regretted the fox-lined interior of the barouche as much as everyone inside the palace regretted their wigs – although not as much as their wigs regretted them. As they waited, Sir Toby wiped his sweating palms on his ruby silk and lace knickerbockers and moaned.

'Good God, this heat is infernal.' A third press-on mole peeled off his cheek.

'Oh do shut up, Tobias.' Lady Annabel was a dry shrew of a woman with little patience for anything that wasn't a beagle. Her gaze drifted out the window. 'A great many worse things happen at sea,' she said, although her mind was full of her dogs and not her husband, who was currently at sea experiencing much worse things.

Sir Toby picked up a marzipan fruit and smiled at the palace. 'It is ravishing, isn't it? Nowhere like it in the whole kingdom. Unless Celador is its like.' He imagined the winter castle to be a place of pine needles, port, roaring fires, and roasted hog. Soon he would see it for himself, with his princess bride.

His mother did not say a word, and the Belair finally lurched on. The Felian family usually spent half the year up at Paloma and the winter in Celador in the South Realm, but Toby had never left the north. Unlike the princess, he had the opportunity, but not the curiosity, for such a trip. He had grown up to be a lazy arse.

Red watched a line of footmen usher the Belair forward to the carriage drop-off point. She watched Sir Toby step out and try a few royal waves at other guests gathered at the bottom of the garden stairs to the hall.

From her roof, Red watched him stumble up the

steps, and she took a long swig of liquor. He was almost unrecognisable now as the boy she remembered coming to stay during the last summer her parents were together. The years he had spent in her step-aunt's company had changed him. For one, he never used to wear make-up. A fanfare sounded, and the herald walked out and stepped up to a podium at the top of the marble stairs. He was flanked by two large men in togas.

'Lords, ladies, counts, countesses, knaves, dukes, duchesses, mistresses, mincers, earls, eminences, knights, and any foreign gentlefolk of great esteem, I welcome you to the Greatest Wigged Ball of All Time.'

There were cheers.

Red groaned. Every one of the half-queen's balls was the 'greatest'.

'No flashers, pets, peasants, children, non-drinkers, or aesthetically unpleasing plus-ones are permitted inside, on orders of the half-queen. Her gloriousness and the half-king hope you have your fill of the delights within, and now it is time to prepare your curtsies for their imminent arrival.'

No one looked that bothered. The doors were opened, the guests entered, and one thousand flutes of champagne were marched into the Great Mirrored Hall on a wave of gold platters.

Red stared pensively towards the river as the sounds of the ball rang out into the dusk and then folded up her spyglass and climbed back through her window. She painted her lips blood red and slipped on a silk dress the colour of sage. No corset, no lace, no frills, no under-wiring, crinoline, or hooped undercarriage. Her dress had a gold sash about the waist and long bell-sleeves that slipped off her shoulders. She did not want to look like a total tramp, but she did not want to look like anyone worthy of a second glance. The last thing she needed at this party was to be chatted up by one of Caroline's entourage. She'd found a dress that matched most of the soft furnishings and asked the herald to find a wig the same yellow as the walls. A pair of round-rimmed glasses and a wan smile completed her disguise. No one expected to see her until the surprise engagement was announced at midnight. She climbed out of the window, tiptoed across a thin ledge that connected her turret to the main body of palace, and, gripping on to the wing of a stone angel, swung inside. She landed lightly on her feet, straightened up, and stared right into the face of her step-aunt. Caroline looked much like a parrot in drag, and the two women's eyes met for one long second before Caroline sniffed and turned away. She did not recognise the girl in the standard-size mid-length blonde wig. Although, glancing back across landing, she felt a chill as if she had caught a glimpse of her own death. Red watched her go, then followed calmly down the stairs and entered the ball.

* * *

William English was wondering where all the torches and trumpets were. The palace ahead was illustrious enough, but the approach was bland and disappointing, and he said as much.

'Don't get none of that flaming lark on the back passage, mate,' came a voice beside him as the wagonette bumped and lilted towards the kitchens. 'This is the peasants' entrance. All the fancy bollocks is on the first avenue.'

He was hitching a ride with a group of peasants. One hundred servants had been drafted in for the night to fill the one hundred additional pairs of purple jodhpurs ordered by the half-queen for the extra staff. Will sat amongst these men, clutching his trunk and trying not to be sick as they discussed the escalating cost of coffee.

'Tried tea but it doesn't cut the slumpy after a long day's peasanting.'

'Yeah, but the half-queen's nicked all the beans, Nigel. Gets through a sack a week, they say. There's more caffeine in that woman than ... caffeine.'

'And the traders won't come anymore because of the fog.'

There was a thoughtful silence. No one liked the traders much, but everyone preferred them to the fog. The fog around the coast could not be explained, and it left an uneasy taste in the mouths of the Landfelians.

'Can't be good for her. Makes my wife's head all full of sharp angles.'

Nods all round.

'I hope she gets an ulcer and dies,' said one, and they all clapped.

When Paloma Palace came into view, a hush descended. Will's mouth dropped open and remained so until they pulled up outside the slop door. High up on the roof of the delicately spiralled east turret, he caught a jolt of red and saw a slight figure with enormous, racket-shaped feet disappear inside. He noted two guards standing below.

One of the men nudged him. 'Everyone off!'

They followed the smell of woodsmoke and steaming delicacies from the kitchens, passed visiting horses stamping impatiently for hay in a wide, immaculate yard. The back of the palace was as lovely as the front – there were sea-green urns filled with thyme, rosemary, lavender, doors of pale ash, and a wishing well. Will forgot about vomiting. He gazed at the summer palace and sighed as the others shouted around him.

'We're on call when the clock strikes eight! Remember that half-brained woman won't pay us in prune stones if we're late.'

'Big C's always late,' a man next to him grumbled.

'Well, I'm not taking my chances. I need the gold.'

The peasants strolled wearily inside to change. They muttered amongst themselves about the jodhpurs.

'Know where you're supposed to be, lad?' asked one.

Will nodded and remained in the yard out of the way of the hustle and bustle until he was alone. The trunk he wheeled behind him looked like a ladies' trousseau. It was midnight blue with a silver buckle and embossed with his initials in the finest calligraphy. One such trunk was bestowed upon each member of The Hey Nonnys, the most infamous company of players in Landfelian.

One of the horses gently burped, rousing him from his thoughts. He checked the yard for guards, walked casually to the nearest stable, and, in the company of an ass, began to warm up.

During the banishment of all actors by the half-queen after an unfortunate play about her parentage, Will had been, what they called in the entertainment business, 'resting', though others called it 'unemployed and often drunk'. He had hobo-ed his way across the land, trying various grades of mead and performing as a street entertainer. They were dark days – especially when newt swallowing had formed part of his act.

The audiences had not been kind; Landfelians had generally forgotten how to laugh, and Will's career as a troubadour had not taken off. He became a glass washer at The Cat's Back, an inn hidden deep within the old citadel of Alba. And there he'd remained until Princess Felian sent him a letter.

'Gobbling gargoyles gobbled gangrenous goblins. Gobbling gargoyles gobbled gangrenous goblins.' He paced around the stable, throwing out his voice.

The ass turned to him in alarm.

'A common weakness, you know, my furry friend,' Will explained to the beast, 'is to miss out the vowel entirely when speaking.'

Will cast an eye around him for any untrustworthy eyes glinting at him from the dark. It was all clear, there was just the slight smell of methane lurking in the straw. He opened his trunk, unpacked two grapefruits and a feather boa, and began to dress. 'This shall be the greatest performance of my career.'

The actor emerged from the stable as the clock began to strike eight. Doves, dyed pink at the request of the half-queen, flew out in shock at the sight of him. Will adjusted his wig and teetered towards a clutch of peasants who were smoking by the slop door.

'Good evening, gentlemen,' he purred. 'Be darlings and point me in the direction of the countesses' entrance?'

Nigel made a wet noise and leaned suggestively towards the lady.

Will's dress was the colour of melted bridesmaids, and it was eye-watering. It was doing something unfair to his pancreas, yet giving him the voice of a baby seal and a twelve-inch waist.

'Urm.' There was a shuffle of interested jodhpurs.

One of the men managed to point a finger to a narrow path between two box hedges, through which the flickering light from hundreds of flaming torches could be seen.

'That's your door.' He coughed. The others stared.

'You are a sweet thing, thank you.'

Nigel curtsied by mistake as Will passed and tried not to look at the countess' bulging corset. He had never met a woman taller than him before or with a hairier chest. She was quite remarkable.

Will fluttered eyelashes as long as spider's legs at the men. He flicked a wave of raven hair from his bare, broad shoulder and giggled helplessly before sashaying off.

'Crikey!' the peasants roared.

A shrill whistle sounded from the kitchens.

'That's our call.' They reluctantly tore their gaze from the corseted, jiggling form sashaying away.

Nigel dropped his pipe into his boot, which began to smoke. 'I'm not one to prophesise ...' he started. Nigel prophesised all the time. As a peasant, he thought it his one right. He looked up at the sky to see a dark, rum puncher of a storm set to hit Paloma right in time for the half-queen's mysterious surprise. 'But I've got a dicky feeling in my jods about this ball. Something big is brewing, lads, mark my words.'

Will was riding high on the reaction of the peasants to his newly created character. Unfortunately, as he surveyed the guests ahead of him, it was not high enough. The steps that greeted Will were not stone, they were marble. There are steps and there are STEPS. These were beyond both. The approach to Paloma's front door was a symphony. It was off the scale, and if you were wearing heels, it was impossible. Will skidded in the six-inch gold lace-up boots he had borrowed from an opera singer and fell up the first five steps beautifully. He joined a line of other countesses, who greeted him with some of the most violent looks he had ever been party to. There were several growing queues, Will noted. The line of mistresses looked the most interesting. Caroline, having been a mistress herself on several occasions, insisted on inviting them all. He complimented a woman on her ermine shrug and was accepted with a giggle into a circle of hand fans and heaving, powdered breasts.

As Will wowed the countesses, on the other side of the palace, a man with hair as curly as fusilli pasta was having a bubble bath. In the adjoining dressing room, his wife picked out fishnet stockings and squeezed a satin bodice over her bullet of a frame before surveying her wardrobe. The half-queen skated on the outer extremes of fashion, and nothing with a skin was safe. She adored animals; they accommodated her taste for leathers, feathers, and tails. No one had seen a flamingo in the lake for years.

'Do you think we should announce the engagement to the girl before or after the entertainment?' she barked at her husband, flinging garters out of a chest of drawers that took up one side of the room and settling on a pair of stockings adorned with tiny purple tassels. Most of the half-queen's delicates screamed 'drag'.

'After, my darling,' he belched happily from the bath, taking a gulp of champagne from a nearby bottle. 'It is a miracle she has not discovered your cunning proposal.'

'I told the servants I would stop their wages if they let a word of it slip.' She snapped a lace garter into place and sniffed. 'Do you know who the herald hired for the entertainment? I hope it isn't that dreadful Acapulco group of nuns from the West Realm.' Caroline's screeching voice explained why Gerald was often found in the bath, his head submerged in the water.

'A lady from Alba, I believe, pootle. Awfully good singer, apparently.' He finished clipping his toenails in the cloudy water and reared up, a flushed, rotund, cherub of a man.

'If she's dreadful, we must start the fireworks early.' Caroline turned away from the naked man to look in the mirror. She mouthed with glee, 'And then, so long, Princess.'

The half-queen had never felt so positive. *Goodbye creamy skin and watchful green eyes. Farewell generous lips and all those happily situated bloody freckles. And as for that den of red hair …* She yanked a comb through her limp locks with small, ferocious hands. It was for the best. She smiled down at her nails. The girl was seventeen and a half and should be married and hosting her own Gin Rummy parties. It was Caroline's duty to see her niece out of the turret and up the aisle. Marriage was the answer. It was so liberating. She plucked an eyebrow bald in her excitement; if the mirror could have cracked, it would have done.

Reading a scroll as lengthy as the tapestry hanging in the Long Corridor, the herald had finally come to the end of the roll call of guests. The last name left to announce was added by his own hand.

'Countess Blanche du Bon Bon of the South Tequeetahs.'

'Hello, Losley, sorry I'm late.' Will appeared before Richard from behind an extravagant hand fan.

'You always had a knack for names, English.'

'It is too much?'

Richard took in the tower of woman, taffeta, and feather before him. 'It's wonderfully fitting. Did you bring enough rouge?'

'Spare tube in my boot.'

'And you remembered a frying pan?'

'Roger that.'

The herald had to ask ... 'Are those grapefruits?'

'Yes.'

'Good choice.'

'They never fail. Now, has the entertainment arrived?' Will's voice lowered.

'She's warming up.'

He looked relieved. 'Excellent. For king and country!'

'Keep your voice down,' hissed the herald.

Will moved back behind his fan as some guests glanced their way. 'What about our young, royal bolter?'

'She's inside, in green, dressed to disappear.' Richard trembled a little at his podium. 'I hope you can pull this off, English.' He looked at the guards by the door and whispered, 'You have no idea what these men are capable of. I don't know what Master Blackwood will do to her if ...' He couldn't bring himself to think of it, let alone say it out loud.

'Who is this Blackwood character?'

'The gentleman in charge of royal security. Thoroughly unpleasant. He walks with a silver-topped cane. Always dresses in black. You won't see him this evening, not until the half-queen announces the surprise.' Richard glanced behind him. 'He'll be doing something unpleasant in the watchtower until then.'

'Fret not, dear friend.' Will smiled like a pirate. 'For this is what I do. The princess will escape.' With that, Blanche du Bon Bon swaggered into the crowd. Heads turned and monocles dropped.

The herald wiped his forehead. Perhaps there was a chance this plan was mad enough to work. He looked up at one of the extremely muscled men in togas. 'Any sign of the half-queen?'

'Nothing.'

'There's a surprise. Maybe she's swallowed her wig.'

'Ha!' The two brothers punched Richard jovially in the kidneys.

Quite early on in her reign, Caroline had decided she needed protecting. The two brothers in togas accompanied her whenever she felt particularly at risk, which was mainly on the stairs and near the servants. She could not remember who was who, so she called them both Joseph after plucking them from Landfelian's most notorious circus troupe.

Men in lilac tights appeared and began to strum their lutes. The balmy night had turned subtropical; the wind had gone. It was the sort of heat you get before the mother of all storms. The powdered faces of the guests turned cakey, and bits of them crumbled off into dripping drinks.

And then the half-queen arrived. Caroline's wig entered the ball before her; it was the same size as her husband. She was wearing enough gold jewellery to make movement difficult, and the stench of her perfume was strong enough to melt the faces of children.

One of the few foreign gentlemen to arrive crossed the room towards her as she entered the hall. She smiled at him warmly, until he opened his mouth and asked where the princess was.

In fact, all the guests wanted to know where the princess was; they'd come to see her and her red hair and have their questions answered. Was the colour natural? Had she inherited the king's chin? Was she real or simply a myth like her lost mother? Caroline had never let Red attend any of her previous balls for fear she would garner all the attention. This had not come as a great loss to the princess, who loathed formal dance.

Caroline gesticulated like an air dancer. 'She'll be down soon enough,' she snapped to anyone who asked.

Sir Toby hovered next to her, and once the crowds moved away, he too asked, 'Have you seen the princess?'

The half-queen howled. It was heard from across the room, and many wondered what animal was being murdered in the kitchen. 'Enough! The guards will ensure she is brought down in time for the surprise.'

'Yes, I know that, but I would like to talk to her,' Toby persisted.

'You will see her for the rest of your life. What are a few more hours apart? Go and sow some wild oats, you silly man, and cease your dithering.'

Sir Toby did not like being called a silly man but did not know what to say. Looking at the half-queen was quite bewildering.

'Do you like my wig? I designed it myself from peahens, peonies, and pineapples.' She laughed and, rocking back, attached herself to a chandelier.

Sir Toby needed to find an open window. The room was stifling, and he no longer felt so well. He felt like a grease stain on an apron, and two things loomed at him from the recesses of his almost sober brain: if the king returned, what would he think of this marriage? And could the princess really love him?

Come to think of it, did he love her?

'I must see her!' Sir Toby yelled, silencing the foreign gentleman and a small crowd around the half-queen.

Caroline took hold of his arm and, smiling politely, led him away. 'And you shall, my darling. I believe she is on her way down shortly.' Narrowing her eyes at him, she whispered, 'What security do you have at Mole Hall?'

'I don't see what security has got to do with anything.'

She gripped his arm. 'Have you experience keeping feral

creatures?'

'Feral? No, my mother keeps beagles.'

'Mmm, how many?'

'Forty-seven.'

'You might want to get a couple of wolves, or blood hounds, and dig a few priest holes.' Caroline was surprisingly practical when she could be bothered. 'She will need to be watched.'

'Are you saying she would try to leave me?' Sir Toby had not entertained the idea that anyone would want to leave him. He had not entertained very much past the end of his nose since the king had left. He spent far too much time in company with the half-queen and her cronies. He rubbed his temples, where the dull throb of a migraine had begun to take hold. Despite knowing the princess since they were children, it was true they had not spoken at length on an intimate level. She did what all young ladies seemed to do when overcome by love; she avoided him. No, the princess clearly adored him, and what had conversation got to do with marriage? 'If it makes her happier, we can remain here,' Sir Toby suggested. Paloma was his home more than Mole Hall these days, and it had the benefit of not containing his mother.

'Out of the question,' Caroline snapped. 'It is time she left.'

'She must be nervous. I've barely seen her these past few days.' He'd only glimpsed Red in the garden, where she always seemed to be planting things or exercising that big horse and climbing onto the roof. 'Are you sure she's still here? What if she's run away?'

The half-queen's bloodshot eyes darkened, and smudges of black eyelash dye seeped out in the direction of her earlobes. 'Run away?' She laughed unpleasantly. 'There will be no runaway bride, tonight or any other night. Come with me, Toby. I will show you something that will make your nose bleed. Josephs!' She blew on a small gold whistle around her neck, and the two large men in togas appeared with a portable throne. 'Take us to the Clock Room.'

Sir Toby was lifted onto a spare portable chair by two servants and swept up through the crowds after Caroline's swaying wig. They left the Great Mirrored Hall and were taken through several quieter, equally beautiful rooms. Sir Toby welcomed the silence. The servants climbed the grand staircase, opening the last door on the landing and taking a number of narrow stone steps up to the darker rooms of the palace. Toby had never seen these rooms before. They hurried along several empty passageways until they came to a corridor where only a few torches guttered. It seemed to grow colder. Along the wall hung the longest tapestry Toby had ever seen. There was only one door at the end; it was taller than most. Toby was helped out of the chair, and he followed Caroline into a room where the walls crawled with shadows.

'Rats.' Caroline adjusted her wig and licked her lips. 'Enterprising little vermin.'

'Where are we?' asked Toby. As rooms went, he did not rate it. 'Not much light.' Toby liked light, and he liked beauty. He sought them unconsciously, as if arranging paint on his palette, back in the days when he used to paint. There was only one window here, which was small, and it had recently been barred.

'The Clock Room,' came Caroline's rather sinister answer, 'does not need light.'

Will English had been working the ball with the level of commitment only an actor of his calibre could maintain under such inhuman conditions. Countess Blanche du Bon Bon had everyone enthralled, and the half-king was on his knees. 'Who is this woman?' the guests tittered. 'Where exactly are the South Tequeetahs?' They all *had* to go there.

'Where are you staying tonight, Countess?' Gerald spoke to Will while holding a firm gaze over the magical land of the countess' cleavage. It promised to pop out and say, 'Hola, Gerry,' at any moment.

'Call me Bon,' Will answered with a breathy red-light of a whisper. 'I hoped to lay my thighs here. I don't need much, just a robe.'

Gerald nearly combusted when Will's silk glove reached out and stroked his waddle. What big hands this woman had. A pearl button pinged off from somewhere and landed on a platter of cheese puffs that had appeared between them.

The half-king reminded Will of a spaniel he had once

shared a dressing room with called Charles. They had the same slightly greasy curls of hair. He looked down at the puffs. 'Oh, how delightful! Ouch!'

Beneath the tray stood the herald, who had kicked him in the shins. Gerald did not notice – he didn't tend to see much else in the presence of a well-assembled woman in a wig. He did not question the arrangement of cheese puffs lined up in a neat arrow pointing to the door his wife had recently exited. Nor did he notice the fervent exchange of eyebrows between Countess Bon Bon and the herald.

'The powder room calls. Back in a tickly tick.' The countess enveloped the half-king with her feather boa, stepped gracefully behind a pillar, and disappeared. Gerald was left holding a tray of deflating cheese puffs, wondering how he was suddenly alone. He slapped a passing bottom for good measure and decided to take a nap on his throne before the dancing.

Will followed the half-queen and Sir Toby at a polite distance, with the agility of a water snake and the silence of a rabbit. Will did not get an 'O' for Out-of-This-World in Movement Class for stumbling during a performance, oh no. He kept pace along all the many staircases and corridors and several quite remarkable wall-hangings, keeping in the blind spot provided by Caroline's wig until they stopped in a cold part of the palace. There, he hid behind an extremely long tapestry and watched the half-queen and a young gentleman in velvet knickerbockers walk through an unusually tall door.

'Goodness.' Sir Toby swallowed. 'What an ugly clock.' An old grandmother clock stood in the room. Alone in the dark, it did not tick. It looked wrong, the wood twisting out towards them as if trying to reach for the door. Why had Caroline dragged him on this unpleasant tour? He only wanted to talk to the princess. He opened his mouth to suggest they return to the ball when something in the far corner of the room stood up – something large with hips, wide ones. It moved slowly towards him.

'What the devil …?'

'Dear creature!' cried Caroline. 'Were you hiding from me?'

Sir Toby tried not to faint. He had to try very hard, because standing over them was the largest woman he had ever seen. 'A giantess.' He found his voice and found it was appalled. 'You keep a giantess in this small room? Why?'

'Why not?' Caroline smiled at the giantess as if she were a baby bird. 'Isn't she marvellous? We've had her for years. Belongs to Daniel. You must have met him,' she gushed. 'Our absolutely fabulous Head of Royal Security.'

Sir Toby was vaguely acquainted with the gentleman who walked with a silver-topped cane. He had never warmed to him.

'Is she mute?' he whispered, looking at the giantess.

'Hasn't said a word since she moved in. Giants are shy things. I've done some reading on the subject.' Caroline had not read a thing about it.

'I have never seen one before,' breathed Sir Toby. 'It was my understanding they do not leave a valley north of Mount Felian, very difficult to reach.'

'Really? I do wonder how Daniel discovers such wonders.'

The room smelt stale. It was not a happy room at all – even the rats were making a run for it through the open door. He took a step back. The giantess moved her chained wrists and feet to unlock the grandmother clock, revealing a hollow shell inside. She appeared to be in pain. Inside there were no mechanics and no pendulum, just a shelf of blackened wood.

'It is not a clock at all.' This threw Sir Toby, who liked and trusted clocks. 'Madame, what is this all about? Why must you keep this large woman here? And what has she got to do with my betrothal?'

Inside the clock was a box made from what looked like polished skull. It was the exact same size and hexagonal shape as a box of Turkish Delight he favoured. Toby looked at it, and the box looked back. He shivered. Boxes shouldn't do that. It appeared to be resting there. Whatever was inside was clearly not Turkish Delight. 'Is it bone?' he asked. The box suddenly shunted forward, making him gasp.

'I believe so – human. It's yours now. Your wedding present. You won't need any beagles with this in your bed chamber.' Caroline's front teeth protruded with glee. 'You lucky man.'

Sir Toby did not feel very lucky. 'Does it belong to the princess? Is it an heirloom, something the vanished queen was fond of?'

'Not exactly, darling.' Caroline could be patient if it worked in her favour. 'Inside, you will find a set of teeth charmed with voodoo. They once belonged to a young boy, one of twins. His sister's teeth are secured around your bride's ankle. And this little box is made from the bones of both the poor souls.'

Sir Toby gasped. 'The Petrified Twins.' Red's anklet, the thing that never seemed to sit easily about her. She wore such sturdy boots that he rarely saw it, although he had always questioned the reasons for such an ugly trinket. 'Great Scott.'

The box began to thrum in the giantess' large hands. It certainly looked possessed. Whatever lay inside was pulsing, wanting to be free. He shrank back towards the door. The giantess followed him with grave eyes.

'I don't understand …'

'A woman arrived at the gates,' explained Caroline. 'Bit of a hag. She called herself a seer, had a white streak through her hair like a badger, I recall. Looked more like a witch to me. She told us she was concerned for the princess' safety and that trouble lay ahead.'

Caroline rubbed her forehead until she left a mark. She looked agitated. 'Strangest thing, I can't remember her name. Extraordinary eyes, though – almost yellow. We had a problem with the girl then, always running off and trying to find her father.' Caroline sighed. 'The seer handed me this box with two sets of teeth clamped together inside like a choker. She referred to them as Hell's Bells.'

Sir Toby went cold. He remembered the disappearance of the twins – it was a tale told throughout the kingdom. There was no trace of them. Their mother had grown so distraught at their disappearance she'd turned mad. The children had been taken in the afternoon, lured from a wood not far from Celador. Toby was a boy when it had happened. He remembered it had upset the queen so much that the heroes were sent out to search for them, but thick fog descended over the twin's village, and they were never found. His father had returned to Mole Hall more subdued than usual after the search was called off. 'Why did the woman call them Hell's Bells?' Looking at the box, the hairs on his arms stood up in protest.

'I never forgot her answer.' Caroline's voice dropped several octaves. 'HELL IS NOT FILLED WITH THE SOUND OF BELLS BUT THE SOUND OF SOULS LOST, THEIR TEETH CHATTERING IN ETERNAL TORMENT.'

Toby wanted to go. The room was cold, and not the refreshing kind – the haunted kind.

'The giantess guards this box. Don't you, dear? Daniel said the teeth required a giant's strength. We've had our fair share of close calls keeping the princess here. The voodoo in this box is very strong – it will stop at nothing to find its counterpart.'

'Attached to Red's ankle. But how ... how?' Sir Toby could not stop asking 'how'. 'How do they keep her *safe* exactly?'

'It's very simple. If the girl was to stray further than the river, the teeth in this box and the ones attached to her ankle will be awoken. They will try to find each other again. There only wish is to be one ...'

'By biting the princess,' Sir Toby finished for her.

'That's it. A form of voodoo. So efficient. It's had some bad press in the past, rogue witches, that sort of thing, but personally I couldn't fault it. Far more efficient than blood hounds.'

'Doesn't it hurt her?'

'A cold pinch she's grown used to.' Caroline looked almost proud.

Toby considered her rheumy eyes. 'You keep her here by crippling her.'

'I wouldn't put it quite like that. If she doesn't run too far from Paloma, the hex will not be woken. It would be a terrible shame to maim the long-limbed creature.' Caroline had not had sleepless nights about this.

'And her ankle?'

'Oh, a little light scarring.'

'Can it be removed?'

'Amputated, certainly.' Caroline was growing impatient, and she was growing sober.

'No,' Sir Toby said, 'The voodoo charm.'

'I'm sure if you give the thing a bloody good bash with an axe it will come off. Ask Daniel; he's escorting you both home after the fireworks. The giantess will follow with the Hell's Bells. They cannot be separated for long, you see.'

Sir Toby thought of his father hunting; something Toby could never do without vomiting a great deal, first from nerves and then from shame. This was inhuman; they were pinning a live butterfly.

'How could you have allowed this?'

'Saint Frank, is that the time?' Caroline squinted at a bejewelled clockface dangling around her neck and rushed Sir Toby out of the room. 'The entertainment is about to start, and God only knows who the herald hired. Warblers from the poor house, no doubt.' The giantess locked up the clock and moved back to the corner, where she crouched down and began to rock.

Sir Toby followed the half-queen, feeling cold and clammy. He would not marry Red Felian. There would be no wedding. The only thing he had to do was inform the king of this woman's insanity. He would leave Paloma immediately.

In a poorly lit corridor of a rarely visited part of the palace, Will English shivered behind an enormous tapestry. He tried to keep his breath shallow, although he needed to sneeze as dust tickled his nose. Will closed his eyes and ran back over the letter he'd received in Alba from the princess.

Operation: Cunning Little Vixen

Dear Master English,

My father's herald, Richard Losley, tells me you are a player of great calibre and experience. I am in urgent need of a skilled man to attend the Greatest Wigged Ball of All Time at Paloma Palace (official invitation enclosed), where your improvisation skills will be essential. I need you to take what sits inside the grandmother clock in the Clock Room on the eleventh floor of the West Wing, opposite the Long Tapestry, and bring it to me.

Do not under any circumstances open the box of bone. It is not a trifle. It is an evil. Take caution. Keep it safe and bring it straight to me.

It is imperative no one sees you. You may disguise yourself as you see fit – Richard tells me you have some talent in this area.

Rendezvous four days from the night of the ball at The Cat's Back Inn, Dead End, in the city of Alba at sunset. Should you accept, you have my word the Hey Nonnys will be reinstated on the king's return* and you will receive three rubies as payment until then.

You are my only hope of escape, Mr English.
Please help.
Yours,

Red Felian

✳ ✳ ✳

Should the king not be found, you have my word as queen.

Yes, Will had thought as much. It was all well and good, but not once did she mention voodoo, cursed teeth, or giantesses.

(Red had worried over this. 'Don't you think I should go into a little more detail? He's going to get an awful shock.'

The herald had waved her doubts away. 'Trust me, Your Highness, the bigger the shock the better the performance. English will rise to the challenge. It is best he does not know the full story.'

Red had raised an unconvinced eyebrow and sealed the letter.)

Will waited until the creak of feet dwindled away, back towards the Great Mirrored Hall, before finally letting himself sneeze five times. He tiptoed towards the door and fumbled into the recesses of his crinoline skirts to locate Amber's hairpins. Picking the old lock was easier than he had expected.

'Bingo!' Inside the dark room, he quickly found the non-ticking grandmother clock. There was no other furniture. Will strode over in all his taffeta and grapefruit glory and gave the clock a good shake. The ominous-looking thing was locked.

'Oh blow, open sesame!' he tried.

Nothing happened.

'By the power invested in me by the ancient hinge-makers, I command thee, door, to release thy locks.'

Not a squeak.

He tried another language. 'حتفا كوجرا.'

'You won't find the powder room in there,' a voice as sad as a cello interrupted him.

'HOOO! WHAT THE ...?' For one confused second, Will thought the clock had spoken. The voice sounded as if it hadn't spoken for some time.

'Christ alive, you scared me,' Will said, calming down as he looked up at the giantess suddenly stepping out of the dark before him. Many would have run away screaming. Not Will. This was *acting*, ladies and gentlemen, and it took a lot to surprise such a player. He did not turn into a babbling merchant of drivel, contrary to the money placed on him by the Gods and three rats in the room. 'Pray, what is your name, lady?'

The giantess looked at her hands as if trying to remember the answer to a question she had not been asked in a long time. She had to stoop to avoid bumping her head on a chandelier shrouded in cobwebs.

Will tried to help. 'What does it begin with? A for Anne? B for Bunny?'

'Ophelia.'

'*Ophelia*. A fine name. You should be downstairs dancing. Dear lady, with those plaits and that belt, you should not be cooped up here.' He heard a clink and looked at her feet. 'In chains.'

'I'm not a guest. The gentleman in charge of royal security keeps me here.'

'I'm appalled!' He was; she looked terribly unhappy. 'Dear lady, a man will never try to push an impractical slipper on your foot if you remain locked up in here. Admittedly, he may have trouble finding a slipper big enough. Nonetheless, I insist you come away from this room with me as soon as I have had a closer look at this clock. I do believe it's a fib.'

The giantess blinked so forlornly, Will forgot about the clock and the guards surrounding the palace.

'How long have you been living in this room?'

At her forlorn silence, he took hold of her hand, which required two of his, and recited a few lines of Benedict Quille, the only playwright to give him comfort when his ferret Emily had died.

> 'O, what noble mind is here overthrown!
> The courtier's, scholar's, soldier's eye, tongue, sword,
> Th'expectancy and rose of the fair state ...'

And, to his complete amazement, the giantess continued,

> 'The glass of fashion and the mould of form,
> Th'observed of all observers – quite, quite down!'

She tried to smile. It had been a while, but she managed a smile well enough in the end.

'You are a player, lady!' gasped Will, spellbound. 'Truly.'

'I was once, before this.' Her eyes shone. 'I had almost forgotten.'

Will was sobbing, really sobbing, and his nose running by the time Ophelia finished telling the story of her past. They sat against the grandmother clock and blew their noses on the enormous tapestry that Will had brought in from the wall outside.

'And your troupe never tried to find you?'

'They believed it was my decision to stay behind with the man with the silver-topped cane.'

'A lady most wretched and dejected. This Blackwood should be put in the stocks and covered in jam,' declared Will.

The giantess snorted. 'He can be very charming. There was a time I would have followed him into the Goby.' She sighed, and a great fanfare of cymbals and trumpets flew in through the tiny window. The rats scattered. 'Midnight already? The princess will be married soon.'

'SAINT FRANK, is that the time?' Will's eyes widened. 'MARRIED, NEVER! We must make haste.'

The giantess peered down at the man next to her. He had two grapefruits strapped to his chest, but a pair of rather more trustworthy eyebrows. Giants surmised a great deal from a person's eyebrows and their response to a sneeze. This player had a good heart. She would let him rescue her. He was tall for a non-giant, taller than Daniel Blackwood too, which could only be a good thing. Ophelia began to sway at the thought of the silver-topped cane. Combined with the heat, the unexpected kindness from a man in a dress, and remembering her own name, it was all too much. Before she could gather herself up, she collapsed face down on the tapestry.

Will could not believe it. He hadn't even needed to use the frying pan. He prized the keys from her hand and opened the clock. The door cried open, and he could have sworn he heard a faint cackle as an object jumped out at him.

It looked like a box of Turkish Delight moving at high speed through the air. 'Hell's Bells!' Will yelled. He whipped out the frying pan from the bustle of his dress and thwacked the piece of evil with all the muscle he had (which was willing but not substantial). Some old teeth flew out of the box. There was no Turkish Delight to be seen. 'Ha, ha! You possessed teeth are no match for my double-handed backhand!' He stared in wonder at his iron-based cooking utensil and the child sized set of teeth crouching motionless on the floor. 'Remarkable! What weaponry! It has stunned the evil out of the twisted thing.'

Will did not trust it would remain quiet for long though. He put the escaped teeth back into the box, secured it shut with his bootlace, and put the whole lot down his stockings. (There was simply no room in his corset.) He took a moment to size up how best to smuggle an eleven-foot woman out of a heavily secured palace, along with a voodoo charm that was twitching about in his boot, making it very difficult to concentrate. It would take time and more than a couple of citrus fruits to get him out of this one.

'I am done,' he wailed. 'This is the end. What will I do?' He took a deep breath, closed his eyes, and asked himself what he'd had for breakfast.

Answering a simple question always worked when Will was close to corpsing on stage. It forced him to think about events prior to the one he was in and thus distract his brain from having the father of all panic attacks.

'Three slices of cold toast and a small apple.'

There. It was clear now.

He needed a distraction. He needed the entertainment to start and, thank his balls, she was only seconds away. Will looked down at the props he had to work with. A grandmother clock, an unconscious giantess, a tapestry that did not know where to end, and a frying pan. Suddenly, as the last stroke of midnight rang out, Will raised his hands to the air and shouted, 'I'VE GOT IT!'

11

A PRETTY VOICE

Outside, precisely twenty-three minutes before Will found the voodoo charm and the imprisoned giantess, Amber Morningstar sat down in her dressing room – an old gypsy caravan parked next to the royal stables. She closed her eyes, took a deep breath, and looked in the mirror. Her lips were painted with enough Carmine Rouge to frighten a geisha. Her hair fell down her back like golden syrup. Her eyes appeared older than the rest of her, although they had enough twinkle in them to break a holy man's sandal straps. A silver tuning fork hung around her neck on a string of tiny sea pearls. It stroked the top of an ample cleavage hocked up and heaving in a white-boned bodice. Two diamonds the size of Brazil nuts and the colour of canaries sparkled from each ear; the half-queen would not be able to take her eyes off them. She smiled.

White gloves ran up her soft, curved arms. She practised a pout and smoothed down her dress – a floor-length marriage-destroyer with a slit, very little back, and two silver threads for straps. Amber Morningstar had been hired to distract a thousand guests gathered in Paloma's ballroom, and, dressed like this, she certainly had a shot. If her dress were an animal, it would have been a fox. If it were a word, it would be *SHWUDDERWING*. If it could speak, it would not need to do any of the talking. It was smoking.

Why am I here? she asked herself. *Dressed up like a fallen angel to give a young princess I don't know a few minutes to jump out of a window and make a run for it, while Will steals something from a clock.*

She questioned the likelihood of her and Will getting out of Paloma without being caught by the guards. She had to use her looks and her voice to stop anyone looking around and wondering where the birthday girl was. Despite all of this and the ominous rumbling of a storm gathering outside, Amber felt as cool as glass. She had never been one to suffer from stage fright. She knew she was good. It was the man with the silver-topped cane she was more concerned about. 'Daniel Blackwood.' She muttered. 'I hoped I would never see you again.'

There was a polite knock at the door.

'Come in.'

The herald's tongue dropped out when he saw her. It had been years since he had travelled to Alba and listened to

Amber sing at The Cat's Back Inn's blues night. Time had been more than kind; it had been glorious. She was still a siren. He bowed so low he practically lay down. 'You look like a recipe for lemon meringue pie.' (Before becoming a full-time herald, Richard Losley used to write the personals.)

She laughed and held out her hand. 'Monsieur Losley, it's been a while.'

He took her hand. 'You are dazzling. We haven't long. Are you ready?'

'Let's get this over with.' She stepped out of her wagon and gave her shire horse, Marilyn, a parsnip. 'Has English arrived?"

The herald smiled. 'Oh yes.'

'Good.' She looked up at the palace. 'Where is he?'

'Inside the Clock Room, I hope.'

'And the princess?'

'She's in the Great Mirrored Hall, waiting to jump as soon as I announce you at midnight.'

'You'd better lead the way.' As they hurried across the courtyard, Amber glanced across at the watchtower.

'If the half-queen tries to announce the surprise engagement early, I'll send on the dancing girls to do something acrobatic,' the herald went on. 'On no account must that woman get one leg on the podium. Do you understand? You must keep singing.'

'Loud and clear.' Her heart leapt when she heard the noise coming from the palace.

To describe the ballroom's opulence would put a person in hospital. For speed, I will say it was like stepping inside a limited-edition Fabergé egg the size of the Teatro La Fenice. Truth be told, King Felian and the queen were rather embarrassed by it. A foreign nobleman from one of the lands west of Landfelian had fallen very much in love with the middle daughter of a past king. The daughter told the foreign nobleman she loved nothing better than collecting the eggshells of wild birds. It prompted the nobleman, Stefanos Thunder, to bestow upon her a love token that would be even more beautiful than bits of old egg. The result was Paloma's ballroom – pale, round, and delicately speckled, with a ceiling that invoked wonder and much Ahhhhhhhhhhhing. All the pastel and silk furnishings gave one such a feeling of light that visitors questioned whether the ceiling was painted straight onto the sky itself.

Amber whistled as the herald led her around the back of the stage. 'Are those geese …?'

'White gold and life-sized, yes …' Richard said. They framed an enormous clock, which had its hands pointing at two minutes to midnight.

Around an intimate half-moon stage, the guests fanned themselves, whispering loudly in blue velvet seats. Richard pointed to the two figures in the royal box. Amber nodded.

He wished her luck and strode towards the orchestra pit.

'Wait, where will you be?'

'Conducting you, my dear.' He winked and withdrew a

baton from his breast pocket.

A hush descended on the gathered crowd as they saw the herald. Every person in the room felt a thrill of anticipation.

Except one.

Sir Toby felt nauseous. Caroline's bright, hungry eyes in the Clock Room. The box made of bone. The teeth … It was wrong, all wrong. He had to talk to the princess – tell her what he had seen, tell her that he had doubts, that something was most definitely, undeniably, up. For the first time, he feared for his life. Sir Toby rose to leave as the torches in the ballroom were blown out by the footmen standing by. Only one light, in the centre of the stage, remained.

Caroline made a small screech from the throne. Gerald snorted and woke himself up.

'Where is the girl?' The half-queen lurched forward and scanned the backs of heads in the audience for a red one. 'She should be here, Gerald, sat next to us. And Toby! Summon Blackwood to find them.'

Maybe it was a bad case of champagne, but Caroline felt terribly on edge. She wanted to announce the engagement, have the marriage done, and get the girl quickly on her way. Then she could dance with the Marquis of Leatherby until dawn and really start to enjoy herself.

But before anyone could be summoned, a woman in white was lowered slowly onto the stage from a gold rope. While no one recognised her name, she was apparently the entertainment, and no one could remember their own name as soon as one creamy leg appeared through the slit of an impossibly avant-garde dress. No one, not even the half-queen, spared a thought for the princess, as a perfectly put together enchantress spun down on the luckiest gold rope in all the land. A soft beat – straight out of a New Orleans summer – grew in volume, joined by several teasing cymbals.

Tsh ti tsh ti tsh . . .

The herald had donned a white top hat and slipped a rose in his top button. He mouthed to the cellist, 'Keep it sultry, Charles.' As a herald, he was accomplished in a little of everything, and music had always been a passion.

Amber had enraptured the guests without even opening her mouth. She spun down to the stage and smiled. And then she began to sing. When she did, anything watching began to dribble. Oh, how the woman on the swing could sing. The gentlemen gawped, and the ladies made a note to get a rope installed in their drawing room as soon as they returned home. A storm blew the scent of green wind-torn things through the open windows – grass and honeysuckle. No one noticed the weather with this vision on the stage. If anyone had been able to leave the ballroom, they may have noticed the barefooted girl in the green dress was no longer sitting by the far window. The window had been abandoned and now swung violently in the wind.

After twenty-two minutes of the sweetest singing, Amber Morningstar disappeared into the slips to change. She returned onstage to a wave of appreciative sighs. The hem authorities of the North Realm thankfully had not got an invitation. The herald picked up the tempo, and the servants gathered in the doorway to watch.

'What an earth are they doing?' a footman asked another.

'I think they are dancing.'

A baron and his seven sons performed a succession of forward rolls on the floor before the stage. The mistresses shook everything they had with the Men of Great Esteem. The whole of Caroline's court was twirling. The guards climbed up the outside wall of the palace and pressed themselves against the windows to get a better look at the woman on the stage. Amber had bewitched them all.

Amber Morningstar was not a romantic sort, in the Landfelian sense, despite looking like Venus' lovechild. The rose-coloured stories her parents had told her about the Age of Romance, about a time of white witches and magical happenings, meant nothing to her.

There was no advance payment for this job, although the half-queen was down a pair of canary diamond earrings and an emerald pendant. It had been so easy to slip into the upstairs chambers while the ball roared on below. She just followed the smell of heated wigs and lily of the valley. It was a start, she considered, as – from what she could see – Landfelian's wealth was otherwise being spent on wigs and profiteroles. But beyond money, Amber had other reasons for helping the princess, and they centred on the man in charge of royal security. The same man who had locked up her family, drawn a ring around her finger with a needle, and claimed her as his wife when she was a girl.

She glanced up at the golden geese and wondered where that rat Blackwood was hiding. Behind one of the cherubs, no doubt.

Hardplace Prison made 'bleak' look like a sunny day, and it was filled with her carnival friends because of that man. She had no intention of taking it lying down, although she was exceptional at lying down when lying down was required.

The kingdom needed someone strong at the helm. Someone to stop undesirables like Daniel Blackwood and the half-king and half-queen from moving in and trampling over everything. Maybe who they needed was this princess. If it was, the girl didn't have a chance in hell with Blackwood decorating the watchtower with tongues.

She would give the princess a chance to change something. And, Amber smiled, she would get her revenge.

Daniel Blackwood was not smiling. He was holding a standard-size mid-length blonde wig which smelt of the princess and staring at hoof marks from an above-average-size horse on the back drive. The hooves of a valien. Neither were present but were galloping away on the other side of the river. The man in charge of royal security was having trouble understanding how this could have happened. He lit a liquorice cheroot, ignoring the violent gale that tore through the gardens around him. Apart from two of his most stupid guards, the rest had disappeared. The wind whipped up his slicked hair – the colour of a rat's coat – like a stuck page. The palace was more impossible to escape than a womb. He had made sure of it, with the priest's holes, black squirrels, and voodoo charm. The princess was hard to miss, and yet she had gone. He chewed at the cheroot and narrowed his grey eyes. He would find out how, and make someone pay.

Before discovering the wig and witnessing the princess' leap over the river, Blackwood had been enjoying a promising night with Agnes the chambermaid. When he heard the music coming from the ballroom, his mouth curled unpleasantly. 'Wait. That voice … I've heard it before.'

Agnes began to say the Lord's Prayer and realised she didn't know all of it. He was a good-looking son of a lawyer, she would give him that, but not a good example of a wholesome Landfelian male. She could see that now as she glanced nervously around for the keys to his chamber.

'I did not order any entertainment,' Daniel snarled and dropped her like a bad book. Agnes breathed a sigh of relief, watching him button his breeches and roll up the cuffs of his impossibly wafty black silk shirt. Blackwood did not possess any clothes of colour; he wore black and nothing else. The young chambermaid had been flattered when he'd asked her to his watchtower for a sherry, but she would never offer to sweep his hearth again. The man was a bad sort and not nearly as kind as Joseph, the half-queen's manservant.

Blackwood stalked back towards the ballroom from the river, stabbing the ground with his cane. The voodoo charm must have been taken. It was the only explanation. Fireworks screamed over Paloma. At some point in the evening, the queen-in-hell's catching devices, an object so dark even he didn't fully understand it, had been stolen – along with its keeper, no doubt, the giantess. What band of rebels could that redhead possibly have recruited, being locked away as she had for the best part of her teenage years? That gardener was involved, he was sure of it.

Amber Morningstar's voice seeped out of the palace and cast its spell over the gardens. Blackwood found half of his guards smeared against the windows of the Great Mirrored Hall. Some had climbed inside and gathered at the entrance of the ballroom like a pack of drooling dogs.

'Who hired that woman to sing?' He pointed his cane at the glittering figure on the stage.

'She's the entertainment, sir. The herald invited her.'

'Well, it is time to put a stop to the entertainment.' He paused, looking back into the Great Mirrored Hall. 'Who opened all these windows?'

'The herald gave the order,' replied the guard. 'It was a hot night and the half-queen started dripping.'

'That bloody herald.' Daniel smoothed back his hair

and stubbed out his cheroot on the nearest guard's shoulder pad. 'Anyone who leaves here tonight loses a tongue. Do you hear me? I want every guest and every servant accounted for. Return to your posts.' He stormed inside.

The palace could have been on fire, with lightning forking through its domed roof and the four horsemen of the apocalypse trotting in and no one would have noticed. Amber stood in the centre of the stage and sang in a piece of gold silk, which might have been a gown, although not by practical standards. It hung from her body like summer rain.

The musicians kept trailing off-piste. The herald threw a baton at the drummer.

'Eyes on me, Hopkins.'

The half-queen and king had no idea where this woman had come from, but they wanted to keep her. Caroline's eyes glistened from their sweating lids. She would hire the singer as her personal minstrel. She would cut off her buttery hair and make a new wig for herself. No one in the royal box remembered there was an engagement to announce. Outside, the firework display had started.

Blackwood climbed noiselessly up to a little-used balcony alongside the domed ceiling, which was concealed behind a spray of playful cherubs. The balcony was used to drop petals over the audience to great dramatic effect. He watched Amber; his grip tightened on Cupid's foot and a tiny gold toe broke clean off. He had never expected to find her again.

No one noticed it fall, but Amber felt Blackwood's eyes on her from the painted clouds above, and she forgot what she was singing. Suddenly it all felt like a terrible mistake – coming to Paloma and facing the man who had once stolen her away and haunted her dreams to this day. What a fool she had been then.

The herald did something creative with a triangle to mask her silence and alerted a footman in the wings to bring on the dancing girls.

Amber's heart pounded. Daniel Blackwood was above her, somewhere in the ceiling. It was time she left. She had done what was asked of her. She had provided the distraction. But now she wanted to find Will and get the hell away before that shadow of a man got down and wrung her neck. She left the stage to deafening applause, and when she looked up at the ceiling from the wings, he had gone.

In the Clock Room, Will was improvising and, so far, very successfully.

'To run or not to run … If that be the question, I shall leave and take this much gifted, wronged giantess with me. No more shall she rot here in this haunted room opposite a large tapestry, with a frankly useless clock. Fear not, Ophelia, you will not remain in darkness on my watch.'

Amber would know what to do, he thought. She was excellent at escaping. While he lingered on the thought of his beloved, two things happened – he noticed the tapestry, and the tapestry noticed Will. Goodness, it was the reigning conqueror of tapestries. If it had been any longer, it would have had to pay taxes.

Minutes later, he was speaking calmly to the giantess while trying to roll her into the tapestry when the half-queen's manservants returned with Ophelia's evening bowl. Tonight it was mutton stew.

Flanking the doorway in their togas, they looked at Will.

Will looked at them, swallowed, and said, 'Hello.'

They looked at the empty clock. They looked at the giantess wrapped in tapestry.

'Do not be alarmed, gentlemen. The lady is quite well,' Will assured them. 'She fainted.'

These large men are going to kill me, he thought. He knew it. Death was squatting on his shoulder and bouncing up and down with glee. *They are going to pummel me into a meaty pulp.*

'The heat today.' The first Joseph observed the giantess and tutted.

Will put his hand on his hips and sighed. 'Yes, it was unseasonably clammy.'

'Giants are very sensitive to high levels of humidity,' added the other Joseph.

'Are they? Gosh.' If they were going to kill him, they were rather drawing it out.

'Not many people know that about giants.' The brothers' expressions remained sanguine.

'No ... it's a good thing the storm is breaking.' Will rolled on his heels and prayed. 'Look, I was hoping to escape.' He nodded at Ophelia and put his hands together. 'With the lady. Do you mind?'

'Not at all,' said one Joseph.

'Glad someone finally came to get her,' added the other. 'She never liked in it in here. The guv'nor always had this door guarded. But tonight, all his guards have gone gaga for the entertainment.'

Will smiled. 'How serendipitous.' He bundled up Ophelia's legs.

'Aye. A lady in a small dress distracted the whole palace.'

'That'll do it.' Will tried lifting the tapestry onto his shoulder and managed to raise one end an inch. He looked at the giantess and scratched his head.

'You'll have some trouble carrying her.'

Will saw a long night ahead; Ophelia's arm was the same size as his left leg. A fireman's lift was out of the question.

'We can help,' the large men offered.

'That's very kind, but I'll manage.' Will tried again, his face growing redder.

'You won't.'

'You're right, I won't. Did you ever see the play 'A Merchant Stole My Heart'? No? Well, they did something very clever with a rug and it worked a treat ... Could you spare a few minutes to assist me?'

The brothers nodded. They bundled Ophelia up, on Will's instruction, rolling her like a roulade until she was completely concealed. After counting to three, they failed to lift her. After ten, they got her airborne.

'HEAVE HO! To the back drive, brothers!' Will grunted. 'If anyone asks, we're delivering the Countess du Bon Bon's wedding present to the ... er ...'

'The Present Room,' supplied a Joseph.

'She has one?'

'Yes.' The half-queen checked the Present Room twice a day, and if it was empty there would be a whipping.

'My, my, you have to admire the woman.'

The actor led the way, groaning politely under the tapestry. His wig had suffered considerably and one of his grapefruits had been left behind in the grandmother clock. Thankfully, they did not pass a soul – no servants, dogs, elves, and not one guard or ghost. Will smiled, fully aware of Amber's pulling power.

'She's still singing.' He stopped when they were near the ballroom. Amber was coming to the end of a song about a hero. It was beautiful. Will sighed, 'That's my girlfriend.'

After a rapturous applause, she appeared through a side door from the wings, bumping straight into Will and the tapestry in the corridor that ran behind the ballroom.

'Will?' He appeared to be dressed as a one-boobed dinosaur in a taffeta dress and carrying a carpet with the Brothers Strongarm. She yelped in surprise at seeing them all.

'Hello, Amber.' The brothers appeared to know her.

The herald launched into a loud bandstand number. Men in tights with ribbons leapt on to the stage, juggling what looked like hedgehogs dipped in gold. He released some doves and looked anxiously at the audience. The sudden breaking of Amber's spell when she left the stage had caused pandemonium. The half-queen was straddling anything she could reach – pillars, her wig designer; Jeremy – in an attempt to get to the stage. The instrumental part of this song about a hero was reaching new heights, but the audience wanted the enchantress back.

The Josephs were not able to catch up with Amber on old times due to the fact that they were carrying a giantess. They had a few minutes of strong left in their arms before they dropped the tapestry. So instead, they gave her a warm smile and tried to get going. Will hesitated.

'How do you know these men, buttercup?' He felt mildly threatened.

'Carnival days. They used to juggle me and Flavia, the hoola hoop girl.' She looked anxiously behind her. 'You must go. Hurry.'

He frowned. 'Well, I think you should put on a little more dress before you go back on stage … Or a cloak? Anything could happen in there. I've spent an evening with these people and –'

Amber slapped him. 'Will! There's no time. The head

of royal security is onto us. Take the carpet and leave. I'll meet you at the river. Do you have the box of bone? Was it in the clock like she said?'

They could hear that the herald was beginning to struggle; the orchestra did not know what they were playing, and neither did he. A desperate baton was hurled through the curtain.

'Yes, yes it's in my boot.' Will lingered over her face. 'Don't let anyone catch you. If you are late by a fifth of a second, I'm coming to get you. I am storming in there and –'

'Go.' Amber slipped back through the door and the ballroom erupted with wails and cheers. Several guests fainted from excitement.

Will blocked out the sound of her sweet voice by humming 'Twelve Green Bottles' to the Josephs. 'To the wagon! Hurry, men, it's not far.'

They heaved Ophelia out to the stable yard and made it past seven abandoned security posts and one lost drunk gentleman searching for the loo. It was as they crossed a courtyard that they saw someone riding towards them at speed. Someone who obviously knew that the colour black worked well for him and wore little else. Will didn't like the look of the rider. He clearly had a good tailor, but he also had a cruel-looking mouth and used spurs on his horse.

'Hold on to your togas, men! Sinister fellow approaching, stage right.'

The brothers watched the horseman approach and

appeared to shrink several inches.

'It's Blackwood.'

Will re-straightened his wig and pulled up his corset. The box of bone jerked about in his stocking. He stood heavily on one side and tried to look nonchalant. The man in black pulled up in front of them on a thin horse with slightly bleeding sides.

'Where are you going, madame?' It was not a warm enquiry.

'These two wonderfully able men were just helping me with my gift.'

Daniel looked at the tapestry and raised an eyebrow.

'It was for the princess, for her birthday, but I'm returning it to my carriage. The half-queen informed me she already has one.' Will shook his head. 'What the youth of today want is anybody's guess. A nice tapestry doesn't cut the mustard anymore. All they want is to travel.'

The man in black seemed highly agitated at the mention of the princess – a muscle began to pulse in his cheek, but he spoke evenly. 'Then excuse me, countess.'

Will curtseyed quite beautifully.

'Josephs.' The man in black's face gleamed in the moonlight. 'When you have finished assisting this … lady, meet me in the Clock Room. There has been an incident.' He left quickly, without a smile.

'What a foul man.' Something popped in Will's shoulder, and he remembered the task at hand. He whistled urgently for

Marilyn, but nothing happened. The shire horse remained where she was – in front of a barrel of cider, drinking. They staggered towards the wagon as fast as they could without falling over and lay Ophelia in the back, checking she was still breathing. A considerable part of her dangled out of the two canvas flaps at the rear of the wagon, but thankfully not the head end. She would be fine as long as they didn't reverse park into a wall. Will made a few frantic clicking, yah-yahing noises and tugged at the reins, but to no effect. 'Gee up or we'll be arrested!'

Marilyn burped gently.

The brothers slapped her hard on the rump and bellowed, 'SHOOO!', which got her trotting. The sight of two burly men in togas can do that to you.

Amber was outside the palace, and she was running towards her wagon. She had left the herald playing her out to the longest encore in Landfelian history. Fireworks fizzed above her as she ran. Gold rain spewed up from all four turrets. A few plinks of rain landed on her bare skin. Her wagon was leaving without her. She tried not to panic. Blackwood would not be far away. She kicked off her shoes, flung them over her shoulder and into a box hedge and started running full pelt for the river.

'If that bloody actor doesn't wait for me, I'll kill him.'

Amber had never been a keen runner; when you're top heavy, you don't jog much. A nervy-looking horse stood alone in shadows at the start of the back drive. It watched her scamper past, holding her breasts. She slowed down. There was something about that horse, its scarred sides and frightened eyes …

Riding like only a woman in a dress with no corset support can, Miss Morningstar flew down the drive on Daniel Blackwood's horse. She could see Will up ahead, weaving from side to side, struggling to control the wagon as a large roll of fabric bounced about in the back.

'Will!' She rode around a very large laurel bush. 'We don't need a carpet!' she yelled after him.

'It's a tapestry!' He tried to turn around and not upend the wagon.

'The princess didn't say anything about taking a tapestry.' Once level with him, Amber climbed over Daniel's horse, jumped onto the wagon, and sat down next to Will – a stunt that posed no problem for an experienced showgirl.

'I love you,' Will told her ardently.

'Shut up. Did anyone see you?' She took the reins and looked behind her.

'I have never wanted you more.'

Amber gave him a look with a deadline.

'One,' he said.

'One what?'

'One gentleman saw us. He didn't suspect a thing; we were brilliant, those brothers and I. Mean-looking fellow in black, silver-topped cane with a little shrunken skull. My guess would be that son of a troll, Daniel Blackwood.'

Amber went cold. She put two fingers in her mouth and whistled like a cocky shepherd. 'Faster, Marilyn!'

Will smelt a rat, and then he smelt himself and realised on this occasion he could be the rat. Nothing usually frightened Amber like this, apart from weight gain and permed wigs.

'Do you know him?'

The carthorse paid attention faster than a moth in a candle shop when she saw the river ahead of them. Amber echoed her confusion. 'Will?' she asked. 'Where's the bridge?'

Outside the stables, Blackwood also found the herald trying to escape.

A voice that no one would want for a speech at their wedding came from behind Richard. 'Are you trying to run away, too?'

'Oh, hello.' The herald was having great trouble mounting anything larger than an ass without his footstool. 'No, no. Leave? What a silly notion. Heralds never leave. Kings, maybe, but never heralds. My hat lies here, and my socks are laundered within. I was merely looking for the entertainment. I believe she is taking liberties with her encore. There are encores and there are *encores*. This has become an odyssey.'

Blackwood gave him a cool smile. 'Guards, arrest the herald.'

'What?' squeaked Richard. 'Why?'

He narrowed his eyes, 'You know perfectly why. The

princess is missing.'

'She's missing? Oh dear me. Someone did say the prawns tasted a little funny, poor lamb.'

'Don't play with me. You invited Amber Morningstar to sing.'

'You're right on that score.' The herald smiled. 'She's the best.'

Blackwood stabbed his cane into the ground as several guards appeared in the yard. 'Escort the herald to the Sharing Room in my tower for questioning.'

The ass gave Richard a sorry look as two men in purple jodhpurs took him away.

'Simon!' called Daniel. 'My horse!'

Simon the stable hand appeared with Socks. Daniel looked at the animal. Socks was the horse that kept the other palace horses company. He was retired. 'Simon, that is *not* my horse.'

'Yours is missing, sir.'

Blackwood got on Socks and rode hard down the back drive. Lightning split the night in two as he followed the tracks of a gypsy caravan heading towards the river.

'What do you mean there's only a raft to cross the river?' repeated Amber. 'How long is this drive?' Amber was trying to work out how long it would take the guards to catch them up.

Will looked behind him; it was difficult to judge

through the flaps of the wagon. 'I would hazard a guess at two miles.'

He tried to extract himself from Blanche du Bon Bon's dress without losing the valuable package in his boot. Once he was out of the corset, he could kiss Amber's beautiful, worried mouth.

'What a pair of swindlers we are!'

The corset got stuck between his neck and the part of arm where his biceps should be. 'Will I never be free of this infernal thing?'

'Will! Climb on the roof and tell me if we are being followed.'

'I would rather not.'

She turned to look at him. 'I've got a funny feeling.'

Will knew not to argue with one of Amber's funny feelings. He inched along the wagon's roof and stared down the back at the palace.

'Nothing but trees and fireworks, my sweet. They've really gone to town. Ah!' He looked up. 'I like those gold drizzly ones.'

Amber let out a relieved breath. The river wasn't far away. Soon they would be on the road home.

'Wait,' called Will. 'No, there is something.' It looked like a horse. 'I need the magnifier!'

'In my trunk.'

Will reached into Amber's trunk and noted Ophelia was

still out cold. He put on the magnifying device. Amber's father, the carnival ringmaster, used it to round up the fleas when they went on strike and hid in the larger animals. Lying flat out on the roof like a twitcher, Will scanned Paloma's parkland.

'It's him!' He nearly rolled off the wagon.

'Who?'

'The man in black! And he's gaining on us.'

Amber hollered at Marilyn. 'Faster! We have to outrun him!'

'I don't know if she can, petal. He's not carrying a giantess, although his horse looks terribly fat.'

'What do you mean, not carrying a giantess?'

Amber took the news about Ophelia quite well, considering. 'How long have we got?' she asked.

'In four minutes, the man in black will be able to touch our wheels,' yelled Will.

'We will get to the river in two.' She yelled at her horse, and they surged forward.

Rain started to fall heavily over them. They could smell the river. Amber looked ahead and saw that there was indeed a raft, but it had been staked into the riverbed and was in no way going to be useful to them. It would take too long to release the stakes.

'Oh no,' she whispered. 'Will! We've got a problem bigger than the giantess.'

Behind them, Daniel took a more leisurely gallop and

smiled, a grim look in his eye.

The giantess opened her eyes and said, 'Where am I?' as the wagon bumped over the jetty and came to a splintering halt upon the raft. Thankfully it was a very large raft made up of established poplar and spruce trunks tied firmly together.

'We're trapped!' yelled Will.

Ophelia scrambled out of the tapestry and quickly assessed her situation. The wagon was standing on top of a floating raft tethered to four stakes to hold it still. She jumped off the wagon and pulled on one of the stakes. 'It's wedged deep in the silt, but I can work it loose. Do you have any rope?'

Amber tried to be civil to the large woman who had rolled free from the carpet. 'I have a trunk of sequinned dresses and a mouth organ. I do not have rope.'

'How about a canoe?' Will began to pace.

'No,' replied Amber coolly.

'Then we will have to swim,' said Will. They eyed the deep, fast-moving water surrounding them.

'What about Marilyn?'

They looked at the shire horse clearly uncomfortable on the raft, and Will resumed his pacing.

'Magic carpet?' tried Will.

'You tell me, you stole the bloody tapestry,' Amber hissed, shivering as the rain got heavier and soaked through their clothes.

'I think we should discuss the option of swimming. I

will drag Marilyn,' announced Will gamely. 'The current will take us east to the Wondering Waters. We will have breakfast on the Bay of Colourful Boats and laugh about all this over a plate of eggs and some hot chocolate. It's a mere stream, look.' He smiled down at the river. A small tree floated past, followed by a hungry fin. 'Nothing to worry about – a few carp.'

He untied Marilyn from the wagon. Marilyn refused to even put a hoof in the swirling water.

Will thought about disguising them all. 'I've got it. We can bury ourselves convincingly in the mud.'

There was a violent jolt from below. The raft began to move away from the bank, Amber swayed dangerously close to the edge. Will gripped hold of her waist and pulled her back.

'I don't want to see him again.' She looked up at Will and shivered.

'Who?' Will saw that Amber could not stop trembling. The raft moved again. The giantess waved up at Will from the water. 'Ophelia, thank goodness, what in Hamlet's name are you doing? This is no time for a dip. Drowning is not the answer.'

'I am loosening the stakes, stay on the raft and hold on.' She disappeared under the black water.

'I see. Carry on.'

Amber held on tight to Will, which he did not object to. Ophelia bobbed up and down like a seal in the Bigeasy river, taking great gasps before disappearing under water. The cold did not seem to affect her as she worked to free the raft.

'I do admire your daring.' The voice oozed down to them from the riverbank. Daniel Blackwood was stood watching Will and Amber. 'Your dramatic flair hasn't dampened over the years, Morningstar.' He made no further move to stop them, they would never manage to free the raft, the guards began to gather behind him.

Will shouted. 'Be on your way, sir, and leave us to our game of pooh sticks.'

The giantess pulled hard at the last stake, but the riverbed was clay-based and it would not budge. Contrary to myth, giants are excellent swimmers. They move with steady grace, their wide hands and feet able to paddle through the strongest of currents. The Bigeasy was a deceptively fast river, but Ophelia took to it like a paddling pool. She took one big breath and swam under to try again.

Blackwood watched from the banks, thinking how best to punish these rebels. He would silence the actor first, using his mouth clamp. From where he stood, they were as helpless as a sack of kittens waiting to be drowned. What he had failed to notice was the giantess in the water quietly setting the traitors free.

Ophelia pulled at the stake with all her might … It groaned free with a *SHLOOP*.

'Hold on everyone!' she bellowed.

Marilyn, Amber, and Will could hear the guards' drums approaching from the palace, beating as fast as their own hearts. And then all of sudden, the banks of Paloma slid quickly from view. They were floating into the arms of the Bigeasy.

'Ha ha! We're free!' cried Will. The river's current was sure and strong.

They watched as a one-hundred-strong army of guards arrived on the banks, clustering around a figure in black.

Will took a bow. 'It seems you have been out-chased and outwitted, you foul brigand! SO LONG!'

He held up several fingers and thumbs at Blackwood as the raft disappeared around the first bend. The merry band of rebels on board began to cheer, Ophelia steering the raft from the water.

'Do you have the voodoo charm?' Amber grabbed hold of Will's shirt and shook him violently.

'Safely betwixt my foot and my sock, my sweet. If you don't mind, I'll spare you the horror in there – it's been a hot day.'

'Thank the gods.' She laughed and wiped the rain from her face. 'We did it.'

'Where to, ladies?' he asked. 'How about a little detour to the Lake of Stars for folk music and mooncakes?'

'We are going straight to The Cat's Back to get rid of that black magic.' Amber gave his boot a stern look and wrung out her hair. 'I want no more of this business. The princess is on her own now. We've done what we were asked.'

Will smiled and got out his mouth organ, paying little attention to their surroundings.

Ophelia floated behind the raft like a giant tiller and relaxed for the first time in years. She had escaped the Clock Room. She was free and on her way home. 'I hope I meet the princess one day. I would like to thank her.'

Will was surprised. 'You must have seen her at the palace.'

'She was kept away from the Clock Room.'

Amber disappeared inside the wagon to change, muttering something about dysfunctional families of high birth. She dragged the tapestry out to air and didn't see the sign that marked a split in the river. No one did.

Right Fork – The Silver City of Alba
Left Fork – Hosanna Falls – Giant Country

The raft went left.

SELINA CARNAL

Daniel Blackwood threw his cheroot in the inky river, where it sizzled and disappeared with the current. Now he would have to inform the witch, and she would be upset. She would be murderous. He returned to his tower and wrote a brief note to her. He placed it in the harness of a black squirrel, which twitched beneath his hands, eager to be on its way.

Black squirrels were the witch's doing. They were her favoured method of courier. She'd sent a drove of them in the direction of the palace once the king had left on his quest. They were shadowy creatures with jagged teeth. Very few Landfelian squirrelgrams remained at Paloma after the black squirrels' squeals were heard approaching the boundary of the royal estate.

* * *

Tallfinger Fortress soared up like a curse. The temperature here dropped to such a degree that bits of the squirrel's tail fell off, leaving a trail of tiny hair splinters behind it.

The black squirrel had been glad to leave Blackwood but couldn't believe its bad luck when it saw the address on the message he'd put in its harness.

Selina Carnal, Tallfinger Fortress, Hinterland – URGENT

The other black squirrels were glad it wasn't them going; it was very sparse on trees and nuts in the Hinterland. None of them were in a rush to go back. There are some dark holes in the universe, some corners you would walk through the night in a hailstorm with no socks on to avoid staying in. Tallfinger Fortess, the home of the witch, made those places look cosy. It loomed out from a terrible and constant fog, beside a frozen strip of sea. No one in Landfelian knew Hinterland existed because no one knew *she* existed. As far as Landfelians were concerned, the kingdom ended at the South Realm, after Big Blue and its range of small summits known as the Mistys. To journey further than these mountains was to die.

Landfelian did not end where everyone thought. The mountains grew more scattered until they straggled into nothing, and there began an ice land. This was the Hinterland,

and, behind a fog like a heavy curtain, stood Tallfinger.

Its structure was formed by the witch with the help of a small, unfortunate tribe of Smoos living in the next-door land. The witch's fortress was composed of one colossal entrance and a twisting staircase of glacial stone. Steps that led up to various chambers in the three-fingered structure. There wasn't a corner that wasn't treacherous – health and safety come no further; 'a bit slippy' didn't cover it. She lived in this dark place alone except for the skreekes and her Smoo, Alfred.

Selina liked her space. She had tried to be sociable once and it hadn't worked out well. She wasn't really a witch – she was so beyond 'witch', beyond that comfortable benchmark with its kooky hats, kitsch broomsticks, vampish dresses, and savvy cats. If only she *was* a witch, then Red could have returned home and slept soundly. Madame Carnal was born in a great storm, with ambitions greater than she could bear – ambitions that consumed her as soon as she became aware of her gift and first saw the man who would rule alongside her.

Sometimes, consumed people can do wonderful things – invent Cloudbusters, make puff pastry, or leap over rivers. For example, Magatha Guiler and January Macloud, the princess's godmothers, on better consumed days, were gifted sign-readers. If Robbie Wylde put his heart into it, he could dine like a king from foraging the contents of a meadow. Will English had made a thousand guests at a royal ball believe he was the Countess Blanche du Bon Bon despite the smattering of hairs on his chest.

Selina was consumed backwards, a way not easily shared with others. She had developed an unwise and insatiable hunger for power. It is very hard to reverse this addiction, even with a fold of white witches and a lot of crumble at your disposal. Little is left of the person – their soul, their heart, and their ability to love. A consumed spirit is capable of forging fortresses in uninhabitable places and surviving on fermented potatoes and bat meat. Selina took being consumed to a whole new level, and she left Landfelian to practise her dark arts, undisturbed by the two peacemakers on the throne. Her magic took the souls of the dead and her own restless desire and twisted them together into an energy that could exert her will. On a good day, Selina could alter whole weather systems.

Evil had got her so far, and then she was rather irritated to discover she needed help with the heavy lifting. Selina sought out a nice, simple clan living nearby, and the Smoos were this unfortunate clan. Their land was not close, but it was a distance Selina could shorten nicely if she put her mind to it, so she set about freezing the small stretch of sea between them.

For hundreds of years, the Smoos inhabited the island of Tum, undisturbed and happy in their Smoo mounds, with their Smoo ponies and goats – until the day the witch attached herself to their coast and tramped through the tall swaying grasses with two beasts in tow. One morning, a Smoo was tucking into a cup of warm mare's milk with a piece of black bread and then came the sound of a sleigh slicing over the snow, heralding the arrival of the witch.

The Smoos had no warning. They were unaccustomed to visitors and were initially excited that such a tall person had made it across the ice without a jumper. She must be a strong, heroic sort. A true adventuress. The sea had never frozen before. It was most odd. In the past, when any weary souls arrived on their coast, the Smoos had invited them in for some peaty ale and a lobster bisque before enquiring, 'What did you come here for? No one comes here.'

Maybe she was part of the endless quest they had heard about. One of the King of Landfelian's famous hero trackers. Maybe all this lady needed was a bath, a tipple, and a nice rub down. Their valiant attempts to introduce her to some of the taller, single Smoo men did not end well. Smoos were not the fighting type. They did not even hunt. When they had to bear arms, it was only for self-defence, and they would give the animal a proper burial. There were more wolves than Smoos in Tum as a result.

The Smoo people were bearded and stout, as a rule, with very rosy cheeks. Female Smoos did not have beards; they braided their hair and had small feet, which they used every Sunday evening for the traditional Smoo Stick Dance. Smoo mounds were made from long grasses – dried and bundled together to form a thatch over a mud home. Inside, they were lined with goat wool. This land had only two seasons – known simply as the White Nights and the Black Days – with about three weeks of normal in between. There were plenty of fish to catch in the summer and jumpers to knit in the winter. It wasn't the South Tequeetahs, but it was home.

When Selina pounded on the door of the first Smoo settlement, she frightened the goats, and the children began to cry. The creatures with her trampled over the paddocks and attacked the wide-bellied ponies grazing there. No one felt like stick dancing around a mound fire after that. Thankfully, she did not stay longer than two days, but she did take an entire community of Smoos away with her as help, after some vague promises about travel and career enhancement. She took them away on the foggy horizon, leaving Tum with nothing but the whispers of impending doom on the wind that blew over from Tallfinger.

'Madame, are you a witch?' a brave Smoo called Alfred had asked what the others were all thinking.

She bared down on him and whispered, 'Witch? Why, no, you astute little man, I am THE witch.'

There would be no rebellion from those remaining. Madame Carnal could do odd things to the weather. She had the ability to alter the atmosphere, and there were the two beasts she kept close to her side. The Smoos continued as best they could, tending the goats and rebuilding their mounds.

The captured Smoos discovered there was no toy-making at her fortress and no healthcare. The pointy woman promised to free them as soon as her home was complete and her bed built. If any of them tried to leave before it was done, she threatened eternal fog and darkness on the island of Tum. Rather than destroy all they held dear, the Smoos remained Selina's slaves. At first, they thought she was just lonely. Loneliness can do terrible things to a person; no one can be strong on their own all the time. A couple from the Smoo Workers Union made the bold decision to invite the witch to join in their game of pick-up sticks. She cut off their beards and gave them the task of digging out a series of squats deep below Tallfinger.

In short, the black squirrel knew not to venture further than the entrance hall. The lower levels of Tallfinger were a labyrinth of frozen caves filled with stalagmites and black, icy pools of putrid water. The two creatures known as skreekes roamed these cold, dripping tunnels, feeding on fish that washed in by mistake. The beasts had mottled, leathery skin the colour of ash and mace-like tails with claws the size of bananas. They were closely related to the dragon family and about the size of a large crocodile. It was rumoured amongst the Smoos that the witch liked nothing more than to spend Sundays with a net and a sharp stick, hunting morsels for these creatures. She had named them Nips and Ammonia and doted on them as if they were her children.

It took a day for the squirrelgram to reach this place from Paloma. Travelling at twice the speed of a domestic squirrel. It was led up to the highest point of the middle finger of the fortress by the witch's head servant, Alfred. There was a balcony that went all the way around the highest tower so Selina could see who was coming and throw things at them. She did not welcome visitors. The breath of the squirrelgram hung in the icy air for a few seconds. On the other side of a stone door, on a chaise longue of petrified wood and ensconced in acres of black velvet, sat the witch. She was not affected by the temperature. In her opinion, one could not be too cold, and she used her power to ensure things around her stayed nicely chilled. The cold sharpened her mind. Landfelian's greatest flaw was its heat – all that ghastly warmth and good will. The white fur of some flattened animal spread about her feet was more for effect than comfort. Interior decorators of the day would describe her style as 'gothic chic', although none would survive there long enough to write a review.

The witch's bed squatted against the far wall of her chamber like a threat. The bedspread looked to be made up from the tails and skins of hundreds of Smoo animals, a bearded goat, a white wolf, and several groundhogs. A gopping headboard made of bone – a fan of bones and a collection of black candles, dripping putrid wax – completed her sleeping area. Selina liked a candle. She'd lived through the Age of Romance, after all, although she did not receive many gentlemen callers; the witch saw no one that had not been summoned or dragged.

This extraordinary woman was enjoying a vase of something close to vodka when a knock interrupted her meditation time. She swung one bony foot onto the cold floor and stretched. Several vertebrae snapped, appearing to lengthen her by at least a foot. Selina was tall for her age and, standing, could look most men in the eye.

'Never a moment's peace, Nip Nip. When will mother rest?' She scratched the upturned chin of the squatting skreeke at her feet with white nails. The creature made a deep clicking noise from the back of its throat and closed it yellow eyes with pleasure. 'ENTER!'

'Madame.' It was very difficult to get the etiquette right when addressing a woman of indescribable age. 'Milady' was generally reserved for the young and pretty. Selina was striking, but she was no longer in her prime. The Smoo, Alfred, faltered at the sight of her, even after nine years in service. Every morning the sight of her sucked the air from his lungs.

'What is it, Alfred? Can't you see I'm busy?'

He looked at her and failed to identify the busy-ness. 'An urgent squirrelgram has arrived.'

'Junk mail,' she drawled. 'You must make the signs clearer.'

'From Landfelian,' he went on.

'How hideous. Probably another *Missing* notice for the queen.' She looked thrilled at the thought.

'It is from Paloma.'

Her eyes bored into him like blades through butter. The leathery beast shifted closer to the Smoo.

'Well, don't just stand there and breathe. Give it to me!'

Alfred unbound Daniel's note from the squirrelgram's harness and handed it to his mistress. As she read, the dark fork of her eyebrow shot up to join her hairline. She dropped the letter and drank what remained in her glass.

Selina swept over to a desk, constructed from the severed trunk of a redwood tree, and snatched up her quill. Alfred knew something was terribly wrong, and so did the quill. The temperature had dropped several degrees. As the quill scratched against parchment, she fiddled with a choker of polished grey teeth around her neck.

'Alfred, come here and hand me your beard.'

The Smoo looked pained as he lifted what was left of his snow-white beard into the witch's hand. She snipped off a lock and tied it round her letter, added a drop of black wax, and pressed an enormous ruby ring in to seal it.

'Return this with the squirrelgram. Then feed the skreekes. I travel south tonight to Mirador.'

He bowed and hurried out, mouthing, 'Thank the gods for that.'

A few flakes of snow scattered over Selina as she sat hunched over her desk, staring out at the fog. The snow seemed to appear from the atmosphere around her rather than any visible gust from outside. Then the walls echoed as her embittered scream splintered through Tallfinger. 'THAT CUNNING LITTLE VIXEN!'

She hurled a couple of candles out the window, gathered up her snow boots, cape, and driving goggles, and left her chamber. Taking the one hundred and seventy-two steps down to her sleigh, she waited for the skreekes to finish eating and take her south to his kingdom.

It grew dark as she waited, pacing up and down the drawbridge of her fortress. Grinding her molars, Selina's mind roared. How could that girl have escaped still attached to the voodoo charm? She had underestimated her strength. If the princess was not captured, her plan would be ruined, and Daniel Blackwood would pay with more than his tongue. The wind began to dance around Tallfinger, stronger and stronger, until the witch stood in the eye of a snow twister. Selina gathered the souls of the dead around her – the souls of those left behind, of those taken before their time – and she used their dark energy like a good sorceress uses a wand, toying with the restlessness left behind by the unhappy dead. Daniel's note remained crumpled at her feet as the witch was consumed by snow.

MADAME, the bait has escaped. I have arrested three suspects. Storm delayed pursuit. If this weather is your doing, please desist. The voodoo box and the giantess are missing. The princess jumped the Bigeasy on her valien. She will be traced and found.

DB

Daniel Blackwood stood in the doorway of Paloma's ballroom and watched his guards round up the guests and servants. He had never failed before. It was not something he wanted to do again. The squirrelgram would return by morning, with the witch's answer. She would summon him to Tallfinger, he was sure. Around him, drunk figures swayed. They had all come to see the princess, and she had quietly run off, outfoxing his plans. His left eye began to twitch in fear.

'Guards! Stop that music. Question everybody inside.'

'The peasants are asking about their payment.' The guard who'd spoken received a look.

The guests began to gain consciousness as soon as the orchestra stopped and guards marched in, shouting at them to form a line for questioning. They looked nervously about for their cloaks, asking politely about coffee. Every gentleman wanted to help in the search for Amber Morningstar. The idea of capturing the woman in the exciting dress was a good reason to go out in the torrential rain. A few fights broke out in the rush to get to the stables, but no one was to leave without first being questioned. Paloma began to feel the effects of the greatest hangover of all time.

The half-queen and king sat slumped on their thrones, mumbling nonsense to one another. Gerald tried to stroke his wife's calf with his foot and slid to the floor like a dead jellyfish.

'What say we have a quick zizz before the surprise? A five-minutes snoozes woulds dos yous thes powers ofs goods,' he slurred and yawned like a hippo.

Caroline looked like a carriage wreck. 'The slurplisz.' Rouge covered the bottom third of her face.

'A nap of any length is out of the question.' The head of royal security's shadow darkened their seats.

'Did I miss the fireworks?' She brightened up and tried to focus.

'The princess has run away. I found this on the back drive.'

The half-queen looked at the standard-size, mid-length, blonde wig being waved in front of her. 'It is not one of mine,' she scoffed. 'Run away? Impossible.'

'The groundsman, Jim True, and his family have been arrested. I believe the herald is also involved, and the princess' valien is missing.'

Caroline's wan smile slipped off her face faster than fat from a griddle.

'How could this have happened? The teeth! The giantess!' She turned grey (with some interesting purple patches). 'Get her back!'

A guard interrupted, holding a grapefruit. 'We found this inside the clock, Guvnor. The long tapestry has gone too.'

'How dare she take my tapestry!' hissed Caroline.

Gerald looked at his wife. She appeared to have missed

the point, but the half-queen was exhibiting classic shock symptoms. She was showing such a shining example, she should have been very proud of herself. In the face of titanic catastrophe, she had become fixated on the whereabouts of an old wall hanging. Her next thought was of the bet she had made.

'The bet! Sir Toby! I have dishonoured the code of Gin Rummy.' Someone should have shaken her then and said, 'WHO CARES ABOUT THE BLOODY BET, THE PRINCESS IS MISSING!'

Gerald was quiet and, for the first time in years, his mind was clear. His only thought was of his stepbrother. 'The king,' he whispered and glanced about the ballroom. 'He will return to this mess and … Dear brother, forgive me. What have we done?'

Something told Caroline's very little brain that she would not be top of King Felian's list of people to award a title to when he returned home to find his only daughter missing. It was assumed that the king would come back eventually, from wherever he was, put on his robes, have a shave, and punch in at the office, even though no one knew if he was even alive. 'On a quest' sounded nicer than 'dead at the bottom of a gorge, partially digested by snakes, and pecked dry by vultures'.

'What should we do?' she jabbered. A gold peacock feather fell out of her wig.

'Place a handsome bounty on her head.' Daniel's voice was stern.

'Yes, yes, whatever it takes.' Gerald tried to stand and waved for a footman. 'The keys to the vault, Simpkins.'

'Wait, how handsome a bounty?' Caroline gave her husband a look.

'I will need the remaining gold,' replied Daniel smoothly. 'It will be necessary to hire outside hunters and bribe the poor.'

'Yes, of course.' Gerald fumbled with the key. 'You must bring her back.'

Blackwood took the key and left them on their thrones, ruined and in charge of a kingdom.

* * *

The storm raged over Paloma Palace's graceful rooftops and rattled against its windows. The lake doubled in size, taking over the grass tennis court, the croquet lawn, and half a ham roll that someone had left in the hands of a statue of Queen Matilda. Swans glided over the fountains.

Inside, the guests waited for it to pass; their carriages were waterlogged. The servants were sent out to try to drain the avenues. It was the gloomiest dawn imaginable. The rain continued into the following day.

The guards waited too. There were one thousand guests to yell at, which kept them busy.

Blackwood paced through the bowels of his watchtower.

The mighty sweep of weather was trying his patience.

The half-queen and half-king managed to make it up to their chamber into a bed the size of a swimming pool. On the rare occasions Caroline let her husband sleep with her, he had great trouble finding her. They clung to one another under the covers, surrounded by fizzing glasses of sherbet-coloured remedies. The heavy curtains and blankets could not muffle the relentless sound of rain on the windows or the sense of doom.

A terrible draught had replaced the stifling heat. The palace quaked as cold shot down the corridors and under the doors as if searching for the missing princess. She had vanished; there were no witnesses. The guests knew nothing.

Sir Toby was thinking. He stood quietly by the far window of the Great Mirrored Hall and stared at the rivers of water coursing through the gardens. He sipped bitter coffee and continued to think. As he looked back at the arc of his young life, he realised how little of it had been spent sober. It was time for a change.

The True family listened to the rain from deep in the cells of the watchtower. June was pensive. 'I think I left the kitchen window open.'

'Don't worry, love. The princess will be with Nin, next to a fire with some sausage pie and a pot of tea.'

'I know that, Jim. But who will feed our pig with us stuck down here?'

Billy was worried about a more imminent problem: they

were locked in the torturing chamber of the man with the silver-topped cane. A damp kitchen and a hungry pig were the least of his family's problems; he didn't even have any of his usual firecrackers on him or his slingshot. At that moment, the cell door cried open, and the True family were greeted by a smile they did not warm to and a lead box they had never seen before.

'What about this weather? Terrible. Although perfect for a game, wouldn't you agree, my boy?' Billy said nothing. 'My personal favourite is the Sharing Game.' Blackwood stepped closer, his grey eyes bright. He placed a lead box down, and they all looked at it. 'This is the Sharing Box.'

There was a gap in the top wide enough to post a thick letter, and there was a cuff and chain to secure that hand to the box. A deep rattle came from inside it. Billy had heard a rattle like it before, near the bog where his father nurtured the compost. He swallowed, shifted back on his seat, and whispered, 'Bullet ants.'

'Clever child.' Blackwood tapped the box with his cane.

During a brief business arrangement with the ringmaster of the Great Cornucopia Carnival, Blackwood had introduced bullet ants to the bill. The act involved a platoon of these insects, a giant or giantess blindfolded, this custom-made lead box, and a great musical number of, 'Oh When the Ants Go Marching In!'

After a month, the ringmaster of the carnival, Theobald Morningstar, asked him to leave. They wanted no part of his act or his business.

Blackwood took the ants and the giantess with him to the darker parts of the city, where for a time they were used to great effect. A giant can withstand countless bullet ant bites without dying from the poison, although it did not lessen the pain. The act pulled in quite a crowd and quite a profit. Bear baiting simply could not compete.

Blackwood took off his black gloves and turned his attention to the groundsman. 'Now it's your turn.' A guard grabbed Jim's left hand and roughly pushed it inside the gap in the box, chaining it securely. 'You've known the princess for a long time. She took a keen interest in the gardens and a spent a great deal of time in your company.'

Blackwood waited.

The groundsman began to hum. 'Sorry, was that a question?' he asked eventually.

The sound of leather slapping across his father's cheek made Billy jump. June's left eye begin to twitch, and a deep rattle came from the box.

'I find it fascinating,' continued Blackwood. 'Why would she spend so much time with an old goat like you, when the pick of society – the crème de la crème, the rich and rare – were lined up on her turret step? Why would Landfelian's princess confide in a common groundsman?' Daniel's eyes narrowed. 'A peasant with a piece of string holding his trousers up.'

Billy had never punched anyone before. He was itching

to have a go now. His father continued to hum a gentle tune that he often sang when working. He did not appear in pain.

Daniel pulled out a pack of cards and began to shuffle. Cards had absolutely nothing to do with the Sharing Game; Daniel was just very good at shuffling. 'Where is she?' He shuffled with such speed that a card flew out of the deck and landed in June's blouse. June handed it back.

'I haven't a clue, sir. I'm a simple man.' Jim continued to whistle the gentle tune.

Billy opened his mouth and closed it. What was his father doing?

His mother started humming too.

'Tell me,' Daniel insisted.

'I can't,' Jim replied honestly. 'When you don't know something, you don't know. There isn't any more you can do about it.'

Red was a clever girl. She had never told Jim or his family where she was going – a decision she'd made from the beginning. The less people knew, the less 'sharing' they could do. The princess had noted down The Honest Sausage on her map, although she'd made no promises to go there. As for the rest of her plan, all they knew was that she wanted to find her father.

Daniel's eyes grew murkier and colder by the second. The groundsman was still the colour of a russet apple. He had only flinched once in pain. By now, Daniel expected him to be convulsing in agony from the insect's bites. The Sharing Game was taking too long. What had happened to his ants? And why was the bloody man still humming?

'I'll repeat the question.'

'You have your answer. Trying to understand a young lady's mind is like trying to walk without legs. I showed the girl how to make good compost. She was loved the gardens and was handy with a trowel. I never presumed to ask what thoughts were in her head or where she aimed her arrow – it was not my place. As you say, sir, I am just a peasant with ill-fitting trousers.'

Billy's mouth dropped.

There was a welcome knock at the door.

'Enter!' Blackwood shouted.

The guard in the doorway was surprised to find the prisoners humming. 'Your squirrelgram has returned.'

'Excellent.' Daniel checked his pocket watch and looked out the window to see the rain had stopped. 'Gather the men, follow the valien's tracks, bring me the girl, and meet me at The Hog's Breath.'

The guard drummed and stood to attention.

'I haven't quite finished.' The guard gulped. 'Lock the tower and let the prisoners starve here. I will find the princess without their help.' Blackwood picked up his silver-topped cane and left the watchtower.

As soon as the door slammed and was bolted seven times behind him, Billy turned to his father.

'Dad? How many bites do you have?' The box itself was strangely silent. He looked at his mother. 'Why are you both still humming?' Tears began to stream down his dirty cheeks. 'I don't understand.'

June stopped for a moment, took his hand, and spoke in an unnaturally calm voice, which further upset Billy, who was used to her bellowing.

'Your father's fine, my boy, just fine. He's singing to the ants, you see. What that piece of cowpat doesn't know is that your pa has built up immunity to them bullet ants. When you spend fifty odd years with your fingers in the soil, you meet a fair few of them in the tall grasses. He's formed an understanding with the little critters.'

Jim took his son's hand with his free one.

'They haven't bitten you? Not once?' Billy's mouth wobbled.

'A little nip, son, nothing to worry yourself about. It'll take more than a box of ants to send me to the grave. Poor fellows are harmless. They keep to their side of the flowerbed and I keep to mine. If they want to cross over my spade, I take my hat off and let them. Right now, they are sleeping. Feel sorry for the buggers, trapped in here. The humming sends them off to sleep. Keeps them calm. And my hands are as rough as bark.'

'He'll be back,' whispered Billy staring at the door. 'That man is as persistent as one of the half-queen's farts. He'll come back and find us all humming and put our tongues in a jar.'

'No, son, you'll see. It will all end well.' Jim winked, lent back on his chair, and closed his eyes. 'Best rest while you can. This is only the beginning.'

Blackwood,

I am most disappointed. Come at once to Tallfinger.
Do not be late.

S Carnal

Blackwood looked down and saw that the squirrelgram's tail was missing. He was not looking forward to a cocktail with the witch of Tallfinger. Her idea of a drink was a tumbler of black ice stirred with a recently gnawed bone. He had no choice, however, and quickly prepared for the journey. The price on the princess' head would appeal to every man in the land with a debt, he thought; nothing would come between him and capturing her. He left in Sir Toby's barouche, with two guards and the last bags of gold beside him. As Paloma Palace shrunk behind him, he did not look back at it standing abandoned in the waning sun.

The king's herald was seated in Sharing Room 2 ½, and he was singing. He pranced up and down the cell, using his baton to drum on the thick walls. The guard stood outside the door was enjoying himself. *What a card! What a fool! What an undeniably small but brilliant plonker!* The small man had clearly lost his mind. He started to put in requests. 'Do that Purple Knave one, "Chink in the Wall"!'

The noise attracted the attention of the remaining guards keeping watch over other prisoners in the tower. They came down to join in the sing-along and laughed so hard it didn't hurt at all when two large men in togas tiptoed quietly up behind them and knocked their heads together.

'What took you so long?' The herald through up his hands in relief. 'I was running out of show tunes.' He stepped over the pile of jodhpurs and gave the brothers a grateful smile and an embrace, which in this case meant hugging two warm thighs. 'Come, men, we have work to do. It won't be long before that snake Blackwood tracks down the princess. I must get to Alba first and warn her.'

13

THE LEFT FORK

Oblivious to his surroundings, Will English was enjoying an inconceivable dream. He was adrift on a raft, floating along the Bigeasy with Amber, a horse, a giantess, a long tapestry, and a box of voodoo in his boot. He snored like a hog and turned over, and something he hoped was Amber licked his face. 'Good morning, ma petite songstress.' He turned towards the licking and smiled. It was Marilyn.

Amber slept uneasily inside the wagon, wrapped in one end of the tapestry. She had changed into her most practical dress – it came with a corset, was burnished yellow, and covered 83% of her body in raw silk. After that, she had put on a pair of stout lace-up boots and fallen asleep. They had done what they'd set out to do, but she could not shake the feeling that somewhere along the line they had made a terrible mistake.

Blackwood haunted every corner of her dreams. He would find her; he always did.

Ophelia was asleep in the water. She was too big to be anywhere else. Her arms and head rested on the raft, while her legs floated out behind.

Through the remaining hours of the night, the raft kept its course. It took them steadily up the left artery of the Bigeasy, away from Paloma. The sky grew light and calm over this unknown estuary of the river, and the water turned an inviting pale green. It dropped in temperature the further north they travelled. Silver fish nibbled Ophelia's toes and darted about her, rousing her from slumber. The water felt too glacial for the East Realm, and she shivered.

Ophelia drank thirstily. The water was cold and clear. Everything in the palace had tasted of salt and strange condiments. She had barely eaten in five years. Her stomach grumbled. 'I could murder a peanut butter sandwich,' she said to herself, kicking her legs to stay warm.

She lay on her back with her face to the sun and looked around her. A few wisps of mist clung to gold cliffs either side of the raft. Great birds with rainbow-feathered tails – and a wingspan as wide as a stepladder is tall – soared high above their heads. They made soft mewing noises as she took in the cliffs, which reminded her of honeycomb and appeared to touch the cloudless sky. So like the giant cliffs of her home country, she took great comfort from them. Ophelia took comfort from anything bigger than her, as any tall woman might on meeting a taller man at a party.

The river flowed fast between the cliffs, and dark green ferns hung down from whatever land lay above. In many ways, it looked like New Zealand, in other ways a lot like Borneo, but in no way did it look like the beginning of the East Realm and the way to Alba.

The rainbow-tailed birds and the bright fish were now making quite a racket. The great birds were swooping down and cawing around the raft, the fish leaping about her. Ophelia wished she spoke bird or fish so she could tell them to clear off and let her enjoy her morning. Paddling on and warming her breasts in the sun, she closed her eyes … and missed the first sign that hung down against the cliff on an old, frayed rope.

WELCOME TO GIANT COUNTRY!
HOME TO THE RAINBOW-TAILED CHICHAW,
THE SILVER DARTE, AND HOSANNA FALLS.

Not long after the first, a second sign came into view, which Ophelia did see.

PARK ALL RIVER VEHICLES AROUND
THE NEXT BEND –
ROPES HAVE BEEN PROVIDED FOR MOORING.
FOLLOW THE TREACHEROUS AND
ERODING STEPS TO THE TOP.

DO NOT FEED THE RAINBOW-TAILED CHICHAWS.

IT ONLY MAKES THEM WILFUL AND THEY WILL PECK YOU.

'Oh no,' she whispered and tried to splash Will, who had fallen asleep at the front of the raft.

Will and Amber were meant to keep lookout for pursuing guards and signs directing them towards Alba. They were both still fast asleep.

Gradually, the left fork became more of a flume than a gentle eddy, and the raft bobbed up and down. Water slapped up against the sides. In his dream, Will was thoroughly kissing Amber when he heard some panicked horse sounds.

'MERLIN'S BEARD!' he cried as he woke up and looked around. 'What is going on here?' He leapt up, tilted unsteadily, and leant back against Marilyn, who was lying down. 'What a ride we are having.' His voice boomed grandly back to him. 'And what FANTASTIC RESONANCE these mighty cliffs have.' Will saw the bright side to every situation and at times did not see the situation at all. 'Amber. Listen. THE ECHO HERE IS ASTOUNDING!'

Marilyn snorted, and the raft darted on. Will wobbled over to Ophelia to tell her about the acoustics, only to find she wasn't in a position to try them out. The giantess was struggling to keep her head above the surface and the raft in a straight line. They were now travelling around fifty whales an hour.

'I say, I say, Captain, it's a bit choppy back here,'

commented Will as a rapid hit the side and soaked him. 'Let me help you. We need to slow this ship down. The tapestry is getting wet.'

'I'll stay here and navigate these rapids. Otherwise we'll sink.' Ophelia turned white and pointed to something up ahead. 'Oh no, look ... another sign ...'

The third sign was clear enough. It swung ominously out at them from a cliff.

WELCOME TO HOSANNA FALLS!
WE HOPE YOU HAVE A PLEASANT TRIP.

Will and Ophelia looked at one another and then looked again at the sign – they were now going so fast the sign was a dwindling dot in the distance. The sun shone down on their shocked faces, the chichaws cawed above them casting graceful shadows over the river.

'Falls? Surely not. As in waterfalls? Are these sign-writers quite sure?' Will cocked his head to take in the cliffs and made a face that suggested he was either listening intently or breaking wind carefully.

'I hear no falls. I see no falls. PAH! Hosanna Falls could refer to many things. Many. It could be the wife of the sign-writer for one or ... Oh blast ... That great misty area ahead.'

Ophelia stared ahead as the raft swung around a bend, heading straight towards a cloud of very spitty and final-looking mist.

'No, no,' said Will resolutely. 'If there was a fall of any kind, we would have heard it by now. This is simply the work of a phantom sign-maker, some joker who goes by the name of Hosanna. There has been an increase of this sort of vandalism recently. I read an interesting article on the disillusionment of Landfelian youth since the quest ...'

Will did not have the giantess' complete attention. 'Can you hear that?' She looked rather weak.

There it was. The roar. The roar of fifty thousand baths overflowing and dropping from a great height into a small, active volcano.

ROOOOOOOOOOOOOOOOOOOOOAAAAAAA AAAAAARRRRRRRRRRRRRR.

HISSSSSSSSSSSSSSSSSSSSSSSSSSSSSSSSSSSSSS SSSSSSSSSSSSSSSSSSSSSSSS.

STEAAAAAAAAAAAAAAAAAAAAAAAAAMMM MMMMMMMMMMMM.

'It' not just any waterfall,' breathed Ophelia. 'It's Hosanna.'

They had reached the end of realm land. They were in her people's country now. So steep was the fall, the water disappeared into a soft cascade by the time it reached the bottom. And at the bottom, a beautiful valley sprawled out – a valley that belonged to no realm, but to the giants. The raft's passengers could not see the valley. They just saw the end of the river on their horizon and the promise of an almighty drop.

Amber was wide awake and staring at the river-end on the horizon. 'WILLIAM!'

'Yes, my love.'

'WE HAVE A SERIOUS PROBLEM!'

'We do?'

'SOMEONE DIDN'T FINISH THE RIVER!'

'Ophelia, hold tight. Try to steer clear of the rocks. I'll be right back.'

Will ran to the front of the raft to find Amber sitting with her horse. The animal knew her number was up and lay with her head down, making a low, pained noise.

'How did you sleep, angel-wing? I woke only a few minutes ago after the most wonderful dream.'

Amber grabbed his shirt and pulled him down towards her. 'What does that sign say? I can't see.' She was short-sighted and often wore glasses when she wasn't performing. Will thought they made her look like a doctoress of seduction and longed for her even more than normal when she wore them. Gripping his calf, she stared at the last slice of cliff and specifically at an old plank hanging from a rope.

SO LONG!
SEE YOU ON THE OTHER SIDE.
GO IN PEACE.

Will decided not to elaborate on the contents of the fourth sign.

'It recommends a fine bed and breakfast not far from here. There is just one small waterfall to get past first.' He sounded like a scout leader.

'Nooooo . . .' Amber whispered and gripped his leg tighter.

'Yes, we've got a waterfall situation here, folks! Nothing to worry about. Although I am not familiar with Hosanna Falls, I am certain it is quite lovely.'

'We are going to die,' Amber whimpered.

'Not on my watch!' Will had once played the part of Pirate King in a theatre above a lobster shack in the small coastal dwelling of Crabbie. He knew it was important for the sake of his crew, who were silent and green, to stay positive. He clapped his hands and climbed gingerly onto the wagon's roof as the raft glided on.

'HOLD FAST, SWAGGERERS! We have faced worse squalls. Do not fear.'

'For Christ's sake, Will, get down. We need to think, fast!' yelled Amber. 'We need to find something, grab it, and hold on. We have to park the raft on something that isn't moving forward and get off.'

They looked around at their options.

There were no options.

'I know!' cried Will. 'If we harness several large salmon, they can tow us to safety.'

There was little enthusiasm for this idea.

There was another sign which they all ignored. It was a lot newer than the previous ones.

HOSANNA FALLS IS A BEAUTIFUL, RARELY VISITED NATURAL WONDER – ONE OF THE SEVEN GREAT WONDERS OF LANDFELIAN.

'Wait.' Amber pointed at something ahead, half submerged against the cliff. 'What is that?'

'A whale!' Will shouted in glee. 'No, it's a rock . . .'

They all craned forward to see.

Amber had spotted – and frankly, thank the fish she had – a partly submerged, flat plateau of rock. It peeked out of the water at the foot of the cliff, shrouded by the swirling cloud of mist. Rapids bucked around it. Ahead there was nothing but a fine view of Hosanna and her fall.

'It's worth a punt,' said Will, looking at Amber.

'I'd say so.'

'Ophelia! STAGE LEFT! We need to bank onto that rock!'

They scrambled over to the other side of the raft and helped the giantess paddle.

The plan was not failsafe. It was the equivalent of trying to land an elephant onto a door wedge. Will wasn't sure paddling was making a difference; the current pushed them straight on. They did not have oars, so Amber used a hand fan and passed Will a vanity mirror.

Certain death waited with a lazy smile – death without a grey area, without a loophole, clause, or amendment; death with no stopover.

Ophelia could see the rock and steered as best she could, conscious that there was a large risk they would slide right over the top and shoot off the other side. The giantess had a strong pair of thighs, but this would test an Olympian's core strength. She put everything she had into it. For a giantess, she was relatively petite – the males, on average, were fifteen foot, and the females between thirteen and fourteen. She was not sure she had the strength to battle the river.

'Can everyone swim?' enquired Will.

The shire horse snorted and tried to stand.

'I am merely interested,' he told Marilyn. 'It will not be necessary.'

Ophelia fought the current, battled the eddies, and slayed the pull of the water to drag them slowly across the river towards the rock.

'She needs more help,' yelled Amber. Their paddling was doing very little other than making them wet.

The roar of Hosanna Falls was all around them now. Will nodded, took a deep breath, and dropped into the water. It felt cold enough to freeze his collectables off. Amber followed, and the three kicked with all their might. When the cloud of mist swallowed them, it was hard to tell if they were even moving in the right direction.

'WE CAN BEAT THIS RIVER, ME HEARTIES!' Will shouted. 'KICK!'

The giantess closed her eyes. Amber swore under her breath.

Will bellowed, 'ON THREE, GIVE IT ALL YOU'VE GOT!' And, in his best heroic voice, he roared: 'THREEEEEEEEEEEEEEEEEEEE!'

The raft surged forward with a speed that threatened their shoulder sockets but wedged them firm and true onto that flat plateau of rock. The wagon, however, followed through with the momentum and rolled straight over the edge, disappearing into oblivion before anyone could shut their ears to the terrible silence that followed.

'My wagon!' Amber cried at the space where her home had stood.

'It may still be alright, my sweet.'

The sound of splintering wood reached them. The current pushed the raft further up the rock. There was a nasty scraping noise. Will looked beneath to find it was overhanging the edge of the falls by an uncomfortable third. He grabbed hold of Amber, and Ophelia helped them both out of the water. They sat on the rock – as far away as they could from the tremendous view.

'Do you still have the voodoo?' Amber trembled from cold.

He dug around in his boot. 'Yes, I've got the ghastly thing.'

'Good, because if I thought for one second that my wagon had rolled off a waterfall for nothing, I would be seriously creamed off.'

There was still another problem, besides the obvious: Marilyn was stuck at the wobbly end of the raft.

'Hold on, Marilyn!' called Amber. 'I'm going to get her.' The raft tilted south as she moved, and the horse whinnied.

'You will do no such thing.' Will held on to her hand.

'If I don't, there will be a drawing of my horse *and* my wagon on the fourth sign!' Amber was shouting, tears streaming down her cheeks. The birds circled noisily above.

'Hold on to this – I will go and get her,' cried Amber. She tied the tapestry around her waist and started to make her way on all fours, calling softly to Marilyn, who was trembling at the misty end. Will held on to the tapestry, and Ophelia held on to Will. Progress was slow and every movement made the raft creak.

'Come on, pet,' crooned Amber. 'Shimmy down this way. There is a meadow with your name on it as soon as we get off this rock.'

Marilyn looked gravely at Amber. As far as she could see, her home was now providing an interesting wreck for divers below. The carnival was a breeze compared to this journey. Still, she began to shuffle slowly towards the three terrified faces.

'That's it. Like the Rings of Fire.' Amber and Marilyn's act had involved flaming hoops. It had absolutely nothing in common with their current situation aside from being one fifth as scary. 'Nearly there.'

A bit of raft snapped off and startled the shire horse, who scrambled suddenly towards them. Amber reached out for her, just as Will sneezed and let go of the tapestry. Ophelia grabbed a leg and pulled. Will found Amber's waist. Amber grasped a hoof. Everyone pulled on what they had and landed in a heap on the rock. The raft did not, though. It tipped and dived headlong into the abyss. Again, there was the sound of splintering wood and swallowing.

No one spoke for a minute – a minute of suspended disbelief. A minute that some refer to as "a close call". After this minute, Will was the first to find his voice.

'That was close.' He wiped his sodden mop of hair from his eyes and took a good look around him. 'What a Sunday we're having.' He sniffed. 'How is morale? High and climbing higher, I hope. There will be a book, a play, and a tea towel about this adventure one day, Hosanna, there will!'

The giant cliffs climbed up behind them, and water surrounded their rock. He felt handsome and heroic and wet. 'We are saved!'

A moment later, part of their rock cracked, broke away,

and disappeared over the edge.

Amber tied up her hair and wrung out the hem of her dress. She patted Marilyn over and over, who was shaking, and held on to Ophelia's hand. Will had never seen her remain quiet for so long. She looked very small and damp. Her lips trembled.

'Okay, Pirate King of the Hosanna Falls, what next?'

'I'm thinking.'

'We are marooned on a dissolving rock, a few feet from the seventh wonder of Landfelian.'

He agreed with enthusiasm that would break your heart. 'I know. I HAVE NEVER SEEN THIS WONDER BEFORE! Glorious, isn't it, nature? Does anyone know the other six wonders?'

Amber was an extremely talented young woman. Her face could say a multitude of things without her mouth getting involved at all. She looked at him now and tried to find the area of his head where the brain was missing. They only had days left to reach Alba and shout at the princess for getting them into this voodoo-ed mess. She had no idea how they were going to get off the river.

Ophelia stood up and examined the cliff. Up close, she could see several footholds and fissures. 'I think I could climb it.' She touched the rough stone. It crumbled beneath her fingers.

'Ophelia, I don't know why you ended up with us on this rock,' said Amber, 'but you are not climbing anything.

Will, you mentioned the acoustics earlier. I think now would be a good time to shout for help. There must be someone who lives nearby. Who made the signs? If we make enough noise, they might hear us and . . .'

'They may rob us,' said Ophelia. 'Bandits are often found around here, thinking they can hide on the borders of Giant Country.'

'I fancy my chances,' said Amber. 'On three.'

'Wait,' cried Will. 'What are we shouting on three?'

'Help, Will,' said Amber. 'We are going to shout HELP on three.'

'Got you.'

'. . . Three.'

'HELLLLLLLLLLLLLLLLLLLLLLLLLPPPPPPPPPPP!'

A bit more rock crumbled away.

The gods and goddesses were quietly confident that help in some shape would find them, so they passed around the canapés and waited. A giantess, an actor, a singer, and a shire horse have four sets of very capable lungs, after all. So for several strained hours, the rebels screamed for their lives.

AFTERMATH

The sun rose over Paloma Palace and the birds sang, all except the doves, who were busy washing themselves clean of pink dye, in the fountains. Hangovers pulsed throughout the guest rooms like lemon juice on a papercut between the knuckles on a cold day. The birds were warned they would be shot if they continued to sing. Figures made their way gingerly out to the carriage park, with pounding heads, hoarse whispers, and unravelling wigs. None of them knew what had really happened at the ball, although they knew for certain there had been champagne. The storm thundered away, giving way to a clear sky. The guards left first, in a flurry of buckles, whips, drums, boots, and leather. A small group of guards believed to be missing were later found tied up in one of the cells under the watchtower, surrounded by a platoon of bullet ants. The man with the silver-topped cane had disappeared.

The half-queen was in the kitchen, which was unusual for her. She was on her ninth short, black coffee – short because she drank it from an egg cup. Every other receptacle was dirty or in a state of ruin. Hunched and shaking, she sat in a gold-satin kimono style gown embroidered with pineapples and stared out at a bright morning. Sud bubbles popped around her as, glassy eyed, she sipped from her egg cup. Maids came and went with mops and dusters.

Elvira was worried, and so were the scullery maids. They were struggling with the aftermath of the ball; its detritus was left all over the palace, and Agnes was still missing. It was the clean-up equivalent of trench warfare in each room. Towers of stacked plates leant over the sink, smudged glasses covered every surface, pots and pans lined up on the floor. Outside the kitchen, stained silk cushions and pools of sour-smelling liquid spread through the beautiful galleries and receiving halls. Exquisite furniture lay upended and covered in stains that an incontinent cat would not claim. Amongst the lost and found were four-hundred-and-two wigs, a grapefruit, and a pet porcupine on a lead with a nametag engraved, *Mortimer*. There were fake moles waiting to be claimed; they had peeled off in the heat and been gathered in a bowl by the front door.

Buckets of soapy water lined the hallway, and great puffs of steam filled the air. Elvira was in her element. She had her skirts hitched up under her apron and wet-weather boots on. The shine of the challenge shone on her round face. She glanced up at the half-queen. It was most strange; she had never spend so long in the kitchen in silence. It wasn't her area of the palace. She looked wrong, sitting there like a dog without a tail.

The servants swept cautiously around the half-queen, scrubbing and polishing; everyone was anxious. Caroline had rubbed a mixture of beaten egg and coarse honey into her face to aid the recovery of her skin. She wore no wig; the devil only knew what that meant. Elvira disappeared outside, where there was a vast bonfire starting up, piled high with broken branches and leaves ripped off by the storm, as well as broken hand fans and orders of service.

'I've half a mind to give her a duster and tell her to help,' Elvira muttered to the parlour maids.

The half-queen felt as if something had scratched, clawed, then curled up and died between her temples. Her feet were bare and bloated like a bullfrog's throat; the gout had finally settled in. Her eyes were open but drowning in gin. When she coughed, it scared the birds and made you suspect death was crouched nearby, idly stroking his beard.

'If that woman is not an example of why it is good to know your limits, then I am an aardvark,' Elvira muttered.

The footmen hovered in the corridor. 'What's wrong with her?'

'She's woken up, that's all. Took long enough,' Elvira

huffed as she straightened up and flicked a rag at them. 'Don't dither, lads – there are glasses sticking out of all the box hedges, and it would be just my luck for the king to return today.'

They kept one eye on the half-queen and carried on polishing. 'Something tells me this is her last ball,' murmured one of the footmen, somewhat prophetically.

Gerald did not recognise his wife when he strolled in at lunchtime for a slice of ham and a small glass of cooking sherry – the only bottle left with anything in it. The half-king had the constitution of a rhino, and nothing put him off lunch. The amount of cheese in his stomach provided a sort of dairy pillow between his head and his hangover. He chuckled politely, assuming the dishevelled form was a guest.

'Hello, there,' he remarked, rootling around for the mustard. When a sound like the sigh of an elderly wasp came from inside the gold kimono, he jumped.

'Run away like her mother. We are ruined.' This last statement was followed by a bout of dry coughing. 'It's all my doing.'

Caroline began to sob. The servants were not sure what was happening at first – it was a noise they were not familiar with. Gerald wasn't sure either; he had only seen his wife cry twice – when he'd asked her to marry him and when she was recognised by some children she used to be a governess to and they threw pencils at her.

'What is going on?' Cook whispered to Elvira.

'The princess has run away,' she whispered.

'Not again.'

'She made it over the river this time.' Elvira's eyes shone.

'Oh blimey.'

Gerald looked around and smiled politely at the servants milling around the kitchen.

'Would everyone be so kind as to leave my wife and I alone for a few minutes? We will make our own lunch.'

There was a great intake of breath. Cook looked doubtful, but he and the servants left discreetly. The noise and liquids streaming out of Caroline were enough to clear the room. Gerald took a chair next to his wife.

Out in the stable yard, Paloma Palace's household staff enjoyed the fresh air and a rare tea break. Elvira bought out a pound cake and slices were handed around. The herald was summoned immediately and informed about the royal happenings and the pound cake by Jeremy the trainee herald.

'The half-queen started to cry. The half-king is making his own lunch. They are in the *kitchen*! Oh and the princess got over the river this time.'

'Jolly good – thank you, Jeremy.' The herald smiled; it was a beautiful afternoon. 'Then all is as it should be.'

Inside, Gerald pulled up a stool next to his wife and gently prized her hands from the egg cup. She turned away and tried to hide inside her robe.

'Don't look at me, Gerry, I'm hideous!' Dried-up egg fell from her face. She wiped her dripping nose with her sleeve and hiccupped.

Caroline had not called him Gerry for years; he loved her more at this moment than he had since they'd moved to the palace. 'You are beautiful to me, Ce.'

'His only daughter, gone. Under our care, lost in the wild. What will the king say? We shall be exiled.' She clasped his hand.

Gerald had taken a long, deep-thinking sort of bath that morning. He'd decided the only thing to do, under the circumstances, was to have lunch. That was what he'd done when his first wife had left him for a blacksmith. Truth be told, his first idea was to go on a long vacation, but on ruminating a little longer in the bath, he knew this to be wrong. His business was safekeeping his step-niece, Paloma, and the kingdom until the king's return.

'We will do what has been asked of us and remain here. She will return. I remember when I was young . . .' He chuckled. 'We must ensure everything is as it should be when she climbs back through the window. Until then, I have had a rather good idea about producing a Paloma cheese. We must earn our keep.'

'Cheese?' Caroline started to cry again.

'Yes, my dear, I am after a cheese-maker.'

She let Gerald hold her; he was good at holding her. He

didn't get to do it very often, but when he did, he was good. She tried to make another cup of coffee, which was a messy business – although, after a lot of snot and tears, the result made her feel much better. She could make coffee and Gerald could make cheese. Her husband was a good and capable man. She had almost forgotten their old life, the dairy. The restless, hungry feeling at the pit of her stomach – the feeling that came over her whenever she entered the Clock Room – had somehow gone. She watched Gerald take a bite of his ham sandwich and felt almost peaceful.

'Blackwood has organised a search of all four realms. She can't have gone far. But there is one thing that troubles me . . .' Gerald chewed thoughtfully.

'Not enough mustard?'

'No, no, flowerpot, no. It's that trinket on her ankle . . .'

Sir Toby strode in and glared at Caroline. 'There is a great deal that troubles me about that!'

In the last twelve hours, Sir Toby had left the window where he had done some of his best thinking and put his mother in a stranger's coach in the direction of home. He had washed his face of rouge and removed his wig. He had taken the ribbons from his knickerbockers and the frills from his cuffs, rolled up his sleeves, looked in the mirror, and said hello to himself once again.

'You imprisoned her, placing her in the hands of that son of a lawyer ... the so-called gentlemen in charge of royal security!' Sir Toby threw a handful of playing cards on the table with a flourish. 'What were you thinking? The man's a brigand, a rat, a silver-topped-cane-owning scoundrel of the first order.' He kicked a stool, then righted it again. 'And selling her to me in a bet? In a game of Gin Rummy!' He spat the last word.

Caroline wailed as if he had trodden on her tail. She pulled her robe tight around her and climbed onto a stool. Height was important to her at this point. 'How dare you accuse me in such a way? Get out of my kitchen!'

'Forgive me, governess, but THIS IS THE KING'S KITCHEN AND NEITHER OF YOU ARE THE KING!' Toby bellowed back.

Gerald quietly finished his sandwich and poured some more sherry.

'May I remind you, Sir Toby, that you accepted the bet. You said yes, how jolly, why not, a princess bride – ROLL the dice!' snapped Caroline.

'I was drunk on the thirteen juleps you thrust upon me!' He slumped against the wall and put his head in his hands. 'I was out of my mind.'

'A little late to blame the aperitifs, you silly young man. You were willing!'

Sir Toby glared at the half-queen. 'I am not a silly man. But I am young, which is more than I can say for you.'

The kettle whistled, cutting through the shouting with its welcome, merry note.

'Ah, wonderful. Tea for everyone,' said Gerald. 'Let's pause for a pot. My dear, why don't you get down from the stool and put that knife down? Sir Toby, it has been a long and trying night. Have some ham, both of you. It's very good.'

Caroline glared at Sir Toby and took a seat. 'A small piece of ham would be lovely, Gerry.'

Sir Toby sat too. 'Milk and two sugars – thank you, Gerald.'

'Wonderful.' Gerald sighed. 'I think we can all agree on one thing: there is a good deal we have done wrong.'

'It's true. I fell barouche and minstrel for all of this splendour.' Sir Toby gestured at a tray of exquisite crystal glasses. 'The avenues, turrets, and peacocks, the walnut bureaus. The princess.' He sighed.

He dunked his ham into a bowl of hot mustard from Engerlande. It took the roof of his mouth off, cleared his sinuses, and revived his spirit. 'I wanted the king to return and my father to be proud. What a vain fool I've been, thinking I could marry the heir to Landfelian. I barely knew her. Who wouldn't want that hair splayed across their pillow, though?'

Caroline hacked through the roasted honey and clove-studded skin of the ham, which was excellent. 'I drove her away.'

'No, no,' said Gerald.

'No,' agreed Sir Toby. 'Not you alone.'

A whole bouquet of Nos was thrown at Caroline's feet.

After guilt comes great forgiveness.

'Yes,' sighed Caroline.

'Well, maybe you did a little,' suggested Gerald, gently.

A small man in tails and still holding a baton appeared in the doorway and skipped quickly into the kitchen. 'You all drove her away.' The herald threw his baton onto the table.

Gerald looked at the herald and the two muscled men behind him and knew there would not be enough ham.

'But she would have left anyway.' The herald sighed and sat down on the next stool. 'Is there a little ham left?'

'I believe there is a second leg in the pantry.' Gerald got to work on another round of sandwiches. 'Allow me.' He felt extraordinarily happy in this simple task. All it needed was a strong cheddar.

'Thank you,' said the herald, surprised. 'Your gravest mistake was hiring Daniel Blackwood.'

'You are mistaken, herald. Blackwood is a charming man with impeccable taste,' the half-queen insisted. (Remember the size of Caroline's brain and forgive her.)

'Madame, you also promoted your wig designer to oversee local land disputes.'

Caroline opened her mouth to object, but the herald continued.

'And paid handsomely for both, from the palace vaults. With gold reserved for war or a state of emergency.' Richard accepted a sandwich and looked at the half-queen. 'Gold that you have only last night given away to Blackwood.'

The last of the face mask fell away. There was nothing to say; recruitment had clearly not been the half-queen's strong point. The strangest thing was that she did not remember with absolute clarity either hiring Daniel Blackwood or agreeing to any of those decisions of state. She only remembered the old hag at the gates, with the horrible little box, who told her help would arrive, and then Daniel turning up with the giantess in tow and new guards later the same day. 'I did not know it was voodoo at first. He was such a persuasive man . . .'

'No doubt he told you the princess was at risk and if she strayed from the palace there would be great and costly ransoms and kidnappings ...?' suggested the herald.

Poor Caroline. It was all coming back to her now, like a regretful one-night stand. Her mouth quivered. 'He did mention something along those lines.' She paused. 'I never understood how he found so many guards at such short notice . . .'

'Prison.' The herald finished his coffee.

'Don't be absurd, the palace guards are not criminals.'

'They are remarkable at beating,' Toby added. 'And cursing.'

'Blackwood uses any resources open to him,' said the herald. 'I believe he meant the princess great harm with the voodoo. The hag at the gates that day, did she give a name? Do you know where she came from?'

'No ... It was all very odd.' Caroline sank further into

her kimono and shivered. 'I was not myself that day.'

Gerald gave her back a reassuring rub. 'I am no king and my wife is no queen. We are not equipped to rule a kingdom. We were never fit for such a task. Herald, what will you have us do?'

Richard thought for a moment. 'Remain here as gatekeepers until the king returns, until the princess is safe. Our housekeeper will show you how to attend the domestic needs of the palace. She will show you how to run the household properly. I understand you make cheese, sir? Well, better start rolling – there is no gold left. The lands surrounding Paloma are destitute, thanks to your spending.'

Gerald looked quite excited at the thought of a purpose. He chuckled. 'Yes, of course. We must try to do some good!'

Caroline looked faint.

'Marvellous,' the herald went on. 'Lock the gates to any of Blackwood's guards, and above all else: no more balls. You will have to earn your living from now on.'

The half-queen gazed out the window. 'Very well. Although you have to admit, I was good at balls.' She smiled.

The ham was finished, the bone given to the dogs, and the coffee drunk. Sir Toby and the herald left the kitchen.

'Herald, you are tall in character and give fine counsel.' said Sir Toby.

'And you are much improved without the powder and rouge.'

Sir Toby laughed. He mounted a willing, silver horse and tried to remember how to ride.

'Where will you go, sir?'

'To Alba. If what you say is true and the guards are headed there, I must follow and try to help the princess. Maybe I can waylay the guards and throw Blackwood and his cane off the trail. I could paint a very unflattering portrait of him and nail it to every door in cities where there are young, impressionable women.' This was as physically threatening as Sir Toby got; he was a gentle man and, before the court had seduced him, something of an artist. 'Truth be told, I am not sure what I will do, but I am sober and hopeful.'

'The un-aimed arrow rarely misses its mark.' The herald shook his hand. 'Amber Morningstar and William English would also be thankful for your help and your purse, sir. Without them, the princess would never have escaped, and they too are in great danger.'

'Ah yes, the entertainment, quite something. I will do my best.'

'God speed.' The herald looked pensively down the drive. 'Long live the king.'

With his shirt billowing in the breeze, a clear head for the first time in five years, and the knowledge that some terrible thing had passed – possibly his mother – Sir Toby left Paloma.

He rode through the curling gates and turned left, the opposite direction to Mole Hall, where Lady Annabel scratched a quill over a thank you note. He had little sense of direction; he had travelled in a barouche until this moment. But the man was observant. In Paloma, he had always managed to find the princess, despite her valiant attempts not to be found, by hiding in hedges or the urns of large palms. He would always find her, and he would do so now.

'This is all very exciting,' he said to himself as he rode unsteadily down the drive. 'I will sleep under the stars, fight in a duel, help a maiden in distress, gather firewood until it begins to smoke usefully, wash in rivers, and say things like, 'I have many miles to go before I sleep,' and 'Make it a double, no, HELL, MAKE IT A BOTTLE, MAN,' and 'May I borrow your sword sharpener? My blade is blunt from sparring.' Although this last one frightened him.

Sir Toby's good intent was strong enough to protect him, at least for a while. The herald watched him leave with the enthusiasm of a setter and asked the gods to watch over him. Returning to the kitchens, he asked Elvira to gather the household.

'I must speak with everyone in the Grand Mirrored Hall. Rustle up all the remaining food. No one will go home hungry.'

'Home? Are you sending us away?' Elvira's lips quivered.

'Yes. We are shutting up shop, closing for business, moving in a new direction; our work here is postponed until further notice. The royal palace needs a holiday; so do the staff, and so do I. And there is very little left in the vaults to pay them. The half-king and half-queen will remain and guard it. They owe that much to the king. The True family will watch over the estate. Those without homes to return to may remain here and help farm the estate.'

'Is that wise? Leaving those two here.'

'There is nothing more they can spend.'

Elvira sniffed. 'For how long?'

'Until someone returns to sit on that throne.'

They both looked at it. The throne was wide backed in burled ash, standing on four mighty legs carved into the paws of a large cat. The arms were bejewelled with jade dragons. It had a worn sea-blue silk cushion and appeared relieved to be vacant of Gerald or Caroline.

Elvira hurried out to inform the household. In the Great Mirrored Hall, the herald sat on the chaise longue, where not so long ago the princess had watched her last ball combust around her. He got up, stretched, twirled around twice, and took a few leaps and bounds around the grand room, until Elvira walked back in and asked him if she should dust the chandelier.

'Maybe a quick once over,' he coughed and quickly left.

Outside, he found a man called Watkins staggering about the carriage park, looking for his hat and boots. The crest of Sir Toby's family was sewn into his tunic; a mole wielding a sword strained over his ample belly.

'Still no luck, Watkins?'

'Not even a wheel spoke, herald.' For losing the barouche, Lady Annabel would make him clean out the kennels. He was not looking forward to returning to Mole Hall. He rubbed his head, and one of his eyes wandered to the right.

'Hit you hard, didn't they?' Richard observed.

'Never had a hit like it. Heard some violin and the sound of corks popping before coming around.'

'No idea who it was?'

'Brigands put a sack over my head. Very bad sort, they were. Couple of guards, I think – I heard their boots squeak, and one of them broke his drum on my head. They swore a lot and talked about their fee.'

'Sounds like Blackwood's men. Fee for what?' mused the herald.

Watkins scratched his bald head. 'Working overtime, they said, and driving to some tree … A purple tree? No, that's not it … Long word, three syllables, sounds like "pet tried hard".'

'A petrified tree?'

'That's it, taking that gentleman with the cane there.'

'Thank you, Watkins. Go inside – we are preparing tea. It would not be wise for you to drive anything until you are fit.'

Five minutes later, the herald stood outside the reinforced door to Daniel Blackwood's chamber in the watchtower with the Joseph brothers. He needed to see if the man had been hiding any further horrors, if he had an agenda involving the princess and this petrified tree. What they found inside made their skin beg not to be taken any further. It wasn't only the tongues in jars. Blackwood's chamber was covered in filth. For such a well-dressed son of a lawyer, the man was a slattern. Sticking out like a snowy egret in an oil spill was Agnes, the missing chambermaid they were all slagging off in the kitchens. She had been gagged by a black silk handkerchief.

'Dear heavens!' cried Richard. 'Hold on, my dear, help is at hand. What an earth were you polishing up here?'

The brothers untied her and carried her out of the stinking tower. Her eyes moved to a smudged glass on the table by the window.

The herald sniffed. 'Opiate, I am sure of it. Agnes, can you speak?'

She could now. 'I could murder a cup of tea.'

The maid sobbed her way through seven clean handkerchiefs and finished a plate of buttered crumpets before being helped into the first carriage bound for Little Snoring. Understandably, she was very grateful to the first brother Joseph for holding her with his strong arms, although by then she could have managed. The opiate Daniel gave her had worn off, and romance blossomed, folks, there is no stopping it. Over the following weeks, it ripened like a peach. I tell you this now because, frankly, there were plain difficult times ahead for everyone else.

Later that evening, the herald stood outside Jim True's potting shed and watched the servants walk down the avenues towards home. He looked at the lovely gardens. 'Can you make it appear derelict? Wild and impenetrable? Blackwood and his guards are no longer employed by the palace, and I do not want them returning to claim squatter's rights. I fear some may try.'

'Don't you worry,' said Jim, with a gleam in his eye. 'I'm good at foliage. In a week it will be a weed-choked and savage wilderness.'

'Try not to damage the foundations.'

'Not a scratch. I shall grow this palace a coat of armour.'

The herald looked back at the palace. The servants had done a sterling job. The stale air was shooed out, and clean, white sheets veiled everything inside. Bundles of sage were burnt in the grates to ward off evil and any forgotten guests.

Richard had folded up his herald's uniform and was wearing a neck scarf and feathered hat.

'Mind how you go,' Jim said to him. It was common knowledge the herald was not at his most confident on the roads, although he was too short to invite any serious trouble.

He waved and pedalled his penny-farthing fast down the Swift Highway into the mother of all storms, where he waited in a ditch for it to pass. There was important business to attend to in Alba. He had to warn the princess of all that Lady Annabel's driver had heard: the Petrified Tree, the kidnapping.

He had to be sure William English and Amber Morningstar made it safely to The Cat's Back to meet her; the voodoo would be wearing her down like an illness. And he hoped to God there was nothing in the ditch hungrier and bigger than him that would prevent him from doing all of this.

15

FATHER PETER

Father Peter floated over the Bigeasy. Below him, Landfelian drew itself closer to the fire and told tall tales of magical happenings. It was approaching Monday night, and the stars were revealing themselves.

Father Peter was not a ghost. He was not that old, for a start, although his hair and moustache were now a distinguished grey. He was floating because he navigated a Cloudbuster through the night sky. The Cloudbuster was an early form of hot-air balloon and his finest invention. With the heat from a small stove, a large piece of silk, a log basket, and the right head wind, anything will fly for a time. The trick to the Cloudbuster, what gave it the edge over every other flying contraption and secured its place in the sky for more than a few seconds, was its four sails and fuel supply. The sails were shaped like giant ears and attached to the main body of the silk balloon. They heard the wind and moved towards it. Other inventions could not carry enough fuel for long flights, but the Cloudbuster was fuelled by Yook poo, and there is nothing more potent for burning.

The rig itself was simple. The ship's prow was nothing more than a log basket lined in sheepskin and large enough to hold five fully grown men. There was a small armchair inside, a bookcase, and blankets for comfort. Father Peter had come up with the blueprint for the Cloudbuster by studying the toadstools that grew abundantly in his garden. Their bulbous shape and the effect of chopping too many into his omelette inspired the first design. It goes to show just what can happen when you sit outside and let your mind drift for long enough.

The inventor was on his way to dinner and terribly late. The weather over Landfelian was at its most ominous, and Father Peter had encountered fierce winds and fog cold enough to kill. These two terrors he found south over mountains he had not mapped, and amongst these, he'd discovered something that caused him to drop his spyglass in shock. The Father did not shock easily, and he rarely dropped things.

Father Peter saw a land of ice – a hinterland, clinging on to the South Realm of Landfelian. He knew bad spirits attached themselves to the weak, but land attaching itself to another land was new to him. What had caused such a place of shadows to appear was the question he asked himself and

Marmadou, the owl perched on his shoulder, as he battled with the weather. Muttering about climatic patterns and tectonic floaters, the Father was bottling up some fog to take home and study when a fortress loomed up below him quite suddenly. It shaved splinters off the Cloudbuster's basket with the pointed end of its tower. He looked beyond, further south at a snow-covered island shaped like a teardrop.

'No,' he breathed. 'It can't be.'

He had read about Tum before, but never visited. It should not have been where it now was at all. It must have floated off course or been dragged towards Landfelian by something unnatural, he surmised. From what he could see, a frozen strip of black sea had formed between Landfelian and the island. Upon this icy plateau, a fortress had been built. A fortress that did not warm the cockles of his heart. A fortress that looked like a middle finger rising out of a clenched fist.

'Great Stoat, who has moved here?' The Father dropped his spyglass in surprise as the Cloudbuster tore over the pointed place. The instrument bounced off Tallfinger's roof and landed on Selina's big toe as she was enjoying a quiet moment on her balcony. Her scream was carried away by the wind. The witch's toe lost a nail because of that spyglass, and Selina Carnal was not a woman you should throw spyglasses at unless you were prepared for something much larger to be thrown back at you.

Marmadou wrapped his wing gently around the Father's neck like a feathered shawl as he hurriedly set their sails in the direction of home. Neither the explorer nor his owl felt comforted by what they had seen. The Father steered his Cloudbuster away from the fortress, back to Landfelian, and straight into a frightful storm.

'Well, Marmadou, at least we are out of that blinding fog!' Swearing and soaked through, he squinted to see through the rain. 'Although once again, we return without the queen.' Minutes later they reached a break in the clouds and floated over an area of considerable natural beauty.

'If my memory serves me correctly, we are passing over Giant Country,' he told the owl. 'Dear me, we should have turned right into the East Realm hours ago.'

The noxious gas carefully collected from a heated saucepan of Yook poo puttered weakly. Marmadou flapped down from one of the sails and squawked, his tawny eyebrows as flyaway as Father Peter's.

'We are losing altitude?' Peter ascertained. 'How many Yook pats left?'

The small owl peered into a bucket and held up both wings.

'Two, eh? That should get us to Magatha. It's not far – I can smell her cooking.'

The little owl hooted and hopped back onto his shoulder.

'I am most concerned about that fog brewing in the south, though,' he bellowed. 'It's spreading. What do you think?'

Marmadou ruffled his feathers until he resembled a

gentle explosion.

'My thoughts entirely.'

Father Peter removed his flight goggles and smiled down at the land below, looking for a pair of plump hills, which were thankfully very easy to spot without a spyglass.

'There it is! Tikli Bottom. Thank the heavens. I thought that trip would never end. We have made it to the East Realm, my feathery friend. Lower the sails.'

Two soft green humps emerged on the darkening horizon as Father Peter hollered further instructions to his owl. He blew out three of the travel matches beneath the stove, and the Cloudbuster began a gracious descent. Two figures could now be seen on top of one of the round hills. They were sitting on armchairs around a fire pit, enjoying a jug of something.

'They've started without me.'

Father Peter was tired and cold and, worse, he was in the dark – a place he never liked to be for very long. The journey had only brought him more questions. The fog was not just an unfortunate natural phenomenon, but the work of a witch. A witch living on the fringes of Landfelian.

This badger of a man was Red Felian's godfather, and he lived in an ancient folly next to a meadow riddled by toadstools. Two Hoots Folly was hidden in the West Realm. It was protected from menace by old, respected magic. The West Realmians were generally a wild and windswept lot, and their lands were rumoured to be full of faeries. Father Peter ate much of his garden and occasionally dried, rolled, and smoked a bit of it too, which made him feel extraordinary and caused the tips of his moustache to stand up and smile. He was most often found in his study, inventing. He had an insatiable curiosity and found the lands beyond his home endlessly exciting. His grey hair made him look more serious than he was, and he wore small, round spectacles that perched on his nose without wires – an invention that had not caught on. From behind these, Father Peter surveyed life with a very clear, blue twinkle.

The Father's front door was covered by a number of brass plaques that read as follows:

<u>FATHER PETER BO FEATHERBE</u>
EXPLORER
MAPPER
INVENTOR
OWL OWNER – FULL LICENCE
FORAGER
CLOUDBUSTER NAVIGATOR (PILOT PERMIT)
WHOLLY UNPOLITICAL FRIEND OF
KING AUSTIN AND QUEEN PHOEBE
GODFATHER TO RED FELIAN
AUTHOR – NON-FICTION:
'Never Underestimate the Map of a Good Woman'
'The Nether Regions'
'What Lands Lie Beyond Landfelian –
A Cloudbuster's Guide … Thus Far'

Beneath these, a weathered piece of parchment had been hastily nailed under a brass knocker the shape of a woodpecker.

FATHER PETER IS CURRENTLY OUT OF
THE FOLLY ON IMPORTANT BUSINESS
UPSTAIRS. HE WILL RETURN SHORTLY.
HELP YOURSELF TO THE TOADSTOOLS.
MRS TWEED WILL PROVIDE TEA AND CAKE
FOR THOSE WHO HAVE TRAVELLED FAR.
SHE CAN BE FOUND AT MARIGOLD COTTAGE
IN THE NEXT VILLAGE OF BROOME.
GOD BLESS.

The Father and Red's godmothers had studied philosophy, miraculism, shamanism, the seven senses, spirituality, and astrology back when the kingdom was full of promise, discovery, and white witches. Magatha Guiler and January Macloud (daughter of the esteemed astrology professor Angela Macloud) were a talented coven of sign-readers. Currently sipping margaritas on top of a hill in the borderlands between the South and East Realm, January Macloud, known by the locals as Psychic Jan, had made a potato salad and crudités. Magatha Guiler only cooked moussaka, and there was one in her kiln, warming. These two women were enjoying the beginnings of a promising second jug when they spotted Father Peter's Cloudbuster.

'There's the old wizard!' cried Jan.

'Oh good,' replied Magatha. 'I won't be able to stand in a minute.'

'What a lovely jug.' Jan fingered the jug dreamily. It was moulded into the shape of a young male torso. 'How is pottery class going?'

'I haven't had that many takers.'

'Is that Mr Twigg from the village still modelling?'

'Yes, poor man. He's very knobbly. It puts some of the younger students off.'

Psychic Jan looked up at the stars and felt dizzy. If she didn't eat soon, she would end up in the flower bed. 'He's late.'

'But here now. He's never missed Margarita Monday.'

'He brings news, Maggie. I have seen.' Psychic Jan always saw a great deal.

Both women were completely whiffled. January wafted a hand towards the heavens and tipped backwards into the lavender. 'This batch is particularly tart. How many lemons did you put in?'

'None, but ten grapefruits. I found them in my cupboard.'

'How queer. Another sign.' January Macloud closed her eyes and squinted hard in concentration.

Oh dear, thought Maggie. She knew what was coming.

'You shall have a visitor ... an artist. He will have a kind North Realmian face and long, sensitive fingers.'

'The last man you said would knock on my door stole

the pony and trap.' Magatha laughed.

'This one will be different. He will stay as long as you allow, paint flowers on your wall, and take his moles off a lot.' Psychic Jan opened her eyes and gave her a serious look.

Maggie took a slurp of her drink and decided it was best not to comment. January was very sensitive about her dwindling powers of foresight.

They were both born sign-readers and accomplished in the skills of witchlore, although their abilities had waned since the disappearance of the queen. The women still saw signs but no longer understood what they meant. It was as if a fog stood between them and their sight.

'What of our goddaughter?'

'Heading this way,' said Jan, waving a moth away, 'although she will miss the moussaka. There is a man with her, delaying things. His name is ... Nobby. No, no that's not it.' Psychic Jan frowned, closed her eyes again, and put her fingers in her ears. 'Eibbor, yes. No ... I've lost it.' She sighed. Her visions used to be so clear she could tell you what you would have for breakfast a week on Sunday and who with.

Maggie patted her arm and hauled her out of the lavender. 'Don't worry, dear, the psychic part of you is struggling with the weather changes. I've heard it's happening across Landfelian. The condiments man told me it is spreading north when he came to deliver the cumin.' She smiled. 'A man, you say? How wonderful. She's bound to be late then. I hope he's got a good head of hair.'

On the top of Tikli Bottom, January Macloud and Magatha Guiler lived with a panoramic view of much of the kingdom. From their two ramshackle houses, each on top of the pert hills, they could see the curve of the Lake of Stars on the horizon and, to the east, the smoke from Alba. They slipped further down into their chairs and watched the lake shine under an early moon.

'Ah. The Monday moon never lets us down.'

Those Landfelians who found their way up to the top of the godmothers' hills came for solace – or a cure for athlete's foot. At least, they did in the days when the two women had visitors. Since the Great Vanishing, the people living nearby had grown afraid and distrustful of their eccentric neighbours. It was an isolated place, and there was a rumour that the two women who lived there were witches. They had bonfires on their hill and sung strange songs. The yokels did not understand that sign-reading rarely involved anything as dark as witchlore. There were some who said the disappearance of the queen was the work of a powerful sorceress and all those associated with being healers were tarnished with her brush. Magatha just enjoyed a fire; she found them very releasing. She was a practical sign-reader, unlike January, whose visions came from astral travelling through the minds of others. Magatha believed the natural world provided all the clues one would ever need to solve the greatest mysteries, but that few people were conscious enough to see them.

'I hope he is trustworthy, Jan. The girl has been under the watch of something terrible at Paloma. If only my letters had got through. The squirrelgrams that weren't captured came back, and the letters had all been opened. I get a terrible toothache when I think about it.'

'Have you been to the molar man?'

'That bluffer? Who knows what he'd take if I opened my mouth for long enough. My teeth are fine, although something has rattled them.'

'Do you think it's a sign?'

'Mmm.' Magatha nodded. 'Teeth are definitely involved somehow; I keep digging them up in the garden. At least she has Julia.' Maggie had sent her cat to watch over their goddaughter at Paloma.

A gust of wind scented with Yook turd, accompanied by the sound of a thousand king-sized sheets flapping on a line, dragged the godmothers back from a tequila-laced melancholy.

'Here he is.'

'*Hola, Padre!*'

'Jan finished the baba ganoush and we're on a second jug.'

'A thousand apologies to the cook,' a faint voice called down to them. 'I'll be right down. Just got to park this thing. Marmadou and I have had the most awful journey.'

'Are the flamingos migrating again?' Jan stood unsteadily on one leg. She had two, but she was doing an impression (which was lost on everyone). She pulled on a branch of wisteria to steady herself and fell over. Her glass was removed by a firm, tanned hand covered in semi-precious stone rings.

'Eat some bread,' said Maggie. 'You are not built for a second jug.'

Fresh bread, cheese-meltingly hot moussaka, and a tomato and strawberry salad had arrived at the table from inside the round house on the hill.

'January is feeling maudlin again. Hurry down, Peter, and cheer us up.'

'Dear me, I'm not sure I'm equipped for cheer tonight.' He rubbed his eyes. 'I did not find her.'

'We have lost our queen?' Jan wailed. 'I'm going back to teaching the harp.'

'It's perfectly possible she is lost somewhere foggy, and that's what we keep seeing,' Maggie said soothingly.

'My visions would still be able to see *her*. I found your house keys during that blizzard when you crashed the broom into a snowdrift.'

'True.' Maggie had tried to forget that. For five seconds, she had flown. For five seconds, the local children truly believed she was a witch. Until she zoomed headlong into a snowdrift concealing a small hedge.

Jan fed a little bread to one of the peahens clucking about her feet. 'The only thing that could affect my foresight . . .' She faltered. 'Is if the queen was . . . If she has passed over.'

'Macloud, if the queen had snuffed it, we would know.' Maggie picked up a strawberry and popped it into her mouth.

'You're right.' Jan nodded. 'I would see light - white light and music. A little violin, the sound of clinking glasses, elderflower spritzers. But this fog is different ... unnatural and hungry . . .' Jan chewed thoughtfully. She felt frail and cold.

'Get closer to the fire, old duck, and tell me more about this man landing on my doorstep.'

'He has a hero for a father.' Jan planted the peahen on her lap and stroked it gently. 'And a mole in his name.'

Father Peter staggered up the hill and sank into a deckchair with windswept silver hair. He was greeted by Magatha's brown eyes and toothy smile.

'Sorry I'm late, ladies, trouble parking.' Eventually, he had landed the Cloudbuster in between the two hills. The silhouette created quite a stir in the surrounding homesteads, who disapproved of the two spinsters enough as it was. Thankfully, the balloon had not stayed erect for very long. Marmadou slept curled within the deflated sails; the little owl had no appetite for moussaka and was tired from the journey.

Tikli Bottom was a challenge to reach if you were in a hurry. The hills' gradient was only just short of vertical. At a brisk walk with crampons, it would take a fit person half an hour to reach the top of either hump. This deterred many sales calls, tax collectors, and drum-beating guards. The godmothers preferred to stay under the radar and indulge in their more avant-garde hobbies – painting nudes, naked dancing, millinery, and primitive drumming, safe in the knowledge that they would not encourage the wrong sort of condiments man up their hill.

'Sit down, Captain! No, not that chair, it's got no bottom. Jan's gone in to rustle up some sort of dip. She's adding some of your dried toadstools, so chew wisely. You look cold. Shall I get my dressing gown? Here, hold the peahen for a while, she's very soft.' Maggie handed him the clucking bird and a margarita.

Father Peter smiled. Wild honeysuckle perfumed the air and lavender waved tall against the lit-up windows of Maggie's living room. He put the cup gingerly down and gathered the hen to his waistcoat with a weary sigh. 'I am glad to be here.' The sight of the round house, overrun with flowers, and its twisted smoking chimney soothed him.

His eyes were dim, and there was a tremor in his voice which had never been there before. Maggie suspected there was a bad spirit clinging to him somewhere. He didn't meet her eye and began to sway slightly in the chair. She watched the firelight lick over his face.

'It is worse than I thought,' he said finally.

January returned, with an incense-smelling shawl and a pot of tea. They all huddled close to the fire. Bad news didn't stand a chance against tea. Bad news needed airing; it needed sky, earth, water, and, if possible, an animal, and then it would simply become news. Bad news can become monstrous and overwhelming if confined to a windowless room with no animals.

Father Peter began to tell them of his journey. 'As you both know, Marmadou and I have been travelling the skies south of Landfelian, searching for clues to help the king on his quest. We have not been home for more than two nights together in the last seven years. I have the goggle lines to prove it. I have been asking myself one question: where is the queen? Why did that dear lady leave in such a hurry and without a note?' He folded his hands in his lap. 'My search thus far has been fruitless; much as your foresight and sign-reading has discovered nothing to help the king.' There was a resigned nod at the fire. 'Only enough blind alleys and false doors to shake a very long stick at.'

Maggie picked at a piece of crusty cheese. 'Apart from a few interesting bits of pottery and some grey teeth in my garden, there have been no clues. I have not trusted a sign for years.'

'Well, I have news. In the south realm, January, the fog you see is not cataracts – it exists. I have seen it. It is growing, and I do not like it one bit. I brought some back with me to show you.'

Father Peter retrieved his expedition satchel and pulled out a small hourglass. He placed it carefully in the centre of the table. 'Allow me to introduce you to the Fog.'

The godmothers leant in and passed around a magnifying glass. Inside the glass vial, there was a substance, and it wasn't sand. It was moving aggressively in a counterclockwise direction. It was thick, billowing, and full of shadows.

'Goodness,' said Maggie. 'Relentless bit of smog, isn't it?'

'It's looking for a way out,' noted Jan, her nose nearly touching the glass.

'Not a run-of-the-mill fog,' agreed Peter. 'And whatever it is, it's not natural. Nature would not create such a substance. See how it moves on its own – without contact with sea, sun, wind, or rain.'

Maggie sat back and folded her arms. 'I don't like it, and I want it off my table. It is scaring the hens.' The bonfire flickered. The hens had all huddled outside the cottage door.

'It is the work of a witch,' January whispered, her pale eyes magnified by the glass. 'Anyone we know?'

Father Peter looked at the two women. 'I may have stumbled upon her lair, although we did not meet.'

'The South Realm has been searched, every inch, by the king,' said Maggie.

'I flew to a place beyond our lands,' replied Peter.

'It is a marvellous thing that Cloudbuster of yours,' sighed Jan.

They stared at the foreign substance on the table. It was strangely hypnotic. 'Does it keep our queen?' asked Jan. 'This fog.'

Father Peter blinked and rubbed his eyes. 'I sincerely hope she is a long way from this magic. It drains one of hope.'

'But there is nothing you have not mapped in the

south,' insisted Maggie. 'Celador has been abandoned. The Forest of Thin Pines and the Misty Mountains have all been searched thoroughly by the quest.'

January looked at the moon. 'I had a fabulous retreat in the Mistys once – rather a lot of goat curd, but wonderfully peaceful.'

The hourglass knocked against the salad bowl. Maggie stroked her dog, a wagging black pillow of a creature called Animal.

'It's moving inland,' Father Peter continued. 'I felt it when I passed over Celador Castle. The fog is creeping in and hovering over the tip of the kingdom. I have met some wonderful clouds in my time, and this is not one of them. I followed it to find the source.'

'There is nothing past the mountains – your sails must have been confused.' January could not tear her eyes away from the hourglass.

'On the contrary, January. I found there is a great deal past the Mistys. I expected to find sea and nothing but mermaidens, exposing themselves in the wash below.' He chuckled.

'Brazen hussies. Are they still at it?' Maggie had once lost an old boyfriend to a mermaiden. She threw a few bottles of turpentine into the sea once or twice a year as retribution.

'I found *land*. The Cloudbuster took Marmadou and I high enough until we saw it quite clearly – a frozen place, unlike any other.'

'What is it called?' Maggie tried to imagine this unmapped place.

'I don't know.'

'Was there no sign?'

'I didn't see one.'

'No sign? Most odd.' Maggie frowned. Everywhere in Landfelian had a sign.

'It is covered in snow, with jagged mountains of black, uncompromising rock.' Father Peter unfolded his map to indicate its position. 'See, right here.'

'The Hinterland,' Maggie murmured.

A gust of wind caused the front door to slam and snuffed out the lanterns in the garden. It was suddenly dark. The peahen struggled to be free, and Animal began to growl. Jan put out her hand to steady the hourglass, but as her fingers touched the surface, it shattered. Shards flew over the table with a force that took their breath away. The fog inside hung over the table for an unpleasant moment. Then it rose like a phantom and vanished quite suddenly into the night, leaving them shocked and speechless.

In times of supernatural panic, Magatha was never speechless for long. She briskly clapped her hands and said, 'Oh, Sally off' – the most efficient way of telling any lurking spirits to kindly leave.

'Right. Who's for pudding? January, dear, you're bleeding. Must have caught a shard in your arm. Come inside.

I will fetch the broom. Hurry now, I suggest we go into the snug for some warm chocolate.'

'Wait, can you smell that?' asked January suddenly.

They all sniffed. 'It may be Animal.' Peter looked accusingly at the fat little dog.

'No, it's a familiar scent.' Maggie sniffed again. 'A mixture of frost and blood. I have smelt it before ... No matter. It will come back to me. Everyone inside – we have aired the worst of it.'

Father Peter struggled to remove himself from the chair.

'It's time for something sweet. A good plan needs pinning to the sides with cream. Peter, you need some sleep. You look like a fossil.' She looked at his furrowed brow and held his head between her hands for a moment.

'The king must know of this.' He clasped her hand. 'I will send Marmadou with a message.'

'How can you? No one knows where the king is.' She spoke kindly and kissed his forehead.

'Marmadou will find him. He can ask the eagles for help.'

She smiled. 'Well, if he does not return soon, those halfwits will claim the throne.' She helped him into the inviting glow of her house.

Father Peter shook his head. 'The evil is spreading; we need all the heroes together under the same sun. We need to open Celador and dust down the throne. We must bring him back . . .'

'We will.' Maggie steered him inside and spoke to her dog. 'Animal, keep watch. That fog lingers somewhere unseen, and it was not invited. The Sea Dwellers are the only clan who know what lands lie in the southern waters. They can tell us when this Hinterland you speak of attached itself to Landfelian and who lives there. I'll get in touch with the pirate.'

'The pirate?' Father Peter looked surprised. 'Are you sure that's wise? Remember last time.'

'He may be a piece of tripe, but he's the only man I know still in contact with the Sea Dwellers. Unless he's drunk himself off his own plank again.' Maggie tutted.

Father Peter's face softened. 'And young princess Red. What news? Is she on her way? Is she safe? I have written every month and not heard a word – Marmadou was terrorised by black squirrels.'

'Our goddaughter has made a great leap.' Maggie's eyes shone. 'I believe she is coming this way.'

He smiled. 'She always wanted to travel.'

'Well, now's her chance.'

Inside, by a flickering fire, their cheeks began to glow. January's boots, propped up by the door, toppled over and landed on the welcome mat, where a leaflet for an all-expenses paid weekend in Alba had lain for several years. Maggie gave the boots a stern look, and as she did, her tooth pounded. 'Boot down. Tooth murmur.'

Jan looked encouraging.

'The princess is being chased by a possessed boot?' tried Maggie. 'She has lost several teeth and is on her way to the Silver City ...?'

'Her wisdom teeth are coming through, and she is being pursued by a one-booted man?' suggested Jan.

Father Peter laughed until his cheeks shone. He dipped a spoon into a bowl of warm chocolate. 'I think I will stay the night. The weather is not to be trusted tonight. I dropped my spyglass in the fog and won't see my folly from my foot if I leave now.'

'Of course, you left your pyjamas here last time,' said Jan. 'Now, let's banish fretting over things we do not yet know. Who's for a game of inappropriate Scrabble?'

PART III

UNDER A FROZEN MOON

'With a little help from my friends.'
The Beatles

16

HINTERLAND

Selina Carnal waited in her fortress for Daniel to arrive. The longer she waited, the more she questioned whether to let him live or not. It was disappointing. The son of a lawyer had shown such promise at the start. Arrogance had weakened him in the end, as was the way with most men.

'Ego or true love; one or the other always gets them in the end.' She stroked the leathery throat of the skreeke at her side and took comfort in the knowledge that her voodoo would do its worse. 'It's of no serious concern. It is unlikely the girl will survive for long, although I will have to think of another way to tempt the king out of hiding."

Daniel lounged inside the stolen barouche, his black boots resting upon the open window. His hand clenched the cane at his side. The velvet curtains flapped about him dramatically as the barouche flew down the western flank of Landfelian. He had never dreaded a dinner date more and sincerely hoped *he* was not dinner. The witch would be weighing up the value of his life because of losing Red. He knew she would not be easily appeased. Why did everyone, even his horse, insist on running away? It was tiresome. He had been so close ... But now, even if he arrived on the back of a black swan, proffering a baby dragon in a cage, Selina Carnal would not crack a smile. He spat out the window and lit another cheroot. If he ran now, she would find him, and he would never have Red Felian for himself – a goal his mind and body were bent on. He would have to rely on his powers of persuasion, which had never failed him before.

'Faster!' he called to the guards. 'Let's get this hell over with!'

Tallfinger Fortress was unreachable if you were not told about the tree. There was an ancient highway that ran from the tip of the North Realm to the toe of the South Realm, hugging the coast. It was used regularly by Theobald's Carnival, who had camped along it during their tour of Landfelian, before Daniel put the entire troupe in prison. Now, apart from the odd merchant, it was rarely used. There were few brave enough to travel along it. If the bandits did not rob you, the fog would. Shards of it hung eerily over the neglected way, rolling in from the sea and causing horses and carriages to plummet to their death. In a barouche drawn by elks, it would be possible to reach the base of Big Blue mountain in just a few days – a journey that would take an average rider on an average horse up to a month.

The shackled animals loped through the night and into the next day. The landscape changed the further south they travelled. It became covered in heather and gorse, with the odd stunted hedge concealing a derelict smallholding. The temperature dropped and the guards' beards became stiff, their faces chapped. The South Realm was a barren place. There were no merrily smoking chimneys, nor signs for logs and hot cider in this corner of the kingdom, not anymore. Every seven straits there were piles of rocks adorned with feathers and bits of bone to mark the way. Tiny icicles formed along the roof of the barouche.

The witch's presence was felt here. It never used to be so cold. Daniel looked outside and, far ahead, saw her ghastly fog hover over the southern mountains. It felt like death sat over this part of the kingdom. The guards wrapped rags around their heads to stop bits of eyebrow and lip freezing and falling off.

Daniel Blackwood barely slept. He considered it a waste of time. Instead, he smoked, sipped a clear, aniseed-smelling liquid from a silver flask, and chewed on salted pork rind. The man thrived on the less wholesome promises of life; there was no brown bread and apples for this gentleman. He was only hungry for one thing: Red Felian. He thought of little else; she had become his obsession. She thrilled him. And the more spirit she showed, the worse it became. That young, breathless, barefooted heir was all he wanted. She was the stubborn, bright spirit he longed to obtain. Living close to her at Paloma over the years, this idle fascination had grown ugly roots. Daniel prodded a cushion with his cane. He had involved himself with a witch to capture her, and now she had escaped ...

He ignored the faint grumbles of frostbite from the guards and their murmurs of, 'We're losing our nostrils out here!' and looked ahead to his return.

After meeting the witch, he'd go to Alba to visit Flint's Hire and Supply and stock up on chains, finger clasps, and opiate. Daniel wiped an icy tear from his cheek and closed his eyes. The elks drove them forward. Hours passed in the stolen barouche, and it began to snow.

'The Frosted Straits! That son of a bucket's fallen asleep.' He was roused by his guards bellowing through a howling wind. They barely had enough lip left to bellow and kept morale up by discussing what they would drink when they got back to The Hog's Breath.

'Something dark and cloudy, high in toxins,' suggested one, shivering.

'Aye, and a nice piece of liver pie,' said another, a frozen grimace on his face.

Where the liver had come from was always the first question on the pub quiz. It was often that of the last foreigner who'd wandered in and asked for directions.

'Barry's got a new ale I might try – The Flattened

Badger. Leaves you trembling for weeks apparently.'

Blackwood's voice crawled out the window to them. 'If we don't reach the Petrified Tree by dawn, you will not have the body parts required to drink again.'

Reins slapped the elk. 'What's got on his goatee?' asked the guard driving.

'The witch,' was all the other replied, and all he needed to. Although the guards had never met her, they knew there was something that lived on the other side of the Misty Mountains and that it was not a school for young virgins or a sisterhood of skiing angels.

The wild yooks of Landfelian knew she existed, too. These elephantine creatures, with four tusks and hair like highland cows, roamed Giant Country and once also roamed the mountains of the South Realm – until her fog drove them away. Even these animals, with their fur as thick as thatch, knew to stay as far away from the pointed fortress as possible.

Selina lived at the point where mountains ceased to become mountains. Where they became pincers of hell, she built her fortress, and she made certain it was cold. Sneeze here and you'd see what came out land in a frozen pile on your boot. The witch sleighed when she had the time and enjoyed flattening the fascinated snow creatures that lived nearby. After introducing the word 'avalanche' to the surrounding lands, she was rarely disturbed. She fed the air around her with fear and glided about the ice in peace, sprinkling haunting whispers into the wind like blossom. Since moving in, she had only ever had two gentlemen callers, Blackwood and a self-exiled hero by the name of Alec Thorne.

There were two ways into Hinterland: the hard way over the mountains, which could kill even the most desperate of men, and the bewitched way through the Petrified Tree. Although, if you did not know about the tunnel within the Petrified Tree, you would just be some chump standing next to a twisted tree, and the wolves would get you as soon as dusk fell.

The Petrified Tree was not a normal tree. After all, what normal tree would let Daniel into it? A calloused, grey trunk was shaped like an upside-down turnip that had been recently kicked down the stairs. This unfortunate tree stood alone on the Frozen Straits. Its roots had been petrified, stretched, and hollowed by the witch to such an extent that a tunnel grew through them, under the mountains and up into a dark, icy land. The tree had a twin, and this sister tree could be found shivering on the other side of the mountains, a short, uncomfortable walk from Selina's fortress. There were few other signs of nature in Hinterland, only pools of black water and the odd ghostly figure of an animal standing frozen, hobbled by snow.

Both trees had a hollow. Animals and people could stand inside and take shelter from cruel weather, but if they were to lean against the wood for long enough and step backwards, they would fall, deep down into the hollow of the Petrified Tree, to a gnarled path below. Almost a day's walk from there, the dark passage begins to climb steadily up and into the hollow of the other tree. If you get this far, you are a very long way from Landfelian.

The bark of these trees was covered in wrinkled markings shaped like eyes. These lines were not the happy result of nature, as seen on the trunks of silver birch. They were the result of Selina screaming at the trees, for years, to keep a lookout for intruders.

Blackwood trudged through the snow to the great shadow of tree swathed inside a thick cloak. The guards watched their master step inside and then disappear.

Selina was plotting in her chamber with Alfred, who had the odious task of rubbing her bony feet and performing all other domestic chores, as her butler. No matter how long he rubbed, the witch's toes never grew warm. She snapped a delicately formed stalactite from the floor, hurled it out the window, and waited hopefully for a scream. Blind stabbing was another hobby she enjoyed.

The voice of Daniel Blackwood echoed up from below. 'You missed, by a small margin.'

'I need your attention, not your brain splattered over my wall,' Selina called in reply. 'Hurry!' She kicked Alfred out of the way.

He scrambled to his feet and bowed. Thankfully, Smoos were an extremely un-brittle tribe, in keeping with their environment. The sharp corners of Tallfinger did not harm them, though not for want of trying.

'Alfred, bring me the lunar calendar.'

'Yes, madame.'

'And some bat wings. For Lucifer's sake, I'm ravenous!' she yelled at him from her chaise longue, which was unnecessary as he was less than three feet away. 'And let Daniel in.'

The Smoo hurried away. Selina's voice carried out of the frozen fortress over Daniel and into the night like a threat.

Selina had been ravenous since birth. It was impossible for her to be full – something that had alarmed her parents when she was a child. It did not alarm them for long, however, as they aged very quickly and died. As their daughter grew, they appeared to shrink, until they became dry and papery and eventually blew away. Selina was outside collecting butterflies in a jar at the time and barely noticed. She had hair the colour of black onyx, but a white streak appeared the day her parents died; the day of her first death.

Daniel stubbed out his cheroot and slicked back his hair as the smoo opened the door. The witch did not smoke, as it was aging and she was the addictive sort already. His jaw ached for a drink; you needed something "on the rocks" before spending a few hours in this woman's company. His feet were frozen from the journey. He looked at his reflection in the cracked mirror, which stood up without any apparent support in the cavernous hall. All things considered, he appeared suitably sinister. Following the smoo, he started the half-hour climb up to her chamber and recalled the night he had first met Selina Carnal.

He'd been leaving The Hog's Breath, in the slums of Alba, and become aware of a figure staring at him from the depths of a dark-crimson cloak. The figure followed him for several days before approaching. She stood in the shadows of a black carriage, her face covered. When he looked into her eyes, they were disturbingly familiar.

'Madam, do I know you?' he'd asked.

'I believe we have similar interests,' she'd told him.

He began to walk away. 'I doubt that.'

Her yellow eyes bored into him, holding him there. 'For a man of law, you're rather good at bending the rules.'

'How long have you been watching me?'

'Since you were born.'

'I work alone,' he said, but made no move to leave. It started to snow lightly over the place they stood.

'As do I. Although lately I've been rather disappointed to realise I need the services of a man such as yourself.'

Daniel found himself growing hungry – it was a hunger that came from the darkest places in him. 'What is it you want?'

'Change.' She looked at the sky. 'Shake things up a little.' When she smiled, her lip curled up over her teeth.

'And what will I gain?'

'The very thing you want more than any of these hollow victories.' She gestured at The Hog's Breath, where he had been gambling, with one of her gloved hands.

'You know nothing of what I want.' He turned his back on her and began to walk away down the dark alley, before a single word pierced the night and his heart held him there.

'Royalty.'

He turned around. 'You have my attention.'

It was true, the witch had observed Blackwood from an early age. As a boy, he was neglected. She watched him torment the moles on his father's land, persuading them up to the surface before clubbing, skinning, and selling their fur for gloves. When he was a young man, she followed him to Alba, where he bent the law like an illusionist, using people's secrets against them to gain power and take what he most desired from them. He would remember every man's shame and their one bad deed, and he would use it to get what he wanted: gold, wine, their daughter, a silver-topped cane. He gathered accessories to his vocation: bullet ants, opiates, and a young giantess called Ophelia.

Unlike Selina, who was about as subtle as a skunk, and with little patience for people, this man had the gift of manipulation. Blackwood worked on his victims for years. He flattered noblemen and seduced the driest of society, allowing him entry into their homes and their most guarded secrets.

But he was unable to steal into the king's company and

the royal palace, to infiltrate the heroes' tight circle and get close to obtaining what he truly desired.

Daniel looked beyond the dark figure at the royal flag flying above the House of Gold, the highest point in the old citadel. 'Access to the princess,' he breathed.

'As you wish.'

Daniel considered the woman before him. He could see very little of her face, only the sharp contours of her cheekbones and whiteness of her neck. 'It is possible?'

'It's very simple. I will remove the king from the kingdom, and you will take control of the royal palace and all who reside there.'

Daniel was dimly aware that the air around them had dropped several degrees and the snow was getting heavier. 'For that, I will need men.'

'I am confident you will find them.'

Their alliance began. Daniel forged a letter demanding the release of the most hardened prisoners locked inside Hardplace and, at the witch's instruction, arrived at the gates of Paloma Palace with a one-hundred-strong army of well-dressed guards. After introducing himself to the newly ensconced half-king and half-queen, the rest was easy. Over the years, the two stewards spent Landfelian gold on wigs, balls, and anything he suggested was for the good of the kingdom and for the good of the court. The rest of Landfelian descended into poverty.

Now, as she watched him cross her chamber, Selina was

damned to admit that she enjoyed his company as much as the way he worked. She decided, then, to let him live a little longer.

'Madame Carnal, you look as ravishing as ever.'

She swung in from her balcony and glared at him.

Blackwood held his breath. What a sight. If Selina was an avocado, she would be black inside and full of threads. If she was a potato, you would not want her in your salad. On the surface, she possessed a fatal sort of beauty and appeared always dressed for a funeral – fur, silk, teeth, nothing else. Her hair was white, but not the white of royal icing – the white of a nasty shock, with several remaining black streaks. She wore it up most of the time, in a severe coronet or a very tight French plait, often with a quiff to add height. Every so often, she back-brushed it. Her lips were the exact colour of a blood clot. Selina Carnal was a portrait not to be missed. As thin as an incision, six foot and a bit more. Side by side, she and Blackwood made a striking pair, if you were at an exhibition for gothic satanic art.

'Stay there before my eyes melt.' It sounded like her voice had been spawned in the furnace of a power station. 'Satan help us. What is that poisonous odour you've emptied over yourself? No doubt some futile attempt to mask the guilt of failing me.' Her yellow eyes flicked up at him. She leant one sharp elbow on a stuffed yook and took a noisy slurp from her drink. 'Guilt does not sit well on your skin.'

He walked in and took off his gloves. As soon as he did, his hands began to tingle with cold. In her company, his thirst became unbearable. He tried to ignore the need for liquor.

'Can you tell what scent I'm wearing?' Selina tapped her nail on the yook's tusk.

'Something with a touch of musk?' He took a cautious step further into her chamber.

'FURY,' she hissed, which was hard because fury contained no 's's. Snapping off the yook's tooth, she squeezed it until a light dusting of enamel fell to the floor.

The hunger in her eyes caused him to flinch. They were not a farmhouse yellow, they were aflame. It was extraordinary, really; everything about her figure was sharp, as if drawn with a needle and cut out with a blade. There were no soft edges. Daniel considered her as very similar to a large fork.

'Oh don't look so serious. Pour me another, will you? I'm parched.' She held out her glass. 'Lots of ice. Don't get yourself one, you won't be staying long.'

As Daniel mixed her drink, a slight tic began to pulse in his left cheek. 'The princess will be found.' Soon he would be on his way to lodgings at The Hog's Breath, he reminded himself. The stinking streets would clear his head of the sweet Paloma air, and he would be able to think clearly. He had only to live through the next few minutes. 'My guards are searching for her. *Wanted* posters have gone up throughout Alba. The price on her head is enough to induce King Felian himself to turn her in.' He smiled. 'And she's alone. All alone.'

Selina stared stonily at him and clicked her fingers

impatiently for her drink. 'She still has that blasted horse.'

'A small setback.'

Selina stamped down on a beetle trying to pass beneath her feet unnoticed. 'Hardly small. The valien is sworn to protect her.' The beetle crunched unpleasantly. 'What happened at the ball has ruined everything.'

At his most charming, Daniel could be very convincing. He raised a confident eyebrow and smiled at her. He was not the son of a lawyer for nothing.

'Although ...' Swinging his cane, he walked towards her, and a little spark of excitement went off in the witch's left eye. She liked it when he tried to impress her. 'Your ingenious piece of jewellery is shackled to her ankle, and it is my belief that she is headed straight for Alba. The city is a slum of lawlessness. Not the sort of place to welcome a royal, not anymore.' He dropped his voice to a hungry whisper. 'The princess is entering a city that has grown suspicious and starving. When my men find her, she will beg for my protection rather than be lynched by her own countrymen.'

Selina gave a little dry laugh, which developed into a terrible cackle. 'I want her name to incite hell. Then will be time for a new lord of Landfelian. And no one will stand with King Felian and his arthritic heroes!' She grew excited. 'They will fall.'

'An age of discontent,' Daniel goaded.

'Yes.' She began to pace. Unlike a lot of women, Selina fantasised about civil unrest and burning flags, rather than a holiday in the South Tequeetahs. 'There will be few left who dare pledge allegiance to the old ways. The people of Landfelian are already turning against each other. The half-queen and -king's last expense claim did nothing to instil trust in the crown.' She had to admit, Blackwood's influence had been irreplaceable on that score.

'Paloma is in ruin. By morning it will be overrun with poachers, squatters, and vermin.' Daniel added.

'The queen will hear of it.' Selina turned from him to stare at a blizzard that had started outside. 'That wretched woman. I hope they stone her.'

Daniel watched the witch's face darken as she mentioned the lost queen. He wondered how the queen could possibly hear of it when no one knew where she was.

'I want that brat here in a week, do you understand? ONE WEEK. No more delays. The kingdom is ready to be taken. He grows impatient.'

'Who grows impatient?'

'You will know, soon enough.' Selina threw her glass out of the window and snapped her fingers. 'Alfred!'

The Smoo appeared at her side, holding a heavy-duty leash. The evening was over. 'It is time to go fishing.'

'Fishing, madame?' Daniel wasn't sure his hands were up to fishing. He could barely feel them.

'Yes, the princess is the worm, the king is the fish, and we hold the line and hook. Let yourself out, and don't ever make me repeat myself again.' She took hold of the leash and swept towards the door. 'It is time I fed the skreekes.'

'You haven't forgotten my reward …?' he called after her.

She stopped and laughed unpleasantly. 'Of course, the princess, your little obsession. It is clear I must bolster your performance … Add some competition, perhaps …' She swung the chain in a lazy circle and turned to the balcony. 'Lidia. Don't dither, dear girl, come in.'

Daniel looked at a slight figure that had appeared, crouched on the balcony. 'I do not need help,' he snapped.

'You have no choice.' The witch gave him a dead look.

'She will get in my way.'

'She will keep an eye on you. I am not a sign-reader. I don't stare at tea leaves and other such tripe. Should the red-headed one soften your will, Lidia will be my eyes.' Selina waved impatiently. 'Stop hovering in the window. Come in. The weather was good, I take it?'

The creature, Lidia, looked into the witch's chamber with twitching eyes. She neatly folded up her wings. 'Could have done without the blizzard.' Her voice buzzed and squeaked, caught between tiny breaths. It sounded like a hummingbird was permanently imprisoned in her mouth. She was lithe like an eel, if that eel were born a human. Due to the unfortunate circumstances of her birth, Lidia had grown no taller than a bar stool. Although, unlike a bar stool, she possessed wings.

She was not afraid of the witch or the son of a lawyer. Her master lived in the farthest corner of Tum, where a constant gale blew. A gale that would make your earlobes fall off and look for cover. Lidia had not known true fear until her master had found her.

She looked at the witch and the lawyer with dark, oily eyes, a nervous smile playing on her lips. Clearly, the princess had not been so easy to snare. 'The swarm await my instructions.' She swung one lean leg over the other and remained on the windowsill. 'Can we hurry things on a bit?'

'There's no room in the barouche for that creature,' Daniel drawled.

'Bring Red Felian to me, Blackwood,' Selina instructed. 'Don't waste any time. Kill whoever gets in the way. Lidia, kindly ask your swarm of spiderlings to patrol the skies over Alba. Help Daniel seek her out. He's failing rather.' She waved a white hand at the Smoo trying to pick up the train of her cloak in preparation for her exit. 'Leave it!'

In that moment, the witch's breath became shallow. Alfred had seen this look before; it came after she returned from one of her mysterious trips south to visit the new master on the island of Tum. She spoke in a voice not quite her own. Neither Daniel nor Alfred were sure who else's voice it could be, but it made them both uncomfortable.

'There is a man. Not a hero. A run-of-the-mill peasant. He has a scar, a whip that maimed him long ago ...'

'What kind of whip?'

Her voice returned to normal and dripped sarcastically. 'A whip, Daniel! Is there more than one kind?'

There *were* several different makes of whip, but Daniel decided it wasn't the time to tell her.

'*He may cause a problem. It's doubtful – I have heard the princess has a big chin and strange hair – but if she can persuade this man to help her ...*'

Daniel clenched his fist. 'Then what?'

'*If the scarred man chooses to take the role of the princess's protector – not for gold, or the king, but for ...*' She choked as the last word got lost in her throat. '*... love ... It would be a problem.*'

'I will kill him,' whispered Daniel.

'*You must not kill this man. Maim him, by all means, but nothing fatal. He may be useful.*' Selina stared out at the night. '*Yes. I may need him.*'

'Is a scar all we have to go on?' Daniel pressed. 'How else will we know him?'

The voice continued. '*He will stand apart from other men; half-angel, half-devil ...*'

Lidia bristled on the balcony. 'My master's only concern is the princess.'

The witch blazed at them. 'Remind your master that he should be concerned with whatever I tell him!' She smoothed back her hair and turned towards the door. 'Do have a bat wing before you go. They are delicious.'

Lidia swallowed in disgust. Her translucent wings snapped open, and her little body dropped from the balcony into the night.

Selina trailed out of the room. She wore clothes that were longer than necessary, leaving everyone with the feeling that she had not quite left the room. Yards of ratty gown wound their way out of the chamber behind her, like a train of black snared animals. She swung around with such force that Alfred, who was still holding her cape, became airborne and landed in a small ball by the door. He unrolled himself as a hedgehog would, rubbed his coccyx, and followed her out.

Daniel stood alone in the dark chamber. One candle flickered in relief. Then he moved quickly. The night howled around him as he hurried away from the fortress to the Petrified Tree, through a blizzard that was almost pleasant if he compared it to the last few hours. The tree was barely visible in the snow. He ran inside and fell, with relief, from Hinterland.

You would expect there to be a soft shower of autumn leaves, a merry rabble of robins, a rainbow, and at least one *WELCOME BACK TO LANDFELIAN* sign. And yet, the man with the silver-topped cane received nothing when he walked out into the South Realm. No complimentary mints, nothing. An old crow on a branch cawed at him. Celador, in all its cloistered majesty, was pretty short on robins at this time. The birds had fled north to escape the bewitching fog. He could barely make out the blueish light from the fire or his guards hunched over it through the frozen air.

'Are you dead?' he asked them.

'Not quite,' came a numb reply.

'Good. We're leaving.'

He lit a cheroot with yellow, shaking fingers, sat back in the barouche, and tried not to think about Lidia following him with her spiderlings. The carriage rolled over the Frozen Straits towards the city of Alba. There would be no tequila on Hoot Street with the spiderlings watching him. No visits to the docks and poker. How dull. That creature and her swarm; together they saw everything. The spiderlings would send word back if he stepped a single spurred boot out of line or if he tried to run from them all with the princess and the remaining royal gold. He stabbed his cane through the roof of the barouche.

The witch was unpredictable. Insanity was the least of her problems. To involve Lidia was out of character, he pondered. She loathed the creature – he knew this from a crude sketch he'd found in her chamber of a large fly-swatting device. This mysterious 'lord of Tum' she wanted to make king must have something to do with it. Daniel Blackwood did not dwell for long on the man who lived in isolation; when he did, his head became very cold and his nose bled a little. Not what Magatha Guiler would deem 'good signs'. The sooner he finished his dealings with Selina Carnal, the better.

Lidia flew fast and low over the Misty Mountains and into the milder climes of Landfelian. The soft breezes of the sleeping kingdom caused her to sneeze and made her want to screech.

'Hateful place!' she hissed. Her home in the south was very different – a nest of web-covered pine needles, moss, and lichen, deep in the Forest of Thin Pines. The forest was not popular with the few locals who lived nearby. The trees let in no light; any birds that flew in were strangled by the thicket. Strange sounds came from within, and the whole forest creaked unpleasantly. People hurried by at quite a pace when they found themselves near it. The acidic, sharp smell of the pines and the musk of something not quite dead leaked out. Choking the foothills of the Misty Mountains – at the edge of the kingdom, almost off the map – the forest never made Picnic Spot of the Year. It grew neglected, as did the creatures living inside it.

Landfelian could blame a lot on neglect. It is a terrible thing. For years, the forest was left alone. No one knew about it; no one stepped inside to say hello or heard the faint cries of an infant left there.

But eventually, someone did.

If the stranger was appalled, he did not show it. The man had tethered his giant horse outside the trees and trekked through the forest, following the cries until he found the small, abandoned thing. The orphan had grown in one way like the creatures of the forest and in every other way like a human girl. A little, stunted girl. He took in her astonishing eyes, her childlike body, and said nothing about the wings or the hundreds of spiderlings that writhed and nested around her.

A spiderling was not a pretty bird or an ethereal insect like a dragonfly or lunar moth. If you put a bluebottle and a spider together and turned the lights down, a spiderling is what you would get. Each black, hairy creature was ridden by a restless spàerit. These spaerits gathered information and passed it back to their new queen – the orphan girl.

A child left alone with the spiderlings. 'Another outcast like me.' The stranger smiled. 'I will call you Lidia.' He held out his hand. 'You have a very great gift.' He looked at her developing wings.

The stranger took her further south, and the spiderlings followed – she was theirs, part of the swarm and part of the forest. They would protect her. No one else would. She would not be the cover girl for the new spring bonnet collection if she remained in Landfelian; there would be no openings for the child to hand out mooncakes at the Lake of Stars festival. People would see her coming and they would scream. Not to say she was a horror; she had certain … *qualities*, but, like an unfortunately placed mole, people would find it hard to look beyond the wings as pale as bone that protruded from her back.

The stranger filled her head with such notions about her former home of Landfelian, the kingdom that had rejected her, leaving her to die in the forest. Before long, bitterness blossomed in the girl's eyes, and she grew up to rely on the stranger for refuge, counsel, and company. Lidia answered to him before all others, and the spiderlings, which had lain dormant in the Forest of Thin Pines for many years, became his spies.

Lidia flew between Landfelian and her master on the island of Tum, listening to the beat of spiderling wings and the hum of their bodies. There was very little she did not see. If you ran out of a bake house with two iced buns down your bodice, bet your bottom a spiderling would have relayed the news to Lidia. The skies over Landfelian were convoluted with eagles, owls, and moustached men flying about in balloons. There was woodsmoke and sounds of revelry and Men of the Road sleeping under the stars. Lidia loathed the sights and sounds of camaraderie from which she had been excluded. If it was not for the Lord of Tum, she would still be alone in the woods.

Despite her unusual shape, Lidia could walk the streets, wear a dress, carry a mop, and pass for a common wench if required. The only telling detail was in her huge, dark eyes, which darted nervously when she was amongst people. If she sensed them staring, she started to twitch. Queuing behind her, you may notice her slight, childlike figure, that her fine hair had a metallic quality to it. If it was a long queue, you might notice her shoulder blades protruded a lot more than most. It would be wise to stop staring at this point.

The spiderlings were brought down by two things. Rain: a spiderling could not fly in wet weather. If it was more than spitting outside, forget it. Once wet, its wings became stuck to its body and it fell from the sky, curled up into a defensive, brace position. Bigger spiderlings could crawl away when they reached the ground, unless a large animal trod on them. But it would take more than a light shower to bring down Lidia.

She flew over Paloma. In the aftermath of the storm, the palace was quiet and overgrown. Several Landfelians were outside collecting windfallen fruits in the orchard. They looked up and stared.

'That's a big moth, June,' murmured Jim.

'What's that, my lover?' They were salvaging the last of harvest before the weather turned again. Jim sensed a Long Wind was due. Billy got his quince collecting done so he could make the most of the empty gardens to experiment with his firebulbs. As he watched the beginnings of a Long Wind approach through the shimmery trails of smoke, he heard his father call him inside.

The groundsman squinted at the stars from halfway up an apple tree, as a lithe shadow glided across the moon. It wasn't the wings that bothered him, it was the legs. He made a quick list of all the moths he knew with legs and couldn't think of one.

'When the moths grow bigger than birds, something's not adding up right in nature's pantry,' he murmured.

Lidia's shadow soared away over Little Snoring, like a dark comet, heading south towards the city of Alba.

June lifted a hip flask strapped to her girdle and took a large gulp of scrumpy. She rubbed her back and turned to look at the palace. It was hard to see through the thicket of ivy and thistle that now swamped the approach. Dark vines crawled up pillars and sticky creepers covered the marble steps. The moss on the first avenue was sponging nicely; all the rain had helped her husband's top-grade manure. The Trues had worked day and night to conceal the pale-gold stone from intruders. It would be hard for anyone to find the doorbell through the ferns now. A faint light could just be seen from one of the bedrooms, where the half-queen and -king remained.

'Everyone in, now,' called Jim, hauling the last of the crates to the shed store. 'There is a Long Wind coming.'

June hurried Billy inside as the howling approached. 'I hope we have enough food until it passes.'

June's biggest fear, besides her sister coming to stay, was not having enough food in a crisis. And a Long Wind was a crisis. Minutes later, as Jim bolted the door shut, it hit Little Snoring. The wind raced through the valley with the velocity of a yook stampede, blowing in like a silent scream. Everyone remained inside. Standing up to a Long Wind was simply not done – it would be like waving a bucket at a tsunami thinking you had it covered.

Blackwood arrived in Alba in time to see the sun rise wearily over the smoking capital. It was Thursday. If a sun could look pained by what it saw, this one was. Two of his guards stood at the city gates. Their job was to check all arrivals and departures by mugging them. Around them the smell of recently beaten peasant hung in the air. A body lay groaning, not far away.

'Any news?' he enquired.

'Nothing,' replied the taller guard. 'No actors, teeth, giant women, large horses, or princesses come through this way.'

'And nothing from the bounty hunter?' Daniel narrowed his eyes, and the guards looked at their drums.

'Nope.' One tried smiling. 'We did rob a gentleman visiting from Engerlande.' It had been a good morning's work on that score. No one liked Engerlanders.

'Find them,' growled Daniel and swept on.

The smell of Alba's greasy streets drew him into its familiar, polluted hug. In the heart of the slum stood The Hog's Breath, corrupt and infested with wrongdoing.

17

GIANT COUNTRY

'Amber, I'm losing my voice! I may never perform again!'

William English was alive, and he was hoarse. His companions were more concerned that no one had heard their screams. They had been yelling for hours. The thunder of Hosanna Falls was quite a sound to out-scream, and the waterfall was winning. The rock they were screaming on was not big enough for a game of Twizzler, and it was getting smaller by the second as bits of it crumbled off into the river.

Amber argued with Will and tried to comfort her horse and keep it together. 'We are stranded here, and no one is coming to help.'

Will tried to be positive. 'It is very *refreshing*.' He opened his mouth and stuck out his tongue. 'All this wonderful waterfall mist.' He received quietening looks from everyone on the rock.

As night fell considerately over them, not a single living thing had passed by the cliffs above them, except the rainbow-tailed chichaws and one flying toadstool. At least, that's what it looked like. The contraption floated high up in the sky. Whatever it was stunned the marooned group so much they fell silent, watching it, and forgot to scream. They then had a lengthy discussion about what it could have been.

'A rare cloud?' suggested Will.

'A very large owl carrying a bucket?' theorised Ophelia.

It was a long night.

'It's no use,' said Will at some point before dawn. 'No one is coming. Not even a Man of the Road. Whoever wrote those signs is most likely dead.' Will kicked the cliff behind him and sat down.

Amber crawled over. 'We have to keep trying.' She looked at everyone and clapped her hands. 'I think we should try yodelling! I have heard it is a popular form of communication with cliff dwellers.' She smiled at them like a tour guide.

'Amber, you're in shock.'

'Shut up,' she snapped. 'We have to do *something*.'

Will had never yodelled before. He cleared his throat. 'Alright. We are not getting any younger or any closer to a cassoulet and carafe of wine sitting here. Ophelia, can you still speak?'

She nodded.

'Good.' He turned to the carthorse. 'I know yodelling will be hard for you, Marilyn, so just give it your best shot.

After three, everyone. Amber, will you give us an A?'

Amber tapped her tuning fork against the rock, and a clear note chimed out. The silver fork was a gift from her mother. She wore it around her neck for luck and, when necessary, self-defence. She never took it off, a thought Will found incredibly exciting.

'THREE!'

'YODELAY YODELAYDAY YODDDELIE YODELLA YODELILIM YODA!'

The cliffs were silent.

'That was marvellous!' enthused Will. Under the circumstances, it was. 'This time, add a little more DIDDLAY.' Will stood before them like a conductor. 'YODDELAY YODDIDDLE ... Dear God, what are we doing here? YODDELIAH YOODLE!'

No one yodelled back. One of the chichaws dropped something on Will's shoulder. It was wet and it was not a rope.

'Oh for the love of – !' He wiped off the bird dropping and sat down. 'We're doomed.'

'**Hellllllllo yooooooodel down there!**' a deep, boom of a voice rang down from above. It reverberated around the cliffs and made them shudder.

'Crikey,' Will whispered and looked up. 'Did you hear that?' He was on his feet again.

'It was probably just an echo. We're delirious. Sit down and take a break.'

'No, I distinctly heard a –'

'**Hooooooooooooow y'all yodel yodel doing down there, yodel?**'

Amber's eyes widened. Will was right. There was a big pair of lungs somewhere above them, yodelling. What were the odds? She looked frightened. 'Is it one of the gods?'

Ophelia stared up into the dark. The voice sounded familiar. They all yodelled back in a flurry of excited yodels.

'Help! Yodel, yodel! Please help us, yodel-diddle!'

'**What, yodel?**' the god replied.

'Must be one of the elderly gods,' said Will. 'Yodel louder!'

'Help us, yodel! We are stuck on a rock next to the falls! Yodel!'

'**Dear me, yodel! Did you not see the signs? Yodel.**' Maybe it was not a god.

Amber was very close to telling the yodeller, god or not, where he could stick his signs.

'Only when it was too late to stop our raft! Yodel!' explained Ophelia.

Pause.

'**That explains it! Yodel! Hang on a second, I will send down another sign. Yodel.**'

'What the hell is he doing?' hissed Amber. 'We don't need another sign. We need some rope. We need a nice set of stairs with a banister. We need to stop this rock dissolving. We do not need more bloody signs!' Amber gripped Will's arm and shook it until she felt better.

Looking up, Will was nearly knocked out by a piece of slate swinging down from the sky. Chalk hung from it by a string.

I am sorry about the signs. We tried to make them as clear as possible.
There have been several complaints and bodies found in the lagoon. Messy business. Do you have any rope?
My name is Erek.

Erek, the god, had tall and dependable handwriting.

Amber was busy gibbering uncontrollably. They were having a conversation with a god called Erek. It was the end. She sat down and prayed.

Ophelia wrote the next message as she had the biggest handwriting. Marilyn could not write, but her yodelling had not been bad at all.

We don't have any rope. We have a shire horse, a singer, an actor, a giantess, and a very large tapestry. Sorry to rush you, Erek, but could you get a leg on? Our rock is dissolving.

Up the sign went. They had to wait a few minutes for the reply.

Put the horse in the tapestry. I will pull her up first.

Will gave Amber a bolstering back rub. 'Our new friend Erek is on the case.'

They waited an agonising seven minutes in the dark and prayed that Erek was a man of his word with no previous convictions. After they positioned the tapestry like a carpet over the rock, Marilyn sat in the middle, looking pensive, as four ropes made a welcome descent. From each end swung a heavy-duty iron hook. Another sign came down too.

I am a weaver myself. A good tapestry is as strong as oak.
Tug when you are ready and I will pull up your horse.
What's its name?

Amber was not sure about this. She was not sure at all. A tapestry winching her horse up the side of a cliff of unfathomable height, in the dead of night, by the unknown voice of a man, or god, called Erek ...

'What if he's a cannibal? What if he EATS HER?' she whispered.

Marilyn whimpered from the tapestry as they secured the hooks to each corner.

'A horse does not a good stew make, my love. If he is a cannibal, he would start with one of us.' Will had never dined on human or horse and had no true idea about it. 'This royal cloth has not failed us yet, and I have never met an Erek I have

356

not trusted implicitly.'

Amber looked at him. 'You don't know any Ereks.'

'I knew one. Played a tree in a play once. A good sort he was, too.'

Will was lying. The tree's name had in fact been Edmund. But it was too late; the corners of the tapestry lifted into the air and scooped Marilyn up with it. She swung a few feet clear of the cliff and wobbled. Everyone gasped, and then up she went, up and up, until they could no longer see or hear her snorting.

After a few minutes, they received another sign.

What a tasty horse.

Amber slapped Will and began to cry. He turned the sign around.

Ha ha! Only having a joke.
I'm a vegetarian.
Send the next one up.

Who was this guy? they wondered. What a rescue. What a tapestry. What luck. Who would have thought it?

When she arrived at the top, Amber fainted. When Will joined her, he was silenced. Maybe it was the altitude, but more likely the fact that on this clear night, under a big moon, he was met by a giant. There were two, tusked yooks

357

pawing at the ground, but the scene was mainly taken by the fifteen-foot man who bent down and offered his thumb by way of introduction.

'You must be the actor!' he cried. 'It is my humble honour to be the first to welcome to you to Giant Country.'

There was nothing humble about Erek. He was too big for it. Will managed, 'Hello.' By the time Ophelia reached the top, she found her friends cowering behind the shire horse.

The giant man looked at her and his mouth fell open. 'Ophelia Butterworth. YOU'VE COME BACK!' It was Erek's turn to faint now. Down he went, and the ground quaked.

Ophelia smiled back with the look of someone cornered at a drinks party by a person she did not remember. She hadn't the faintest idea who Erek was. She muttered an apology and stepped awkwardly over him.

'What did you do to the giant?' asked Will.

'I don't know.'

'Poor chap, he seemed to know you.'

Amber came round and gazed mistily at the length of Erek, flat out on the tapestry. She stared at his solid, muscular legs and arms. He wore a poncho. 'He is the biggest man I have ever seen ever in Everland. Look at his feet,' she whispered.

Will was determined to regain some control over the situation. 'It's been a long night, ladies. Let's get the giant man and these large animals away from the cliff edge and back to wherever they came from. I will enquire about the nearest inn. We've few days left to meet the princess and are clearly a long way from Alba. Ophelia, do not worry. You are under no obligation to go anywhere with this Erek or any others like him claiming to know your full name.'

Will felt mildly threatened; height had always been his thing, but in an audition against Erek for the part of Beanstalk, he wouldn't have a hope. Erek was a mast. Somehow, between them, they hauled the giant over the biggest yook and climbed onto the other. The docile beasts fell into a loping stride and the lost Landfelians lilted down the cliffs into a green, misty valley. Other yooks grazed here, lifting their hairy faces to watch the strange ensemble pass by. Smoke soon sweetened the air, whispering up from a meadowland dotted with hundreds of yurts. They had arrived at the valley where the giants lived.

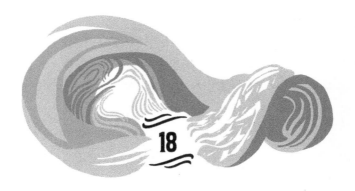

18

THE LONG WIND

Red Felian stood out like a healthy tooth in a mouthful of fillings as she rode east with the Man of the Road. And yet, due to the weather, she remained blind to the guards and the spiderlings scaling the roads and skies for her. The Long Wind forced both man and beast, guard and bird, and anything else outside with legs, to seek shelter, which is what they were doing when it hit them – and it hit them like a wall.

After ten minutes, every part of Red's body felt burned. She tried to not cry out, to keep her head down and trot on. It was hard; the Long Wind came at them from all directions, like bullies in a playground. She had already been kissed by an amphibian, drowned, died for a minute in a leafwell, been chased by one hundred guards, and been rescued by a man with unruly hair, who forced her to drink coffee that would stop hearts. The week was still young, but there was simply no room on Red's dance card for a Long Wind.

Her valien pushed on, his back legs trembling with the strain. She glanced back at the Man of the Road, and he shouted at her to cover up her neck. Her hands were so chaffed and sore, he rode alongside her and gave her his gloves. Red concentrated on her horse's head, bent low against the wind, and the man next to her – leading them, she hoped, out of danger.

Robbie looked nothing like the able men and women her father had elected for his quest. He did not have a sword or feathered hat. Instead, he had a set of kitchen knives. He must be a poacher too, for he had a bow, a handful of mismatched arrows, and a lunging whip. There was a fishing line sticking out of his bag, which contained a set of saucepans and a grubby sack of potatoes, onions, and other fodder from the road. His spare clothes were tied to the rim of his saddle, where they dried in the wind and turned the colour of the earth. The wind tugged at the clothes they were wearing, and she noticed a vicious scar around the ridge of Robbie's shoulders and neck. As she wondered how it got there, he turned around and caught her looking. Red quickly looked away. This man had not undergone any formal hero training. His skin had the sort of quality you only get from sleeping in the sun and under the stars. Although, he did smell clean – of land and heather ... Like Jim, but sweeter – a wet corn field. His eyes would glint green, dragon green, when they were not moody and bracken.

'It's not far now.'

'Where are you taking me?'

'To a friend of mine.' He paused. 'I'll tell her you're my cousin.'

'Your cousin?' she bellowed back.

'By marriage.' Robbie smiled under his hat. 'Cousin Mary. Mary Drew.'

'You looked through my bag!' Did this man have any manners? She would go on alone as soon as the Long Wind left Landfelian.

Red had never used the 'princess' card to get her own way. She tried to avoid being associated with the title completely. Being a princess only got her into trouble. But riding over the empty hills in the dark in a Long Wind, with her ankle pulsing in pain, she felt close to the edge. She was, in fact, a few strides away from throwing a complete princess paddy and calling the whole thing off. But she guessed what Robbie thought of her and had no intention of giving him the pleasure of seeing her weakened. So Red rode painfully on; her ankle started to weep long before the wind found it.

It was impossible to see where they were heading. She couldn't fully open her eyes into the wind for longer than a few seconds. Anything fully exposed would be lost.

'Who is this friend of yours?' she shouted. 'Can they be trusted?'

Robbie didn't answer; he wasn't very sure it was a wise idea to visit Maureen, but he was out of wise ideas. In fact, he'd never had one before and wasn't about to start. Of course, the lady of Boondongal would ask questions, but there was nowhere else they could reach before the weather left them bald and raw, in a ditch. White Sands was the only safehouse for many miles. Waterwood was behind them, but that was the last place you would want to be in a Long Wind. Dropping treetoads were a high enough risk at the best of times. Robbie trusted Lady Maples. She may have a vendetta against the king and be a trifle eccentric, but these days, who wasn't? 'Don't worry. We won't stay long.'

Red closed her eyes and spoke softly to her horse. A Long Wind could last days – up to a month, if it chose. They were not nature's doing. The winds began one year before the queen disappeared, after which they grew more frequent and more violent. Father Peter suspected the Long Winds were a warning of some kind. A message from whom or saying what he did not know, but the wind always drove through Landfelian from the south, with the full force of a cold and draughty hell behind it, picking up small rodents, clothes left on the line, chimneys, and carriage wheels. But worse were the tiny shards of ice hidden within it.

A Long Wind alert was declared in every town and village; bells were sounded across the land. Pathways were closed, travel stopped, the Long Wind flag went up, and the Long Wind flag was ripped off. The Landfelians whose job it was to raise the Long Wind flag questioned, again and again, why they bothered with the flag. Children stayed under the covers and were read stories about the Great Howling, an invisible beast that roared in from the south.

The sky was lost. If there was a dawn, neither Red nor Robbie could see it. The trees they passed sounded pained, their branches creaking as their roots clung on. They looked at one another as two yowling cats flew past.

'We should go faster,' Red said.

'Mm-hmm.' Robbie was struggling to keep up with the valien.

It was impossible to ride in a straight line; the horses struggled on as if running through wet sand. They battled towards the coast. Red clung to her horse, whispering encouragingly into his tense neck. Legs was a far smaller horse, and she stopped frequently to rest against the wind. Robbie's strength alone stopped her from lying down.

Robbie wondered if Lady Maples would be home. He could just make out a faint yellow light a long way off.

Whatever it was, Red saw it too and hoped it was attached to a strong roof. 'Look out!' she screamed and reached across to shield Robbie's head as a fence post whistled over them. 'It's getting worse.'

'My horse can't go any faster,' Robbie cried.

'You shouldn't ride her – climb on with me. We'll lead her.'

'Alright.' Robbie hauled himself up on to the valien,

grabbed hold of Red's waist, and wound his whip around his horse's bridle, who followed behind.

The princess' hair brushed his cheek. 'It's not far. Keep moving towards that light. I've got you.'

He certainly had. Red tried to relax, although she was aware of his warmth against her. Keeping her head down and her body as far from him as possible, they pressed on as the wind ripped across fields. She tried not to think about the fact that she couldn't feel her ankle anymore. She felt nothing, not even a twinge.

The yellow light grew brighter. It was not a lamppost, but the mast of a ship staked in the ground – the mast of a great ship that had wrecked itself on the rocks not far from where they stood. A lantern forged from thick, green glass had been soldered on the top of the mast. Inside, a sea-candle burnt low and constant. She remembered her father telling her about each of his heroes and how there was a different marker for every hero's land.

'It's the Mast Light! One of the markers of a hero of Landfelian.' She felt relieved at the sight of it and the smell of the sea. They were in the East Realm. This marker signalled the start of the Boondongal estate and the house, White Sands. The weather-beaten, pebble-dash pile was owned by a Man of the Sea; the king's hero, Captain Mark Charles Maples. The captain was one of the seven selected to follow the king and search the seas for the queen. If any man could lead a confident quest over the water, it was the captain. If the queen was offshore or if she was marooned in a spate of difficult water, he would find her.

His wife, Maureen, was still waiting for his ship to return as Red and Robbie made their way to her front door. She kept the Mast Light burning constantly and had watched the horizon every day for seven years. The sea-ravaged walls of the house were covered in lichen and home to thousands of speckled barnacles. The observatory room at the top of the house had one chair, which sagged in the middle, a soft blanket, and a small table for a lantern and brass spyglass. Maureen had rigged up a tray and hatch system for whichever member of the family was on duty – tea and water biscuits with fish paste sustained her through long hours watching the sea – and there was not a moment the observatory was left unmanned. Either the lady of the house, her children, Ship and Sail, or the servants took the post.

For the first three years, Maureen sent letters. She folded them inside empty wine bottles and sent them out to sea with her news. She knew the odds of her husband finding them were slim, but they were still odds. If they failed, her bottles might be found by another soul, who would pass a pleasant morning reading them. She received guests and rode to the city once a month to buy a new hat or novel. Her children went to school, and life carried on. It was not until halfway through the third year of the quest that White Sands began to feel like a mausoleum and the lady of the house began to worry. Not one of her bottles had come back with news. She would have been satisfied to find her husband's breeches washed up on the beach, anything to confirm he was real, alive, or dead – but the quest had vanished. No one had heard a peep. Income from the estate petered out. Eggs and kippers were replaced by seaweed broth and grape nuts. The dogs collected abandoned gull's eggs for the occasional omelette. Most of Boondongal's tenants abandoned the white-washed cottages dotted over the cliffs and went to earn a living elsewhere until the captain returned. Lady Maples had no choice but to let them go, and she could not afford to keep them.

Maureen had attended a farewell dinner with the other local wives and families of the missing men. The party drank red wine and dined on cheese soufflé, roasted duck and chocolate sauce, honeyed-roasted parsnips, crisp potatoes, and syrup pudding with custard. They pooled together what little they could to enjoy one last feast in each other's company.

'There has been no word.'

'We must wait. There will be an end to this.'

'The end is taking its time.'

'They will come back. Have faith.'

The sky was pale by the time the party left The Cat's Back Inn, gathering up their skirts, children, and in-laws and bundling them into carriages to return home. Addresses were left and one-thousand compliments paid to the cook, Mr Wylde, and his whisk.

Maureen Maples collected a seashell every day the captain was away and plastered it to the walls of her house. There was little wall left that had not been shelled. She wore his clothes, his blue seafaring cap over her dark, wavy hair, a coarse jumper, and a pair of fisherman's trousers. Her children grew thin and feral. Boondongal was a tired reflection of its former self, as was its mistress.

'What is this place?' Red shouted. The house looked abandoned.

'White Sands,' Robbie answered softly in her ear.

'*This* is White Sands? Who lives here now?' His breath was under her collar again. She almost sat on her valien's neck to avoid leaning back into Robbie.

'The sea captain's wife and family.' The house sat on the top of a sandy hill amidst three leaning Scots pines, the cliffs beyond dropping away. It looked wrecked.

'Do you know the captain well?'

'I know his wife.'

Red felt dizzy. Her horse was foaming at the mouth but still grunted valiantly up a sandy path. Soon they would stop and rest. It was not long before they clattered into an ancient forecourt, overgrown with weeds. A wishing well stood in the middle. The Long Wind roared around the crumbling collection of buildings. Looking up at the house, Red was not sure she wanted to take shelter somewhere that looked so abandoned and sad. Either side of the door stood two enormous green bottles, each of which contained sand and a beautiful model sailing boat. The sails were made from parchment, on which a skilled calligrapher had written the words:

When the storm clouds roll in, I would not
be caught outside without a shovel.

And

It is not gold you find at the end of the
rainbow, it is an old friend.

Robbie jumped down, grabbed on to a peeling pillar and yelled, 'Stay here!'

Red had no intention of going anywhere; one false move and she would be decorating the Mast Light. The wind shuddered against the windows, several of which had been boarded up. Robbie tried to open the door by throwing himself against it. Red and the horses watched him. At around the seventh go, he stopped.

'It's locked!' he shouted.

'Why don't you try the key?' She pointed to a large copper key inside one of the glass bottles.

'I doubt it's the –' He reached into the large glass bottle, tried the key, and the heavy door opened with a groan. 'Quick, get inside, these old hinges won't last.'

'The horses too?'

'Everyone!' Robbie reached for her hand.

Red ran inside, leading Legs, who trotted into the hallway. They had trouble with the valien. Robbie pushed the mighty horse from behind until he thundered into the flag-stoned entrance, his ears low and his nostrils flaring. As they yanked the door shut against the wind, something popped in Robbie's shoulder, probably a useful tendon. Grabbing a couple of swords hanging on the wall, he slid them through the door handles and leant against the door, breathing heavily. On the other side the wind wailed like a jealous lover. He pulled away the rag covering half his face and looked at Red.

'Anyone would think it was after you,' he tried to smile but winced at his shoulder. It was very quiet in the hallway. Quiet, dark, and a little awkward.

'Shall we light a fire?' Red sounded nervous as she looked around the damp receiving hall. Sleeping in the wild with a Man of the Road was less inhibiting than being alone with him in this large house. His eyes were bright in the gloom, and his shoulder looked wrong. 'I think it's dislocated,' Red said, nodding towards it.

'No.' Robbie patted it and his eyes streamed. 'It's fine.'

'Let me help.' She stepped closer and put her hand on his shoulder. 'It happened to the groundsman's son when he fell off the wall.' She pulled hard. There was a crack, and then silence quickly filled up the space between them.

'Thank you,' he croaked.

Her hands lingered at his shoulder as her eyes studied the back of his neck. 'How did you get this terrible scar?'

'I ran in to a whip, long time ago.' Robbie's voice closed the subject, and his eyes did not find hers.

19

WHITE SANDS

Red let go, her heart thumping. 'Is there anyone still living here?'

'Yes, they must all be asleep.' Robbie tied the horses to the banister.

It smelt of the sea. A faded family crest hung on the wall, showing a stork nesting on the poop deck of a beautiful ship. Red gazed at solemn paintings of dark foreboding seas, pirate ships, and one haughty-looking parrot.

'I know this house.' She wiped more grit away, unwrapping the scarves from her head. 'I came here once as a girl.' She did not finish her story – to be honest, it was no showstopper – because the princess then fell neatly onto the hard floor.

Robbie did not see her fall. He was busy brushing

his horse down. Her fetlock was hot and had a nasty graze. Over the last few days, he had grown used to the sound of the princess' voice dancing away behind him. The roar of the wind outside masked the sound of her fall. 'We need to eat.' He muttered. 'Then sleep.'

'That sounds like a fine idea.' The lady of the house was on the stairs holding a candelabra. She saw everything; she had not camped out in an observatory for seven years to miss a young woman with red hair faint in her hall.

'Lady Maples.' Robbie turned around to see her silhouette on the stairs.

'Kindly explain why you have brought two horses and an unconscious young woman into my house.' Her voice sounded like an oboe. She had watched them arrive in her hallway with quiet interest. Never before had she seen her Man of the Road with company, except for his horse and a sack of potatoes.

'There is a Long Wind.' The front door rattled. 'We needed shelter.'

'I am well aware. And the young lady?' The wiry woman walked slowly down the stairs towards him. 'Green dress, bright hair, strong chin. She collapsed in front of the portrait of Mark's mother?' Maureen stooped down to look at Red. 'Bleeding a little. How did you acquire her?'

Robbie ran to her. 'What happened?' He lifted the princess gently from the floor, away from the concerned nose of one of the biggest horses Maureen had ever seen, which, she realised, would make it a valien.

'I presume she fainted.'

'How long has she been like this?' He gazed at Red's pale face.

'A few minutes.' Two intelligent, dark eyes of ocean-blue looked at the bedraggled heap suspiciously. 'Who is she, Robbie? You've never bought anybody here before.'

'She's my cousin, Mary. Could you help me – she's quite important.'

'As opposed to your other cousins?' Maureen thought several things. *Cousin Mary, my foot,* was the first of them. She gave a shrill whistle and two sheepdogs arrived at her feet before shooting off as she pointed up the stairs.

'Bring her to the kitchen. The dogs can keep watch from the observatory.' She smiled and shook her head. 'Goodness, you look terrible.'

Robbie carried Red through to a long room with a dying fire with help from the lady of the house. A line of mackerel hung over the pale cinders.

'Cousin or not, this girl does not look the right colour.' She looked at Robbie and frowned. 'Do something with the fire and let me see to her.' She scraped her hair back and tied it with a blue ribbon.

Red lay on the kitchen table, dimly aware of voices. One of them she knew; it sounded safe, a little tired. It needed brandy, if only she could wake up and suggest it. The servants always suggested brandy in the palace when anyone was under the weather. The second voice she did not know, although it was reassuring, brisk, and deep. The breath of a woman who had recently had kippers spoke over her.

'It's a deep gash. The wind and the sand must have stopped it bleeding out. You are lucky; she would have left a trail for the wolves. She'll live. Keep this pressed to the wound. I'll boil up some seawater and give it a clean.'

Red did not like the sound of that. Where was the brandy? Her head throbbed.

The tired voice spoke again. 'Thank you, Maureen. Come here.'

'Get away, pirate.' There was quiet laughter of a flirting sort then the sound of a gentle slap.

Red frowned.

'Who is she and why did you come here? It's not my month – not that it isn't a lovely surprise. I thought Lady Hamilton was May?' She washed Red's forehead with a hot cloth.

Red was aghast. Who was this Man of the Road? What did the lady mean by 'not my month'?

'I was on my way there when Mary needed my help.'

Red tried to look as dead possible so that they might continue talking.

'You've grown thin.' Robbie looked at the lady of the

374

house carefully. 'How are the family?'

'The children are fine. Young enough to think this is all a grand adventure. Sail drew a picture of her father the other morning and gave him a grey beard.' She sniffed. 'At least she didn't give him a halo. I fear they will forget him soon.'

'Come on, let's have a drink. There's got to be a bottle round here that's still got some good in it.'

Red heard the clink of glasses. She guessed what kind of Man of the Road Robbie Wylde was. A gigolo-shaped one. He was a travelling, philandering, basket-weaving bandit of the worst kind, and he preyed on the lonely, vulnerable women of the quest. The industrious rotter.

Maureen paused to look at the girl on her kitchen table. 'Is Mary from Aquila? She looks like an islander, with that hair and those freckles. Fresh off the boat, I'd say.'

'From the North Realm, on her way to Alba. She's got a new job as a chambermaid at The Cat's Back. I am going with her as far as the city. You know how the roads can be.'

'You never told me you had family.' She gave Robbie a look that said, *If she is your cousin, I am the Queen of Engerlande.*

'Came as a surprise to me, too. She's a good girl, though. A bit haughty, but the city will soon spank that out of her.'

The first chance she got, Red would ask her horse to kick him, and then she would use her tennis racket.

'You've got good timing. Some of Blackwood's Guards

were here earlier, snooping around, looking for Princess Felian. She's run away from the palace, helped her set sail apparently. Rumours are rife. Left her fiancé and jumped out a window.' Maureen took a slurp of tea and looked carefully at Red.

'The princess was to be married?' Robbie could not believe it.

'According to the *Palace Times*, though unless you hear directly from the king's herald, it's bound to be some of the half-queen's propaganda. Your cousin does look remarkably like her. Look at the state of her dress. You could rear a litter of swamp wallabies in her hair. Covered in grime, poor thing. Where she will park that horse in Alba, I don't know ...'

Red opened her eyes at that point and smiled. 'He's a lot smaller in daylight.'

Lady Maples raised an eyebrow. 'Oh. You're awake.'

'It's a pleasure to meet you, milady. Cousin Robert told me so much about you. I'm grateful for your kindness.' Red did a passable farmer's daughter accent. 'After a good night's sleep, I'll be out of your house. Don't want to be late for my first day at work.'

She swung off the table with as much dignity as she could.

'Dear girl, you must be exhausted. Take the first room on the left at the top of the stairs. You must rest. We'll talk more in the morning. Don't either of you leave until the Long Wind passes over. Goodnight.' She handed Red a lantern and a blanket.

'Thank you, your ladyship.' Red curtsied like a comely maid.

Red limped past him towards the horses in the hall. She could not look at Robbie. Her face was flushed with anger. She unknotted her valien's mane and tail, cleaned out his hooves, and removed the sand from his ears and nostrils. Face looked sadly at some stale bread and a bucket of water that had been brought out for him.

Red stroked his nose. 'Just be thankful it's not seaweed.'

Her head throbbed, and she was experiencing a new feeling, which could be found under the word *piqued* in the Landfelian dictionary. Climbing the creaking stairs, she fingered the sharp wall of broken shells and thought of the lady living here, waiting day and night for her husband to return. He had no right to take advantage of such a lady. She did not say a word to Robbie. As she walked into a large, musty room, it took every ounce of willpower she had not to slam the door. Someone had lit the fire. Hot water steamed up from a small tin bath, and there was a note on the bed that said, *Curl up well, cousin Mary.*

She bathed her ankle in the water. It stung in shock. The swollen skin peeking between the bandages was a dull colour, the voodoo charm a sharp shadow that gripped her skin. She was too tired to tend to it now. She undressed, got into the bed, and suddenly became weak with laughter.

HYSTERIA

1. **A person suffering from hysteria may suffer fits of uncontrollable laughter. Sometimes this can be cured by:**
-   **A shot of vinegar.**
-   **A sudden surprise – a stranger kissing them, for example, or a bucket of icy water being thrown over their face.**

The Long Wind banged against the windows as she slept. During the night, she could have sworn someone was standing next to the bed crying. Red was used to people crying when they saw her. It was her face; something around the eyes reminded them of the queen, and some wept openly for happier times. If her mother ever did come back, Red would let her know that, growing up, she could have done without this. She opened her eyes and found no one crying there, only one of the house sheepdogs, which panted beside the four-poster bed and whined in a mournful way.

'Come on, then.'

The animal jumped up beside her, keeping her back warm through the night. She lay awake for a time and listened to the wind. This was not the journey she had imagined when she set out. For the first time in a long while, she did not think of her parents. She considered her future before eventually falling into an exhausted sleep.

2. Hysteria can be a sign of an infection reaching the bloodstream. Mild hallucinations may follow the uncontrollable laughter. The area around the infection will become very hot and swollen.

In the morning, Robbie knocked on her door. The sky outside was pale blue, and gulls mewed over Boondongal. The Long Wind had gone and been replaced by warm gusts smelling of the sea. The paths and byways were open for business.

'Cousin, it's time we left.' He waited, then knocked louder. 'Are you ... quite well?'

His shoulder was stiff, and his hands ached from holding the reins tight against the Long Wind, but after half a night's sleep, he at least felt almost rested. The door swung open.

'Very well, thank you!' Red rushed past him and limped down the stairs. If the banister had been up to it, she would have slid down. Robbie followed carefully, at a distance. Something was wrong. She looked very flushed.

'There's tea, bread, and eggs in the kitchen.' Robbie watched her. She was almost panting. 'Are you sure you're not unwell?'

'Fit as a fiddle.' She didn't look him in the eye. 'Eggs, how wonderful!'

There was a lot he did not understand about women. Wasn't there a part where they became flushed? Hadn't his mother treated ladies of a certain age with a similar problem? 'I think you should sit down,' he said carefully. 'You look feverish. Here, Maureen has lent you some clothes for Alba.'

'She is very kind.'

He sat down with a weary sigh. 'She is a remarkable woman.'

Red thought about throwing the eggs at his sleepy face, but she was starving, and they smelt too good to waste. She swallowed them down, barely pausing to breathe.

'I put in a dash of cream and nutmeg.' He smiled, watching her eat. 'Get changed, and then we should leave if we are to make Alba in time. I'll go and ready the horses.'

Red looked at the pile of clothes and chewed thoughtfully. This is how he came to know so much about cooking, she thought. From other men's wives feeding him. She pierced a mushroom.

'Mary, good morning,' the lady of the house said, coming into the kitchen. 'Goodness, you look hot. It must be the Man of the Road's breakfast. How did you sleep? Have you tried the bread? It's seaweed sourdough. Your cousin is a god in the kitchen.' Lady Maples smiled and picked up a piece of bread. She took a seat at the end of the table and wrapped a frayed silk robe around her wiry body.

'Sleeping in an armchair is not good for my old back. Give this to Robbie, will you? He left it here last time.'

Red swallowed a scorching gulp of tea and took the pastry brush.

Robbie appeared in the doorway. 'Are you ready?'

Before waving them off from the Mast Light, Lady Maples pressed a smooth white pebble into Red's hand. It sparkled in the sun like quartz.

'It's called a sea diamond. Take it, for strength. The city can be a lonely place.' She kept hold of her hand. 'Be careful there, Mary. Alba has changed considerably. I can't stand the place myself, but then I never did like people all that much. I prefer the sea.' She gave Red's hand a firm squeeze. 'I hope you find what you are looking for.' She smiled sadly and walked back to the house, closing the door.

'You told her,' said Red as they set off.

'I did no such thing.'

'It was written all over her face after she passed me your pastry brush.' She threw it at him. 'You told her who I was.'

Robbie started to object. 'No, I ...'

'Don't say another word. What you do with these women and your utensils is your business.'

'Well, it's pancakes, mostly, sometimes meringues ... She may have guessed.'

Red made a point of overtaking him. Reaching the end of a sandy path, they both saw the black, retreating wall of the Long Wind filling the northern sky. It was a forbidding sight, although the sun was high in the east and the air dry. It warmed her skin. Despite her anger, Red squinted happily at the sky. When Robbie caught up with her, he was laughing.

'What is it?'

His eyes shone. 'Nothing.'

'It's the hat, isn't it?'

'It's the whole package, really. I couldn't pinpoint a particular part.' He raked a hand through his hair and grinned. 'It's some disguise you've got there, Mary Drew.'

'There wasn't much of a choice.' She grimaced.

Most of Lady Maples' clothes had tiny barnacles living in them. For Red, she had pulled out the garments she had worn to the 'Clinging to the Wreckage' dinner, where they went down a storm with the other wives: a stripy blouse and a skirt embroidered with sailing boats, trimmed with a blue sash, topped off with a seafarer's hat and her riding boots. Red looked like a maid on a pirate ship. She stood out like a jingle. If Will English had seen her, he would have auditioned her for the part of Sally in 'Starboard Dreams'. Her hair, almost clean for the first time since leaving Paloma, swung in a glossy plait.

She was in no mood to be laughed at. 'You've got a nerve! Travelling around, flinging your *AT YOUR SERVICE, MILADY* cards and dirty tunics at a different wife every month. Well, don't think for a second you can pull the yook wool over my eyes, Man of the Road. I heard everything Lady Maples said. You keep their beds warm while their husbands search for my … for the queen. And I thought you were a gentleman! A bit of a sarcastic son of a beekeeper, but overall … honest.' She took a breath. '*Well.*' Then she growled a fraction.

Robbie waited for her to finish. The horses trotted on. There was a pause as they reached a barley field. 'Well, what?'

'I was mistaken.' She narrowed her eyes.

They turned left and began to canter. Red flicked her hair out of her face and tried to keep her distance, but he soon caught up.

'So that's what you think of me,' he began quietly; there was no point exploding without a good, solid build-up. 'May I remind you, Princess, that it was your family who caused this?' He waved at a forlorn little crofter's cottage with one roof tile left rattling in the breeze. 'Oh yes, BRAVE King Austin took his heroes away on a wild, seven-year-long queen chase. Those men are following nothing but the dying hopes of a mad old man.'

It is not a real argument until somebody says, 'HOW DARE YOU!', which Red did now. She stopped and tried to turn her horse around so she could say it again to his face.

Robbie had not reached grade five on the irked-off scale yet, but he was close. 'Leaving hundreds of families at the mercy of those dogs of guards, with a pair of gold-wasting cheesemakers in charge, WHAT A HEROIC SON OF A …' He couldn't quite bring himself to finish. The loveliest of rainbows whispered over the fields ahead of them. 'Your precious father deserted them, and he deserted this land.'

Red had actually forgotten that step-uncle Gerald used

to make cheese. She closed her eyes and galloped on. She did not want to listen to this Man of the Road anymore.

Robbie had not finished and pushed Legs to a gallop, too. 'Running a big estate is no long lunch and a quick once-around with the duster, *Your Highness*. Working this land is not like being at Paloma, where you and those wig-wearers sit back, sip the good juices, and powder your big noses while someone else sweats over a poor harvest.'

The nose comment was unnecessary. The princess' nose was in proportion to the rest of her. It was, if anything, a strong nose. 'There is much to be done at the palace ...' she whispered.

'What, giving balls? You need to *grow* some balls, sweet-cheeks, because your family's precious Landfelian gold has been spent hiring criminals to secure the kingdom for the wrong people. Giving the guards a set of drums does not hide the fact that those men are from Hardplace Prison.' Robbie ended quietly: 'You have no idea what it is like to live, breathe, and make an honest living on the road, so don't think you can judge me or my life .'

The word 'balls' still rang in the air between them.

It was left at that. The remainder of the clear, blue morning was spent in quiet contemplation. Some silences are magic and some are golden; this one was shattering. It crackled. It was passionate and painful. It was hell, and a little exquisite. They endured it for the rest of the day.

At a shady copse of beech, they stopped for the horses

and sat looking at the view from different sides. The Man of the Road and the princess did some serious thinking on this astoundingly beautiful day under a dappled light.

No one had ever spoken to Red like that before. No one had ever questioned her father's sanity or judged her upbringing. She had so much she wanted to say and ask Robbie, but she was struck dumb. She felt ashamed at her ignorance and angry at being criticised. He knew so little about her.

Robbie sat against the tree and took a deep breath. The air was dry and sweet. How dare she judge his living? What he did with his days, how he survived – it was his own business and no one else's. She knew nothing about it. So why did he care? And he did care. He did not want this woman to think ill of him. For the first time in his life, he wanted to tell someone everything.

A few peasants walking along the coastal path waved as they passed the shady copse and wished the silent pair well. Two farm boys repairing a dry-stone wall whistled when they saw the princess and doffed their hats. 'Aye, aye, Captain!' they called. Children played in the field around them, and to their left, the sea was calm, the horizon clear of fog.

Robbie yearned to be upon that horizon.

Red thought of her parents. Were they out there somewhere? Where would she go if they never returned? What shape would her life take?

The horses dealt with the silence as best they could by

grazing around it.

Without a word, they remounted and continued their way. The destruction caused by the Long Wind was a sobering sight. Thatch roofs lay in fields, like lost toupees. Displaced farm animals roamed around, bleating, after being picked up and dropped in the wrong field. Robbie helped a shepherd gather what was left of his flock.

As evening drew in, they arrived at the viewpoint, and Red gasped at a shimmering city ahead. She could see the smoke of many chimneys. 'Is that ... Alba?'

'Yes, milady,' replied Robbie. 'There it is, the silver city.'

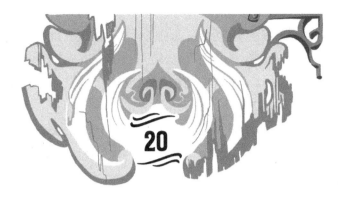

20

THE HOG'S BREATH

The city of Alba was not as silver as it used to be, but there lies the way of the world. It was still the greatest city in Landfelian. It was the one where they kept all the gold, flew most of the flags, and made the important decisions. It was a city that took itself seriously, unlike Kande in the West Realm, where almost everyone played in a band and wore attention-seeking waistcoats. Alba housed a citadel, an impressive life-sized statue of a dragon, an imposing cobbled square, and an opera house. The Bigeasy river ran through it, dividing the old, beautiful part of the city from a sprawling, smoking slum. The Bay of Brightly Coloured Boats lapped into the city's shore. If Bath had married Venice, they would have made Alba. Most visitors arrived by water; those that did not had to travel through the slum and over a bridge before reaching the quartz streets. It was known as the Silver City from the silver reflections that the cloudy quartz cobbles made on the waterways and the sea surrounding it.

Alba's citadel was built in tiers, like a cake, with layer upon layer of winding streets. Tall, pale houses stood within its fortified, all-encompassing wall, alongside hidden squares with lemon trees and rose-windowed Still Places. Two entwined leaves of gold and silver adorned the highest spire, where the House of Gold, the seat of Landfelian's wealth, stood amidst the other domes, spires, and fluttering flags.

The skyline alone had inspired gasps of wonder from poets and strangers to the city. But the smoke, stink, and grime no longer left the same impression. If there were gasps, they were asthmatic. Most of the poets had left or become gewgaw men. From far away, in a flattering light, and if you closed your eyes, the city still looked promising, boasting a decadent, if faded, glamour. At dusk, anything looked hazy and interesting. With the sea breeze upon her face, Red forgot about the silence between her and Robbie when she came to the outskirts of the city. They stopped at the start of a cobble-less road.

'There it is,' she breathed. 'Alba!'

Robbie wondered if she realised the smoking part of the beautiful view was the street fires of the scrapers. He looked down at the missing cobbles and frowned.

'How far are we from The Cat's Back?'

'A day's travel.'

'Goodness.'

'The slums go on forever.'

Red and Robbie started their way through the outlying area known as the Chimmeries – a network of shanty towns divided from one another by narrow waterways. It was then only a matter of getting over Fortune Bridge and entering the city proper. If they could do this without getting mugged and beaten, it would be reason to sing 'Kumbaya'. Over the years, the Chimmeries had become like a dangerous formation of wasp nests surrounding the ancient citadel. The lanes were no longer filled with trailing wisteria and pots of lavender, and waterways were no longer teeming with river trout. It was unwise to dip your toe in the water or eat anything that lived there now. Things with more than one head slunk below the surface, and the smell of cat permeated the walkways.

Red soon realised that right outside the greatest city in the kingdom was an ever-growing slum. The paths were dotted with large holes where cobbles had been taken. When dusk moved on, the sun ran for the hills; nothing lingered for long in the Chimmeries. It was eight o'clock, peak thieving time, and the evening was filled with the sound of pain and thwacking.

Robbie led them on, wondering how the princess would deal with the daily horrors of Alba. She had begun to act strangely, riding with a vacant smile on her face. He watched as she swatted imaginary flies away from her face. 'It's so hot,' she kept exclaiming. She removed several shawls and dropped them, obliviously, into the waiting arms of hags. 'I expected the East Realm to be cooler somehow,' she added listlessly.

Robbie was not hot. He needed a coat as a slight frost was forming on the ground. This came as a relief to the homeless. A frost killed germs; they could sleep sound tonight and not fear another plague. In many houses fires were being lit. The city had become colder over the years, like most of Landfelian.

Robbie noticed the bright colour of Red's face as they passed the warm blaze of a man recently set on fire. 'Look at me.'

She tried and looked intently at his ear. Her hands shook terribly. 'I can't see ...'

Robbie caught her before her head hit the ground. She fell from her horse and into his arms, full of fever. You could have sautéed onions on her skin. He struggled to both hold her and stop the horses shying away from small street fires. 'Hold on, we are close.' It took at least three days for the bubonic plague to kick in here; he didn't understand what could have happened.

They were, in fact, opposite the only passable stopping place and not close at all to anywhere good. Robbie tied the horses up in an alley where they would hopefully not be stolen.

He looked up at The Hog's Breath. He did not want to stop here, but he had no choice. It was the only place with rooms still open in that part of town. It served bitter ale and gristle pies to a belching crowd of accomplished thieves and bandits before they went out into the night to hurt things. The rooms were therefore cheap. Once through the door, Robbie tried to ignore the smell and steered the princess towards the bar. He balanced her against it with his leg and a stool. Barry, the landlord, watched them with interest. He had a wart with a hair on his chin that had been there as long as he had.

'Hello, Robbie, mate. Been a while.'

'Hello, Barry. Yes, I've been out of town …'

'Moved up in the world, have you?'

'Not exactly.'

'No need to go any further, boyo.' Grinning suggestively at Red's damp blouse, Barry rubbed down his bar rather vigorously with a grey smelly cloth. 'I've got just the room for you and this little strumpet. She looks expensive – did you get her down at Madame Mim's place?'

'Not this one.'

'Nah, thought not. They're all trolls there.' He winked at Red. 'What can I get you? We now do sharing platters of offal, and Sarah can make coffee.'

There was nothing about The Hog's Breath that summoned up the casual sophistication of a café. No musicians tooted discreetly away in a corner, and there was not a cappuccino or mille-feuille in sight. There was froth, though, plenty of froth – froth at the sides of Barry's mouth, swimming along the gutter outside, and floating on the tops of glasses, like whisked bone marrow. Barry liked to think of his home as being more than an inn for outlaws, so he'd added the word 'cafe' after overhearing a foreign gentleman describe one in Fronze.

As her nose became aware of her surroundings, Red began to sway.

'Are there any of Blackwood's Guards on your books, Barry?' asked Robbie. 'I'd like to keep a low profile tonight. Didn't pay my horse tax last month; not on their Christmas list, if you know what I mean.' Robbie pulled his hat a little further down and looked cagily around the room. 'We just need a room for a night.'

'Say no more, mate, say no more! MUM'S THE WORD!'

Robbie wished Barry would stop shouting.

'Those drunkards don't come by this early. Got a room at the back with a bath, for you and the little strawberry cream here. Looks like she needs a good dunk in the tinny.'

Robbie lifted Red away just before her head landed in a bowl of dry roast maggots moonlighting as peanuts.

'Thank you, Barry.' He threw a ruby across the bar without thinking. It shone in the air like the last pure thing in a dirty world. A few men looked up from their drinking to watch it catch the light. The room went quiet.

Barry's eyebrows reached his hairline as he handed over a rusty key. 'Pay your bill and it's all the same to me.' He pocketed the jewel quickly. 'One more thing, purely regulation, you understand … Are the two of you related?'

'Far from it.'

'Well then, enjoy your stay at The Hog!' He fingered what might have been gristle stuck in his back molar and smirked at Robbie. 'Sarah! Hot water for Room Thirteen and a bottle of our finest.'

Robbie stumbled up the stairs and felt his shoulder twang again. 'Whatever they say about princesses being full of grace and light is absolute buckweed,' he mumbled to himself as he heaved her onto the bed.

Room Thirteen was a pit worse than he could have possibly imagined. Cockroaches would sue. There wasn't much in it between Red's general appearance and their lodgings. She was shaking uncontrollably, her eyes big and dark, darting between him and some interesting damp marks on the ceiling.

'My feet,' she cried. 'Please, they burn!'

'Shh.' He wiped the slick of her hair from her face. 'Christ.' Her skin was boiling up like caramel. Nursing wasn't Robbie's area; he had no idea what to do. They were in an armpit of a brothel, where the stains alone could kill her. Nothing was clean, and it all smelt of death.

There was a knock at the door. 'No room service, thank you!' he shouted.

'Hot water.'

Robbie opened the door to Sarah, Barry's long-suffering wife, who had a moustache and a kind smile.

'Thank you, Sarah. Could I bother you for something clean – anything at all?'

'I washed a sock today. I'll get that.'

'Great, thanks.' Robbie was so grateful he hugged her.

He closed the door and started by taking off Red's boots. He saw the problem immediately, and the problem saw him and snarled. It stared at him from what was left of her ankle. The voodoo charm, it's teeth black and sharp. The smell of infection took up most of the room. He stared at the throbbing, raw, blistered mess, which was edged with some nasty-looking green gunge.

He looked at Red's face. 'How long has it been like this?'

Her eyes struggled to focus on him, and she moaned. There was a second knock at the door.

'NO, THANK YOU.'

'Sock for you.'

'Thank you.'

Barry's wife hovered outside and wondered what else she could bring the Man of the Road to get another hug.

Robbie locked the door once she had gone and tried not to be sick. 'Why didn't you say something?' he yelled, which was no good as she was unconscious. How could he have missed that her ankle was in such a mess? She must have been feeling the pain for days. He had to start being more useful. He rolled his sleeves up, washed his hands, and tore up the sock. People tore rags up and tied them just above the wound, didn't they? He was sure he'd seen that. Before they amputated ...

Red could no longer remember how to spell the word

'ouch', let alone yell it. A stoic voice in her head told her to think of schnitzel with noodles as she floated up and out of her body. She looked down, watching the man with unruly hair and tanned hands attend to her sorry foot.

Robbie did his best to move the cursed teeth away from the damaged skin. He soaked the rags in what he prayed was boiled water and added some salt. 'This might sting a bit.' He held the cloth firmly around her ankle. She flared back into consciousness and screamed so hard Robbie gave her his sleeve to bite down on.

Face whinnied in the alley below and tried to kick through the wall.

Barry short-changed a customer for a pint of tepid water with aspirations to be beer and looked up at the ceiling. 'Newlyweds!' he explained to the bar.

His wife banged out the pastry for another batch of gristly pies.

Outside, it grew late and dangerous. Blackwood's Guards approached the door of The Hog's Breath to drink. They were followed by a man with a silver-topped cane and two frostbitten guards thirsty for a barrel of the new ale and a seat by the fire.

'Any arrivals?' The man with the cane lingered over Barry's face and sniffed. He narrowed his eyes at the landlord. 'Is that garlic? It smells like a Man of the Road in here.'

'Nah, mate! Saw your poster – only princess I got on the premises is Mitzy. Other than that, just a couple of newlyweds from the country, very poor and full of lice.'

Mitzy, Barry's dog, a Landfelian Pekinese, continued to bark at Blackwood. He turned to sit at a table in a dim corner and lit a cheroot, sipping a clear, blue liquid that splintered the glass. Mrs Barry dropped her tray when she saw him and hurried back into the kitchens. 'Oh dear,' she whispered. The son of a lawyer had returned to Alba.

Upstairs, Robbie was doing his best, and Room Thirteen was not being supportive. After cleaning up her ankle as best he could, he tried to keep the princess semi-conscious by talking to her.

'Live until sunrise, do you hear me? That's all. It's not long. Don't die on my watch – your horse will trample me and your father will have me killed.' He looked at her. 'And it would be darn right selfish of you.' An eye flickered. 'You're missing this beautiful room and the start of a promising Friday night in the city.'

He forced a little water down her, which she sweated out seconds later. As the rest of the night and much of the next day wore on, Robbie drank from a bottle labelled *Barry's Finist* and gave her some for the pain. He opened the greasy windows to let the air in. It wasn't fresh, but it was cold, which was an improvement. On and on he talked to her. He explained his theories on efficient estate running and how to milk a cow without pinching it and then getting kicked, as well as how to use a mildly different milking technique on a goat and an entirely different approach with an almond. Why marriage was not for him. His failsafe top five suppers to get a bed for the night – 'Cheese omelette followed by coffee with cream and whisky never fails.' His plans to journey to the foreign lands, to places where they dip snails in garlic and butter. By dawn on Sunday, he was flagging for anything left to say. The shadow of teeth around her ankle remained; it had spread all over her. Robbie knew if the princess were to live another day, the teeth had to be removed.

Red dreamt she was back at Paloma turning compost with Jim, surrounded by apple and cherry blossom. She yearned for the sweet scent of the gardens and the sounds of birds. One afternoon, Jim had leant back on his rake and given her some advice.

'You're going to need a bandit.'

'A what?'

'A bandit, Princess – for the road. A bodyguard, a heavy, a wingman, a loose cannon, a loyal defender, a strong heart, a helping hand. You know, one of those Man-of-the-Road types.'

'What for?'

'Elbow grease. To carry the heavy bags, change your horse's shoe, watch your back … and sometimes your front.'

'All I need is my valien,' Red had assured him. 'In any case, I can change his shoe.'

Jim smiled and picked up his rake. She was stubborn as a dock root. 'Aye, you have your horse, but someday you might want an extra pair of hands. Someone to talk back to you.' He paused and looked at her. 'To help, milady. No one is unbreakable.'

She had carried on digging. It was hard going. There were root vegetables tied to her wrists and ankles to increase her strength for the great escape.

'Swimming for hours in the lake, riding, running – it's too much, milady. Give yourself a chance to rest. Pause for a moment and lay in the blossom. And when you're on that road …' Jim waved towards the fields beyond the river '… accept help when it's offered.' He took the spade gently from her. 'It won't go away, you know, missing your folks. No matter how tired you make yourself.'

'It's important to be strong when the time comes to run.' She stared at the marrow tied to her arm. 'I need to withstand days on the road against the voodoo. I'll stop once I find them.' She looked at her feet and wiped her nose.

Jim handed her a muddy handkerchief. 'I didn't mean to upset you. I worry, that's all. You're too young for such a burden. Try to keep your eyes open to the life around you and enjoy it a little.'

'I'll try.' She could not imagine waking up with her mind free of worry. But if the quest never returned, she would have to try.

For two nights in The Hog's Breath, Robbie got no sleep. He was becoming accustomed to sleeping beside the princess, and it was not as fun as he had imagined. And he *had* imagined. He mentally wrote down what sleep was so that when he found it again, he would recognise and enjoy it.

The sun rose reluctantly over Alba as if forced to kiss a very smelly uncle. As the sky grew light, Robbie stood up and glanced out the window. Most people in the Chimmeries were still working hard at being drunk – when you lived in their neighbourhood, it was better not to wake up sober – but the path to the bridge was empty. Well, almost empty; a few tramps were setting up tramp stalls and a fight was about to break out for the best position. Inside The Hog's Breath, all was quiet, except for some loud snoring from Barry. If Robbie could get them inside the citadel before the guard's woke up, they were home free.

'Okay, cousin Mary, rise and shine. It is time we got you out of this hole.'

Red blinked painfully.

'Put your hand around my neck. Try to look conscious and happy. We are newlyweds.'

She moaned as he lifted her up and sagged against his chest. Her skin burnt brightly. 'I can't.'

'You can.'

'Actor. Sundown. English.' She frowned, trying to make

sense of the nagging thoughts in her head.

Robbie promised the heavens he'd pay all his taxes and make regular donations to Alba's donkey sanctuary if they got through the next ten minutes. 'Yes, we're on our way to him.'

She tried to stand, buckled, and cried out as the cold floor made contact with her ankle. Robbie put his hand over her mouth before she screamed.

'I know it hurts. Hold on.' He covered her legs and the offending bloodstains with his coat and gently picked her up. 'We'll do this the old-fashioned way'.

Outside, a door banged. There was a grunt. The Hog's Breath was stirring, with the sound of hoicking gullets. Whatever stayed there during the night would soon be demanding breakfast – and a bloody nose if they didn't get it sharpish.

Robbie crept out the door. Red lolled against him, the captain's hat covering up her damp scarlet hair. He sighed as he carried her. He was now very familiar with her weight. 'Come on, highness, let's go.'

The stairs creaked. The bar was empty, and the curtains were closed. A ball of dirty grey fluff was fast asleep by the door; Barry's dog growled in its sleep. Every floorboard that could have squeaked did as Robbie made for the door. The floorboards, like the stairs, had one job to do, and they were bloody well going to do it. Four guards were slumped at a table, drooling out the night's excesses, a couple of feet away. Robbie tip-toed, which was hard while carrying another person, but he made it to the door. The door wailed as it opened, and the dim light of an overcast morning greeted them. There was smoke in the air.

Sadly, Red chose this moment to shout out a delirious, 'NO!'

Mitzy opened one gluey eye and bared her teeth at them.

Robbie took a deep breath and stepped outside. The door slammed behind him – an award-winning slam. Red's feet knocked against it, sending her into the bright hold of pain once again.

Mitzy began to throw herself bodily against the door, baring her fangs at the couple creeping away down the street.

A guard stirred and yelled 'SOMEBODY KILL THAT DOG!' before falling back to sleep.

Before sunrise, Fortune Bridge was manned by Alba City Guards. These were not the drum-beating kind, they were a far nicer breed. Alba Guards were family men who enjoyed boules and the occasional smoke of a pipe. They volunteered for the job mainly for the free sword and the pale blue uniform embroidered with the crest of King Felian. There was no one else on the bridge; the toast sellers were not yet awake. Robbie rode the valien towards the two men. covering the horses coat covered with a blanket. Red lay asleep against his chest, and Legs followed innocently behind. He gave the guards his most laid-back smile. Behind the guards, the old citadel stood like a stately gentleman from another time, tantalisingly close, the other side of the water.

'Good morning, good sirs.'

Two ruddy faces saluted him, in slightly frayed blue and silver tunics. Their swords rested by their sides.

'Good morning to you, sir. Isn't it a beauty? An even, grey sky, few corpses clogging up the river, a gentle mist, and the city alive with the sound of music.'

Robbie strained to listen. There was a sound, but it was not music; it was groaning and something gushing out.

Alba Guards were good at welcomes. They got a small commission for every visitor they persuaded to pay the toll and enter the citadel, so it was worth their while to dust each welcome with icing sugar. The toll had arrived with the half-king and half-queen at the suggestion of their security advisor, Daniel Blackwood.

'I am afraid I must ask you to dismount, sir. We need to see permits and identification. Regulations from the palace, you understand, and they've just put the toll up again, would you believe.' The first guard slapped the railings of the tarnished bridge fondly to illustrate his point. 'Several thousand years old, this drawbridge. The engravings are all original oak, and if you look carefully, there's still some gold medieval bits.' This was not true, but admirably said. 'Five gold pieces to cross.'

Robbie stayed firmly mounted and leant down to hand

the men a piece of oily paper claiming to be his birth certificate. Face was a twenty-hand horse – it was a very long lean, and he was not sure he could get back up.

He gestured to the nearest guard. 'My cousin is tired after a long journey. Forgive her for not dismounting. She's a delicate sort – not royal, though, nor infectious. Have you ever travelled with a weary woman before?'

The guards made sympathetic noises and patted Robbie's boot, which was all they could reach. 'You have our understanding on that score, son.' They looked at the horses. 'Big ride you got there. Take a morning to just climb off.'

'Yes, he's big for a carthorse.'

They looked unconvinced. 'The lady looks a bit peaky.'

Robbie threw them a leather pouch of coins stolen from a sleeping guard at the Hogs Breath. 'She's alright. Only minutes ago she fell asleep. Moaned herself out. I beg you, good men and true, give a Man of the Road a few hours' peace in the city before she wakes up and starts complaining again.' Robbie pushed his hair back from his eyes. They were wrecked and bloodshot. 'I haven't slept for a week.'

Poor chap did look a bit rough, and there was no doubt his cousin had the face of a right old princess. Determined chin, freckles – clearly a bit fiery.

'Give us a minute, son.' The guards went to confer in a place they had conferred often – under the arch that led into the citadel. Robbie rubbed his eyes and waited. After a long silence and a synchronised nod, they returned.

'I travelled beyond Alba once, with my wife Beryl and her sister. They wanted to go to Boondongal for a picnic.' The guard spoke gravely. 'I will never take that woman on a picnic again. Not happy with any of the perfectly pleasant spots we stopped at. Not happy with the cherry cake. If it wasn't rheumatism giving them grief it was piles. The view was too hazy. Then there were the flies. Yap, yap, yap they were at it all day …'

The second guard got out a little stool to sit on. Robbie tried to look interested, but the sound of a drumroll behind him caught his attention.

'It was after midnight by the time we had lunch.'

Robbie prayed. 'I see. I have your sympathy, sir. This one's got quite a set of teeth on her too.'

'I can well believe it, my boy.' The Alba guard looked around the bridge. 'Go in quickly, before any of Blackwood's Guards get here. That lawyer would have my tongue if he found out I hadn't followed procedure.'

'Thank you.'

'And be glad she's not your wife! Or a princess. Apparently, there's one on the loose.' The guards waved him off and patted the vast, muddy horse. 'Take my advice and stay single. If you meet the princess, lock your door and run for the hills. That royal lass will only bring you trouble. The lengths they are going to in order to find her – posters everywhere, big reward …' they shouted after him.

Robbie saluted, for some reason, and led the horses quickly over the drawbridge and into the old city. A maze of narrow alleys, false front doors, trapdoors, cellar doors, and twisting stairwells leading up to seemingly solid walls greeted them. It was the area where anyone with good reason to hide did just that. It was easy to disappear in the old city.

He arrived at The Cat's Back with a few hours to go before sundown. He had not expected to be early. He was not an early man generally; he planned his life to be a race until the end, with no time to potter. He checked in and asked for boiled salty water, some bread, butter, a pot of tea, whatever stew was left from the night before, and an unopened bottle of whisky.

'It's good to see you again, Robbie,' said Mrs Dibble the landlady, looking at Red with concern. 'I didn't know you had a cousin.'

'Neither did I,' sighed Robbie.

The Cat's Back was an old coaching inn. A sprawling citadel house with thick silk curtains, high ceilings, and generous fireplaces, it stood down a quiet dead-end road, helpfully named Dead End. The grand house did not want any trouble, and so naturally troubles were all it got. Since the king had abandoned Landfelian, every one of the rooms had been occupied by those fleeing some sort of strife.

Laura and Timothy Dibble managed the inn. They did their best to accommodate the constant stream of runaways and made sure a welcoming fire burnt day and night. As the years of the quest wore on, the temperature in Alba dropped. They added an extra quilt to each bed and doubled the log order. The soot caused by the scrapers – the people living on the streets – setting fire to things blackened the walls of the house, as well as the water. Gloves, gleaves (a sort of ear hood), and snoods (a nose sock) became a necessity amongst the homeless. Will English put a notch on the beam every time a lost-looking person blew through the door with their shoulders hunched and face pinched, exclaiming, 'Cor blimey. It's got more of a bite out there than I remember.' The inn was running out of beams.

The Cat's Back was formerly the private home of an art-loving impresario known to all simply as the Duchess. Childless, she had left everything to her maid and valet, who'd always been kind. It was now named after the Duchess's cat, an elegant blue Persian called Napoleon, or Naps to those who knew him. On the same foggy morning the queen disappeared from Celador, Naps vanished from his seat by the window. No one knew where or why he decided to go, but he did, and he was gone, so they couldn't ask him why. Mrs Dibble was beside herself; she thought he had been stolen by scrapers for his fur, which was the colour of oyster shells. Signs went up around Dead End: *Naps come home*.

The Dibbles had decided to shut the great house and travel across the Four Great Realms, get some country air, and hopefully bump into their adopted cat. They had grown accustomed to the sight of Napoleon rubbing himself up against the chair legs. The pillow on the windowsill still had his indent and fleas. Six months passed and the Dibbles returned to Dead End smelling of the road and with some new ideas for the menu, ready to open the house once again, though with all hope of finding their cat lost. The sign creaked in welcome, and an old street-sweeper approached.

'You'll never guess what ...' He pointed to the door with a withered finger and a gummy grin.

'What is it, old man?' asked Mr Dibble, weary and thirsty for tea.

'The cat's back!' And off the man cackled, chattering to himself. 'Her ladyship's old mog ... He's back.'

Napoleon had a leather patch over one eye now, but the other was bright with adventure. He had a few ticks on his nether regions and a whisker was missing. He had purred like a Bengal tiger upon seeing the Dibbles again and returned to his pillow to lick himself. The Dibbles repainted the sign and the establishment changed overnight. The Cat Naps became the The Cat's Back and reopened immediately with a few new members of staff. Dead End remained seemingly innocuous to unwelcome ears and spying eyes; the house's gently smoking chimneys and hanging baskets of forget-me-peas were protected by the maze-like map of the citadel.

Will English was employed as a glass washer, a job that restricted him to the butler's sink in the back room. As a waiter, he'd overwhelmed the customers with his poetry.

Amber Morningstar sang most nights and helped serve the drinks. Richard Losley used to run show tunes on Sundays, bringing his baton and making use of the grand piano. And a Man of the Road was given a bed in the attic each time he returned to Alba with a bloody nose on the run from Blackwood's guards.

The Cat's Back had never housed a princess. The Dibbles were too polite to say how like the king's daughter Robbie's cousin looked.

'What happened to you?' she asked Robbie with a curious smile. 'It's been months since you paid us a visit. You look different.'

'Age. I won't stay long,' he said quietly. 'A few days.'

'I'll call for a doctor,' said Mrs Dibble. 'Your cousin isn't well.'

Robbie caught her gently by the arm. 'You can't.'

She nodded in understanding. 'Then you'd better come upstairs.'

21

THE SWAN BOAT

'I asked for one thing, Will.'

'I know, sunflower.'

'What was it?'

'A kiss?'

'No. To stay on dry land.'

'Well, I –'

'Dry land. Where are we?'

Will thought for a moment. 'We are on an area that was formerly land but is now sea. They are very similar. One is just covered with a light glaze of water.' He smiled as gently as possible. 'I do hope we see a mermaiden.'

'SEA IS NOT LAND!' Amber snapped. 'It is a deep, dangerous, never-ending swell of salty water.' She paused for breath. 'With cross-currents, whirlpools, underwater trenches, sharks, giant octopi –'

'I believe the plural of octopus is octopoda.'

Amber then said something like, 'OH BLOOOOOOOOOOOOOOOW OFF.' When Will tried to hold her.

'It is not true what they say about sharks; they are victims of bad press. I, for one, have never met a mean one.'

Amber was not listening; she was hysterical. 'We only recently survived a waterfall. Clearly, that was not challenging enough because …' She took another gasp and shuddered. '… for the better part of the day, we have been floating across the Sound of Whale in a Long Wind!'

'And I have not told you how lovely your hair looks. Remarkable, quite something. Like a shooting golden star.' He reached out for her hand.

She pushed him away and began to sob.

Will and Amber were on a boat. Amber had not slept, and the memory of her few possessions flying off a rock into Hosanna Falls did not find her in the best of moods, topped off by Marilyn's decision to stay with the giants in their peaceful valley until things calmed down. The river and the cliff ascent had forced the shire horse to take a long hard look at mortality. Early retirement in a nice meadow, with some giants and yooks, appealed. She liked the yooks; they made her feel petite and safe. The yooks thought Marilyn was a hoot.

The previous day had been spent in the valley where the giants lived. After the fainting of Amber and Erek the giant, Will had become quite upset on top of the cliffs.

'Enough fainting. Everyone still conscious, listen carefully: you have one faint allowance and that is it. Ladies, you have had yours. Marilyn and I have one to go, and this Erek character has just lost his.'

They wrapped the giant Erek in the tapestry like a sausage no roll should ever see and hoisted him onto one of the yooks. Giants faint for two main reasons: when they overheat (the menopause is a dangerous time for the female giant) and when surprised, and Erek had been tremendously surprised. After pulling up his ropes to help some unfortunate small people off an eroding rock by the waterfall, he had come face to face with a very pretty and very famous giantess. One who had been lost for many years. Erek had a drawing of her on the wall of his yurt. Ophelia was a poster girl in Giant Country, a reason to get up and whistle. The other giants in the valley had not heard from the rising star of their Amateur Dramatics Club, Dream Big, for years. Not a byline, a clipping, a postcard, nought. And then there she was, climbing out of a tapestry with some small Landfelians. Erek had not expected to faint, but he had, nonetheless.

They rode down to the giant encampment, along a path where the chichaws left colourful feathers amongst tall, swaying trees. The camp was a meadow filled with canvas dwellings.

Feathers poked out of the top of each one, distinguishing each of the one-hundred-and-seven yurt homes from its neighbour. Yooks grazed happily amongst them, on some of the richest grass in the kingdom.

Amber, who was ever so slightly short-sighted, had wondered if she was looking at giant anthills. She relaxed only when she saw one smoking gently with a washing line beside it.

The next morning, Will was woken by a yook having a quiet dump after its morning feed. Yooks were large animals; to anyone else, a poo or a bleat sounded like a landslide. Disorientated, he wandered into several of the wrong yurts before finding Amber beside her horse, fast asleep. He became dimly aware that she had abandoned him in the night to lie in comfort in a guest yurt, leaving no room for him. 'In the last two days, I have rescued you all. And have I heard but one word – one note – of thanks?' The sleeping pile did not stir. He went back to sleep, outside, under the tapestry.

A few hours later, 'Morning, Wilf!' a voice boomed down at him. The ground shook.

Will screamed and tried to sit up quickly; during the night, he had dreamt about a man-eating valley of giants. 'Don't eat me!' They would cook him in the tapestry with a few chives and call it Crêpe William.

The giant Erek had red hair – not like the princess, not like a roll in the leaves, not what you might call maple red, but red like a happy carrot. He began to laugh. Will hoped if he kept laughing the ground below might crack, allowing him to fall through to somewhere safer. He could make a run for it, then save Amber and still meet the princess. The giant's head was the same size as a Grecian urn he had seen in the palace.

'I will taste terrible.' He tried stalling for time. 'I have no experience at being eaten.'

Erek liked the actor and his little head and waggly eyebrows. 'You wally, I don't want to eat you. It's alright, my friend, you're safe in Giant Country. We don't go in for man meat much up here.'

'Very wise. What, if you don't mind my asking, *do* you dine on?'

'Spinach, fish, and peanut butter.' The giants lived, loved, and breathed peanut butter. It was believed to play a key part in their size. A noise like a bear waking erupted inside Erek's belly. He patted it. 'Come with me, it's breakfast time. I'm famished.'

Will's racing heart slowed as he took in his pleasant surroundings. 'I like what you've done with the yurt feathers. Although, those signs on the river if I'm honest, need improving.'

'The elders have called a sign meeting. I've come to invite the rest of your raft for breakfast.' Erek went a little pink around the ears. 'Did you know Ophelia's the finest performer in Giant Country? Maybe the finest of the non-giants, too.'

Will was coming around to the giant. 'Erek, my good

man, I'll have you know *I* was the queen's favourite performer.' He thought it important to add, 'And amongst my people, I am considered one of the tallest of men.'

'Head to the orange-feathered yurt.' The giant gave him a gentle slap, which tipped Will over, and he bounded off.

Will considered his life for a moment. There were two days left to reach The Cat's Back. The last thing he should be doing was attending a sign meeting in Giant Country. Although a spot of tea and toast wouldn't go amiss, and these big people had saved his life from a watery abyss. He checked on the voodoo charm. The horrible box of bone had blistered his foot, although it was safe and sweaty inside his boot.

He scoured the area for the yurt with orange feathers, taking in the yooks grazing in the misty meadows edged by a gentle cascade of water. Hosanna Falls looked very different from the bottom up. He walked to its lagoon to wash and came upon a giantess staring quietly at the water.

'Can you swim?' he asked. 'Only I haven't had any breakfast. If you can't swim, I may not be fit to rescue you.'

'Hello, Will.'

It was Ophelia. She looked different. She looked terrific. The butch belt, drab dress, and stern plaits had gone. She looked like a playful hippy – all blousy sleeves and colourful skirts, feathered earrings, and rosy cheeks. She was still enormous.

'You look better.' He smiled. 'Between us, I think Erek may have a stonking great –'

She held out her hand. 'Come, I want to show you something before you leave.'

'Is it far? I'm late for a sign meeting and need to find some peanut butter before heading off for Alba …'

She was already climbing the rocks on the other side of the lagoon and beckoning him to follow. There was a crude set of steps cut into the cliff overlooking the valley. Will hoped they weren't going for a hike; he felt faint, and he only had one left. It took him twice as long as Ophelia to reach the top – he had to scramble up each step like mounting a wall – until they stood on a high plateau where a cool breeze blew and looked down at the lay of the land at their feet.

The other side of the lagoon was a natural amphitheatre. Will gasped. 'It is GIANTASTICAL.' It felt like he was standing on the top of the world. 'I have never seen anywhere like it.'

The giants' amphitheatre was the largest in the land and in the parts of the world thus far discovered. The heavens and all the best ethereal wispy things living in the clouds had held a meeting at the beginning of the beginning and decided about it thus:

'Well, if there must be actors, Celia, if there *really* must, then we might as well give them a decent-sized stage.'

'Very well, Laurence. As long as we are able to watch, too.'

Which they did. And if it was a bad show, the ethereals threw things like hail, lightning, and locusts, or they would rub together some thunder until the acting stopped.

A smile spread over Will's face. 'You performed here?'

'Many times before I left for Alba and met Blackwood.' A very small, very ominous dark cloud skulked across the sky at the mention of the man with the silver-topped cane. Ophelia shivered and then turned to Will and smiled. 'I'm happy to be back, although I'm not sure I fit in this valley anymore.'

'I can assure you, dear lady, you fit beautifully.' Will looked down at the grand setting under a bright blue sky. 'It is glorious. Come, let us yodel together to celebrate your homecoming, dear Ophelia.' Will and Ophelia had a quick yodel, then he took as much of her hand as he could fit in his own and led her quickly down the steps. 'You will always be welcome in Alba, although I would not advise you come with us today. That Blackwood character is still lurking somewhere.'

The sign meeting was in full swing when Will strolled in.

'Sorry I'm late, everyone!' He clapped his hands and looked around him. 'Now! What is the deal with these signs?'

Erek passed him a tower of peanut butter and bread. Amber nodded at an antique clock hanging from the wall of the yurt. The clock said, *Saturday*. 'We need to leave,' she whispered. The giants had kept them too long.

He nodded and addressed the crowd. 'In my opinion, less is more, my giant friends. One large sign before the left fork of the Big Easy is the way to go. A sign not even a blind mole would miss.'

There were mutterings of, 'But how?' and 'We don't have the ink for it.'

'Fret not, I have an idea.' Will smiled in the patient silence. 'A parting gift. Amber, the tapestry, if you please!'

With the help of Erek, the tapestry was rolled out and silence descended on the yurt. It was the longest tapestry the giants had ever seen.

'What the river needs is a textile warning on a grand scale. An embroidered *TURN AROUND OR DIE – WATERFALL AHEAD* – something along those lines, though maybe a smidge more positive. It will showcase your skills as weavers, increase tourism, and prevent future unnecessary deaths.' He winked at Amber.

'Yes,' the giants agreed. 'No one would miss that.' The small people from Landfelian received a rousing applause and preparations were made. 'Summon the weavers!' they shouted. The minutes were written up and pinned to the yurt door. The peanut butter sandwiches were finished.

'And now we need your help,' said Will. 'What is the best way to reach Alba from this valley? We must reach the city by sundown tomorrow and rescue the princess.'

The giant men and women looked grave, and murmurs of, 'Oh dear, but you'll never make it' and 'It's a week's trek on a yook' filled the yurt.

Erek stepped forward and smiled. 'I have a boat.'

Amber let go of Will's hand when they were shown the boat. 'No.'

'What a beautiful vessel!' Will jumped on board, marvelling at the handiwork of what appeared to be a large floating swan.

'No, and a heavily laden tray of NO chucking NOs,' said Amber. 'Is there another way? A fast yook? A pair of chichaw birds? They could fly us to Alba, could they not?' She appealed to Erek by gripping his thumb.

'I'm afraid the birds would drop you,' said Erek. 'They are very wilful creatures. The yooks would be too slow, and there are the mountains to consider. My boat is the fastest way out of the valley. The current will take you straight into the port at Alba.'

She looked at it. 'Don't expect me to row.'

'There is no need, my love,' announced Will. 'It's a pedalo, look.'

One of the giant women passed Amber a bundle of yet more peanut butter sandwiches. 'Food of giants.'

'Thank you.' She sat down forlornly. 'You've all been very kind.'

Quite a crowd had gathered to wish them well. The giants knew it was unlikely the humans would make it in Erek's swan, but they wanted to give them a good send-off. Will had no idea that this was the case, but Amber's doubts escalated when she realised the boat was in fact a prop from one of the many water-themed productions of Dream Big. It had never seen open water before; it was a papier mâché swan pretending to be a boat. There were two wings and a canopy for shelter. The hull was deep enough to conceal a giant lying flat and pedalling hard to keep it moving without being seen.

Will couldn't wait to get going. 'How came you by this boat, my friend?'

'It was for a play Ophelia was to star in called "The Swan is a Lonely Hunter".' Erek looked at his feet. 'And I kept it for personal reasons.'

'It is quite brilliant. No guard will see us coming – no one will suspect a thing! You must visit when the Hey Nonnys are back in business. We need your skills as props master.'

The giant beamed and pulverised Will's hand.

Ophelia came forward and kissed them both. 'Go carefully. There will be a manhunt out for both of you. Leave word at The Cat's Back if you ever need our help. I know the landlady well.'

Amber gave her a shaky smile. 'Look after Marilyn. She's a greedy mare but gentle and about the right size for the young ones.

'Anchor's away!' cried Will.

'Will, there is no anchor,' sighed Amber. 'Just start pedalling.'

Five hours later, the canopy had been ripped off. It went in a hurry, caught in a vicious gale. It disappeared into the horizon before Amber and Will had time to shout, 'Wait!' and 'What the … That's our canopy!'

Those friendly giants had not mentioned anything about a Long Wind. They'd said to follow the gentle current down the Sound of Whale into the Wondering Waters and past the chalky downs of the east coast until they reached the Bay of Brightly Coloured Boats and spires of Alba.

'THOSE GIANT BRIGANS WERE MISTAKEN!' Amber yelled into the wind, several hours later. 'THOSE GIANT PEANUT MUNCHERS LIED TO US, WILLIAM!' she screamed. 'We'll never make it. We will die here, starved and wind-ravaged. This boat will sink. We are fish food.' She ended her speech with a sob and laid back down.

Will was not sure where they were exactly. At sea, yes, he could tell that much. But which one, he could not tell. If he lifted his head out of the swan for one second to check the coastline, the Long Wind would blow it clean off. And I mean CLEAN. He fingered the hair around his temples gingerly. The last attempts to look up and navigate may have kickstarted the receding hairline he had nightmares about. He hoped they weren't on their way into the White Ocean.

Maureen Maples watched the swan boat as it passed her observatory window and waved merrily. Amber and Will did not see her. They were squashed together like pilchards in the hull, having a heated discussion about death and love – which brings us up to speed.

Amber tried to put her head above deck, resulting in very red cheeks.

'Move up!' she snapped at Will, who tried not to look surprised or smile when he saw her ruddy face. 'I can't see a bloody thing. Are we even moving?' She sank back down onto him. It was very snug in the boat.

'Amber, if we die in this swan, there is something you must know.'

'Mmm?'

'I have never wanted anyone ... I have never loved anyone ... and I have never wished to argue with anyone ... but you.' William English was not acting, although his voice was a little sat-upon, as the most beautiful woman in his life, dreams, and heart lay on top of him and scowled. It was a rare and blessed event when William English stopped acting for long enough to be taken seriously. His eyes grew wide, and his face took its clothes off. He looked lovely when he was not acting.

Amber Morningstar stared at the man beneath her and kept staring for some time. She liked the way he appeared now, with no theatrics or falsity. She leant further down onto his chest and decided to kiss it. She had thought about kissing it before, but he always put on an act. And Amber found it hard to trust an act. Blackwood had taught her that. She kissed slowly up to his surprised mouth. Will blinked back at her. His hair blew about, and his eyes were a warm, muscovado brown. 'You're a fool.' Amber leant closer and looked again to be sure he wasn't really acting.

Will mumbled something and swallowed as her eyelashes grazed his cheeks. 'I ... am. Sorry.'

'William Theodore English.' She laughed gently into his neck. The laugh turned into a heaving, tears-rolling, eyes-gleaming, quick-get-this-woman-a-glass-of-water-and-a-sprig-of-thyme full-bodied guffaw. 'Come here.'

If a voice can regain control and drop an octave over the words 'come' and 'here', Amber's could. No one expected her to kiss him. Not even Amber, or the land, the wind, the sea, or the swan boat. She had sworn off kissing. The closest Will had got to her lips before was a misjudged peck on the nose. Those are the best sorts of kisses – the ones that take you by surprise, provided those involved have not recently eaten any smoked fish. Will kissed Amber back. He was unsure at first, and then, with great passion, he kissed her. Holding her close, which had never been allowed before, he kissed Amber like his life depended on it.

'Blimey,' said Amber several minutes later, a little dazed.

'I'm sorry. I might not get another chance.'

They carried on until they could no longer hear the wind. They kissed until they did not know what day or colour it was. When you're enjoying something this much, death himself could tap you on the shoulder and you wouldn't look up. After a fizzing length of time, they heard a voice – someone was asking them a question.

Amber sat up quickly, rearranged her hair and her dress, and looked around. A weathered man in a rowing boat with the royal crest paddled up beside them. He blew a whistle at her.

'Good afternoon. Parking permit, please, for the … swan.'

'But we haven't got a permit.' Her lips were pink and tender, and she had very rosy cheeks.

'You haven't got a hairbrush either, have you, miss?' The man looked at her and smiled like a walrus. It was not every day he got a swan and a rumpled blonde washing in on the Sunday shift. It was normally filthy, corpse-heavy work.

'First bay on the left, then, if you would.' He looked at the pedalo and smiled. 'It's not exactly a boat, is it? Put your swan between *Lysander* and *Buxom Wench* and enjoy your stay in the smoking capital.'

'Thank you.' She smiled sweetly back at him and pedalled away. 'Will. Wake up! We're in Alba, it's Sunday, and the sun is setting! Pedal, man.' She kicked him.

The actor allowed himself a minute to bask in the memory of the last few hours while the swan floated slowly into the Bay of Brightly Coloured Boats and moored up between two larger vessels. Amber and Will clambered out and finally stood on dry land. The light was fading, and the lighter kinds of crime had already begun for the evening. Will drew in a deep breath.

'Ah, rotten fish and the dish of the day from Marlene's Soup Kitchen. It's good to be home.'

Amber grabbed his hand. 'We must hurry, there's little time. Here, put this on.' She had retrieved two sailor caps from a sleeping crew next to a merchant ship. 'The guards will be everywhere.'

THE SPIDERLINGS DESCEND

The swarm would not fly in a Long Wind. The wind forced Lidia to return and shelter in her bower in the Forest of Tall Pines. If this was the witch's doing, it was ill-timed. She twitched about her vast needle kingdom impatiently, then folded up her wings, crossed her legs, and remained in a disconcertingly still pose, shrouded by dusty webs, until the sky grew quiet again. The swarm lost a day and a night due to the weather.

The forest was dark when Lidia opened her eyes and heard the storm had passed.

'It is time,' she addressed the swarm. 'Find the girl. She's hiding in Alba. Return with news.'

A horrible buzzing filled the Forest of Thin Pines as a thousand bony wings began to beat as one. They rose slowly, in a black mass. Lidia watched the spiderlings ascend through the trees and into the night at her command and prepared herself for the journey to Alba.

Daniel Blackwood was polishing the skull on his cane in his room at The Hog's Breath. There was time for an aperitif before he met the bounty hunter. He buttoned up a wafty black shirt and looked out the window. The evening scent of open drains and street fires greeted him like an old friend. The Chimmeries ... there was nowhere quite like it. He would take a stroll to Madame Mim's and then down to the docks to meet the bounty hunter. A slight gust of wind caused him to glance up at the blue-black sky, and his eyes narrowed at the sight. A moving shadow, flying towards the citadel. The spiderlings had arrived in Alba. His abduction of the princess was no longer a private affair. The entire city was being watched.

Will was out cold before he could even question why. After such a nice day, it had to end with a punch in the face.

'Robert Wylde? Is that you?' asked Amber. 'What the devil are you doing here? You look terrible.'

It was a very small, convoluted world in The Cat's Back, and no one inside batted an eyelid at the conversation going on in the entrance hall next to the hat stand.

'Amber? I should have known you would be mixed up with all this. There's no time to explain. Is this the actor,

William English?'

'It was, yes, until you hit him.' They looked at Will, who still had a smile on his face.

'I had to be sure he wasn't a guard or bounty hunter. Quick, she's upstairs. Does he have the teeth?'

Robbie had not returned to Dead End for several years. He had never met the actor, although he had known Amber long enough to think him a vast improvement on any of the other gentlemen she attracted.

'Of course he's got teeth,' said Amber, unsure how much Robbie knew of the voodoo. 'Everybody has teeth.'

Robbie gripped her arm. He looked very tired. 'There is another set of teeth upstairs, and I'm not talking about your average, run-of-the-mill pearly whites. These are hexed with dark magic, and they are consuming the life of the only known heir to Landfelian. I brought her here because she is under the illusion that your actor, William English, can help her. She said he was to meet her with the means to remove it. Now, give me the god damn teeth.'

Amber took a step back. She had not seen him this anxious since he had lost his horse to a thieving butcher for a week.

Robbie took her arm and pulled her towards the stairs. 'Come with me.'

When Will opened his eyes, it was clear he was on the floor. A blue Persian with an eyepatch was sitting on his chest, purring.

'Hello, Naps.' His nose felt tender. 'You're looking well.' Sharp splinters stabbed between his temples. It came back to him once he sat up and the little wrens stopped twittering. 'If I remember correctly, I was recently punched. Where is that knave now?'

Mrs Dibble bent over and handed him a steak for his eye. 'Room Seven, with Amber.'

'Ah, hello, Laura. Is he now? We shall see about that! Where is my frying pan?' He scrambled up from the floor, and a few regulars raised their glasses and waved. It wasn't the same when English went away. He was always bellowing about something or spouting poetry.

Will ran up the stairs and kicked the door to Room Seven open, which was completely unnecessary as it wasn't locked. Amber was opening it to get more hot water. He flew in, landed on Robbie, and shouted, 'Take your Man-of-the-Road filthy hands off my woman, you cadbandit!' and slapped him across the face with the steak.

There was a moan. It was pained and pale and from the bed. It was the sound of something in trouble. A woman was on that bed, and she was suffering and making the sort of sound no one wanted to hear unless there was going to be a baby at the end of it. Robbie stopped glaring at Will. Will stared at the bed and saw blood. He saw a long slim leg, and he couldn't for the life of him see a baby. He recognised something around the bloodiest part, an object of darkness and horror.

'Oh no,' he whispered. 'I'm too late.'

'No. You're right on time.' The Man of the Road stood in front of the princess like a very fierce shield. He looked capable of throwing Will through the wall, capable of breathing fire from his nostrils. 'Now you are here, you can remove it.'

Will tried not to look at the mess that was her left foot. 'I don't know how.' Her beautiful hair was dull with sweat, and her skin as white as the pillows. 'I was only told to bring the princess this box.'

'Think.' Robbie clenched his fists. His eyes did not leave her. 'Weren't there some instructions?'

'No, nothing, I swear. Look.' With trembling hands, Will pulled off his boot and fished into his sock – a sock that had seen better days. He held up the box. Inside it sounded like a rattle snake had got hold of some maracas. The room darkened. Something scraped against the window. Will looked desperately at the princess. 'Oh dear. I don't know. I was only told to bring it to this place before sundown. I'm not versed in the ways of magic.'

'Give it to me.' Robbie held out his hand.

'What are you going to do with it?'

Red whimpered, and more blood seeped into the sheets. Amber rubbed her hand and did the best she could with a cold flannel and some humming. She gave both men a stern look. 'She will lose more than a foot if I can't get to the wound soon and give it a good clean. Find a way of removing it.'

Amber knew about wounds; she knew about exposed bones. She had seen it all. Back with the carnival, every day, one of the animals, rope walkers, or high swingers tore something. What she saw now was far worse than a stubbed toe. What she saw was infection and something unnatural holding the girl hostage.

'I will open this box. On three.' Will trusted three; it had not let him down so far.

He put it on the floor, and Robbie hovered over it.

'Wait!' cried Will.

They all jumped. Amber glared at both men. 'Stop shouting. You're scaring her.'

'I'm sorry,' he whispered. 'I have just remembered – the frying pan!'

'This isn't the time for frying anything.' Robbie held his hand over the box and stared desperately up at Will.

'Trust me, it worked last time I opened it. Whatever is inside jumped out. I thwacked it hard with the frying pan and stunned the evil thing stone-cold for a minute.' He looked hopeful and mad.

'Is that it?' asked Robbie. 'We knock the voodoo out of these teeth with a frying pan?'

'That's all I've got. Here.'

Robbie looked at Red and took the frying pan from Will. He held it in his best hand, if we're talking pancakes.

'Everyone ready?'

Room Seven held its breath.

Will opened the bony box. Inside pulsed a set of teeth identical to the ones around princess' ankle. It paused for a quarter of a second, then leapt high above everyone's heads and landed on the bed. It happened too fast to swear even a short word. What the room heard will stay with it to the grave; a clawing, dry howl as the thing jumped across and attached itself to Red's ankle, with an ominous crack. Red screamed and squeezed Amber's hand so hard, the singer yelled in shock, which set Will off.

Robbie gripped the frying pan. 'Everyone, stop! Look!'

The teeth were locked together, and, for the first time, completely still. The spell appeared to be broken as the two souls trapped inside were united again. The teeth were just teeth once more, and darkness left the room.

There was only one thing left to do.

Robbie lifted the frying pan above his head, the lip hovering level over Red's ankle. Amber closed her eyes and hummed louder. Will put his fingers in his ears and recited something.

'Princess, forgive me.'

He brought it down hard.

His aim was true.

Crack!

The sound of an elephant snail being stepped on by a steel-capped boot was followed by a relieved silence and a lot of heavy breathing. No one dared to look.

Will yelled at Robbie with his eyes closed. 'What did you do! Is it off?' He tentatively took his fingers from his ears and heard weak laughter. 'She's hysterical. The princess is hysterical. She has lost a foot!'

Robbie sank to his knees next to the bed, his face buried in his hands. 'What have I done?'

Red turned and looked relieved to see him there. A small, exhausted tear rolled down her cheek into the pillow. 'Thank you, Robbie.'

Will opened an eye. She had two ankles. The teeth had cracked into four pieces and lay lifeless, like a fossil from another time, around her foot. The voodoo had left the room; they could feel it. The hunger and the shadows had gone. The spell was broken.

'Did I hurt you?' asked Robbie.

A toe wiggled. 'No.'

Amber stood up and opened a window. 'Right, I need you two to clear off while I burn these sheets and clean up this mess.' She tied her hair up. 'Will, pour the princess some of that whisky and give the rest to the Man of the Road. Both of you go and wash; my room's free.'

Robbie didn't move. It was over, and whatever had been travelling with them had taken flight out the window. He looked at the princess' sleepy, relieved face for a beat more than most looks require. She looked different. She looked free.

'Go on with you, Wylde,' said Amber. 'Have you seen yourself? I don't know how you got roped into this business, but you're in it now. We all are.'

The actor slapped Robbie's recently dislocated shoulder. 'Welcome to the royal club, my man. Operation Cunning Little Vixen. Come, the lady has spoken, and in my experience, it is best to acquiesce.' Will herded him towards the door. 'Now, I'm interested, how exactly do you know my future wife?'

'I used to cook here a long time ago.' Robbie didn't want to leave her so soon.

'Cook? Excellent! I can see we are going to be great friends, Robert of the Wylde. We favour the same weapon.' He retrieved the frying pan from the floor. 'And not the same woman, of which I am glad. Come. Let us get clean, and then let us get drunk!'

They left Amber in peace to wash away the worst of the infection and wrap the young heir's ankle in dry, clean muslin with a drop of myrrh oil.

'Let the healing begin.' She lifted her glass and drank before offering the bottle to Red. 'Bottoms up, Princess.'

'What is your name?' Red drank the fiery liquid gratefully.

'Amber. I sang at the half-queen's ball a week ago, though we never met formally. The herald is an old friend.' She gathered up the sheets and placed the broken voodoo charm next to the princess' things. 'Goodness, and I thought *my* family was batty. Don't worry, you're in a good place. The old Cat's Back will keep you safe, for now.' She smiled.

Red felt too weak to run anywhere else, which made her anxious. She could always hobble to the window, jump, and hope for the best, but then again, this Amber woman did not look like a guard. She appeared to be ten or so years older than Red, and her voice had the worldliness of a traveller.

Amber sat on the end of the bed and smiled. 'Drop those shoulders. I'm sure there's a neck in there somewhere.'

'You are the one that distracted the guards. You sang to them.'

'Guilty as charged.' She winked at Red.

'The herald said you have an extraordinary voice. I didn't believe him.' She looked guilty.

Amber shrugged. 'It's something I've always been able to do, like breathing.'

'I would love to hear you one day.' Red was struggling to keep her eyes open.

'Sleep now. You've had a rough week.'

'It started well.' Red looked at her bandaged foot.

'You'll have to do something about your hair before you leave; it's a bougainvillea.'

'I lost my wig jumping the river.'

Amber laughed. 'And your tennis racket, no doubt. I lost everything in a waterfall a few days ago.' She threw the last bloody rag into the fire. 'You picked a good Man of the

Road, mind. Surprised he hung around for so long. Robbie's not usually one for company.'

'I called him a gigolo.'

'Oh, he's been called worse.' Amber smiled. This princess had pluck; she was ballsy for an aristocrat.

'I was horrible, and I didn't pay for my sausages.'

Red looked so tired and sorry that Amber poured them both another drink. 'That man has got a good heart but a dozen wicked habits, let me tell you.' She took a sip. 'May I suggest something?' She did not wait for an answer as she placed a clean towel on her lap. 'Shall we give that royal head of hair a wash? It'll do you the world of good.'

'I –'

'Go on. Before the wallpaper starts curling.' Amber began unbottling something that smelt of roses and prepared the water for the bath. 'You'll sleep better for it.'

'Thank you.' Red shyly climbed in and allowed the water to wash away every remnant of the road and enfold her.

'That's better.' Amber smiled at her. 'Keep your foot dry and leave the bandages on for three days. There will be a scar, but what's life without a few of them? Your ankle will be strong enough to walk the tightrope in no time.' She packed up her bottles and made for the door.

'Thank you.' Red had never met a woman like Amber before or experienced the same kindness from the ladies at the palace. 'My father will repay you for your help. I mean to find him.'

Amber stayed for a while and she generally doubted most that life had promised her, except for Will. There was something about this Red Felian. She still had hope.

'You're not out of the woods yet. Keep your rubies until then. No woman should leave the house without something to barter with besides her body.'

Red looked down doubtfully; her body was not exactly screaming out as a siren of lust. 'No one knows who I am.'

'Don't you know.' Amber closed the curtains. 'There are posters of you everywhere, many unsavoury gentlemen are sniffing your trail, and there's a bounty on your head, Princess. Tread carefully.'

'A bounty?'

Something scraped against the window, making both women jump. Amber rubbed the faint black line around her ring finger. She looked spooked. 'Bats,' she whispered. 'There's a lot of them about. They nest under the eaves. Keep the curtains closed, do you hear me? Don't leave the room until tomorrow night. You are not strong enough, and that sea shanty of an outfit draws far too much attention to itself. I'll find you some new clothes. There are some people that wish you harm ...' She smiled. 'And many who would see you on the throne.'

'I doubt anyone remembers who my family is ...'

'This kingdom has a long memory. You'd be surprised. From where I'm sitting, you've got the king's chin.' She looked at Red's lightly muscled arm. 'I'm not sure about the rest of you … A disguise is a must in this city.'

Amber left the room and closed the door. The Cat's Back was open, although the blackout curtains suggested otherwise. Landfelians from every realm needed drinks. They needed lamb stew and treacle tart. They needed to listen to a beautiful voice. Timothy Dibble was tuning the piano for her. She went to change and wondered if the runaway in the bath would one day be Queen of Landfelian.

The spiderlings flew by the old inn again. The curtains were drawn. They hovered in the shadows with the bats.

Red glanced at the window and wondered what caused the scratching noise. A lover with a handful of stones? Well, they had the wrong room. A large moth, the fingernail of a witch? Her nerves were still on edge, but she was too exhausted to leave her bed. The drink soon lulled her to sleep.

The spiderling crawled into the gutter and waited. Whoever was hiding inside would not be able to resist opening the window, and when they did, the witch would be ready.

ACKNOWLEDGEMENTS

- CC Book Design – Cherie Chapman for designing the most beautiful cover.

- Sally Parker – map illustrator extraordinaire. Thank you, Sally!

- For Maddy, Carl, and the Softwood Self-Publishing team for finally making it happen.

- Philippa Donovan at Smart Quill Editorial for reading the first draft of this monster and believing in it.

- Melissa Hyder and Tilda Johnson at the Golden Egg Academy for all the editing, bolstering, and brilliance.

- To my family and friends for the inspiration.

- To the Tripod.

- To Fred and Bridget for choosing me.

- To Ben, my husband, for everything else.

10% of every book bought for the first 2 years will be going to Ormiston Families, a charitable trust devoted to helping children and families in need in the East of England where I live.

Join Red's journey in book 2 of
the series, *Missing Midnight.*